Praise for Blood in the Valley

"I was a big fan of Fire on the Island, book I in the Vigilati Series, and Blood in the Valley was even better. Raven was a perfectly imperfect heroine and one I loved from the first chapter. And Drew gave me the happy sighs. A slightly geeky Cajun determined to get his girl? Yes, please. But my favorite thing about this series is that is really is a girl's fight. The heroines are on the front line in the good vs. evil war, and while the heroes do support and fight beside them, the battle is won or lost based on the heroine's intelligence, strength and courage. There's no sitting around, waiting for the white knight to save the damsel in distress. These damsels save them-selves, along with everyone else, thank you very much."
~Romance Reader at Heart, Novel Thoughts and Book Talk

"I found myself resenting every interruption while I was reading because I wanted to see what was going to happen next, with the romantic developments, the archeological dig, and the paranormal aspects. Hogan struck a wonderful balance between the different elements that satisfied both my romance reader and my paranormal/fantasy reader."
~The Book Pushers

"It's an exciting paranormal romance with passion, heart, and humor. The characters are complicated and relatable and my emotions were all bound up for their journey. I couldn't put this book down!"
~The Book Tart

"These heroines roll with the punches, get back up, acknowledge their weaknesses, kick some major butt, and love their men."

"[The female characters] are beautiful, intelligent, and can kick-butt and take names. They are right there on the front line protecting those that they love! This is an excellent read you will not want to put down!"

Praise for Fire on the Island

"Fire on the Island is a paranormal tale that mixes together a good brew of essential elements—love, death, mystery, intrigue, magic and demons, to name a few—that brings the reader into a modern day world with the age old battle of good vs. evil. The reader will love J.K. Hogan's pairing of romance with the paranormal as she weaves a tale that pulls us into this mysterious and magical world."

"This is an action-packed paranormal romance book with a very lovable cast."

"I love to read a good paranormal romance. One that will sweep me into it and take me on a magical adventure. Fire on the Island does exactly that and I loved the journey. This book is rich in detail and world building. It has a unique take on witches and demons and I was captured by this story."

~The Book Tart

"Unique, with lots of action, a strong heroine, and a sexy hero, Fire On the Island is a recommended read. I will be picking up book 2 when it comes out in May. Hogan has created a world that I want to revisit frequently and I have high hopes for this series!"

~Romance Reader at Heart, Novel Thoughts and Book Talk

"In a nutshell, I can't wait to read this again. And again. The simple beauty of Hogan's writing transported me from my apartment into the beautiful wilds of the Scottish islands, sitting on the back porch with Isla and Jeremiah. Absolutely stunning. "

~The Canon

Also by J.K. Hogan

THE VIGILATI SERIES
Fire on the Island
Blood in the Valley

THE COMING ABOUT SERIES
(Available beginning March 2014 from Wilde City Press)
I Survived Seattle

THE SERPENT'S FATE

A Novel of the Vigilati

JK HOGAN

Copyright © 2014 J.K. Hogan

Cover Art by KHD Graphics
www.khdgraphics.com
Male model photographed by Andrei Vishnyakov
(www.vishstudio.deviantart.com)
Female model & photographer, Janna Prosvirina
(www.kuoma-stock.deviantart.com)

Edited by Karen Harper

J.K. Hogan

http://jkhogan.com/
http://twitter.com/JK_Hogan
http://www.facebook.com/OfficialJKHogan
http://www.goodreads.com/jkhogan
http://www.amazon.com/author/jkhogan
http://officialjkhogan.tumblr.com

The Serpent's Fate/ Hogan, J.K. — 1st ed.
ISBN 978-0615972596

Dedication

To all of the wonderful readers, authors, reviewers, and bloggers I've met along this journey. Without you, none of this would be possible.

To my D.A.M.N. girls, you know who you are. Thank you for all your support!

From the Journal of
SFC Matthieu J. Rousseau, Army—Ret.

December 16, 2006

I am Matthieu.
I am a finder of the lost;
A killer of the innocent; a soldier for hire.
I am a shadow. I am dust.
I am the Cobra.

I am...no one.

CHAPTER ONE

New Orleans
March 30, 2012

MATTHIEU ROUSSEAU SAT AT A TABLE IN THE BACK of the darkened club, his shrewd eyes scanning the poorly lit room for his prey. Without glancing down, he fingered the dossier in front of him. He'd only brought it along for photo identification.

He didn't need to look at the file now, he had it all memorized. *'Fate Farrell, 25, 5'6", 145 lbs. Last seen six months ago in Boston, Mass.'* Matthieu eyed the picture that was paper-clipped to the manila folder. The woman had short, spiky blond hair that swept down over one eye. The eye that was showing was a smoky grey. Though her face was soft, she had high, sharp cheekbones, a square jaw and full lips that were stretched into a smile over straight white teeth. One of her canines had a tiny chip in it, which seemed to give her smile that much more character.

Matthieu jerked his eyes away from the photo, startled to find himself fixating on the mystery woman. He had no idea what the client wanted with her. His job was to find her and report back to his handler. But the one solid rule that applied to every 'find' was never, ever, personalize the mark.

She was good, he'd give her that. He could find anything, anyone, but Ms. Farrell had proved to be elusive, even for him. A breakthrough had come when a tip pointed him towards the small, privately owned jazz club on the outskirts of New Orleans. So far, though, his mark had yet to make an appearance.

To top it off, it was open-mic night, which brought forth an endless string of hopeless aspiring singers and 'next-big-things'. It really was almost enough to have Matthieu considering blowing off this job altogether. Almost. It wasn't as if he had any choice to speak of. His ass was well and truly owned by his former commander, Lieutenant Arlen Ward.

Matthieu had been stationed in Afghanistan when was approached by Lt. Ward. Ward had heard about Matthieu's particular skill set, and wanted to recruit him for an elite Special Ops team called G9X Corps. They had been charged with tasks such as tracking enemy hideouts, rescuing POWs, and the discreet removal of persons of interest in the opposition.

What Matthieu didn't know at the time was that G9X Corps was an 'under the table' operation. While some of the higher ups in the U.S. military were aware of their existence, and in fact gave them their assignments, the operations were not sanctioned by the government. It was the military leaders' way of circumventing higher authority and due process. They could get the job done, without it being traced back to them.

This meant they received no support from the military and no leniency when it came to the law, regardless of how many lives they saved. Should information about their operations ever leak out, they would all be essentially fugitives from U.S. military police. After retirement, Ward had joined the private sector, taking mercenary jobs and forcing his former soldiers into service. They completed the jobs in return for his silence.

Matthieu didn't mind it much—and he was certainly good at it—because it was more than he deserved after destroying the lives of so many in the name of war. He always figured he'd die on one of these missions. That's how he spent most of his life, surrounded by regret...waiting to die.

So here he was, in a little dive club—in his hometown, no less. He was less than fifteen miles away from where his brother lived with his new wife, whom he'd never met. A few miles from where his mother lived. Matthieu shook off such thoughts as his heart was squeezed in a vice grip. No, they were better off without him tainting their lives with his corruption.

As he wrestled with the sentimental thoughts of his family, a sweet melody floated back to him as it filled the room. Helpless to control the reaction, his head snapped back toward the stage as if yanked by an invisible string.

The source of the voice was an ethereal looking yet curvaceous woman dressed in a simple black evening gown. Her blond hair fell in thick waves over her shoulders and swept across her face, obscuring most of it. It didn't matter. The spotlight shining down over her cast her face in shadow, yet she seemed to glow with some sort of inner radiance. He was sure the stunning package was home to a soul of pure light—the complete opposite of him.

Once again, Matthieu tried to push aside his traitorous thoughts, but this time the song interfered. It swirled around him, threatening to fill all of the empty spaces. He guarded those empty spaces carefully, felt he deserved them for all he'd done, all he'd hurt. They were his cross to bear.

Anger washed through him—though even he recognized that it was ridiculous to feel anger towards a song—and he steeled himself to get back to the business at hand. He once again tried to concentrate on scanning the faces in the room. The club didn't get a lot of play, so it didn't take long for him to figure out that his mark was not among the current patrons.

Matthieu started to get up and call Lt. Ward with a progress report, when he heard a sound behind him. Years of war and subterfuge had turned his body into a machine—one that would do what was needed before his brain even registered a threat. Muscles tensing, he whipped around, one hand already inside his leather jacket and resting on the butt of the SIG Sauer pistol that was cradled in his shoulder holster.

He saw no movement in the darkness behind him, but his body was still sending fight or flight signals, so he sat back down and watched. Matthieu noticed a flicker of a shadow near a load-bearing column behind him. As his eyes adjusted to the darkness, the shadow formed into the shape of a tiny person. No, a child. A little girl clung to the column and unabashedly stared at him from behind it, naked curiosity in her eyes. And what eyes they were. They were huge; open wide and rimmed with thick black lashes. Their color was a blue so light and clear, it was almost white. Her tiny white face was framed by blunt, chin length black locks and a thick fringe of bangs.

What a peculiar looking child...not that Matthieu had any knowledge of children whatsoever. He tended to look on them with the same reverence and trepidation as he would a unicorn, or a two-headed cat. He watched as the little thing gathered her courage—curiosity clearly outweighing caution—and took a timid step towards him. What was a child doing here at this time of night? This creature should be in a frilly pink room surrounded by dolls and ponies, not in a dark club tickling the seedy underbelly of New Orleans.

As she crept towards him, intense focus in those gigantic eyes, Matthieu felt a smile trying to tug at the corners of his mouth. It felt odd...rusty—like the muscles hadn't been used in far too long. Hell, that was probably true. It must have looked as bad as it felt, because the little girl froze in her tracks. She seemed rooted to the spot, unwilling to turn back but too scared to continue.

With his own curiosity eclipsing self-preservation, Matthieu placed a booted foot on the bottom rung of the chair across from him and pushed it out. The girl's smile was brilliant as she tiptoed to the chair that was much too high for her, and hoisted her tiny body up to face him. In a comically adult gesture, she plunked her elbows down onto the table, folded her hands together to rest her chin on them, and stared at him with unnerving focus.

"Hi," he said, in a voice that sounded like the love-child of gravel and sandpaper. The girl didn't even flinch. Someone needed to teach this little one about stranger danger because, as it stood, she didn't seem to be scared of much of anything.

"Hi," she squeaked. "Who're you?"

Matthieu had to cover a laugh with a cough. Whoever this one belonged to had their hands full, to be sure. "I'm Matthieu," he answered, having no idea why the hell he'd given his real name. "Who are you?"

"I'm Ridley Callahan. I'm seven," she announced, as if it were a matter of the utmost importance. "You gots a snake," she pointed out.

"So I do."

The child had seen the king cobra tattoo on his neck that he had earned in combat—Cobra had been his deployment code name—and still she showed no fear.

"I draw'd a butterfly on my arm once...but Mama got real mad and I had to wash it off." As if mentioning her mother would conjure the woman, Ridley shrunk down in her seat, eyes darting around the room to rest on the stage. "I'm not s'pose t'be out here. If Mama sees, I'll be in a bunch of big trouble."

"Yeah? Where is your mom, anyway?"

"Promise you won't tell?" she asked in a small voice.

"Cross my heart."

Ridley gave him a stunning, snaggle-toothed grin as she pointed to the stage. For the second time, Matthieu turned rapt attention to the woman singing, and everything else in the room receded into the background. It was like the aftermath of getting too close to an explosion—you have tunnel vision, can barely see through a haze of smoke and sand, and the only sound is the ringing in your ears. Or in this case, the mournful song of a smoky voiced beauty.

Attraction. He recognized the signs of course—the rapid breathing, the skittering pulse, dilation of the eyes. Arousal. Matthieu hadn't felt either in the longest time. He didn't deserve pleasure. He didn't deserve happiness. He was a monster. So his rendezvous with the opposite sex had been as such. In the dark, from behind. No faces, no names. Certainly no arousal— at least not of the mental variety. He'd been fulfilling a biological function, nothing more. But somehow, in the presence of this divine creature—this woman who seemed to be calling to him— it felt so much emptier. So much more damaged.

The music she made was so genuine, so raw and provocative; it was touching places in him to which he'd thrown away the key. But she seemed to clutch the melody to her, as if it was the only thing holding her together, and if she let it go, she'd fall apart. Something about the sadness in her called to him. He could relate.

Matthieu didn't understand why this woman, or her child for that matter, was in this dive. The way she was currently slaying ""I'd Rather Go Blind," she should be selling out places like Tipitina's or the Rock-N-Bowl, not slumming it at open-mic night in Nowheresville.

The song was building a crescendo and when she hit the bridge, she flung her hair back and raised her face to the light. Matthieu's body when utterly still and his blood turned to ice. He knew why she was in that dive. She'd aged well, the hair was longer, the look more refined, and she'd filled out nicely. But it didn't fool him. She was the mark.

Matthieu cursed under his breath, but he must not have done too good a job of it because the child's eyes popped. Though she was only seven, those eyes...they seemed ageless; like she knew too much of the world and what lurked within it.

Without warning—which was the way it always happened— Matthieu was transported to another time and place; to another set of fathomless eyes...child's eyes.

He was staring into the eyes of a little afghan girl, the one who turned to head into a building that was supposed to be cleared of civilians. The shabby, drooping apartment building was serving as HQ for a high-level enemy commander, and G9X had been deployed to take him out.

The little girl locked eyes with Matthieu as she toddled past her mother and into the building. Shit! He'd done a lot of things he was going to burn for, but he wasn't a child killer. He broke his cover, ignoring the orders to stand down barking in his ear piece, and sprinted full speed toward the building. His lungs burned, his thighs ached, but there was nothing on his mind but getting to those civilians.

He was a couple of strides from reaching the door when it blew. The blast threw him thirty back, and when they found him, he was covered in burns, plaster dust, and blood. The noise of the explosion had rendered him deaf—lasted for three days, that time—so he couldn't hear himself screaming, but he felt it. He screamed and screamed until he was finally silenced by the butt of an AR-15. It wasn't his comrades that had found him. It was the Afghani soldiers.

The ringing of his phone jerked Matthieu out of the flashback and back into the present, where he found Ridley Callahan, seven, staring at him like he'd lost his very last marble. Well, wasn't he just Mary fucking Poppins? Giving the phone an annoyed look, he rose from the table, mumbled something along the lines of 'gotta take this' and bolted for the door.

"Rousseau," he barked into the phone once he'd stepped outside, still trembling from the impact of the flashback. There was a pause, and he figured the LT was deciding whether to address his *tone* or just get to the point.

"What's the status?"

"I'm locked on, just waiting for orders."

There were muffled voices on the other end and Matthieu figured Lt. Ward must be talking to the client. When he came back on, his voice was a bit unsteady, which gave Matthieu a very bad feeling. "The client wants you to get rid of her."

"*Come again*?" Matthieu had searched out, tracked, gathered intel on civilians before, but never had he been asked to kill one. And he wasn't about to start.

"You heard me, Rousseau. Take. Her. Out."

"Bit of a problem there, Lieutenant," he answered, playing along to gain as much information as he could. "She has a kid—a little girl." Matthieu's lips twitched at the thought of the feisty, fearless Ridley.

More mumbling over the line and this time, it sounded more like an argument. Ward's voice cracked when he spoke the next order. "Then get rid of her too."

2 CHAPTER TWO

FATE RUSHED THE END OF THE SONG. SHE HAD TO. Singing was as essential to her as breathing, always had been, but when she'd looked out into the audience, she'd seen her daughter sitting at a table and conversing with a strange man.

She groaned inwardly when she thought of her little girl's propensity for plunging into anything like a tiny, blue eyed wrecking ball. Despite the circumstances of Ridley's birth, that child was her treasure, her heart. It didn't matter how many times Fate had tried to impress upon her a healthy dose of caution, Ridley had no fear.

The girl would talk to anyone as if they'd been best friends for ages, and dive into any situation with the full force of her exuberance, without considering any of the dangers. There were some days, she was ashamed to admit, that she envied that quality. For the past eight years, Fate had lived with fear as a constant companion—first from her attack, and then her abusive marriage—and it seemed like it had become a permanent part of her.

But there were other times, like the present moment, in which she had to protect Ridley from herself. While she negotiated the stairs that led from the stage, Fate had to take her eyes off her daughter. When she looked back at the table, both man and child were gone.

With an outward calm that she certainly didn't feel, Fate made her way through the club, smiling politely at intoxicated patrons who tried to speak to her. Reaching the table, she looked around for signs of where her daughter was hiding.

Finally, she heard the telltale rustle of clothing behind one of the large cinderblock columns. Busted, Fate thought.

"Ridley Jane, come out here right now." She spoke in a quiet but stern voice, not wanting to create a scene. The club owner did her a favor by allowing Ridley to sleep on a cot on the office when Fate had late night appearances. She couldn't always afford a babysitter.

Most mothers would expect a child to be sheepish or regretful after being scolded. Not Ridley. She was a hurricane as she exploded into Fate's arms and hugged her tight.

"Hi Mama! I heard you sing!"

"Yes, I see. You're supposed to be in bed, though."

Ridley blinked like an owl and gave her mother her best innocent face. "But the man said he wouldn't tell," she said, looking a bit crestfallen.

"The man didn't tell. I saw you. And now that we're on the subject, my love, who was that?"

The tiny face screwed up with intense concentration as she thought about it, and then light dawned. "Matthieu!"

Fate hoisted Ridley up on one hip so that she could look her straight in those piercing blue eyes. "Ridley Jane Callahan, what have I told you about talking to strangers?"

"Um...to not do it?"

"Exactly right, and what did you do anyway?"

"I talked, but it wasn't a stranger! It was Matthieu!"

Fate heaved an exasperated sigh and deciding to pick her battles, since the man had obviously left. "All right, love, I have one more set so you need to go on back to bed. Scoot!" She swatted her daughter's rear as she scuttled off to her bed in the office.

Checking her watch, Fate saw that she had about fifteen minutes until her next set. It was just enough time to grab a bottle of water from the bar and get some fresh air. She'd taken only two steps when the front door swung open, and her head swiveled around as if pulled by an invisible magnet. Stepping through the door was one of the most intimidating men she'd ever clapped eyes on—and apparently her daughter's new best friend.

Matthieu, Ridley had said. It was such an elegant name for such a rough looking man. His hair was dark, almost black, and longer at the top as if he was growing out a military brush cut. His height was probably just over six feet, but the bulky muscle across his chest and shoulders made him seem much larger. A jagged scar marred the smooth skin of his face as it ran from the corner of his left eye to his jawbone. As her eyes traveled just lower, Fate stifled a gasp when she saw the image of a king cobra coiled to strike tattooed over his pulse point.

Even with those chilling imperfections, he would have been handsome—sexy even—if it weren't for his eyes. They were so dark she couldn't determine the color but, more than that, they were empty. No, that wasn't right. Not empty, just hollow. She could see anger and pain, and resignation, swirling in their depths, and it chilled her. Unable to help herself, she took a step back as those orbs of misery snapped to her face and locked on.

He was even more terrifying in motion, as he strode with purpose...straight towards her. He wore black—black t-shirt, black fatigues, black combat boots—and he obviously had a destination in mind. Her. His powerful legs ate up the ground as he came to her, stopping just in front of her and lowering his brows to give her a menacing stare. Well, little did he know that Fate had been bullied one too many times in her life, and she just didn't take that kind of crap any more.

Crossing her arms over her chest, she stared right back and raised a brow at him. "Can I help you?"

His eyes widened momentarily before they shuttered again, but his aggressive posture eased a bit. "Fate Farrell?"

She tried not to show her surprise that he knew her name— her former name though it was. "Callahan. Farrell was my married name. I'm not married anymore. And you are?"

"Matthieu," he bit out. Nothing more. Just Matthieu.

"Okay. Well, Matthieu, mind telling me how you know my name and just what you're after?

"You're probably not going to believe anything I tell you, but both our lives depend on whether or not you do as I say." He raised a hand when she would have protested. "Just hear me out. You've made an enemy, Ms. Callahan. I don't know who and I don't know why, but I was hired to track you down."

Fate's heart dropped, not from fear but from the inevitability of the situation. Eli had finally caught up with her. She thought her ex-husband had given up when she disappeared, as he'd never made any move to find her in recent months. But who else would possibly hire this…P.I., detective, whatever…to come after her. "Christ, Eli," she breathed.

"Eli?" he asked, pegging her with that intense glare again.

"Eli Farrell, my ex-husband. Long story," she said, dismissing it with a wave of her hand. "Do finish, please."

"I just checked in with my…employer, reporting back that I'd found you. According to him, the client has given the order to have you eliminated."

Fate sighed and pinched the bridge of her nose. Of all the crazies in the city, of all the clubs in New Orleans, why did this nutcase have to walk into hers? With a tired sigh, she looked up at the stranger with the haunted eyes, and was astonished to see nothing but sincerity. "Okay, I'll bite," she said. "What did you say to that?"

"I said absolutely the hell not. I don't do hits on civilians. It's kind of a rule." He said it with such a wry tone that she almost laughed. Almost.

"Thing is," Matthieu continued, "if I don't do it, they'll send someone else. And since I've refused, my name will be on the list right next to yours. So we've got to get out of here, like yesterday."

"But my daughter--"

"Has to come with us. They've put a bulls-eye on her too, the sick fucks."

Fate closed her eyes as spots began to swim in her field of vision. She couldn't believe Eli would go this far. She knew he hated her for leaving him, for bursting his perfect little bubble and refusing to be his trophy wife in public, only to get beaten on in private. No, she *could* believe it; she just hadn't planned for it. But how could she possibly trust this menacing stranger. He said they were on the same side, but how could she be sure? Was that a gamble she was willing to take?

"Look, I'm sorry, Mr....er, Matthieu. I can't just grab my daughter and take off with you. I'm not going to play Russian roulette with my daughter's life! How do I know you won't kill me as soon as you've gotten me some place private?"

"You can't know," he said in a gravelly voice. "None of us can know if we'll live to see another sunrise. But I can tell you most assuredly that if you stay here and do nothing, you won't. Besides, if I were here to kill you, you'd already be dead and you'd never have seen me."

"You have *no* idea how comforting that is," she said, glaring at him. She was gearing up to tell him where he could stuff his threats when a soft light appeared behind him. It was the angel. Or at least that's what she thought it was. Fate had been seeing her since she was a little girl—always in times of great trouble or indecision—and she'd always figured the woman was some sort of guardian angel. Either that or she had a brain tumor.

The woman materialized behind Matthieu, her milky white eyes barely visible over his shoulder. Her glowing face was framed with long ebony ropes of magnificent hair. "*Te n'effraie pas*," she whispered. It meant don't be afraid, Fate looked it up once. But how could she not be afraid of the very man who'd been sent to kill her?

"*Te n'effraie pas*," the woman repeated, more emphatically this time. "You *must* go."

Before words had left the specter's mouth, she whipped her head around to face the door, and then she vanished. Moments later, a man in a dark suit and wraparound sunglasses entered, immediately scanning the room as if he were searching for someone. Her startled gasp drew Matthieu's attention, so he turned and looked as well.

"Shit, time to go. There a back way out of here?" he asked, holding a hand out to her. She just stared at it as if it would jump up and bite her. Finally he grasped her by the shoulders and gave her a light shake, forcing her to look up at him. "Fate. I've done a lot of terrible things in my life, things that are not to be forgiven. So I would happily go to my grave knowing that the last thing I did was save yours and your child's lives. But I can't do that if they kill us both first!"

Shaking out of her stupor, Fate realized she'd have to trust the troubled stranger and the angel, because the most obvious danger was pressing in on them. "There's a back door through the office. That's where Ridley is. We can pick her up on the way out."

"Let's go," he said, grabbing her hand and pulling her in the direction of the door marked 'Office.'

CHAPTER THREE

MATTHIEU HAD JUST TRANSFERRED THE CAR SEAT from Fate's dented Civic into the backseat of his Jeep SUV, and was helping her hoist a sleeping Ridley into it when he saw the black unmarked edge around the corner to the back lot.

"Get in," he snapped, though he tried to keep his voice low so as not to wake Ridley. When Fate glared at him, he jerked his chin toward the car that was slowly creeping up on them. Her eyes widened and she nodded, climbing into the passenger side. Without waiting for her to buckle up, Matthieu slid behind the wheel, fired up the engine and peeled out.

Fate had to brace a hand against the window to keep from cracking her skull, and she whipped around to snarl at him. "Drive much?"

"Quite a lot, actually..." was his droll reply, "which is going to come in real handy right about now. Buckle up, for God's sake."

Matthieu ignored her indignant sputtering and focused on the set of headlights following close behind them, in the rearview mirror. He swallowed convulsively and wondered what the hell he'd gotten himself into. Not only did he have a target on his back now, but he was responsible for a woman and a young child. He could barely even be relied on to be responsible for himself, most days. They needed a plan, and fast.

"What about my car?" Her question jolted him out of his thoughts, though he still paid attention to their tail.

"Leave it. We go back for it, it'll be bugged, tracked, or wired to blow, I guaran-damn-tee it."

Her sharp intake of breath was the only indication that she'd heard. She remained silent for several minutes, leaning up against the window and staring through the glass. Eventually she turned weary gray eyes back to him and sighed. "So where are we going?"

Matthieu could tell her nerves were beginning to fray, and he really couldn't blame her. So he summoned what little people skills he had and tried to be nice. "As soon as I lose the tail, I thought we'd make a run to your place so you can grab some things for you and the kid. Don't know how long we're going to have to stay out of sight."

"Lose the...we're being *followed*?" Without waiting for an answer, she turned as far as the seat belt would allow and let out a little squeak when she saw the lights behind them. "How can you be sure that's them?"

Actions speak louder than words, Matthieu thought, changing lanes. Almost immediately, the car behind them slid into their lane. He repeated the action with the same result. "Believe me now?"

"Oh my God. We're in a mother-loving car chase."

Matthieu felt his lips twitch, remembering his mom would use the same type of phrases when trying not to curse in front of her boys.

"Looks that way."

"Oh, no, I can't do this. Not with my daughter. I've got to find somewhere safe for her to stay."

"You have any family?" Matthieu inquired, knowing that if she did, Ward and the client most likely knew about it.

She shook her head and drew her knees up to rest her feet on the dash. It was an odd position for a woman wearing an evening gown, but she seemed to want to curl up around herself. "My mother's alive but we haven't spoken since, well, before Ridley was born. I have an aunt that I've never met. That's it. "God, what am I going to do?"

Matthieu had an idea and he wasn't sure if it would fly, but it may be their only option. While Ward may know all about Fate's life and family, Matthieu took great pains from the very beginning to keep his fucked up world well away from *his*.

"I may have another option. Just hear me out," he said when she gave him a wary look. "My brother and his wife live less than fifteen miles from here and they owe me a favor. He's...they're not like me. They're good people. I know they would protect her like she was their own."

He heard a sniffle, and winced when he looked over to see tears streaming down her face. "I'm sorry. Look, if you have another idea —"

"No, it's not that. It's just that I've never been separated from her. I don't know how to do this."

At a loss, Matthieu racked his brain for something comforting to say. He came up with nothing. Zilch. "Um, well, don't think of it as leaving her behind, think of it as keeping her safe."

Turning her head, she gave him a long, inscrutable look. Uncomfortable, he just shrugged and went back to monitoring the tail. They were nearing the on-ramp for the freeway and Matthieu stayed his course, hoping the person following them would think they were staying on the city street. At the last possible moment, he jerked the wheel sharply to the right, cutting across solid white lines to the on-ramp. He stomped on the gas, accelerating as fast as the jeep would let him, and then cut over to the carpool lane, pushing ninety.

After a few miles, he determined that he'd lost them for good and slowed down. Chancing a look over at Fate, he noticed she was as pale as a ghost, but hanging in there. She still hadn't released her white knuckled grip on the hand-hold but it looked like her breathing was returning to normal. "Sorry," he said. "I think we lost them. You're going to have to give me directions to your place."

She opened her mouth to answer but nothing came out. Clearing her throat, she tried again. "Get off at the next exit and hang a left," she croaked, glancing back at the still sleeping Ridley.

"Can't believe she slept through that," Matthieu muttered, not able to remember a time when he'd slept so soundly.

"Oh God, she'd sleep through a nuclear holocaust. I'm jealous, really," she said, mirroring his thoughts. "Here's my street coming up. Take a right."

They turned onto a street populated with lower middle class townhomes in various stages of disrepair. One of them was older, but shone as if were taken care of regularly. He wasn't surprised to find that it was hers.

"Mine's the third on the right. Right here!" she exclaimed when he drove past it.

"Going to make a couple of passes first, make sure no one's staking it out yet. Believe me, they will be. There an alley out back?"

"Ah, yes, it's where we park."

"Perfect. We'll park back there and I'll watch the front while you get your stuff together. Once we get inside you have five minutes, got it? Once they figure out they lost us, they'll probably give up and come straight here."

"Okay."

He saw a slight tremor in her hands as she tucked her hair behind her ear. "Hey," he said, waiting until she turned those stormy eyes to him. "It's going to be okay. This is the easy part. I do the same job as these people, only I'm much better at it. I can get us out of this."

He'd meant it to be comforting, but he guessed it probably wasn't, coming from a perfect stranger. She blinked a few times and jerked her chin in a curt nod. Shortly after, Matthieu pulled the jeep up to the back of the townhouse and let the engine idle. "Hurry up," he urged.

She glanced at him, then back at Ridley, and her eyes snapped back to his face. "With all due...*whatever*, I'm not leaving her alone in this car with you."

"Fine," he said through clenched teeth, "we'll all go."

He climbed out of the car as Fate unsnapped the harness of the car seat. When she went to try and pull Ridley out, he stopped her with a hand on her shoulder. "Let me. I'm sure she's heavy and, besides, you've got to do the packing."

A muscle twitched in her jaw as she reluctantly stepped back to allow him room to move. Matthieu gently lifted the sleeping girl and hitched her up on one hip, while trying to ignore how big and clumsy he felt.

He froze when he felt thin arms wind around his neck, and Ridley nestled her face into the crook of his shoulder. Feeling Fate's eyes on him, he cleared his throat and started walking. "Remember," he said in a whisper, "five minutes."

"Got it, Chief," was her sarcastic reply as she gave him a smart salute before unlocking the back door. She headed straight for the stairs, presumably to start packing.

Still carrying his delicate burden, Matthieu walked to the front door. Reaching to the window beside it, he pulled aside the curtain just enough to see the road in front of the house. Ridley stirred for a brief moment, snuffling into his neck before quieting.

Unable to help it—or even explain it—he held on just a little bit tighter. He'd never been trusted with, or even close to, something so precious. It scared the hell out of him, but in that moment he knew that he would die to protect this child. Her life was worth so much more than his.

As if she could sense his inner turmoil, Ridley raised her head off of his shoulder and blinked to clear the sleep from those enormous blue eyes. When she finally focused on him, she dazzled him with a brilliant gap-toothed grin. "Matthieu," she whispered, touching his scarred cheek with tiny fingers, as if nothing else needed to be said.

Matthieu had to clear his throat a couple of times before he could reply. "Hey there, jelly bean," he said, making her giggle—and feeling like he'd been given the greatest gift.

"Where's Mommy?" she asked, sleepily rubbing her eyes.

"She's just upstairs getting some of your things, and then we're going to go on a trip."

"Like a sleepover?" she inquired before yawning so wide, her tiny jaw cracked. She had settled her head back down and her eyelids were drooping before she even heard his answer.

"Something like that."

Fate made quick work of the packing. In fact, she was downstairs in under four minutes. And not a moment too soon. Matthieu noticed a similar unmarked car roll down the street in front of them, sweeping past the house, likely to turn around and come back.

"Time's up," he hissed, turning to see Fate stuffing a cell phone into the back pocket of her worn jeans. "The phone stays here."

"I'm not going to leave my daughter with strangers who've no way to contact me," she snapped.

With a sigh, Matthieu prayed for patience. "Phones," he said, plucking it from her grasp, "can easily be used to track you through the signal, especially if it has GPS. We'll pick up a prepaid for you on the way out of town."

She calmed a little at that, but narrowed her eyes at him. "What about yours?"

"Mine *can't* be tracked."

Hearing car doors slam outside spurred him into action. He held on tight to Ridley with one arm, while picking up Fate's suitcase with the other, leaving her to carry the smaller pink Hello Kitty bag.

While Fate locked up the house, Matthieu hurried to the car to secure Ridley in her seat. Once they were all loaded up, he threw the jeep into reverse and crept down the alley. His hope was to be long gone before their pursuers noticed they'd been there.

He watched in the rearview for several minutes before reassuring himself that they weren't being followed. What was to come next was a much bigger hurdle in his mind—facing his brother after all these years, and the wife Matthieu had never met.

CHAPTER FOUR

S HE DROVE TO HIS BROTHER'S TOWNHOUSE ON THE other side of town, Matthieu gripped the steering wheel so hard that he thought he might break it. Nothing made him nervous. Nothing...except the prospect of seeing his brother.

When their father had died, Matthieu had really been too young to understand. All he knew was that the big, boisterous man who'd had such a presence in his life was just...gone. Although only two and a half years older than him, Jeremiah had stepped in to try and fill James Rousseau's size twelves.

He'd done everything he could to be a father figure and a role model for Matthieu, and Matthieu had tried so hard to let it be enough—and to be enough himself. But it wasn't. Somehow, he'd turned out broken. Hell, maybe he'd been broken at birth. Who knew?

His overwhelming feelings of inadequacy and emptiness had led him to distance himself from Jeremiah, Esme, their mother, and their foster brother, Drew. Matthieu knew that Jeremiah would blame himself, still did, for not being able to take care of him—to fix what was wrong—and that only added to his guilt. Eventually, he'd stopped coming around altogether.

Oh, he'd kept tabs on them of course—Jere, Esme, and Drew—and he knew what they were all up to. This was precisely why he stayed away. They had good lives, all of them, and they certainly didn't need his perpetual thundercloud hovering over him.

But now he was about to storm the beach, swoop in out of nowhere and drop a bombshell or five. Matthieu could feel the cold sweat begin to trickle down his back. He snapped out of his musings when he heard Fate clear her throat and he felt his cheeks heat.

"You okay?" she asked. "You can't freak out on me now. You're driving this bus, private."

Trying for humor, Matthieu pretended to look offended. "I was ranked a bit higher than private, thank you."

Her eyes widened, and he figured she was pondering how a decorated soldier ends up a hired gun on the run. Yeah, he'd wondered that a time or two himself.

She kept her eyes on him, raking over him so thoroughly that he felt more than naked. It was like she was burrowing her way inside—and no one was allowed inside.

Brow furrowing, she cocked her head at him, and he caught the motion in his periphery. "When was the last time you talked to your brother?"

"Officially? Years."

"...seen him?"

"Longer."

"Then how can you possibly know he'll help us?"

She looked like she was about to panic, so Matthieu reached out and patted her knee. Heat radiated into his hand and up his arm from the point of contact, so he jerked it back as if she shocked him. He guessed she kind of did.

"Because he's that kind of guy. Trust me, family is everything to Jeremiah."

Nothing else was said, and when he pulled up in front of the elegant two-story, Matthieu cut the engine but didn't move. He sat there staring at the house for so long, he jumped when Fate placed a hand on his shoulder.

He raised his gaze to her face and was surprised to find comfort there—something he'd had precious little of since he'd left home. "Hey..." she said. "If your brother is the kind of guy you say he is, he'll be happy to see you, yeah?"

"Yeah, I guess." *Time to man up, Rousseau.* Gathering his courage, he climbed out of the jeep and went around to scoop Ridley from her seat, only to find that Fate already had her daughter in her arms. He couldn't help but feel the slightest twinge of disappointment, but he shoved it down. There were bigger things to deal with.

Matthieu steeled himself and rang the doorbell, realizing too late that it was very, *very* early in the morning. Cursing himself ten times a fool, he could do nothing but wait, with Fate standing expectantly behind him. God, he hoped she was right about Jeremiah.

A light came on under the cover of the porch and the door swung open to reveal a tiny woman. She had black curly hair and her brilliant green eyes were framed by a thick fringe of bangs. Her eyes widened with obvious surprise at the sight of him, but then two dimples winked out when she gave him a stunning smile.

"I'm so glad you're here!" she exclaimed in a charming Scottish brogue, and threw her arms around his neck, squeezing with surprising strength. "Jeremiah will be so happy."

Matthieu was unsure of what to say, especially when he saw tears gathering in her eyes, so he gently set her away from him. He noticed that she laid an unconscious hand protectively over her rounded belly. And, wow, that was new. Obviously he hadn't been keeping close enough tabs on his brother after all.

Suddenly remembering Fate and Ridley, he stepped aside to allow them to enter. "I'm sorry if we woke you, but we have a bit of a problem we need some help with. Um, this is my...friend, Fate Callahan and her daughter, Ridley."

"Isla Rousseau," she explained, shaking hands with Fate and patting Ridley on the back. "And no, you didn't wake me. I'm a bit of an early riser, you see. But as far as Jeremiah, I'm afraid I'm going to have to go poke the bear," she said with a smile.

"Too late," said a voice from behind her. "The bear has been poked."

A rumpled, sleepy Jeremiah padded down the hallway toward his wife, shaggy hair standing on end and a couple of days' worth of stubble on his jaw. Matthieu realized in that moment just how much he'd missed his brother, and the feeling stabbed through him like a knife.

Jeremiah stepped up behind Isla while rubbing sleep from his eyes, and blinked a few times as if he was trying to focus on the people standing in front of him. When his gaze finally connected with Matthieu's, he froze.

They all stood there, still as death, for so long that Matthieu looked down and began to shuffle his feet. When he could no longer stand the silence, he cleared his throat. "Maybe this was a bad idea," he mumbled, "we should—"

He was cut off from further conversation when Jeremiah stepped forward, grabbed him by the back of the neck, and pulled him into a bear hug that took the wind out of his lungs. It was the kind of hug that only a big brother—or a father—could give.

The embrace seemed to go on forever, long enough for Isla to usher Fate and Ridley into the kitchen. Matthieu took a deep shuddering breath and allowed himself to lean into his brother, just a little bit. Jeremiah smelled of Irish Spring and cedar and, to Matthieu, it smelled like home.

Realizing he was letting himself feel too much, want too much, Matthieu took a step back, breaking Jere's hold on him. They stood staring at each other for a few more tense moments before Matthieu spoke.

"Nice place," he said, feeling shy and awkward, and hating it.

His brother's hazel eyes lit up and his wolf-like grin made an appearance with its overlong canines. "Yeah? It's just temporary, we're building just outside the city, but we like it. Are you needing a place to stay?"

It was a subtle prompt to get to the point of matters—why had Matthieu showed up at his doorstep after all these years, with a woman and child in tow? Matthieu shook his head and rubbed a hand over the stubble on his jaw.

"No...no, not exactly."

Jeremiah crossed his arms over his broad chest and raised a brow, just waiting for Matthieu to speak.

"I think I may need to cash in that favor. The one you said you owed me for tracking down that guy for you last fall."

"Go on..."

"We—Fate has someone who wants her dead. They're after us. We have to disappear for a while until I can figure out who's behind the hit."

"How do you know this?" Jeremiah asked, and Matth eu could tell that his perceptive brother knew there was more to the story.

"Because I was the one who was hired to find her." Ignor ng Jere's muttered curse, he pressed on. "When I reported back to my superiors, I was given the order to take her out—and the child, too."

Jeremiah's sharp gasp was like a gunshot in the darkness. "Matty," he growled, "tell me you didn't consider it.

Recoiling, Matthieu's eyes widened and snapped to his brother's face. "Oh, fuck me; of *course* I didn't consider it." What the hell kind of person did his brother think he was? "I may be damaged, but I'm not a monster."

"You're not either," Jere whispered.

With a sad shake of his head, Matthieu frowned at the declaration. Jeremiah always gave him too damn much credit. Matthieu flinched when his brother grasped his arm.

"You don't have to do this, you know—live this way. You could stay with us; we'd love to have you. I've even got connections in the security business that could sure use your talents, in a legit kind of way."

With a defeated sigh, Matthieu gave his brother a half-hearted smile. "You know I can't do that, big brother. I don't belong in polite society...I've got too much blood on my hands." He held up one of said hands to stop Jere's protest before it started. "Besides, you know I've tried it before. Didn't work out. So let's just drop it, yeah?"

Jeremiah shoved his hands through his shaggy hair with a curse. "*Fuck*. Fine. So where do I fit into this whole hitman scenario?"

"When I refused to kill Fate and Ridley—meaning when I politely told my boss and his client to go fuck themselves—I sort of made myself a target as well."

"Of *course* you did."

Ignoring the sarcasm, Matthieu continued. "We're going to have to ghost for a little while until I can figure out who's behind the hit."

"Got any ideas?"

"Fate seems to think it's her ex-husband, but I'm not sure. I can't imagine a guy being so fucked in the head that he'd order a hit on his own child, and I've seen a whole lotta fucked in the head. I haven't had a chance to get the whole story from her yet."

Jeremiah stared hard at him for a long moment, and then his expression softened. "What do you need us to do?"

CHAPTER FIVE

FATE'S HEAD SWAM AS SHE ALLOWED HERSELF TO BE lead into the warm, homey kitchen. Grateful for a moment to sit, she hitched Ridley up further on her hip and plunked herself down at the kitchen table.

As soon as she was comfortable, Isla pegged her with a direct stare—Fate had always appreciated direct. Isla softened the expression with a friendly smile. "Now that we're alone, would you care to tell me what brings you and Matthieu to our doorstep at this 'ungodly hour,' as my husband would say?"

Unsure as to how much she should reveal, she decided to start off with ambiguity. "We're in a bit of trouble. Someone is after us, and I didn't want to drag my daughter into some kind of cat and mouse game. Matthieu suggested that you two would maybe...let her stay with you for a few days."

Isla's riot of black curls bounced as she gave a noncommittal nod. She startled Fate by leaning forward, placing her own hand over Fate's, and looking directly into her eyes. "Understand that Jeremiah and I would do anything for Matthieu. But first, I need you to be honest with me."

Fate discreetly pulled her hand back. She'd never been comfortable with strangers touching her. She wasn't sure where Isla's question was leading but strangely, she didn't feel threatened, so she nodded.

"Good," Isla continued. "I need you to tell me if you're here against your will."

"Um, well, I guess. Sort of. I certainly didn't ask to be chased by some unknown bad-guy and forced to go into hiding."

"No, what I meant was, did Matthieu—"

"Oh, God, no!" Fate answered, cutting Isla off because she finally realized what the other woman was getting at. "Of course Matthieu didn't force me to go with him. I mean, it took some convincing, sure, but he's being chased as well.

Wondering what kind of life Matthieu had led to have his family question him in that way, Fate quickly explained what had gone down at the club.

"And you think Matthieu's *client* is your ex-husband? Why?"

"I can't imagine anyone else hating me that much. He's the only one in my life that I've ever had cross words with. And it wouldn't be the first time he's gotten...violent."

Isla flicked worried eyes to Ridley, who was still sleeping against Fate's shoulder. "No, never her, thank God."

As if she knew they were talking about her, Ridley stirred and lifted her head, blinking to focus on her mother's face. "Mommy?"

"Hello, angel. It's time to wake up now; I have some friends for you to meet. This is Isla," she said, nodding towards the other woman.

Still blinking, Ridley looked over at her and cracked a toothy smile. "Auntie!" she said with a sleepy squeal.

Isla laughed and smiled back. "Not exactly, sweeting, but you can call me that if you like. I'm married to Matthieu's brother," she explained.

Ridley yawned and nodded, as if that was all the explanation she needed. The child's eyes widened suddenly when an enormous cat leapt onto the table. On its hind legs, the thing could probably look Ridley in the eye.

The regal looking animal licked at his paw, blinked at them, and then bounded off the table to chase another equally humongous cat. Fate could feel Ridley practically vibrating against her with the need to go play with the animals.

"Are they friendly?" she asked Isla.

"Oh, of course. They're still adjusting to being American cats now, so I'm sure they could use a friend."

"Go on then," Fate said, and Ridley was off before she'd finished speaking. Casting a worried glance down the hall after her daughter, Fate chewed on her lower lip.

"Don't worry, there's no trouble for her to get into back there," Isla said with a kind smile.

Fate let out a gasp when a young man padded into the kitchen wearing nothing but a pair of shabby pajama bottoms. His body was trim but sculpted, and covered in an expanse of bronze skin that hinted of a Mediterranean heritage. Intricate tattooing covered one arm and part of his neck, and it rippled as he yawned and stretched.

"Um..." Fate was at a loss. Supposedly only Matthieu's brother and sister-in-law lived here, but Isla didn't seemed surprised to see this man.

"*Amarelúpo*, we have company." Her voice held a gentle reprimand but was full of love as well. The young man looked up, blinking sleep out of his eyes, and froze when he saw Fate.

She never knew someone with that skin tone could blush, but hey, you learn something new every day.

He ducked his head in embarrassment. "Apologies, *domina*. Ma'am," he murmured, before slipping into what Fate assumed was the laundry room to grab a shirt. Chuckling, Isla treated him to an indulgent smile.

"Don't mind him; his manners are a bit...savage at times. This is Marduk. He's a relative of mine who's staying with us for a while." Fate noticed a strange look cross the other woman's face before she turned to Marduk.

"Marduk, this is Fate. She's a friend of Matthieu's. He's here."

Fate noticed the young man's eyes widen at that, but he showed no other reaction—until the Tasmanian devil that was Ridley bounded into the room, squealing at the cats as she chased them.

Fate nearly laughed out loud at the look of horror that colored Marduk's features, and he gave the little girl a wide berth, as if she might attack at any moment. Isla wasn't nearly as polite when she snorted out a laugh.

"He's not been around children much," she explained, obviously amused. "Marduk, would you make us some tea? And maybe some cocoa for the bairn?"

"Of course, *domina*," he answered, looking grateful to have something to do.

"This may be a strange question, but that name that you called him...Well, I studied Latin for years in school. I don't understand the dialect, but it seems like you said something along the lines of 'lovely wolf.' That's...odd."

"It's just a little pet name I have for him. Sort of an inside joke." Isla laughed it off, maybe a bit too casually, but Fate decided not to push. Beggars couldn't be choosers, after all.

Fate looked up as Matthieu entered the kitchen, followed by Jeremiah who had a hand on his brother's shoulder. It was almost as though he felt like Matthieu could disappear at any moment. Ridley immediately ceased her frantic chasing of Smitty and Atticus, the cats, and ran over to attach herself to Matthieu's leg.

Without seeming to give it much thought, he lifted her up and tossed her in the air, before setting the squirming bundle back on her feet only to collapse in giggles. Fate looked back and forth between Jeremiah and Isla as they shared equally dumbstruck expressions. Ridley tired of the tossing game and walked over to Isla, climbed into her lap and placed a tiny hand on the woman's belly. "What's in here?" she asked with the curiosity of youth.

"Ridley!" Fate hissed, discomfited by her daughter's boldness.

Isla simply smiled and patted Ridley's hand. "That's perfectly all right. What's in here? Hope is in here."

"Hope?" Fate and Ridley asked at the same time, confused.

Isla nodded, her dimples winking out. "A baby girl. Her name is Hope."

"When can she come out?" Ridley asked, causing Fate to again flush with embarrassment.

Isla's laughter was music as she looked down at the curious child. "Not for a while yet, I'm afraid. Two months, maybe a bit less."

Ridley frowned at that, but turned and smiled, distracted by Matthieu's voice.

"So what do you guys think?" His question was tentative, as if he wasn't sure they wouldn't get turned away, despite the glowing description of his brother that he'd given.

"I think we'd be happy to have a little house guest, don't you Jeremiah? It'll help us prepare for this little one," Isla said, patting her belly.

"Are you sure it's not too much?" Matthieu asked.

Jeremiah shook his head, his eyes searching his brother's face. "Nah, not at all. Between the cats and the w— er, Marduk, we're already running a funny farm as it is. Mama an' Ray will help out too."

Matthieu's face darkened as a line of confusion formed between his brows. "Ray? Not that two-bit hustler I tracked down for you last fall?"

"Easy there, Tiger. That's Drew's future father-in-law you're talking about. He had sort of a close call awhile back and he suffered some kind of PTSD breakdown. The hospital kicked him out, and Mama agreed to take him in for a while so Raven could be close to her father."

Matthieu didn't seem convinced, but he said nothing else on the subject. "Well," he said, turning to Fate, "I guess we should get on the road. Don't want to sit around and wait for those spooks to track us down."

Fate's heart lurched when she realized that it was time—time to leave her little girl for the first time ever. She just hoped Ridley would understand that it was for the best. Kneeling so that she was eye to eye with her daughter, she broke the news.

"Okay, my love. Matthieu and I have to take care of some things. How would you like to stay here with Isla for a little while?" She braced herself for any number of reactions; she thought the most likely of which would be tears or a tantrum.

Ridley blinked her huge blue eyes a couple of times, looking up at Matthieu who nodded, and then over at Isla. It seemed to Fate as if she were weighing her options. Sometimes she seemed so impossibly grown up.

"With the cats?" she finally asked, cracking that snaggle-toothed grin of hers. Wow, Fate thought, she'd been thrown over by a couple of uppity felines.

CHAPTER SIX

MATTHIEU TRIED TO FOCUS ON DRIVING, BUT IT was difficult with Fate sitting next to him. She was curled up in a ball as best she could with the seatbelt on, and was leaning against the window, quietly sobbing. She'd changed from her elegant evening gown into a sweatshirt and yoga pants, and she looked...fragile.

Matthieu had handled bombs, air raids, assassins, even being a prisoner of war, but he was at a loss when faced with a crying woman. He really had no idea what to do or say to make it better—to assure her that her daughter would be all right.

Hell, he figured that Ridley was definitely the safest of the three of them. Wanting to say something, anything, to try and reassure Fate, he turned his head toward her. "You can stop crying. She's gonna be fine."

He guessed it came out terser than he'd intended, partially because of his scarred vocal chords. The damage had happened during the explosion in Kandahar, although he never recovered his full memory of exactly what had caused it. Most of the time his voice came out sounding like it had been scrubbed with sandpaper.

Fate flinched at the sound of it, and then began scrubbing her cheeks and sniffling. While he realized he hadn't comforted her like he'd intended, his comment seemed to have snapped her out of her misery.

"Sorry," he whispered and then fell silent.

"Where are we going?"

"For now, we're heading down the bayou, out below Houma. I have sort of a safehouse about an hour from here. We should be safe there for a few days until I can figure out our next move."

He watched in his periphery as she pulled out the prepaid cell phone he had picked up for her on the way out of the city and began to fiddle with it. "Planning on calling someone?" he asked, raising a brow.

She glared at him, obviously resentful of having to answer to him. Well, that was just too damn bad. They couldn't afford any mistakes. "I was texting Isla the number so she can call me if there's a problem."

Nodding, Matthieu turned his attention back to the road. "Just don't call anyone but her without telling me. I can't keep you safe if I don't know what risks you're taking," he added when she looked like she might argue.

He looked over at her again and noticed a peculiar tattoo on the inside of her wrist. It was a tribal-looking design that had three nested circles with three slashes across them. There was a symbol inside the smallest circle, but he couldn't make it out.

Curious, he tried to urge her to talk about it. "Nice tattoo. What's it mean?" It was a simple question, but her whole body seemed to freeze for a moment before she glared at him.

Without answering, she tugged the sleeve of her sweatshirt down so that the hem covered the ink, and then turned her face away from him. Okay, no tattoo talk. Noted, he thought, and let it drop.

They lapsed into a somewhat comfortable silence, but Matthieu grew more and more agitated with each passing mile. The adrenaline of the chase had begun to wear off, and he was starting to realize just what he'd gotten himself into.

It wasn't as if he couldn't handle the spooks, couldn't track down Arlen Ward and his mysterious client. No, with his expertise, that was the easy part. Matthieu was worried about Fate and her proximity to him.

Anyone who came within a thirty foot radius of him could tell he had issues—that was no secret. But no one knew the half of it. No one could. The devils that tortured his mind were only for him to see, to hear.

And he could always hear them, their insidious whispers always fluttering around the edges of his consciousness. They'd been with him nearly as far back as he could remember, and every day, he felt another piece of his fragile sanity slipping away.

That was the real reason he'd cut himself off from everyone and everything that mattered. He could never be sure when he'd finally snap. When he was younger, he'd passed it off as grief over the death of his father, and more recently, the PTSD. God knew he had plenty enough of both to cause an average man to lose his sanity.

But Matthieu wasn't an average man. So every day he fought back the voices that called to him, hissed depraved promises in his ear. But at night, when he slept? He had no defenses. They seemed to take over, bombarding him with images, sounds, and smells, regaling their evil deeds. They wanted him, he knew. Just as well as he knew that one day—in his sleep—they would take him.

Matthieu flicked a nervous glance at Fate as he white-knuckled the steering wheel. He hadn't shared a residence with another human being since the barracks in Kandahar. And those were men. Soldiers.

He'd tried only once to sleep in the same bed as a woman, and it hadn't ended well. There'd been a few other half-hearted relationships, but only one that he thought he had a chance of taking further. Her name was Emilie, and he'd fancied himself in love with her. They were going to run away together, get married, and Matthieu was finally going to have a normal life.

Only that didn't happen. He never slept much, couldn't stand the violated, dirty feeling he had when he woke—after the demons had been crawling around under his skin and using his mind as a playground.

But one night, after a particularly acrobatic round of sex, it finally caught up with him. He'd woken up with his hands around her throat. Once he realized what was happening, he released her immediately and stumbled into the bathroom, where he promptly emptied the contents of his stomach.

When he came back into the bedroom, Emilie was gone. Matthieu never saw her again. He thought that was probably for the best, not only for her but anyone associated with him. So he ghosted and never looked back.

"I'm going to sleep for a bit."

Fate's voice cut into his thoughts so sharply that he jerked his hands on the wheel. The jeep swerved when he overcorrected, but he quickly righted it.

"You okay? Where'd you go?" she asked, her stormy eyes narrowing in a wary expression.

"Yeah, fine. Just zoned out I guess," he murmured, embarrassed. Holding the wheel with one hand, he leaned forward and shrugged out of his leather jacket. Balling up the supple material, he handed it to her. "Use that as a pillow."

He cursed himself inwardly as her eyes locked on his shoulder holster and his twin Sigs. Looked like Fate Callahan had just been reminded just who the fuck she was with. Her throat worked in a convulsive swallow, but she took the offering and croaked out a thank you. Matthieu nodded and turned his attention to the road. He doubted she'd get any sleep now, but they were almost to Houma which meant they were close to their destination—his daddy's old fishing shack on a hidden canal in Theriot.

CHAPTER SEVEN

WHEN FATE AWOKE, THEY WERE DESCENDING DOWN an overgrown drive. One side was lined with huge twisting oak trees draped in Spanish moss, while the other side bordered the swamp and was lined with bald Cypress trees.

Matthieu still had a death grip on the steering wheel and she had to wonder what that was all about. Surely a hitman would have sturdier nerves. Right? She was beginning to wonder if he wasn't more nervous about her than she was about him.

The sun was sinking low and the oaks shaded them from the waning light, so Fate had to strain to see where they were going. Finally Matthieu pulled up in front of a house and stopped the Jeep.

Upon second glance, Fate realized that, no, it wasn't a house. It was a shack—a barely upright one at that. The tin roof was rusted and sagging, extending out over a porch that was missing a few columns—so many that she wasn't exactly sure what was holding it up.

Grayish, rotting wood siding covered the outside of the structure and though the windows were covered with dilapidated shutters, Fate was sure that they would be broken. She couldn't see the back of the "house" but it seemed as though the dark, fetid swamp water came right up to the foundation.

He must have heard her sharp gasp because, in her periphery, Fate saw his lips twist in a sardonic parody of a smile. "Welcome to *La Maison de Rousseau*," he said, and she rolled her eyes. But he still made no effort to stop the car, to get out.

Taking the time to study him, Fate's eyes were immediately drawn to the scar across his cheek. It wasn't quite as prominent with a light beard growth over it, but it was still gruesome looking. *Had to have been a pretty deep cut*, she thought.

It looked like it had happened a long time ago, and had grown with him over the years. Fate had the inexplicable urge to reach out and trace it with her fingers. It was something she could hardly help—she felt connected to things when she touched them because she could determine the history of something or someone by linking to it on a metaphysical level. She kept it to herself because one person looking at her like she was bat shit crazy had been more than enough. She'd tried to tell Eli once and it had gone...badly.

She was pretty sure her attentions would be unwelcome—she'd learned that lesson the hard way over the years—so she tried to focus on something else. Her gaze landed on the dog tags that hung from a chain around his neck and rested against his sternum. They hadn't been visible when he found her in the club, so she wondered about them now.

Unable to help herself, she reached out and closed her hand around the tags. She was startled when he snatched her wrist in an iron grip but, before she could react, she was plunged into darkness.

After blinking a few times to clear her gaze, she looked around and saw not the interior of the Jeep, but a cloud of viscous black smoke. It engulfed everything around her, burned her eyes, poured into her lungs to the point that she could barely breathe. All she could hear was a piercing ringing in her ears.

Fate was jolted out of the vision when Matthieu gave her a firm shake. "Hey! Where'd you go?" he asked, repeating her earlier question. His inky eyes were wide with alarm and he regarded her as if she were about to start speaking in tongues.

"Sorry. Just spaced out there for a minute. Did you say something?" her voice sounded thin and thready to her own ears, so she could only imagine what he was hearing. He gave her a dubious look, clearly not buying it, but he didn't press.

Matthieu faced forward again and studied the house for a few intense moments before looking at her again. He clenched his jaw and Fate swore she could actually see the moment his face closed up and he distanced himself from her. "Look, I think it would be best for both of us if you don't touch me."

Ouch. Fate glared at him, and wondered why in the hell he all of a sudden thought he was God's gift. It wasn't as if she'd wanted to touch *him*—well, after she'd talked herself out of it, of course—she just wanted to see the tags.

But when she looked at him again, she saw none of the conceit or cockiness that would come from that kind of attitude. She saw only pain, he only looked haunted. Deciding to give the guy a break, she said nothing more.

When Matthieu stepped over the threshold and held the door for Fate to enter the house, she was shocked at what she saw. Apparently the façade of the house was just a clever ruse. The inside was in perfect condition and immaculate.

The living room and kitchen were all one room beneath the low ceiling with only a bar separating the two areas. The house was furnished in a modern style but with the low lighting and the fireplace, it was extremely cozy.

Confused, Fate turned around to question Matthieu. "Why do you leave the outside looking that way?"

A shadow crossed his face and she thought he might not answer, but he did. "My father used to take Jeremiah and me fishing here, and the inside looked much the same as the outside back then. When he died...he left the shack to me because Jeremiah hated fishing—he only ever did it to be close with Dad. Anyway, I remodeled the inside so that I could use it as a safehouse, and the point of a safehouse is to hide."

She raised a brow at that but said nothing. What had this man been hiding from?

"I figured leaving the outside as it was would be good camouflage," he finished.

"I see your point. I can't imagine anyone caring enough to break in. How do you keep it up?"

"I have a neighbor who comes in and takes care of things a couple of times a month, stocks it up for me when I need to use it. And in return, I don't turn him in for his off-season poaching— and his on-season bookmaking."

Fate turned a slow circle around the open great room before putting her bag down and sitting down on the overstuffed sofa. Matthieu walked over to join her but he sat on the coffee table across from her.

"We need to go over some house rules real quick, and then I'll let you get settled in."

Her head swiveled around slowly to peg him with a glare. Just who the hell did this guy think he was? *Rules*, like she was some kind of child.

Clamping down on her ire, Fate just raised a brow at him. "Such as?"

"One—keep all doors and windows locked when you're inside. Two—don't leave the house without letting me know—"

"Oh, you mean I'm going to be allowed to leave at all?" she asked with a little more snark than she'd planned, but she wasn't sorry. She'd had enough of men trying to bully her and control her life.

Matthieu didn't flinch; he just gave her a long, hard stare. "Of course. You're not a prisoner, no matter what you may think. We're relatively sheltered here. However, that leads me to rule three—do not, under any circumstances, leave the property without me. We'll go on a walk later and I'll show you how far the land goes."

He stopped and waited, as if he thought she might protest again. She thought about it, but was pretty sure it wouldn't do any good. When she didn't, he frowned and continued.

"Lastly—and this is the most important—do *not* wake me if you find me sleeping. In fact, get as far away from me as possible, preferably behind a locked door. I don't sleep much, so don't forget."

What in the hell? Fate had never heard of such a thing. But then she remembered the dog tags, and the vision, and decided it must be some sort of PTSD thing. But she was still curious, to a fault. "But why—?"

"Don't worry about why. Let me ask you this. Do you remember the movie *Gremlins*?" He waited until she nodded. "Remember what happened when they broke the rules?"

Fate nodded again.

"Good. Keep that in mind," he said, and she rolled her eyes. As if she was going to be scared by some bad horror movie reference. She didn't say anything, though, because he suddenly grew very serious. "I mean it, Fate. You can't trust anyone. No one."

"Except for you, right?" she said with a wry twist of her lips.

He shook his head, the action laced with sadness, with regret. "Fuck, no. *Especially* not me."

She was speechless, and he clearly wasn't going to say more on the subject. Conversation. Over.

"You can take the back bedroom, just down that hall. Why don't you unpack and grab the first shower while I make us some supper," he said in that gruff tone that never failed to intrigue her.

"You're going to cook?" she asked, skeptical that this rough military man would have any cooking skills to speak of.

His lips twitched, which was about as close as he ever came to a smile. "We don't exactly have pizza delivery this far out in the swamp."

CHAPTER EIGHT

MATTHIEU BUSIED HIMSELF FIXING SANDWICHES for a light supper, and tried to ignore the sounds of the shower running. The fact that a beautiful woman was less than thirty yards away, naked and wet—hell, he may have sworn off relationships but he wasn't dead.

Clamping down hard on that train of thought, he continued stacking meat until he heard Fate's soft footfalls on the hardwood floor. She was wearing a robe that he hoped to God had something underneath it, and her wet hair was pulled back into a low ponytail with the end draped over one shoulder.

As she moved towards him, the scent of vanilla drifted ahead of her and he breathed deep, unable to help it if he tried. She gave him a shy smile as she approached the kitchen bar, and cocked her head at him.

"You really are making dinner," she said, clearly astonished.

Matthieu shrugged, feeling heat creep into his cheeks. "'S not much. Just sandwiches. Once I have time to get to the store, I'll make you my famous étouffée, guaranteed to roast your tonsils."

She blinked and stared at him, as if she couldn't quite figure him out. *Join the club*, he thought. He slid a plate over to her and didn't take his eyes off of her until she was tucking into the heaping sandwich. She was just the right combination of smoothness and curves that never failed to make his mouth water. And damn, if he didn't like to see a woman eat. Really eat, though—none of that salad with the dressing on the side kind of crap.

As he studied her, he couldn't help but compare her to Emilie. Emilie had been waspish and delicate, like a hesitant flower, so easily wilted or broken. That's what he'd done...broken her. Fate, on the other hand, was only a few inches shorter than him and quite obviously tough. She was just *there*. Present. Her presence seemed bigger than life. Though he instinctively knew that she had a sturdiness and a strength that most women didn't—even if she did seem a bit frail at present.

He knew he would have to question her about her ex, sooner rather than later, but he wanted her to be able to enjoy her meal, so he brought up the only topic guaranteed to make her smile.

"You check on Ridley?"

The smile that lit her face was instant and heart-stopping— and was a stark reminder to Matthieu that this woman was so far beyond his reach. He knew he'd never do anything worthy of a smile like that.

"I did. Isla said she's been running the cats ragged, but they're all having a great time. She sounded good. Happy." Fate turned smoky eyes to him, an intense scrutiny that made him want to squirm, and he hated himself for it. "Thank you."

"For what?" he asked, genuinely confused. He hadn't done anything, not really.

She narrowed her eyes at him, as if she thought he was being deliberately obtuse. "For getting us out of the club. For finding Ridley a safe place to stay. For all of it. We could be dead if it wasn't for you."

Matthieu had to shut that right down. She shouldn't be feeling gratitude to him, not when he'd finally, for once, did the right thing. Nothing more, nothing less.

"Don't thank me yet," he said in his sandpaper voice. "I've still got to figure out who's after us and...neutralize them."

Her eyes widened and, yeah, she knew what *neutralize* meant. She was already freaked out so he figured he might as well drive in the final nail. "Tell me about Eli."

Fate lowered her eyes, studying her empty plate. "Not much to tell. He was abusive, I got out. End of story."

Matthieu sighed and ran a hand over his rapidly growing former brush cut. She wasn't going to make it easy for him. "Fate." It was a plea and a warning all in one word. "It was you who said you think he could be the one coming after you. I need the whole story if I'm going to protect you. And Ridley," he added, for the win.

She looked sick...like green, and he instantly wanted to take it back. He wanted to tell her she didn't have to talk about it; that he'd fix everything and such ugliness would never touch her again. But he couldn't, and even if he could, Matthieu never made promises. It only made it worse when he let people down. "Please."

He thought it might have been his quiet supplication that finally did her in. She seemed to collapse in on herself a bit as she clutched at the steaming mug of coffee he'd handed her. Her lips quivered for a moment before she took a deep breath and squared her shoulders. Damn it, he didn't want to be impressed by her.

"I was studying voice at Juilliard when I met him. He was in the audience at one of the school's summer concerts." She gave him a soft smile but her eyes were far away as if she were remembering.

"I didn't know it at the time, but he was trolling for talent for his many nightclubs—both the classy ones and the seedier ones. He tracked me down after the show and...sort of swept me off my feet. He said all the right things, and I was just...dazzled," she said with a self-deprecating smile. "I'm not proud of how easy I made it for him. It had just been so long since I'd felt...beautiful, wanted, not completely alone—take your pick."

"So you dated?"

She snorted, and he raised a brow at her. "Nothing that formal. He just sort of assimilated me into his life. It was hard not to be charmed—he took me to all of the best places in Manhattan, bought me things—and he was *so* good to Ridley."

Matthieu's eyes snapped to her face when he heard that. "Wait, what? I thought...I guess I just assumed that he was her father. Then, who—?"

He didn't think it was possible, but her eyes looked even more haunted. It was the first time that he had the feeling she could break. "I can't...not now. That's a story for another day. Let me get through this one first," she said with a half-smile, and he nodded.

"Eli even convinced me to leave school and sing at one of his clubs exclusively. I think that was the beginning of the end of the life that I thought I was going to have. We got married three months after that, and then he just...changed."

"Changed how?" Matthieu asked, completely engrossed. It was such an unbelievable story and they hadn't even got to the part where Eli suddenly decided to put out a hit on his ex-wife.

She passed him her coffee mug for a refill and he obliged, giving her a moment to collect her thoughts. "He got really possessive, worrying about where I was going, what I was wearing. It was like he wanted to control everything, to mold me into his perfect little trophy wife."

"I can't imagine that there was anything wrong with the way you were," Matthieu said, looking her up and down, meaning it more as a confidence booster than a come on. He was delighted when she blushed to the tips of her ears.

"Don't think that was really the point, at least for Eli. He felt like he *created* me, for lack of a better term, and because of that, he could control me. But I'm not easily controlled," she said, eyes flashing. *Good girl*, he thought. *Get angry.*

"When I wouldn't cooperate, that's when he started hitting me. Always in private, always where the bruises wouldn't be seen. Never in front of Ridley. I don't think she saw—she was so young. God, I hope she didn't see."

"Why didn't you leave?" He couldn't help but ask. It was the one thing that always bothered him about battered women. He knew it was easier said than done, but it was possible. Just walk away.

"At first, I wanted to make it work for Ridley's sake. Eli was the only father figure she'd ever known. So I just found little ways to strike back at him."

"Like what?"

"He used to love to grab me by the hair, to force me to do things, to drag me around. So one day, I just chopped it all off," she said with relish. Her wicked smile made Matthieu feel a bit better about putting her through this. She hadn't just lain down and given up.

Matthieu snorted and again, *damn it*, he didn't want to be impressed. But he was. "I bet he was pissed."

"More than. That was the first time he ever hit me in the face. At that point, I knew it was a matter of time before Ridley saw something or, God forbid, he hurt her somehow." Matthieu couldn't control the violent jerk of his shoulders at the thought of someone hurting that child. He didn't have a parental bone in his body, but he knew he'd do anything to keep that little girl from harm.

"So I packed us up and we headed for Boston to stay with one of my few remaining friends. I hired a lawyer and filed for divorce. Eli didn't want to cooperate at first, but when my lawyer told him that I'd documented the abuse, he agreed to sign the papers. I didn't want his money; I just wanted to be free of him."

"Wow..." Matthieu didn't know what to say. He didn't think he'd ever met anyone with her kind of strength. It was kind of humbling in a way. He'd been a soldier—would be viewed by many as an American hero—but he didn't have a fraction of the strength that this woman had.

She blew out a shaky breath. "Yeah. I thought it was over until he started trying to contact me, ask about me; about Ridley. So we moved again. And again. I thought perhaps he'd given up, until you walked into The Blue Note and changed everything."

Matthieu looked her over, checking for cracks in her resolve, but he found none. She looked wrung out and a little bit miserable, but she'd pull it together. She'd survive. *And that, folks, is the fundamental difference between her and me.* While Matthieu was slowly crumbling under the weight of his demons,

Fate was soldiering on. Some fucking soldier he turned out to be.

Suddenly unreasonably angry with himself, Matthieu walked away from the bar. "I've got work to do," he barked, not meaning the way it sounded. "You're going to have to tell me about Ridley's father, sooner rather than later, but I'll leave you alone for now.

Turning his back on a bewildered, and probably more than a little pissed off Fate, Matthieu stalked off to find his computer. He paused when he heard her voice from behind him. "I'm going outside. I need some air."

His shoulders slumped a little when he caught the edge of hurt in her voice, but steeled himself against it. Neither of them could afford to forget who and what he was. "Remember the rules...and watch out for gators."

ಬಂಧ

With a growl, Fate picked up one of her discarded lime green Converse shoes and hurled it at Matthieu's retreating back. It bounced off of him like it had hit a brick wall. He snorted and waved over his shoulder, but kept on walking.

She bit the inside of her cheek as she forced herself to calm down. She was not like him—just because Soldier Boy had no people skills whatsoever, didn't mean she had to forget her own. If he wanted to walk around acting like a colossal asshat, that was fine. She'd just smother him with fricking sweetness.

Thinking back to their conversation, Fate realized that he had been decent enough through most of it. It was as if something just flipped a switch, and his mood completely shut down. She didn't know what his damage was, but she'd always been too curious for her own good. She'd find out before too long.

When she first met Matthieu, she couldn't tell a thing about him other than that his look screamed military. He had no accent to speak of, no facial expressions other than those tormented eyes. Since he'd been back in New Orleans, she'd slowly seen bits of his personality emerging.

Hell, there was even a hint of Cajun in his accent now, a diluted version of his brother's. Watch out for gators, he'd said, and her lips had twitched at the way he said *gatuhs* in that gravelly voice.

He was a strange duck, Matthieu. He had secrets—*that,* she knew for sure. And while it would be easy to take them from him, she'd prefer he tell her himself. But that wasn't happening anytime soon, so she decided to follow through with what she'd told him and go outside for some air.

CHAPTER NINE

WALKING BAREFOOT OUT ONTO THE SAGGING back porch, Fate surveyed the landscape of the hidden bayou. Bayou Trépas, Matthieu had called it—he'd also said that the name meant death, which was ever so comforting.

Matthieu mentioned that few people knew about the secret canal because it was so hard to reach by boat. When the tide was low, fishermen were lucky to even be able to reach it by pirogue—a lightweight, flat bottom canoe-type boat. The pirogues could navigate deeper into the swamps and go where propeller boats couldn't.

Attached to the porch, in a rather precarious position, was a long pier that extended out into the muddy water. Tied to the dock was a houseboat that appeared to be in a similar condition to the shack behind her. Fate wondered if the inside of the boat matched that of the house. Regardless, the tub was aptly named *The Crooked Ace*.

Lashed to the other side of the dock was a pirogue that had seen better days—*Double Down* was painted in crude lettering on the back end.

As Fate descended toward the dock, she studiously ignored the flashes of the past that tried to push their way into her brain through the contact of her bare feet with the warped wood of the pier. She'd long since learned to block out the more latent visions—it was the strong ones that pushed through, like Matthieu's.

After she cautiously made her way down to the dock, Fate rolled up her jeans and sat on the edge so she could plunge her feet into the water. Bayou Trépas was overrun by bald Cypress and banyan dripping with stringy Spanish moss. It was like being in the middle of a gloomy jungle, and Fate found a strange sense of peace within the natural shelter of the narrow canal.

A hawk watched her from a low-hanging branch, and she could see the ripples in the water that were most likely created by trolling alligators. But for some reason, she wasn't afraid. Leaning back on her elbows across the creaking boards, she stared up at the canopy of trees and she swirled her toes in the water.

A few moments of silence went by until Fate began to sing. The song was an adaptation of an old Reggae tune— *Redemption Song.* Not her usual forté but it had always seemed to lift her spirits. After a while, all the sounds of life in the bayou quieted, as if the animals and the trees were all listening intently.

It was comforting, even if a little creepy. She felt a tingling at the back of her neck that made her glance back towards the house. She couldn't see, but somehow she knew that Matthieu was there, watching her. *Let him watch*, she thought with a smirk, and continued singing.

Fate realized she must have dozed off when she was startled awake by a sound coming from the opposite bank, across the small canal. She thought it had probably been her imagination but she sat up to look.

"*Jiminy Christmas*," she hissed when she saw a boy standing there, watching her. While she'd been startled, she wasn't frightened, though she knew she was probably supposed to be. The boy was just...stunning.

He had longish black hair that flopped over his forehead almost, but not quite, covering striking golden eyes. Knife-edged cheekbones rode high under those eyes, and they were offset by a straight, sharp nose and full lips.

Barefoot and dressed simply in a white tank and jeans cut off at the knee, the boy couldn't have been a day over sixteen. But Fate was astonished to see a beautiful network of tattoos that ran up one arm and peeked out at the collar of his shirt.

She remembered the rules, and she knew she was expected to run inside and tell Matthieu like a good little girl. But she didn't want to—and as soon as the thought crossed her mind, the boy flicked a wary glance up at the house and slowly backed away until he was swallowed by the dense foliage.

🙰🙰

Matthieu tried to ignore the confusion swirling inside him. He'd watched Fate relax on the dock and, for some reason he'd had the overwhelming urge to go to her. Before he knew it, his hand had been on the doorknob—and then she'd started singing.

The sound was so stirring and pure, he felt it sink into his bones and threaten to turn him inside out...laying him bare. That feeling lasted for one dizzying moment before he remembered. He was tainted. Marked. Claimed by evil that most certainly should never touch Fate.

Miserable and resigned, Matthieu forced himself to turn away. Sitting down on the couch with his laptop, he put on his reading glasses. He hated the things, but he'd left his last pair of contacts in a hotel room in Sydney when he'd had to leave in a hurry, and he sure as hell wasn't going to get more anytime soon.

Since he was in such a piss-poor mood, Matthieu figured he may as well get some work done. He brought up Arlen Ward's banking website, and called up a program he'd written that would search tens of thousands of password combinations to match the correct one. No guarantee it would work, but he had a feeling that Ward wasn't very creative, or stealthy.

Sure enough, the program signaled a match within minutes. *Jessica.* Ward had used the name of his estranged daughter as a password. Hell, Matthieu could have probably figured that one out without the digital intervention.

He barely glanced up when Fate came in from outside and sat beside him on the couch. He could feel her gaze on him, but he ignored it. If she had something to say, she'd just have to pony up and say it.

"What are you doing?"

Matthieu looked up from his screen and considered her. There really was no reason to lie. What was she going to do, turn him in?

"I'm hacking into Lt. Ward's business account—although he's made it so easy, I can hardly call it hacking."

"You can do that?" She turned an astonished expression to meet his eyes, and he just smirked.

"I can do a lot of things that might surprise you," he said with an exaggerated leer, having no idea why he was toying with her. He watched her to see how she would take that statement. She cleared her throat and dropped her eyes to her lap.

"Who's Lt. Ward?"

"Ward is—was…my handler. He was the one who arranged the jobs. I never met any of the clients. If money changed hands, there'll be evidence in this account."

Fate fell silent, presumably to let him work, so he did. Scanning the account records, he found the date on which he'd been assigned to tail her. "Bingo."

"What?" She leaned closer to him, so close that he could smell her, and he had to force himself to focus.

"On the day I was given the assignment, a sum of ten thousand dollars was transferred into Ward's account from DraconusCorp. Ever heard of that?"

Fate shook her head, and he frowned at her. So much for the easy Eli angle. Pulling up a search window, he ran a search on DraconusCorp and learned that it was an acquisitions corporation, owned and operated by one Drake Maxwell.

"You know Drake Maxwell?"

"No," she said. "I was so sure it was Eli." This came out as merely a whisper.

"Still could be. Eli may be affiliated with Maxwell somehow. Maybe he's using the company as a front." Matthieu went back to scanning the transaction list until he saw something he hadn't expected to find. "Huh," he murmured, and Fate's eyes snapped to his face.

"Did you find something else?"

He definitely did. He'd scrolled down to the date he'd made contact with Fate—the day he'd been ordered to kill her—and was shocked by what he found. "They *are* in it together."

"What? How do you know?"

"An additional five thousand was transferred to Ward from the personal account of Eli Ferrell on the day I was given the order for the hit. Your Eli wasn't very smart."

Fate glared at him, and he was glad to see the fire return to her smoky eyes. "He's not *my* anything. Never was. And no, he wouldn't be smart about something like that. He's too cocky, thinks he's indestructible."

Matthieu rubbed a hand over his stubbled chin as he considered the implications of the partnership. "We know what Ferrell's motive is, but Maxwell is the red herring. What in the hell does he get out of this."

Sighing, he took off his glasses to rub at tired eyes. He could feel the need to sleep creeping in, blurring the edges of his vision. *No. Not going to happen.* "Well, that settles it. I'm gonna have to go to New York."

"What?! Why?" Her voice was laced with panic, but he couldn't help that.

"I've got to find out what Ward has on these two. He doesn't trust computers so he keeps a lot of hard copy records that I obviously can't hack into. Besides, if I can make it into his office, I can bug it, maybe set up some cameras."

"Rousseau, you can't leave me here alone in this God-forsaken swamp."

Matthieu turned to look at her, and he saw genuine fear there—and felt like an ass for putting it there. He answered her in a quiet voice that was meant to be soothing, but wasn't. "Relax, you're coming with me. But you *will* have to stay in the hotel while I break into the office. I can't have you distracting me."

She was obviously recovering from her panic, because she gave him a look that was just edging toward seductive. "So I'm a distraction, huh?"

Oh, he *so* was not going there. He scowled at her and turned back to his computer. "Don't flatter yourself. I don't trust you not to cause trouble."

She deflated a little, picked up a magazine and started reading. "We'll stay here for a couple more days while I set up travel arrangements that can't be tracked, and then we'll go. One night, in and out, and back here for remote surveillance."

She didn't respond, so Matthieu continued to scour the account listing to see if he missed anything. He had no idea how much time had passed but eventually the words and numbers begin to blur together.

Matthieu could feel sleep tugging at the edges of his consciousness—so much so that he felt his eyes trying to roll back in his head. How long had it been? Three days, maybe four. He knew that he was going to lose the battle, but he could only hope to hold out until Fate went to her room, and hopefully locked the door.

Snapping his computer shut, he got up and headed to the kitchen. "I'm gonna pour myself some more coffee," he said, his voice slurring from exhaustion. "You want?"

Startled, Fate glanced at him, looking for all the world like she thought he'd lost his mind. "Coffee? Cheese 'n rice, Matthieu, it's nearly midnight?"

Matthieu blinked and had to lift his coffee cup in front of his face to hide a smile that was determined to come out. "Sorry, cheese who?"

"Oh, shut up. I have a seven year old. It's habit."

Matthieu snorted and returned to his place on the couch. He sipped his coffee in silence, letting the warmth the scalding liquid fill his body; letting the steaming mug warm his chilled hands. The room was comfortably warm, but he found himself wishing he could build a fire. He could practically feel the toasty glow fill the room, relaxing his muscles and easing his mind.

He was jerked out of his daydream by the sound of an explosion, the familiar sting in his ears as his eardrums burst, the burn in his throat as he breathed fire, ash and accelerant. His daydream had turned into a nightmare.

Pushing his way to the surface, Matthieu's body jerked as he returned to consciousness, causing his coffee to slosh out of the mug he still held. Breathing rapidly, he cut a glance to where Fate was sitting to see if she had seen. She had.

She studied him closely, a line of concentration forming between her brows. *Please, please let it go*, he chanted inside his head. He was too strung out to explain it to her, his whole body was like a raw nerve.

Oddly, she seemed to take pity on him. After giving him one last concerned look, she stood and dropped her magazine on the coffee table. "Think I'll go to bed. Don't work too hard. 'Night."

"Goodnight." She turned to head back to her room but he stopped her with a whisper. "Lock your door." She froze with her back to him, and for a moment he wondered if she hadn't heard him. But the tension in her shoulders told him she had. "Please."

She sighed, but didn't turn around. He watched her disappear into her bedroom and didn't release the breath he'd been holding until he heard the lock click into place.

When the nightmare began, Matthieu knew it was happening. Just as he knew he'd be trapped and helpless. When he realized it was Kandahar, he was actually relieved. While this was a fresh hell in its own right, it was so much better than the alternative. There were no demons here—only soldiers and civilians, death and guilt.

The dream took him to the moment after the bombing—after he'd been love-tapped by the AR-15—when he was being held captive by Afghan insurgents. He could barely see, his corneas still scorched from the explosion, but he could tell he was in a dark, dusty cave-like room; a militarized bunker.

He could hear raised voices from behind him, men arguing in *Pashto*, but because he was tied to a chair, he couldn't turn to see. Finally, one of the men stepped into Matthieu's line of vision, pointing a rifle at his face.

The swarthy soldier was kitted out in full fatigues, but also wore a light blue turban and an eye patch. He rolled out a medical tray filled with various rusty instruments. Matthieu sighed and rested his chin on his chest. So, it was to be torture then. Well, they were going to be disappointed—this was what he'd been trained for.

Matthieu had a working knowledge of *Pashto*, but the soldier wouldn't know that, so he spoke in broken English. "Bazir want to kill you," he said and tipped his head toward the man that Matthieu knew was standing behind him.

"His wife, daughter, was in that building."

Closing his eyes, Matthieu hung his head. The little girl and the woman he'd seen—there was no way to know if that was Bazir's family, but somehow he did. "What was her name? The girl," he croaked from his ruined vocal chords.

"Riksa," the man behind him growled.

"Riksa." Matthieu repeated the name, knowing he would never allow himself to forget.

"Yes, Bazir want to kill you. But I say you better alive. You give us information."

Matthieu raised his head and stared into the man's eyes, before speaking in perfect *Pashto*. "That's not going to work out the way you want it to."

The first man—Patang, he later learned—stared at him in stony silence, before finally speaking again, this time in his native language. "Who do you work for?"

"Fuck off," Matthieu answered, and spat at the man's feet.

Patang shook his head and turned to the tray of tools. Bazir moved in front of Matthieu, his face obscured by a black scarf attached to his turban. Taking out a sharp knife, he sliced Matthieu's t-shirt down the front, exposing his torso to Patang, who was approaching with what looked like a rusty scalpel.

And yeah, *fuck*, that was going to hurt. It was his last thought before the scalpel began ripping into the space between his last two ribs. After that, Matthieu knew nothing but white hot pain, which did nothing to overpower the ever present guilt.

10 CHAPTER TEN

FATE SHOT UPRIGHT IN HER BED, ON INSTANT ALERT AS she looked around the dark room. Something had woken her, she was sure of it—but there was nothing there. Her room, seemingly the whole house, was dead silent, yet she knew she had to have heard something.

While her eyes adjusted to the darkness, she climbed out of bed and put on a thin robe over her tank top and shorts. She crept towards the door to her bedroom, treading lightly while still listening for anything out of the ordinary. Her hand froze on the doorknob as she remembered Matthieu's whispered plea to keep the door locked.

She'd planned on obeying—but what if their pursuers had made their way into the house? What if they'd taken out Matthieu? Fate wasn't about to wait in her bedroom for them to come and get her, the perfect gift-wrapped sitting duck.

She had to make a quick decision. Turning the lock, she stepped out into the hall and listened. Finally, she heard it...a pained moan coming from somewhere in the living room. It was barely audible, yet excruciating—as if someone were gasping out their last breath. *Matthieu.*

Fate hurried into the open living room which was awash in pale moonlight from the large picture windows. She didn't see anything at first so she started to turn toward Matthieu's bedroom, when she heard the sound again, much more faint.

It came from the couch. Panicked, she rounded the end of the overstuffed sofa and looked down; sure she was going to find Matthieu bleeding out on the supple leather. He was there, but with no physical injuries that she could see.

His body was completely tense, back bowed off the couch but arms and legs straight, as if they were bound. But his face...his face was screwed into a twisted mask of indescribable pain—jaws clenched, teeth bared, eyes squeezed tightly shut.

She watched as he seemed to struggle against the invisible bonds, and he let out another one of those death-moans. The sound tore at her and she was helpless but to try and stop his pain. Yes, he'd made her promise never to wake him—but maybe she didn't have to. Maybe she could soothe him, ease his pain, while he still slept. It was worth a shot.

Climbing onto the couch over him, she straddled his hips and stared down at his pain stricken face. "Here goes nothing," she whispered, and grabbed his thick wrists, one in each of her hands.

She felt her body convulse as she was violently ripped from her own consciousness and thrown head-first into Matthieu's.

I'm in the dream, Fate thought. She was in Matthieu's nightmare and, more than that, she *was* Matthieu. For that moment in time, she had his thoughts, his memories. She was inside him.

She found herself strapped down by the arms and legs to a metal table, surrounded by men chattering in a language she'd never heard, but somehow understood—because Matthieu did. Looking down at her body—Matthieu's body—she saw that it was covered in blood that oozed from dozens of open wounds. They were too shallow to be fatal, but enough to cause immeasurable pain. No wonder he'd cried out.

Finally, the men stopped yelling, and one who seemed to be the ringleader—Patang—approached. He gestured to one of the other men, who opened the door of the dank, dungeon-esque room. A third man came through tugging a bound soldier, an American, and pushed him to stand in front of them.

Fate felt Matthieu's stomach constrict and his heart begin to pound. A name flickered through her mind, just a whisper. *Striker.* One of Matthieu's team members—a brother in arms. Striker's captor kicked at the back of his knees, forcing him to kneel in front of the leader, before taking out a wicked looking knife.

"Last chance, Sergeant," he said in that guttural language. "Who sent you? Who's pulling your strings?"

Matthieu hesitated, and the man holding Striker pressed the knife closer to his jugular. Fate could hear Matthieu's thoughts racing as he stared at his friend in what could possibly be his last moments alive. Striker knew that Matthieu wouldn't give up his unit—in fact, as Matthieu's eyes connected with the other man's, Striker stared him down and gave him an almost imperceptible shake of his head.

You were trained for this, Rousseau, he told himself. They couldn't sacrifice the entire unit, the entire mission, for two men, and they both knew it. Slowly, with his heart clenching in his chest, Matthieu turned his face to the leader and glared, then looked back at Striker.

The leader obviously took it as confirmation that neither soldier was talking. With a stiff nod to his subordinate, Patang stood there, detached, as the man pulled the sharp knife across Striker's throat and let him drop.

Fate felt Matthieu's pain, but also his conviction. He wouldn't grieve much for Striker, knowing the man had died the way he lived, protecting his country. But he would grieve the rest of his life for Riksa.

She'd had enough. She wanted to be back to herself. *I need to be me*, she repeated, and concentrated on pulling her thoughts from Matthieu's. Finally, she felt herself separate, but much to her disappointment, they were still in the dream.

The insurgents had gone and left them alone with Striker's cooling body. Fate cringed and tried not to look. Instead, she concentrated on Matthieu. She could see him now as she stood beside the torture table. He was strapped down by his arms and legs, covered in blood from the agglomeration of wounds that marred his body.

His face was turned towards her, but his eyes were on Striker. She wasn't sure if he'd be able to see her anyway— then again, she didn't really know the rules of invading someone's dream. It had never happened before.

Matthieu's body was racked with violent tremors and tears were running down his face, mingling with the blood to create ghastly red streaks from the corners of his eyes. After a few moments of silence, he threw his head back and let out an anguished roar.

It was too much for Fate. No one deserved to suffer this much. Heedless of the blood, she stroked his face with a gentle hand. "Matthieu, it's time to wake up. Let it go, for now." She was startled when he stopped screaming and grief-stricken eyes locked onto hers.

Fate was slammed back into her own body with the force of a freight train. But it didn't dislodge her from her perch on Matthieu. Her hands remained wrapped around his wrists. Good thing, too, because he came up swinging.

Well, he would have, but Fate concentrated all of her energy on holding him down. His body raged and bucked beneath her as he tried to dislodge whatever was weighing him down. She just held on as tight as she could.

"Matthieu," she said in a calm voice that belied her trepidation. She repeated his name over and over until his violent motions stilled and his eyes began to focus. A deep, dark chocolate, his eyes finally rested on her face and widened. While still cautious, Fate let go of his hands but kept her position on top of him.

Matthieu looked disoriented as his eyes bounced around the room, likely trying to get a handle on exactly where—and when—he was.

"Hey. It's me. You had a bad dream, but you're here in New Orleans. *La Maison de Rousseau*, remember?" she asked with a quirk of her lips.

Finally he nodded and threw a heavy arm over his face. She couldn't see his eyes, but the tears that seeped down his cheeks were clear as a bell. His muscles took up that full body shudder he'd had in the dream, and his big chest began to convulse.

Swallowing down her fear, Fate lifted his arm away from his face and held his head still so that he was forced to meet her eyes. She stroked his scarred cheek—realizing that this injury had to have happened before the torture incident—and spoke softly to him.

"Matthieu, you have to let it go."

"How can I?" he said. His voice cracked as his body was shaken with another brutal shudder.

"Tell me," she answered. Without a thought, she ran her fingers through his hair and found it softer than she would have imagined. He tensed and she was sure he wouldn't speak, but then he did.

The whole story poured out of him in stuttering gasps and sobs—he told her about the mission, the bomb, the civilians who'd been killed. *So that was who Riksa was.* He told her about his injuries, to his eyes, ears, and throat—and, yeah, that explained the voice.

He told her about getting captured, and being tortured by Patang and his crew. She was horrified by what they had done to him, but she forced herself to keep calm. Finally, he told her about Striker—SFC Vincent "Striker" Perelli—and how he'd essentially signed the man's death warrant.

When it was all done, he looked so destroyed, so miserable, that her heart went out to him. She leaned forward and took his face in her hands. "You were doing a job and still, you did everything you could to try and save Riksa. And you did exactly what Striker had wanted—expected—you to do. You have to let this go, and forgive yourself."

"I don't think I can."

"Try," she said, and leaned over to touch her lips to his.

When they touched, she felt a punch of awareness sweep through her and she froze. That was…unexpected. Once she'd made the move, she really didn't know where to go from there. It wasn't as if she had much experience in the area. Her first sexual encounter—well, she refused to think about it. And Eli, he hadn't ever been too concerned with her pleasure.

Fate felt rather than heard Matthieu's faint gasp of surprise, and she froze. She'd wanted to soothe, to comfort, and yes, assuage her own mounting curiosity—as she was keenly aware of her position straddling the man's hips. But what now?

Matthieu was a live wire, feeling strung out and flayed open, bleeding from a thousand different places. He always felt that way when he dreamed of Kandahar; when he dreamed of Striker's death, and of Riksa's. But it had been different this time. *She* had been there.

Just when he thought he might drown in the misery once and for all—never to wake up, trapped in the dream forever—Fate had been there. She'd calmed him, coaxed him, and brought him out of it. He was still confused by it when he'd woken up, when he'd finally stopped struggling beneath her, which was why the kiss had caught him off guard.

It was just a gentle brush of her lips, tentative and unskilled, but it set his blood on fire. The press of her lips against his, the weight of her body on him, was more than his raw emotions and hollowed out mind could take. Then she went still, as if not knowing what her next move should be.

Well, Matthieu had a couple of ideas on that. He knew he shouldn't touch her, that he'd regret it, but only a fucking saint would turn her away. Mind made up, he tunneled one hand into her mass of blond hair that was deliciously rumpled from sleep. His other arm slipped around her lower back to pull her closer—and then, for the first time in who knew when, he took something for himself.

Because he could sense her hesitance, Matthieu pressed soft kisses to her upper lip and the corners of her mouth, before sucking on her plump lower lip. This pulled a sharp gasp from her as her body stiffened, and then relaxed.

When she melted against him, her weight pressed harder on an area that was becoming painfully aroused. Trying to keep it together, to keep from scaring her, he resisted the urge to buck up against her. Just barely.

Matthieu pulled his hand from her hair, and gave her jaw a light squeeze, urging her to open her mouth around a surprised gasp. He took the opportunity to slip his tongue inside the wet heat of her mouth. She didn't mirror his movements, but she didn't push him away. It was as if she was...unsure but curious, waiting to see what he would do next.

Matthieu certainly didn't want to disappoint her. He angled his head to deepen the kiss. He explored her mouth with tongue and teeth, drowning in the needy sounds that escaped her throat. Fate seemed so innocent—but she had a daughter, so he knew she wasn't *that* inexperienced.

When he thought about it more closely, he remembered what an asshole she'd been married to—a man like that wouldn't care about his partner's pleasure—and the experience with Ridley's father was something he'd yet to even get her to talk about. Maybe she was as innocent as a virgin when it came to taking her own pleasure from sex.

The thought saddened and aroused him at the same time. He knew he should back off, but he wanted *so much* to be the one to show her how much pleasure could be found in the arms of another. She tasted like honey and sunshine, something so bright and beautiful that she threatened to burn him up inside. He knew he shouldn't mar her loveliness with his touch, but he was lost to sensation.

Although she trembled, she was getting braver, chasing his tongue back into his mouth. He had to bite back a groan when she gave it a gentle suck. Damn, now he was the one acting like a horny virgin. Gathering the ends of his fraying control, Matthieu concentrated on giving Fate the most pleasure from a simple kiss that he could manage.

It started—as it always did—with the whispers. Skittering through his mind were the voices of the demons as they murmured their most depraved desires to him. Like before, he did his best to ignore them, to concentrate on what was real and ignore what was not—what couldn't be.

When he felt them slithering underneath his skin, scratching his bones and clawing at his mind with their obscene presence, he realized they wouldn't be ignored this time. But it was when they started reaching out for Fate, coveting her, desiring her, that he realized he had to break the connection. He had to make sure she never got this close to him again.

It took all his willpower to break the kiss and push her away, maybe a little rougher than he'd intended. He swung his legs over the side of the couch to sit upright, placed his head in his hands and tried to catch his breath. Finally he gathered the courage to look at her.

She sat staring at him, her eyes still unfocused with lust and confusion, a hand raised to touch her kiss-bruised lips. Her breath came as fast as his but, he imagined, for an entirely different reason.

"What's wrong?" she asked, insecurity creeping into her voice.

Steeling himself against her inevitable pain, he gave her a hard stare. "I meant what I said before. It's best for both of us if you keep your hands off me."

Instead of the shock he expected, there was only sadness in her eyes when she looked at him. And not saddened by him—

saddened *for* him. Before he had a chance to digest the meaning of that, her voice interrupted his thoughts.

"Don't you want me?" she asked with a raised brow that seemed to know what his answer would be.

Going for cold indifference, Matthieu allowed his gaze to slide up and down her body. "Of course I want you. Who wouldn't? It's like I said, I don't need any distractions."

She crossed her arms over her chest—causing her smoothly rounded breasts to swell above her tank top—and looked unconvinced. He had to deliver the kill shot or risk everything by taking her right there on the couch.

"Besides, I need to focus on the mission, and if I'm going to risk my neck breaking into Ward's office, I need all of the information. You still haven't told me about Ridley's father."

He kept a close eye on her, so he saw when all the color drained from her face. *Direct hit, center mass*, he thought. Her lower lip trembled a bit, but her eyes sparked. "What's that got to do with any of this?"

Matthieu shrugged, because he didn't have a good answer for her. "Won't know until you tell me."

She was quiet for a long moment, but when she opened her mouth, Mathieu mistakenly thought it would be to answer him. Wrong. "Who the heck is this Ward guy really?"

Matthieu sighed. It was a valiant attempt at changing the subject. "I told you. My handler."

"Sorry, but that means jack spit to me—I don't speak assassin. What does that mean, and how did you hook up with him?"

"That's classified. Enough. Start talking," he said, giving her a hard stare and pointing a scarred finger at her.

Her entire body seemed to collapse in on itself, her demeanor suddenly turned dark and haunted. It was much, much worse than when she'd talked about Eli. Still, she didn't answer. She just sat there and shivered, chewing on a fingernail.

Matthieu was trying his best to be sensitive—but unfortunately his *best* wasn't much to work with. "Look, I don't care about your dirty little secrets, I really don't. But I do need to know if there are any other asshole exes running around making threats and putting out hits."

"I was *raped*, okay!" she shouted it at him. She used the words like a knife to strike out against her tormentor. She curled up into a ball and hid her face, but he could see her shoulders shaking with silent sobs.

Matthieu scrubbed both hands over his face, feeling like the biggest tool. He should be locked up—he truly wasn't equipped to live in polite fucking society. There on that couch was possibly the strongest person he'd ever met, reduced to a crumbling ball of agony, in part because of his insensitivity.

She'd even been strong enough to hold him down during one of his nightmares—a feat that both Striker and Dodge had failed to accomplish—and he'd brought her down with one careless statement.

Matthieu hoisted himself onto the couch next to her, shoulder to shoulder, close but barely brushing against her. He didn't think a direct touch from him would be welcome. Her body tensed at first, then slowly relaxed on a ragged sigh.

"Tell me," he said in a voice that was nearly a whisper, echoing her earlier command.

She raised her head from the pillow of her arms but her eyes were hollow, staring out into the past. "There isn't much to tell. I had a late rehearsal one night, and by the time I got back to my apartment, it was well after midnight. I was exhausted, so I came in and headed straight for the shower. Stupid. I didn't lock the door behind me."

He winced and her lips twitched in a self-deprecating smile. "Some New Yorker I turned out to be. After I finished showering, I put on my robe and went to the bedroom to get ready for bed. He came from behind." Her voice trembled just once, but stayed strong and clear. "He attacked me from behind and I never even saw his face..." her voice trailed off, and Matthieu assumed there really wasn't much else to say.

It shocked him how close her attack was to the encounters he'd had with women the last few years. Nameless, faceless sex, with the women blindfolded and him behind, fulfilling the most basic of biological functions. Those women hadn't been forced, not by violence, but who knew if they'd been forced by circumstance to make a living that way. He'd never asked, nor cared.

Shame burned like acid in his gut, along with the molten ball of anger that quaked inside him. It made him want to squeeze the life out of her attacker with his bare hands—and fucking love every minute of it. But he just paced, unable to meet her eyes lest she see the guilt and shame, or the demons hiding there.

ॐ

Fate watched Matthieu surge up off the couch to pace, his body vibrating with frustrated energy. She finally saw how fitting his tattoo was. He was like a cobra himself, bunched and coiled to strike. Only there was nothing and no one to strike at. They'd never found the guy. As if reading her mind, he froze in his tracks to question her.

"Did they...did you call the police?"

She nodded, biding herself some time to find the right words. "I did. Went to the hospital, got the exam, looked at the mugshots—the whole nine. They tried, but there was really just nothing to go on. No witnesses, no hit on the DNA—it was like he never existed."

It was almost comical, the way he cocked his head at her nearly completely sideways, as if he could see into her memories, figure out the mystery himself. The gaze was as unsettling as it was mesmerizing. It made her want to tell him everything, and it was suddenly important that he not think her...damaged. "I'm fine. I survived, I did the therapy and I've moved on. I can't even bring myself to wish it never happened, because then I wouldn't have Ridley."

"You kept her," he said in a gritty whisper. "Not everyone would do that."

"No, I guess not everyone would."

He simply continued to stare, unblinking, head cocked, and she knew he was waiting for some kind of explanation. Fate wasn't sure there was one—not one that he would understand anyway.

"It's not that I didn't consider other options...I'm not a saint. But as soon as I felt her growing inside me, it was like...we were in it together, and I wasn't quite so alone. She was my reason to not fall apart.

"I think that may have ultimately been what drove me to Eli so easily. I just didn't want to be alone with the memories—wanted to take a stab at normal, for me and for Ridley."

"So you had her, and raised her alone...for the most part." Matthieu's brows drew together, low over piercing eyes that appeared pitch black in the low light, as the sun was just beginning to rise.

"Yeah, basically. My mother was always overly conscious of what all of her high-brow friends would think of anything resembling a scandal—and this most certainly qualified. Hell, my deciding to study music almost caused her to disown me; the fact that I got in to Juilliard was my saving grace. Once she found out I was keeping the baby, she finished the job and cut me out of her life. So it was just Ridley and me, for a while."

Matthieu let out a streak of inventive curses, and Fate could only nod. What else was there really to say? Tired and wrung out, she was anxious to get the spotlight off of herself.

"So what about you?"

He gave her a look that she could only described as a quizzical sneer. "What *about* me?"

"Tell me, Sergeant Rousseau, what skeletons are hiding in your closet."

He narrowed his eyes at her and frowned. "How did you—?"

"Dog tag," she interrupted, wagging a finger towards the chain around his neck. "I also know your blood type is O-neg. Useful information." She wasn't ready to explain that she'd heard the Afghan soldier call him 'sergeant' in the dream.

Clearly, he wasn't amused at her ingenuity, if his stone-faced silence was any indication. But Fate was happy she wasn't the subject of discussion anymore, so she pushed. "For instance, who's this Ward character and how'd you have the bad fortune of coming to work for him?"

He glared at her and she was sure he wouldn't answer, until he shrugged a shoulder, as if the information wasn't any big deal. "I served under him in Afghanistan. After our unit was disbanded and I was discharged, I went to work for him in the private sector."

Fate saw a muscle twitch in his jaw, and she snorted, knowing he was lying. "Yeah, I think there's a little more to that story." She hadn't thought it possible for his expression to close up even more, but it did. His eyes hardened and he spoke through clenched teeth.

"The less you know about me, the safer you'll be."

And just what the hell did he mean by that? "Why?"

Rounding on her, he squeezed his hands into fists as if he were resisting popping her one. Somehow she still knew he wouldn't lay a hand on her in anger. "Do you have to question everything?"

"Yes. Why?"

He sighed and swiped a hand over his exhausted expression. "Because you can't tell what you don't know...among other things."

Shutting down any further questioning, he shuffled into the kitchen to start making breakfast. Fate stared after him, more than a little gobsmacked. How could this man infuriate her to the edge of reason, yet she still couldn't help being curious—or if she were honest, fascinated by him?

Giving up on the interrogation for the time being, Fate decided to go outside. Maybe the mystery boy would come back so she could have someone to talk to besides the great wall of silence that was Matthieu Rousseau.

CHAPTER ELEVEN

FATE MADE HER WAY DOWN TO WHAT SHE'D BEGUN TO think of as *her* spot on the dock below the house. She sat there and listened to the sounds of the living swamp, pondering her would-be killer turned savior. The man was a puzzle wrapped in an enigma and Fate couldn't, for the life of her, figure him out. He was abrasive, rude, and uncaring—to a point where she almost felt as if he *wanted* her to hate him, to fear him. But then she would occasionally get a glimpse inside to the man behind the scars and the scowl; inside that invisible well of pain that he kept so well hidden. And that—well, that just made her want to pry it out of him and be the one to heal his wounds.

Of course it was ridiculous, and she'd told herself that over and over—Matthieu Rousseau had absolutely no redeeming qualities. Except...he could have just killed her, but something inside him had kept him from it, and she guessed it was that something that she was trying to find.

She abandoned her circling thoughts when they began to give her a headache, and gave her full attention to her surroundings. The weather was clear and the trees swayed with a gentle breeze that caused the muddy water to ripple around the dock. Nearby, she saw the head of a small snapping turtle breach the surface and, in one of the trees across the canal, the hawk sat silently watching her.

It was a stunning animal with burnished bronze feathers over a proud chest, but the eyes were what intrigued her. They were an intense gold with an almost anthropomorphized clarity in them. The bird watched her with its head cocked sideways in a position that absurdly reminded her of Matthieu and his inquisitive posture.

Humming to herself, Fate lay down on her side facing the water and propped her body up with an elbow. She twirled her fingers in the water, watching the floating twigs and leaves circle in the eddy she created. Lulled by the warmth of a Southern spring day, Fate found herself yawning.

Beginning to pick up Matthieu's sleeping habits—or lack thereof, she thought to herself. *Gonna have to convince that man to sleep more before I turn into a zombie myself.*

Intending to go inside, she pulled her hand out of the water. Gasping, she saw the water twist up and away from the surface, as if chasing her fingers. Carefully rising to her feet, she lifted her hand higher, but still the water reached for her.

She stood, transfixed, unable to look away from what was happening—what *couldn't* be happening. Startled by the hawk's shrill cry, Fate jerked her hand back and the spell was broken. The water dissipated into mist, and she scrambled backwards across the creaky dock.

"What in holy hades?" she breathed, looking up to the hawk as if it could explain it to her, but the bird was gone.

She didn't know how long she stayed that way, sitting on the creaky dock with her knees drawn up to her chest, staring at the water in utter confusion. Fate didn't know what was wrong with her—first, the strange ability to access an object or person's history just through touch, and now the crazy water magnetism. She was beginning to feel like she just stumbled onto the set of the latest *X-Men* movie.

She was startled out of her panicked thoughts by the faint sound of splashing. She glanced up to see a flat-bottomed pirogue coasting around the corner from the adjacent cove. As the boatman rowed closer, she realized it was the same boy from the other day.

He was dressed similarly in nothing but ratty overalls and skin, and his feet were bare again. With a deft turn of the oar, he skirted the boat alongside her dock, reaching out a trim but muscular arm to catch the side.

"Hi," he said with shy smile. She returned his smile with a bright one of her own, glad to have someone else to talk to.

"Hi." She reached out to shake his free hand. "I'm Fate."

"Étienne," he answered with the distinctive French-Creole accent that was common in the area. "You live here?" He jerked his chin at the house behind her.

"For a little while, yeah."

He frowned and continued to stare at the house. "Didn't think anyone lived there. Never seen nobody."

Fate didn't entertain the constant paranoia that Matthieu did, but she was wary about giving away too much to a stranger. "Uh, well my friend owns it, but he doesn't stay here. We're just visiting for a while."

He seemed to accept that with a thoughtful nod before turning his attention back to her. "Was just out for a fish, thought I'd say hello. Ain't many folks in this canal, so I figured it'd be neighborly."

"Do you live close to here?"

Étienne pointed to the woods across the canal. "Over yonder."

Fate looked, but all she saw was thick forest and swamp. "In the woods?"

He shrugged a single shoulder and tossed a glance over at his fish bucket. "Mother Nature, she provides. Got everything I need to get by—food, water, shelter."

They settled into comfortable conversation, and Fate found herself learning a lot about her mysterious new friend. His name was Étienne Agnier—pronounced *ahn-YER*, thank you very much—and he was an orphan. He'd been living in Louisiana for as long as he could remember, but he knew he wasn't born here.

She couldn't get him to budge on his age though. For all Fate knew, he could be anywhere from fifteen to a hundred. She kept the conversation going while revealing only tidbits about her own life. Eventually, Étienne began to look tired, his expression drooping as he tried to stifle yawns.

Taking pity on the kid, Fate rose to her feet and gave him a wink. "I've got to get going. We're going out of town for a few days. Will I see you again?"

He gave her a grateful sigh and pushed off the side of the dock. "Might just."

CHAPTER TWELVE

AS FATE ENTERED THE LIVING ROOM THROUGH THE back door, she had to bite back her shock as two things became abundantly clear. Matthieu was a consummate professional—and he was going to New York loaded for bear.

An array of equipment was laid out on the large square coffee table; some she recognized and some she didn't. Matthieu sat on the couch sorting and he hadn't looked up when she came in, so she knelt down on the floor across the table from him.

"Whatcha doin?" she asked in a singsong voice. He flicked his eyes briefly to her face and raised a brow at her.

"Packing." He nodded at the pile on the table. She recognized several cameras and what looked to be digital recording devices. The rest of the gadgets were unfamiliar to her.

"So what've we got?"

"Three remote controlled digital video cameras, one thermal imaging device, several mobile listening devices, motion detectors, various lock-picking tools."

"Oh." Her eyes swept past the hardware to the arsenal and noted there were quite a few semi-automatic handguns, a double barreled pump action shotgun, and a long range rifle complete with a scope and a laser sight. "Um...are we doing surveillance or storming the Bastille?"

She thought she saw a faint twitch of his full lips but it was gone so fast, she could have easily imagined it. "It depends on what we find when we get there, Fate."

Fate knew he was trying to drive home the seriousness of what they were about to do, but she couldn't get over how her name sounded in that gritty purr, and what it was doing to her insides. Shaking her head slightly, she tried to focus on the task at hand. "What's the plan?"

His dark eyes assessed her for a few uncomfortable seconds, as if he was trying to gage how much she could handle. Finally he nodded towards the arsenal and looked back at her. "Ever handle a gun?"

Swallowing hard, she gave him a slow nod. It was one of the few childhood memories she had that were worth the remembering. "I had a stepdad once—for as long as my mom could stand being married, which was all of about five minutes. Steve was a collector and since he had guns in the house, it was important to him that I learn to respect and use them correctly. It's...been awhile though."

He pushed one of the firearms towards her—a sleek, compact piece of hardware. "This is a Glock 19, a semi-auto compact nine-millimeter. Should be easy enough to handle."

She reached for the unloaded weapon, but paused with her hand hovering over it. "Have you used this one to...you know—"

"Kill someone?"

Fate nodded, ashamed at the need to ask. She'd been controlling her visions from objects for some time now, and they rarely got through without her allowing them. But she didn't want to take the chance if the gun had a violent past—especially given the way her *ability* seemed to go haywire around Matthieu.

"Not that one, no." When he offered no further explanation, she picked up the gun. He patiently walked her through loading and clearing, racking, field-stripping, and cleaning. "Unfortunately, there isn't time for you to practice. I have a couple of rules for you, though."

Unable to help herself, Fate rolled her eyes. "Shocker."

He narrowed his eyes at her, but she saw that ghost of a lip twitch again. '*Just turning into a big teddy bear, aren't ya?*' she thought.

"First, always assume it's loaded, even if you cleared it yourself. Second," he used his index finger to push the barrel of the gun down towards the floor, "don't point it at anything you aren't prepared to shoot."

"Sorry," she mumbled.

"Dead people can't be sorry."

"Thanks for that, Mr. Sunshine."

His contemptuous look spoke for itself. "I want you to keep this with you at all times. You shouldn't need to use it—it's really just to make me feel better about bringing you."

"Let's put aside the fact that I don't have a license for a firearm—what makes you think that TSA is going to let us waltz through airport security armed to the teeth?"

Matthieu snorted and gave her a smirk. "What makes you think we're going to the airport?" At her puzzled look, he took pity on her. "I've chartered a plane. We'll leave from a private strip in Thibodaux this afternoon."

"Oh."

Unrolling an old fashioned leather folio, he pulled out a couple of cards and handed them to her. In her hand was a Connecticut driver's license issued to someone named Abigail Ross—with her picture on it—and a concealed carry permit.

Then he handed her another license with his face on it, and the name Jackson Ross. "We'll check into the hotel under the guise of a married couple, Jack and Abby. When we get there, I'll head to Ward's office to break in and plant the equipment while you will," he jabbed a finger in the air to point at her, "Stay. Put."

Fate looked down at the false documents, and a sudden feeling of unease twisted her gut until she began to feel a bit nauseated. "I'm starting to feel like an accessory."

The look he gave her was a cross between impatience and thinly veiled derision. "The only thing you'll be an accessory to is getting us both killed if you don't do as I say. Let me worry about everything else."

"Point taken. I'll go pack."

Clutching her phone to keep her hands from shaking, Fate decided to call Isla to check on Ridley, and to let the Rousseaus know where they were going to be. Matthieu wouldn't approve, but what he didn't know wouldn't hurt him.

After a brief conversation with Ridley that left her smiling through blurry vision, Isla came back on the line.

"I hope she isn't being too much trouble."

Isla's laugh tinkled in her ear. "Of course not. She's adorable and you well know it. How are things with you?" she asked, her voice growing more serious.

"Um...fine, I guess. Why do you ask?"

"Well, we love Matty of course, but he can be a bit...trying at times." Fate was pretty sure she heard a male voice grumble *'crotchety' bastard"* in the background.

"We're getting on all right. I mean, Matthieu's still, well, Matthieu—but after we talked a little about what happened to him during the war, I understand better why he acts the way he does."

"That's gr—wait, *what*?"

"Um..." Fate wasn't sure if she'd overstepped, talking to Matthieu's sister-in-law about his problems.

"Matthieu talked to you about Afghanistan?"

"Um, yeah. So anyway," she said, quickly changing the subject, "I wanted to let you know that we've got to go to New York for a few days to try and find some information about the person who's after me. It will be a quick trip, and you can still reach me at this number."

Isla sounded a bit dazed when she answered. "Oh yes, sure. Well, be safe and we'll talk to you soon."

"Bye." Fate stared at the phone for a few seconds after the line went dead, going over the conversation in her head. "That was weird."

Letting it go, she started packing a small duffle bag for the trip. After gathering the essentials, Fate mulled over just what the fictitious Abigail Ross would take for a weekend jaunt to the Big Apple.

She imagined Abigail as a socialite on holiday, and tried to channel some of her mother's general snobbery for the part—though she loved music, Fate had always had a secret interest in acting.

Scanning her meager wardrobe, she picked out a simple black dress. It was understated, but form-fitting, and it dipped low in the front for a hint of décolletage. It was much colder in New York in the spring than it was down south, so she topped off the look with a light black trench-style coat.

Stepping into the dangerous black pumps she'd been wearing at the club the night she met Matthieu, she surveyed the results in the mirror. "Not half bad," she said to her reflection, but she decided the look needed just a bit more class. She twisted her long blond hair up into a loose chignon to the appearance of effortless chic.

"Perfect." Fate grabbed her bag and stepped out into the living room as Matthieu was just emerging from his own bedroom. She stopped dead in her tracks when she saw him, and had to forcibly keep herself from swallowing her tongue. This couldn't be the same man—without the cammies, the dog tags, and the bad attitude, he was...handsome. More accurately, this Matthieu was drop dead gorgeous.

He hadn't seen her yet—he was fiddling with his lapels and scowling down at himself. He'd chosen an impeccably cut black suit that fit him like a well-worn glove. Instead of a dress shirt, he wore a black turtleneck underneath his suit jacket. The choice was presumably to cover his tattoo, which was most definitely an identifying marking, but the effect was a layer of danger underneath the classy exterior.

He had shaved his face smooth, and his hair—which had grown out of a high-and-tight and taken to sticking out at odds and ends—was slicked back away from his face. The style emphasized his startling bone structure and the hollows underneath his high cheekbones.

She sucked in a breath and he must have heard her because he looked up, pinning her in place with those dark chocolate eyes. And then he froze, just as she had done, with his hand still resting on his lapel.

Those eyes made a slow trip from her face down to her toes, lingering over every curve. When he reached her face again, the master of cold detachment seemed unable to hide the heat in his gaze. Attempting to diffuse the tense moment, she tried for a light-hearted approach.

"Great minds," she said, referring to their similar state of dress. When he didn't speak, she crossed the room towards him, and his eyes began to dart around as if looking for means of escape.

"Here, let me," she said, gently removing his hand from the supple material of his jacket, and running her hands along the lapels to straighten them. "You clean up nice, Mr. Ross," she said with a touch of humor, smiling up at him.

Matthieu actually shuffled his feet, looking away from her. He cleared his throat and swallowed. It was almost as if he were...shy—but that seemed impossible to Fate. She'd never met anyone more self-assured.

"Um, yeah, well we'd better go," he said.

His voice was grittier than usual, causing an involuntary shiver to run up her spine.

"The plane will be waiting at the strip."

ℝ℞

The air strip was nothing but a dirt runway bush-hogged into a wide open field. And the plane—well, calling it a plane was more than generous, it was absurd—was nothing but a puddle jumper, with twin prop engines.

Fate stopped when she saw it, turning to Matthieu to protest, but he kept on walking. Apparently she had no choice in the matter, so she hoisted the strap of her bag further up on her shoulder and followed him. It was a good thing she didn't have a fear of flying, although she might after this experience.

Climbing up the metal staircase that descended from the hatch, she had to duck her head to enter the plane. Just as she'd suspected, it was a six-seater, not including the seats in the cockpit.

As she stuffed her bags in the overhead bin and took a seat, she noticed that Matthieu was sitting up front with the pilot. *Okay, fine, so he wants to keep an eye on everything.* As if he sensed her gaze, he turned and looked at her.

"Get buckled in, we're about to take off."

Fate did as she was told, and watched in confusion as Matthieu said a few words into the radio mouthpiece. *So he really likes planes...I guess it's nice of the pilot to humor him.*

She braced herself as the tiny tin can started to roll down the runway. As the nose tipped up and she felt the landing gear leave the ground, she noticed that the pilot wasn't touching the yoke—but Matthieu was.

He was flying the plane. The man she'd thought was the pilot was actually the *copilot. Fan-freakin-tastic.* Fate found herself, not for the first time, wondering what exactly Matthieu had done in the army that had required learning all of these special skills.

Images flashed in her mind of government operated pro-grams turning out military super-soldiers, á la Jason Bourne. Clamping her jaw shut to keep from blurting out stupid questions that he wouldn't answer, she closed her eyes and white-knuckled it the rest of the way to New York.

CHAPTER THIRTEEN

MATTHIEU CLOSED HIS EYES AND LEANED HIS HEAD against the cool window of the cab as it wound its way through the Manhattan weekend traffic. He'd chosen the Belvedere hotel in the theater district because it wasn't high profile or flashy, but was charming and still fancy enough for a couple of Connecticut socialites to patronize while in the city to catch some shows.

He'd known it was a bad idea to take Fate with him because she was beyond distracting—especially in that outfit. When she'd come up to fix his lapel back at the house, it had been all he could do not to drag her back into his bedroom and find out just what she looked like *out* of her little black dress.

But he couldn't exactly have left her behind, and he didn't trust anyone else with her safety. So he'd jail-broken her prepaid phone and uploaded a tracking program he'd written, that would send updates of her movements to his phone. That way, he wouldn't be distracted on the job worrying about where she was.

So there they were in Manhattan, posing as a married couple, and he had to find a way to keep his hands off of her. So far, his regular routine of making everyone around him think he was a colossal asshole wasn't working with her. Somehow she still tolerated being near him—*too* near.

"Hey, buddy. This is you," the cabbie said, interrupting his thoughts. He passed the man some cash and exited the cab, skirting around the front to open the door for Fate. She glanced up at him in surprise, giving him an indulgent smile, and Matthieu felt his body react.

Get a grip, Rousseau. It's an act. She's playing the part. Two can play that game. He didn't smile, but he let his eyes soften with warmth as he looked at her. He held out his arm so she could slip her hand in the crook of his elbow. "Shall we?"

"Lead the way."

He led her into the warm lobby and excused himself to go check them in. The concierge smiled with polite disinterest as he looked up the reservation. "Ah, yes, here it is. Mr. and Mrs. Ross in the Executive Suite, correct?"

"Yes, sir." Matthieu handed over his falsified ID and a wad of cash. The older man gave him the hairy eyeball for a moment—probably wasn't used to people paying cash, but Matthieu sure as hell wasn't going to leave an idiot trail for his potential killer. The concierge eventually got over his suspicion in the face of cold hard cash and gave Matthieu two key cards.

"Enjoy your stay, Mr. Ross."

"Thank you," he said, forcing a smile because he knew that Jack Ross would be expected to be somewhat personable—not a cold-hearted bastard like Matthieu.

As he made his way back to Fate, he was struck again at how beautiful she was. The light seemed to follow her everywhere, as if it reached for her warmth like a flower did the sun. He knew he couldn't touch her, his hands weren't near clean enough, but maybe just for the weekend...he could pretend that she was his.

Giving her his arm again, he escorted her to the elevator. She turned to him as the doors were closing and spoke softly. "What's the plan? Are you going to go to Ward's office now?"

He found himself almost hypnotized by the smoky gray eyes that were trained on him, waiting for an answer. Fuck, he needed to get it together. "No. We're going to go down to the restaurant and have a nice dinner. It's Brazilian, you'll love it," he said when she looked at him with a slack-jawed expression.

She chewed her lip nervously and he was unable to tear his eyes away from the motion. Yes, he wanted to see what it would be like—just for a little while—to be out with her under regular circumstances, but his plan did have other motivations.

"Relax. We're supposed to be a married couple on vacation, remember? It would look suspicious if I dumped you off in the suite as soon as we got here, and went out by myself. We have to keep up appearances."

She mulled it over and nodded slowly. "Do you really think someone could be watching us?"

"Not now, no. But if someone does come sniffing around, I don't want to give anyone at the hotel any odd behavior to focus on and remember."

"Makes sense," she said as the elevator chimed and the doors opened.

They quickly found their suite, dropped their bags inside and went right back out again. Matthieu made sure to hang the do not disturb sign on the door. He didn't want to come back only to find out that an overzealous maid had stumbled onto his bag of goodies.

Matthieu took careful sips of the Lagavulin he'd ordered with dinner while they sat in their cloistered booth at the *Churrascaria Plataforma*. It wasn't a luxury he allowed himself often—alcohol being a depressant and him avoiding sleep at all costs—but he was so tweaked on endorphins for the mission, he doubted a short glass of scotch would slow him down. He should be watching the room, looking for anything out of the ordinary, but he was fixated on Fate's animated face as she talked.

She'd been telling a story about her college friend Danny's brief foray with erectile dysfunction, and how he was cured by the national anthem and the US Olympic swim team. He'd tried to listen, really tried, but the unconsciously sexy way she formed the words was more than distracting. He'd have to try harder.

"So he says, 'Doc, I'm getting it all mixed up in my head. Now, whenever I hear it, I don't know whether to put my hand over my heart or pop a stiffy!' And the therapist says, 'Now Daniel, a patriotic erection is better than a nonexistent one.'" She then reached for her glass of club soda, but ended up taking hard swallow of his scotch. Between the punchline, the choking and the eye watering, Matthieu couldn't help but laugh.

Sure, the muscles were a little rusty but he still remembered how to do it. Fate froze with her napkin at her lips and stared at him, wide-eyed. The smile disappeared and he rubbed a hand over his face, wondering if he had something on it. "What?"

She seemed at a loss for words for a moment and just shook her head. "Nothing. Just—you should smile more, that's all. It's nice."

Embarrassed, but unaccountably pleased, he ducked his head to study his lowball glass and did what he did best— change the subject. "We need to go over how things are gonna go down tonight."

Disappointment flickered over her face for a brief moment and then it was gone. "You're the boss."

Matthieu didn't believe that for a second, but it seemed as though she'd decided to play along for the time being. "After dinner, we'll go back to the room together. I'll get my things together and head out around midnight. I should be back by oh five hundred at the latest. You are to stay inside the room at all times. Understood?"

He could tell she wanted to say something snarky, but she reined it in. "What if you don't come back?"

"I'll come back."

Her eyes narrowed and she clearly wasn't backing down. "But what if you don't?"

Sighing, Matthieu finished off his scotch before answering. "Fine. If I don't come back as scheduled, wait until dark tomorrow and then hit speed dial 3 on your phone. That will get you to Rick, the copilot. Just tell him the situation and he'll make sure you get home. But I *will* be back. This ain't my first rodeo."

"I really hope so. I just don't want to get stranded."

"It'll be fine. When I get back, I'll spend the day checking the feeds and making sure the cameras don't get spotted. We'll head back tomorrow night."

They finished the rest of their dinner in relative silence and as if there was an unspoken cue, they rose to leave at the same time. Matthieu started to walk past but Fate stopped him with a hand on his arm.

The heat of it seeped in right through the material of his jacket, and he had to suppress a shudder. She waited for him to look at her and, when he did, he felt the undeniable pull that sparked between them.

"You'll be careful?" she said. Though phrased as a question, it was more of a command, and all he could do was nod.

CHAPTER FOURTEEN

MATTHIEU TOOK THE SUBWAY—WHERE PEOPLE avoided looking at each other—as cabs were easily tracked. He'd swapped his suit for his worn leather jacket and a pair of black BDUs. The twin SIGs were a familiar weight across his shoulders, and he also had a suppressed pistol strapped in at his lower back.

For once, he hoped he didn't have to use them. They'd gain more information if he were able to get in and out, undetected. Ward might be a giant tool, but he hadn't gotten where he was by being an idiot. Matthieu would have to be careful.

Ward's office was located on the second floor of a million dollar Brownstone on the upper west side. The lieutenant shared the building with a law firm that occupied the ground level. Matthieu would have to break into the lower office and make his way upstairs for another bit of B & E. *Piece of cake.*

After getting off at his stop, he took the last few blocks at a crisp walk. He hopped the wrought iron fence around the tiny garden to find the electrical box mounted on the side of the concrete steps. Opening it, he identified the wires running to the box from the alarm system—a skill born of many years of practice.

Instead of cutting the wires, which would leave evidence of him having been there—he took out a tiny black device from his bag. The thing had cost him an arm and a leg, but it was worth its weight in gold. He clipped the wires into the device and armed it. It would interrupt and loop the signal from the alarm system, without alerting the monitors of a problem.

Blending into the shadows cast by the street lamp, he made quick work of the front door, deftly picking the lock and slipping inside. Moving like smoke with nothing but a whisper of sound, he crept through the richly appointed law office and climbed the stairs, always keeping to the shadows.

When Matthieu reached the door to Ward's office and was surprised to see the thick wooden panel adorned with only a single doorknob lock. "You're slipping, Ward," he whispered. Either that, or there was nothing in the office worth protecting. Luckily, Matthieu wasn't there for his file—that day. His goal was to plant the surveillance equipment and get out in one piece.

He slid his fingers along the door frame, checking for any hidden antitheft measures and found nothing. Pulling out a pick and a tension wrench from his kit, he popped the lock and went inside.

He'd honestly expected some kind of *Indiana Jones*-esque booby trap, and fought the urge to duck an imaginary spear flying at his head. Nothing. Ward was seriously off his game. Or maybe the man had just gotten too comfortable since his biggest threat was on the run. *We'll see about that, big guy*, he thought.

Once he was safely inside the dark office and had the door locked behind him, he pulled out his phone and brought up the tracker app. The flashing red dot told him that Fate was still safely ensconced in the hotel room. He left all of the lights off because he didn't need them. After years of covert ops, his night vision was so finely tuned; it was almost as good as his regular vision.

He tackled the file cabinet first—his instincts told him that his personnel file wouldn't be found there, but he had to check. First, he checked under his given name, followed by his ID number, codename, and unit name. Nothing. Matthieu had a feeling that wherever Ward kept the G9X personnel files would be locked up like Fort Knox. He couldn't be the only one the Lieutenant was blackmailing this way.

Matthieu turned to the sleek laptop that sat atop a monstrosity of an oak desk. He shook his head, remembering all too well Ward's "little man" syndrome. His movements were quick and economical, but unhurried, as he unscrewed the bottom panel of the computer.

Inside, he strategically placed a chip of his own making that was designed to allow him to follow the movements of the user—and remote in if necessary. After replacing the panel, he wiped the outer shell clean of fingerprints.

The mission was going well—almost too well for Matthieu's liking—but he couldn't fight the itch at the back of his neck that told him trouble was just around the corner. And worse still, the demons were closer to the surface than they'd ever been. They liked this place, which meant it was a place he shouldn't be for long.

Matthieu knew he needed to finish up quickly, so he bugged the phone and placed another listening device inside a light fixture. He found discreet places to hide the live-feed cameras and the thermal imaging device.

Just as he finished placing the last of the equipment, he heard muffled voices and the jangling of keys from outside the office. *Fuck, Ward can't catch me here*, he thought. Whoever it was, they'd cut off his most effective means of escape. *Time for plan B*. He made his way to the back window just as he heard a key turn the lock. Slipping out the window and onto the fire escape, he carefully closed it back and made for the ladder.

The ladder was pulled up, but he heard keys in the door and there was no time. Slinging his bag over his shoulder, Matthieu jumped and caught a rung of ladder on the way down. The rusty metal structure groaned and gave way, sliding down under the force of his weight.

When he was about fifteen feet from the ground, he was jerked to a stop hard enough to jar his teeth together. "Goddamn old fire escapes," he grumbled as he realized the bottom of the ladder had rusted through at some point and broken off, because it no longer reached anywhere close to the ground. He'd have to jump.

Cursing some more, he let go and dropped to the ground, landing on his feet in one piece, although his legs would be feeling that in a few hours. Before someone thought to check out the fire escape, Matthieu ghosted down the back alley and rounded the corner of the block of Brownstones.

Staying in the shadow of the old buildings, he snuck around front to retrieve his signal jammer—that was one piece of equipment that was too valuable to leave behind. Once he was sure he'd left nothing behind, he set off at a fast clip and disappeared into the nearest subway tunnel.

When Matthieu slipped into the hotel room just shy of four in the morning, Fate was asleep in the king sized bed. She'd protested the single bed at first, until he reminded her that they were supposed to be a married couple. It wasn't like he was going to sleep anyway.

Standing by the bed, he watched her for a moment. She had her hands tucked under her head like a child, and her long mane was spread out over the pillows. A small smile graced her lips, and it made him wonder what she dreamed about. He couldn't imagine dreams that made someone smile.

Her skin was so smooth, glowing in the moonlight, that he caught himself almost reaching out to touch her. Jerking his hand back as if he'd just discovered he was about to pet a rattlesnake, he turned away from her. *One more time—not for you, buddy.*

Instead, he dragged one of the plush hotel chairs to the foot of the bed and positioned it facing the door. Lowering himself into it, he pulled the shotgun across his lap and waited. He was pretty sure he'd gone undetected, but if he was wrong, he'd be ready. That was where Fate found him when she woke up, hours later.

CHAPTER FIFTEEN

MATTHIEU WAS RUNNING ON FUMES. HE TRIED TO think back to the last time he'd had even a little bit of uninterrupted sleep. It had to have been the night Fate had caught him in the nightmare. He knew if he didn't lie down soon, he was going to fall down, but it was so dangerous to sleep with someone else in the house.

After they'd returned to the bayou house, unpacked, and had a bite to eat, Fate had disappeared outside. Matthieu hadn't protested. He meant what he'd said before, she wasn't a prisoner. Besides, he could hear her—the rustle of her clothing, her soft footfalls on the deck, and always, her singing.

The melody was one he often heard her singing to herself when she wasn't paying attention, and the sound of it soothed him. Closing his eyes, he listened to the melancholy tones as they washed over him, threatening to pull him under.

Whispers, hisses, and the inevitable explosion—Matthieu sprang up from the couch, his eyes wide and his chest heaving.

"*Sonofabitch!*" It was happening much easier lately. It seemed like the more time he spent in Fate's company, the closer his nightmares and demons were to the surface, straining to get out.

He needed a distraction. Pulling out his laptop and setting it up on the coffee table, he decided to check and see what Ward was up to. It was optimistic to expect to find out anything useful this soon, but it would at least keep him awake.

Matthieu brought up the surveillance program that gave him a screen divided into sections with the feed from each camera. As expected, Ward sat alone at his desk, working on his computer. Leaving the screen on, Matthieu started to get up for more coffee when he noticed movement on one of the feeds.

Ward had gotten up to let two men into his office. The newcomers took their seats in front of Ward's desk, while the man himself resumed his spot at his computer. His interest piqued, Matthieu clicked a button to switch on the audio. He kept it low, because he wanted to screen what he heard before telling Fate what happened.

The man on the left was slender, with pale skin and brown eyes. His black hair was cut artfully in a way that tried and failed to look effortless. Matthieu recognized him immediately to be Eli Farrell, Fate's ex-husband.

Matthieu couldn't positively identify the man on the right because he was in profile, but based on his perceived age, height, and build, it was safe to say that this was Drake Maxwell. He also had black hair, but much longer, combed back away from his face. Where Farrell was fair, Maxwell's complexion was the perfect golden brown of an expensive tan.

It was clear from the first that Farrell would defer to the older man, and that Maxwell was in charge. The man leaned forward, eyes intent on Ward. "Have you found them yet?"

Ward didn't exactly cower before Maxwell, but he definitely looked uncomfortable. "Not yet. My people are still on it. Rousseau's good—the best—but asking him to do the hit was a gamble that didn't pay off. He has more incentive than ever to go off the grid."

Matthieu was unable to see the man's eyes, but Maxwell's entire body tensed. Eli Farrell, whose eyes he *could* see, cut a nervous glance toward his partner. "Hit? *What* hit?" Maxwell growled.

Lieutenant Ward just seemed confused, casting a helpless look at Eli. "When Rousseau located them, I asked you what the next move was—you said take them out," he said, addressing Farrell.

The room became so dead silent that Matthieu turned up the volume on his computer just to make sure that wasn't the cause. It seemed as though minutes ticked by before anyone reacted, but in reality it was probably only seconds.

So fast that Matthieu couldn't even track it, Maxwell's arm shot out to clamp a hand around Eli's throat in a grip that threatened to crush his windpipe. The man writhed and gagged, clawing at the arm of steel that held him.

Matthieu thought that he just might be about to witness a murder, and he had no idea what he would do about it—or what Ward would do, for that matter. But, for the time being, Ward seemed to be content to watch with detachment and only a mild concern. Probably more for the cleanup than anything.

Maxwell squeezed harder and Eli's eyes bulged out, while Matthieu heard a sickening crunch over the audio. He was sure when Maxwell let Eli go, that the man would be dead, but he just coughed and sputtered, and glared.

The picture of calm once more, Maxwell leaned back in his chair and steepled his fingers. "What the fuck, man?" Eli croaked. "I thought that's what we were doing here. I couldn't care less about the other two, but the child—"

"Enough," Maxwell said, his voice was as deadly as it was quiet. "I want the woman alive, and her pit bull as well. They're both mine."

As if he sensed Matthieu watching, he turned his head to look directly into one of the cameras and smiled. Only it wasn't a smile—it was a gruesome sneer of a mouthful of fangs. Almost instantaneously, the man's face changed as well, his features becoming sharper, his gray eyes becoming translucent and full of writhing shadows.

Matthieu knew all too well what those shadows meant. They were the demons or, at least, *of* the demons. While Maxwell continued to leer at the camera, a symbol emerged on his forehead. The symbol of death—the jackal, the symbol that haunted Matthieu's dreams. As if sensing his thoughts, the thing that had once been Drake Maxwell looked into Matthieu's eyes straight through the camera, and winked.

"Holy Shit!" Matthieu slammed the lid shut on the laptop, threw it to the other end of the couch, and scrambled back away from it. He even stuffed a pillow on top of it for good measure. With his knees drawn up to his chest, he sifted his hair with shaky hands while he waited for his heart rate to come down off the roof.

What the fuck had that been? It was if the guy had known he was watching. "Either I'm losing my ever-lovin' mind, or we're in way over our heads," he said to the empty room.

Maxwell didn't want to kill Fate and Matthieu, he wanted to capture them. Ridley had a target on her back, but the scariest part was that Matthieu knew he and Maxwell had met before— on the worst day of his life.

CHAPTER SIXTEEN

IT WAS EARLY EVENING WHEN FATE CAME IN FROM OUTside. She was so sure that Matthieu would read it clearly on her face that she'd spent the afternoon talking to Étienne. She knew she should tell him about the boy, but she just couldn't bring herself to do it.

Matthieu would see him as a threat, and demand that she stop talking to him. With her daughter so far away, and her *current* roommate so distant and cold most of the time, Fate was lonely. Étienne gave her someone to talk to besides herself, or the wall.

Still, she was feeling guilty about keeping secrets from a man who was protecting her, and she expected for him to jump on her with accusations that she couldn't deny as soon as she stepped inside.

What she found instead disturbed her much, much more. Matthieu was huddled against the arm of the couch in an almost fetal position, hugging a pillow to his chest. His eyes were wide and unfocused, staring into some distant corner of the room, and his skin was leeched of all color. He was so still that if she hadn't been able to see him breathing, Fate might have worried that he was dead.

Taking a couple of cautious steps toward him, she lowered herself onto the coffee table. "Matthieu?"

Her heart lurched when there was no response. Was he having some kind of stroke? Or maybe another side effect of the PTSD. Clearing her throat, she spoke louder. "Matthieu? Sweetie, what's wrong?"

This time, he jolted at the sound of her voice. Blinking several times, he turned his head and looked at her through bleary eyes. "Huh?" His voice was nothing but a gritty whisper.

Drumming up some false confidence that she surely didn't feel, Fate gave him a weak smile. "You were a million miles away. Did something happen? A flashback...a nightmare?"

She could see the very moment he finally pulled it together and came back into himself. His expression quickly shuttered, and he uncurled his tense body. "It's nothing. Don't worry about it," he said, still distracted.

When she would have pushed him more, he surged to his feet and left the room—she heard the storm door bang shut as he went outside. *Storm door, indeed*, she thought. Fate was so dumbfounded by his abrupt departure that she stayed where she was, contemplating the riddle that was Matthieu Rousseau.

If she was confused then, she was even more so when he returned. He stomped into the living room and tossed some heavy coils of rope onto the table beside her. Thinking that nothing good could come of this, she swallowed hard and looked up at him through widened eyes. "Um..."

He closed his eyes and took a deep breath—and when he opened them, they were as haunted as she'd ever seen them.

"It's been nearly four days...I think. I've got to sleep—I'm no good to either of us like this."

He looked at her as if that should explain everything, but she sent a dubious glance back to the ropes and hoped it conveyed her confusion. "So sleep," she said, gesturing towards his bedroom. "I don't understand the problem."

"No, you don't," he said with a sigh. "It's not safe. Things happen in my sleep—things I can't control. What you saw the other night was just the tip of the iceberg. Things can get...dangerous."

"So," she said, drawing out the syllable, "what do you plan to do about it?" She flicked another wary glance at the ropes. Was he going to tie her up and lock her in her room so she couldn't bother him in his sleep? Fate didn't see how that would help.

"You're gonna to tie me to the bed."

"I'm going to *what?*"

"You heard me. I need to get some sleep to be able to protect you. You need to be protected, from them and from me. It's the only solution."

A number of protests ran through Fate's head as she grasped what he was asking—demanding—of her, and it was on the tip of her tongue to let them fly. But then she thought better of it. What was the point? If the man wanted to be tied to the bed—if that would make him feel better, then who was she to complain. She didn't have it in her to fight another losing argument with him.

"When, now?"

He jerked his head in a stiff nod, and walked to his bedroom door. When he put his hand on the knob, he looked over his shoulder to answer her. "I'm to the point that I can't wait any longer."

After he disappeared into his room, Fate was left alone to gather the ropes. Trying not to think about what she was actually doing, she picked them up and followed him. When her eyes adjusted to the dim light of the room, she saw him—and immediately squeaked and dropped her armload on the floor.

Completely naked with the exception of the sheet that was pulled up between his legs to cover his hips and groin, he was spread out like a sacrifice. He grimaced when he saw the look on her face. "Sorry," he said, genuinely apologetic. "I didn't want to get tangled up in clothes when I couldn't move my arms or legs. If you wouldn't mind..."

As his voice trailed off, she noticed his arms and legs were pointed at the posts of the queen sized four poster bed. Trying not to look at the expanse of bronzed skin that covered his muscled body, or the network of scars that peppered it, she grabbed his right wrist and made quick work of tying it to the bedpost.

Testing her work with a jerk of his hand, he nodded his approval and raised an eyebrow at her. She shrugged and moved on to his right ankle, now *really* trying not to look. "The stepfather with the guns...he was a yachtsman as well. He'd often take me sailing, so I learned a thing or two."

Fate rushed through the remaining two limbs, and he tested each binding for strength. When he was satisfied that everything was secure, he looked back at her and the well of gratitude in his expression shook her. She realized that he really was so afraid of himself and what he was capable of, that he truly felt like this was the only way he could get a good night's sleep.

It broke her heart a little, but she was glad she could help give him this. He may be a socially stunted would-be-assassin, but he'd done a lot for her since they'd met. Before giving herself a chance to think better of it, she placed a chaste kiss on his forehead and brushed his hair back from his face.

She might have imagined the way he leaned into her touch, just for a moment, but she didn't think so. Needing to get away from him before she made a fool of herself, she forced her feet to back away. "Sleep well. Just yell for me when you're...you know, ready to get up."

He breathed a sigh of relief and his lips curved up into a half smile. "Thanks. Really." As she backed her way out of the room, she saw his eyes drift shut just before she closed the door.

Making her way to the kitchen, Fate surprised herself with a jaw-cracking yawn. Apparently she was more tired out from their trip than she realized. She made herself a quick sandwich, and headed for her own bedroom. She expected to have trouble sleeping, knowing there was a sexy—however unapproachable—man tied to a bed in the room next door. But she was asleep by the time her head hit the pillow.

$$\infty\!)\!\infty$$

It was pitch black when Fate was shaken loose from her pleasant dreams by a rhythmic banging sound that reverberated through the house. Startled she sat up and blinked into the darkness, trying to orient herself.

The thumping never ceased or lost its cadence. If she didn't know that they were alone in the house, she'd have thought there were some *extracurricular activities* going on in Matthieu's room. As it stood, Fate was worried—their enemies were still a constant threat.

She shrugged into a light robe over her tank top and bikini briefs, and tiptoed out of her room toward the sound. It was indeed coming from Matthieu's room.

Slipping through the door without making a sound, Fate searched for what caused the noise. The moon had risen and Matthieu kept his drapes open, so his body was awash in moonlight.

His muscles twitched and rolled as his body bucked up off the bed, and she could see that he was obviously in the throes of another nightmare. As he lurched, the bindings on his arms pulled the headboard forward and slammed it back, which created the pounding noise.

It was hard to tell in the dark, but she thought there might be dark red marks, and maybe blood, where the ropes abraded his skin. It bothered her—but not enough to untie him. While she hesitated to invade his thoughts again as it felt like a violation, if she could help bring him out of it, then she had to try.

Just as she had the other night, she climbed on top of him and straddled his hips. The erratic bucking subsided when her weight settled on him, but he continued to thrash his head from side to side. Instead of holding on to his wrists, this time she gripped his face in her hands.

Fate felt a familiar queasiness as she was once again ripped from herself and thrown head first into another turbulent nightmare.

CHAPTER SEVENTEEN

THIS TIME WHEN SHE WAS SUCKED INTO MATTHIEU'S consciousness, Fate was ready for it—as much as one could be ready for dropping into someone else's dream. She realized that this one was less of a dream, and more of a memory.

So far, the dreams had seemed to have a hazy quality, as if she were looking through a fine sheer curtain. This was different—everything was sharp, stark, and in clear focus. She didn't know how she knew, but Fate wasn't inside Matthieu's mind this time, although she could feel him.

She found herself alone on a long gravel drive, shrouded in low hanging trees draped with Spanish moss. After a cursory look around, she realized it was the drive up to the very house that they were staying in.

Fate wondered if it was winter, because she shivered as a bitter wind blasted her from behind—even New Orleans had a few weeks of cold weather. Hearing gravel crunch up ahead, she noticed a man and a small boy about Ridley's age walking away from her.

Curious, she followed them, treading quietly although she didn't think they could see or hear her if they were part of the memory. As she got closer, she could see the man carried a tackle box and a fishing pole that had seen better days, while the boy carried a shiny, new pole.

When the man turned to smile down on his boy, Fate gasped as she saw his face. He had an uncanny resemblance to Matthieu, although he was older. His face was tan and weathered, suggesting that he spent a good bit of time outdoors, but his dark brown eyes were very familiar.

She had to assume it was Matthieu's father, so that would make the little boy either Matthieu or Jeremiah. Considering she was crashing Matthieu's memories, she imagined it was him.

Young Matthieu's attention was drawn to the edge of the woods to a copse of blackberry bushes. Smiling indulgently, Mr. Rousseau followed, handing over a small backpack that Matthieu could load up with berries. *So, not winter then*, she thought.

Fate settled in to watch the loving exchange between father and son, glad to have even a brief glimpse into a happy memory for once.

And then the dark clouds began moving in much too fast to be natural, casting rolling shadows across the darkening road. The hairs on her arms stood up from the sudden static crackling in the air. Maybe not such a happy memory after all.

Fate noticed a man emerge from the shadows and saunter towards the pair. She felt a ripple of uneasiness through the air created by the stranger's presence, and when Mr. Rousseau looked over his shoulder, it was obvious that he had felt it, too.

As discreetly as possible, he pushed Matthieu back into the cover of the trees.

The man who seemed to be stalking Mr. Rousseau wore jeans and a simple black t-shirt. His longish black hair was swept back away from his face, revealing razor sharp cheekbones over hollowed cheeks. He looked positive-ly...predatory.

Mr. Rousseau waited, his posture tense, as the stranger came to a stop in front of them. It looked to Fate as if they were speaking, but she couldn't hear what was said. Matthieu's father was shaking his head and made as if to turn away.

The newcomer wrapped a hand around the back of his neck to hold him in place, and then brought both hands into a caging grip on Mr. Rousseau's face. Fate could hear frightened whimpers from Matthieu in the trees as he watched his father stare into the stranger's eyes.

Widened brown eyes stared into translucent shadowy ones, as if he was unable to look away, and tears began to slip down his cheeks. During the deadlock, an image took shape on the strange man's forehead. Fate had to choke back a cry, because it was a symbol she was all too familiar with.

Suddenly, the stranger's brow furrowed as he looked at Mr. Rousseau. Shaking his head, he released his grip, and the older man crumpled to the ground, unmoving. He raised his face to the wind as if he were scenting the air. His eyes locked onto the spot in the trees where Matthieu was hidden.

Oh God, not the child, she thought. But she knew it would be—they wouldn't be here in this memory if it wasn't.

The man crossed his arms and leaned his weight on one hip, and waited. He presented like he had all the time in the world, but if Matthieu didn't come out, he'd go in after him. After seconds, or maybe forever, the little dark-haired boy emerged from the trees. His jaw was set, mouth in a grim line, but he flicked wide eyes between his motionless father and the stranger.

Fate could feel the fear bleeding out of Matthieu, and the man relishing it. As she watched, he changed. His bone structure became sharpened, more hollowed out, and his cocky sneer turned serrated, like the shark that stalked a helpless seal.

The man-who-was-not-a-man made a thoughtful study of Matthieu, shaking his head and scratching his chin. "Interesting. It's you, little pup. I thought it was *him*," he glanced at Mr. Rousseau's body, "but it's you."

The voice was warped—probably from the nasty grill—and it caused a shudder to ripple through Fate, mirroring young Matthieu's reaction. Who—*what*—was this? She'd never been one to believe in things that went bump in the night, but she instinctively knew that, even through the distortion of a child's memory, this had really happened.

Matthieu glanced at his father again, his tiny body tensing, and Fate could almost taste his indecision. Should he run to get help, and risk getting caught by the monster? Should he try and help his father and risk the same? Could he stand his ground and protect his father from another attack?

It was all too much for a seven-year-old to take in, so instead, he remained frozen with fear, warily watching for the creature's next move. "What is your name?" it asked.

Matthieu's lower lip trembled but he raised his chin a fraction. "Matthieu Rousseau."

The creature nodded as if that made perfect sense. "So it is. You may call me Draconus."

"Who are you?" was his brave reply.

"Who am I? I am a king...and you shall be my prince." The man-monster extended his fingers, capped with claws like ice picks. With an index finger, he sliced a deep laceration in his own wrist, hissing out a breath at the pain.

When he withdrew the claw, it was dripping with his own blood. He began surreptitiously closing in on Matthieu until he was close enough to grip the boy's face in his bony hand. Using that hand to distract the boy and hold him still, Draconus raised the bloody claw and carved a long furrow in Matthieu's flesh from the corner of his eye down to his jaw, commingling their blood.

The only indication of any pain Matthieu gave was a twitch of his facial muscles and the tears that gathered in his eyes. Then his gaze hardened and he met the creature's eyes in stony silence, as blood dripped steadily down his chin and onto his shirt. In that moment, those eyes changed forever—from an innocent boy's to a tortured man's. *So this is where it began*, Fate thought.

Draconus stroked his fingers through the blood on Matthieu's face in a sickening caress. "We are connected now, you and I. When I need you, you'll come...until then, I'll always be with you," he said, dissolving in a cloud of smoke and brimstone.

Matthieu stood there, chest heaving, looking impossibly small and old at the same time. He stared at the place where the creature had once been, and then he stared at his father's body slumped on the side of the road. He made no move towards his father, maybe because the boy knew—as well as Fate knew—that he was gone.

A wave of guilt hit Fate so hard, it would have knocked her off her feet—had she been corporeal. Instead of mourning his father, Matthieu turned that pain inward onto himself, hating himself for his inaction, his ineptitude, his childishness. He blamed himself—always would—for his father's death, and for his mother and brother's loss. *This* was it. *This* was the source of all of the hatred, the self-inflicted torture. Not the war, not even being assaulted by a fantastical boogie-man, but a seven-year-old's guilt over letting his father die.

It was more than Fate could take. She couldn't—*wouldn't*—allow this to continue. It was enough. He'd been through *enough*. She did the only thing she could think of—she placed an evanescent hand on the young boy's shoulder and shook, even though he wouldn't feel it. She did her best to solidify herself and her thoughts, and called out to him. *"Matthieu!"*

ℬ☽☾

Fate was nearly thrown off the bed by the rigid bowing of Matthieu's body underneath her. He gasped for air as if there wasn't enough to fill his lungs, and again thrashed his head back and forth. She had to use her hands on his shoulders to steady him.

At the feel of her touch, his eyes flew open, unseeing. Only they weren't his eyes, they were the monster's eyes, crystal clear and swirling with shadows. Terrified, she grasped the sides of his face in her hands and brushed her thumbs over his lips.

"Matthieu…" she said with a hitch in her voice. "Please look at me."

And he did. The translucent shadows dissolved back into the deep brown she was so familiar with and he looked at her, but he wasn't really seeing her.

"I've been dying since that day...," his voice came out as a hoarse whisper. "It's infected me. That's why I keep my distance—all that devil wants is pain. Mine. Theirs. Yours."

Fate had reached her limit of how much of his torture she could watch. She stroked his scarred cheek one last time before popping it with a light slap. "Matthieu. Snap out of it!"

Finally, his eyes seemed to focus on her face, and realization dawned. She watched first the confusion, then embarrassment, then guilt. And that was quite enough of that.

"No. You are *not* doing this. Your father's death was not your fault."

"How did you—"

"Later. We'll talk about it later—full disclosure. But right now? Tell me you don't feel responsible for your father's death."

When he spoke, the words were thick with unshed tears. "I can't tell you that. I should have done something. I should have stood up instead of hiding in the goddamn woods."

"Damn it, Matthieu, you were just a child—Ridley's age. Would you blame her for this?"

"Of course not, but—"

"But nothing. What was your father's official COD?"

"Officially? A stroke."

"There, you see?" Fate asked. "If that were the case, there was nothing you could have done. You've got to let this go."

He sighed, the movement lifting her with the soft rise and fall of his body. "It's not that simple."

"No, of course it isn't. But I'll help you figure it out."

"Help me," he repeated, considering. "You've already helped me. That day would have played on an endless loop, all night, until I managed to claw my way to the surface. Somehow, you got me out."

He looked at her with such gratitude—as if she'd pulled him from a burning building, rather than simply woken him from a nightmare—that it rocked her back. That reminded her just how precarious her position was, once again, only this time there was much less in between them.

Her breath hitched as she was compelled beyond her control to look down at him. His chest, deeply tanned and riddled with scars, rose and fell rapidly with the adrenaline that still lingered in his system. Abdominal muscles rippled and twitched as he tried to get that breathing under control. She was surprised to see the striking cobra tattoo that began at his neck flowed over his left shoulder and coiled around his bicep. She'd never found tattoos sexy before, but the evidence was irrefutable.

Looking over shoulder at his tied ankles, and then back at his tied hands, she realized that this man was completely at her mercy—and the irony of the reversal of roles was not lost on her. It was a heady thing, that.

Without thinking, she reached out, determined to feel the silky skin, but her hand froze in midair. What was she doing? The man was tied down for heaven's sake. This was hardly any different than what had been done to her.

As if sensing her turmoil, he glanced at his restraints and looked back at her with a smile—and it stunned her no less than it had the last time, all the more special for its infrequency.

"Go ahead," he said, the smile taking on a mischievous edge. He seemed happy to have a distraction from the nightmare. "Look, touch...do whatever you want." He studied her thoughtfully before continuing. "It might be good for you— like replacing a bad memory with a good one...maybe."

When Fate thought about it, she believed he could be right. Almost all of her relationships with men had been one-sided and controlling, and certainly all of her sexual experiences had. While she chose not to dwell on the rape, she thought about Eli.

In hindsight, she knew that Eli was a selfish lover. Her first encounter had destroyed her adolescent ideals as to what sex would be like, and she'd tried to get them back with Eli. She told herself she liked what they did, because she knew she was supposed to.

However, reality was the great equalizer. She knew now that he'd only cared about his own pleasure, and made her do things she wasn't sure of because it was *expected* of her—because it was what lovers did. But he'd never been concerned with what *she* thought lovers should do for each other. Hell, she wasn't even sure she'd ever had an orgasm. And if she had to think about it, she was pretty sure that was her answer right there.

Embarrassed beyond reason, she put a stop to that thought process, feeling the heat rise in her cheeks. Looking down at the man below her from a completely new perspective, she saw naked emotion in his eyes—those eyes of warm chocolate brown that crinkled just so at the corners, probably from too much squinting in the desert sun.

She realized that for once, his expression wasn't tortured—it was just calm, open, welcoming. And here he was, offering himself to her *carte blanche*, whatever she wanted. She might be scared and inexperienced, but a fool she was not.

When she met his eyes again, he must have recognized the change in her, because his eyes darkened and he unconsciously pulled his lower lip between his teeth. "Put your hands on me."

His words were a rasp across her skin that abraded the last vestige of her uncertainty, and she found herself more than willing to obey.

CHAPTER EIGHTEEN

MOVING WITH UNCONSCIOUS REVERENCE, FATE placed her hands on Matthieu's chest, to where she could feel his heart racing beneath her fingers. It eased her mind to know that he wasn't unaffected.

Now that she had him at her mercy, she wasn't exactly sure what she wanted to do. Deciding to go with her initial impulse, she smoothed her hands over the taught skin, marveling at the gentle expansion and contraction of his powerful ribcage.

She sneaked a peek at him from beneath her lashes and saw that his head was slightly raised, and his eyes were following every move of her hands. His lips had parted, allowing heavy breaths to rush through.

Growing bolder, she swept her hands over his shoulders and down his biceps, eliciting a contented sigh from him. Fate found herself barely able to suppress a satisfied smirk. Matthieu liked her hands on him.

During her gentle mapping of the hard planes and smooth lines of his chest, her fingers trailed across a nipple. He expelled a ragged breath and his head fell back onto the pillow. *I did that*, she thought, marveling at his responsiveness. That was certainly something she hadn't experienced before. It was like a drug, and she wanted more.

Her own body was suffused with a feverish warmth as she felt him respond to her, and for a moment, she was ashamed. She wasn't sure of where to go, what to do. How could she possibly consider taking advantage of someone who was restrained? And how could she want to, so badly?

Her indecision must have shown on her face because when she looked back at him, his expression held a Mona Lisa smile's worth of secrets and promises. He looked at his bound wrists one more time, and then back at her, raising his brows toward his hairline.

"You're in control, Fate. No one's going to take that from you. It's your move—you could walk out of here and leave me tied up for a week...or you could do...whatever..."

Giving her a cheeky grin, which was just one more expression that she wished he'd wear more often, he relaxed his posture, laying himself out for her as best he could with the bindings. Just to emphasize his point, he gently raised his hips just enough so that she could feel his arousal. "I'm not afraid.'

That really made all the difference, didn't it? It was exactly the right thing for him to have said, and it made up her mind for her. He knew what was happening, and he wanted it as much as she did. He wasn't being taken advantage of—any more than he wanted to be.

Decision made, she swung her leg off of him and knelt beside him on the bed, looking her fill. He was a maze of long, ropy muscles that, for once, weren't stiff with the tension that was his constant companion. With the sheet leaving just the slightest bit to the imagination, he was stretched out before her like an offering to some merciful higher power.

Leaning over him, she stroked a hand down his hip where it was exposed by the sheet, and she was rewarded with a ripple of his stomach muscles. This time, she savored her arousal—it wasn't a luxury she'd had in previous encounters. Holding a man such as Matthieu captive with only a touch—and some rope—made her feel powerful in a way she never had before.

Feeling braver, she continued her slow assault by running her hands down the cords of tendons and sinew in his strong thighs and calves, enjoying the brush of coarse hair against her palms. Fascinated, she mapped his body with her hands, sliding them over his ankles and feet.

Her lips curved in a slow smile when she caught sight of his hands gripping and releasing the pillows. As she traveled back up his legs, her hands skirting along both sides of the sheet that barely covered him, he took a deep breath and held it. She could practically hear the gears spinning in his mind, wondering what her next move would be. Would she or wouldn't she?

She allowed her knuckles to brush just the lightest touch along the side of his erection, and his entire body went taut. He let go the breath he'd been holding on a curse, and then he was exhaling in gasps.

Panicked, her eyes flicked to his face, wondering if she'd hurt him somehow. "I'm sorry! Should I stop?"

When he met her eyes, his pupils were so blown his eyes were almost black, and his expression was tight. "*God*...don't ever...stop," he stuttered.

So the panting is a good thing. She smiled to herself. *Good to know.* Following impulse, Fate crawled up his body until her face was poised just above his. She smiled with satisfaction when his eyes immediately dropped to her lips.

She moved closer until their mouths were just a hair's breadth apart, their breath mingling, but stayed just out of reach. "You can't push me away this time," she said.

Riveted and speechless, Matthieu just shook his head. "Don't want to," he managed.

Fate pulled her lower lip between her teeth and raised a brow at him. "What about distractions?"

He seemed confused at first, until he remembered how their first kiss had ended. His chest rose in a deep, shuddering breath. "Fucking distract me. Please."

No less eloquent for its crudeness, the statement was exactly what she'd been after. She lowered her lips to his and poured everything she had into her kiss. All of her frustration, fear, arousal—and yes, desire as well.

She was still inexperienced, but she prided herself in being a fast learner. He opened for her immediately, and she swept her tongue inside to tangle with his. It was a rough kiss, full of urgency, both of them dueling for control—but she eventually won out, drawing his lower lip into her mouth for a nip. She soothed the pain with a lick while she felt the fine tremors in his muscles under her hands.

Breaking away, she sat back on her heels and looked at him, savoring the aftermath of their kiss. His chest was still heaving, and his lips were swollen from their spirited joust of a kiss. She couldn't suppress the smile as she thought again, *I did that.*

Matthieu stared at Fate as she knelt over him. Her hair fell well below her shoulders, tangled and rumpled from sleep, her lips were bruised and bee-stung from the force of their kiss, and there was new light in her eyes.

She'd discovered her feminine power, something that she'd never been allowed to do before. He was happy to offer himself up as bait for her hook—especially since, for once, the only blessed sound inside his head was his own racing heartbeat.

There was a wicked gleam in her eye as she climbed over him to hop off the bed. Turning to face him and making sure he could see her every move, she held his gaze as she cast the robe off her shoulders and slowly lifted her tank top up and off.

Swallowing hard, Matthieu squeezed his bound hands into fists as the futile urge to touch her came over him. She wasn't perfect—she was better than. Her brows arched high over those stormy eyes that slightly tilted up in the corners. High cheekbones were offset by a nose that could only be described as cute; though he was sure she'd hate that. Her mouth was just a bit too wide, but that was what made her smile so incredible, and her lower lip was enticingly plump.

Like an angel, her pale skin reflected the moonlight, giving her an ethereal glow—yet she had a body built for sin. Her breasts were voluptuous, and her belly was taut and smooth with a subtle curve. Her hips were a soft flare that gave way to miles of leg. She was all the more perfect because of her refined imperfections.

The best thing by far was her current total lack of fear. She was in control and she knew it, and Matthieu was more than ready to let her have it. She chewed on her lip, and he knew that while she was embracing control, she still didn't have much of an idea about what to do with it.

"Come here," he said, though it came out as more of a plea than he'd intended. She took a step forward but stopped. He frowned until he saw her hook her fingers in her simple white panties and push them down her long legs. Matthieu was pretty sure he'd just had a small heart attack but God, it was worth it.

He couldn't keep his eyes off of Fate as she climbed over him to her original spot on the bed. Her heated gaze was a caress from head to foot and back again as she studied him. Feisty though she was, her innocence made him ache. She was like a kid in a candy store, given free rein and unsure of what to try first.

"What do you want?" he coaxed.

Those white teeth sank into her lower lip again, and he wanted to get down on his knees and beg her to let him do that for her. Considering his question, she trailed her fingers through his hair, making him never want to cut it again. "I'd like to touch you some more, I think."

He grinned at her—he'd done that more since he'd met her than he probably had in his whole life. "Have at it. All yours," he said, and meant it.

So Fate began her slow torture again, stroking her hands over him just enough to tease, to arouse, until he had to clench his teeth to keep from begging. She stretched her long, lithe body out along his side, still lazily stroking her fingers over his chest and belly.

A change had begun to come over her—she was finding her power—and the engrossed look in her eyes made Matthieu shiver. A lock of her hair fell over her shoulder and brushed against him, causing goose bumps to break out over his skin.

Nerves warring with desire, she kicked the sheet off of him, tentatively placed a leg over his thigh and inched closer to place kisses along his stubble-roughened jaw. As it stood, she was coming dangerously close to...*fuck*...his neck.

She'd discovered one of his most sensitive spots, and was exploiting it to the best of her ability. She drew her tongue along his flickering pulse and sucked up a mark on the sensitive skin below his ear, and he was cursing his inability to touch. He knew having the control was good for her, but it was fucking *torture* for him.

Tilting his head just right, he nuzzled his face into her hair, drawing deeply of the intoxicating scent of vanilla and sunshine. He'd never wanted anyone this much—never been so concerned with another's pleasure—but he was well and truly under her spell.

With a barely audible moan, she shifted further on top of him, sliding a knee between his thighs as she dove in for another kiss. While her lips on his drove all thought from his head, the pressure her leg was putting on his unyielding erection had him choking out a pained groan.

At the sound, her entire body went still. He tore his lips away from hers, trying to find enough blood north of the equator to form a coherent sentence. "Please don't ask me if I want to stop," he rasped in her ear between pants, thrusting up against her leg to show her that he was feeling just fine.

Matthieu sent up silent thanks to whoever was listening that she didn't say anything, she just fell back into the kiss and started up her sensual rhythm once again. It was the single most erotic experience of his life, and they were really just making out.

God, how he wished he could touch her. She began seeking her own pleasure by rocking against his hip, which was putting delicious pressure on his cock. It was exquisite misery—and when he began to see sparks behind his eyelids and feel a tingling at the base of his spine, he knew he had to rein things in.

From the flush of her ivory skin, to the sexy little moans she didn't know she was voicing, he could tell that she was in the same predicament.

"Fate," he whispered into her mouth.

When she raised her head, her gorgeous sex-rumpled hair fell around them like a golden curtain. The flush of her cheeks and the glistening redness of her freshly kissed lips were almost enough to finish him.

"You know there's more."

She turned her head to look down his body, eyes lingering on his erection that lay heavy on his stomach. When she looked back at him, there was a question in her eyes—she seemed beyond the power of speech in that moment, and he wasn't far behind her.

He just nodded and whispered, "Whatever you want." Matthieu held his breath and could have sworn his heart stopped in the brief moments that he waited for her decision. After long moments, her lips curved in a sly smile as she raised herself onto her knees.

She straddled him again, poised just inches from his aching body, close enough to drive an anguished growl from him. Making eye contact with him through heavy lids, she raised a brow.

Matthieu had never been so turned on—he felt as though he was on fire from the inside out, and he welcomed the burn. He gave her an infinitesimal nod coupled with a subtle jerk of his hips.

Finally, *finally*, she reached down to steady him as she slowly enveloped him in her snug heat. It was agony. It was bliss. It was more than he deserved but as his eyes rolled back and his teeth clamped together painfully, he just couldn't bring himself to care.

Fate struck up a slow—try torturous—rhythm that had him testing his bindings in an effort to get his hands on her and speed things up. The headboard creaked with the force of his struggle, so he backed off, determined to enjoy the gift that he was being given, and not be greedy.

Her eyes slid closed and soft, surprised gasps were escaping her lips as she moved. Though his body was straining with the effort not to break the bed just to get free, he lifted his hips to achieve just the slightest change in angle. Her eyes flew open and connected with his, and her breath rushed out of her on an amazed "*Oh*," before her head fell back on her shoulders.

As she rocked on him, discovering the pleasures of another's body that she'd been denied on the past, Matthieu floated in a twilight state—blissed out on arousal and contact that wasn't quite enough to ease the burn.

He watched her discover herself bit by gorgeous bit, her face flush, muscles tight, and her body ripe with pleasure. She moved over him, this exquisite, ethereal creature, and he would have thought it was a dream—except Matthieu never, *ever*, had good dreams.

He knew she was close by the way her muscles rippled around him, and she let out an agonized whimper, as if searching for the one thing that could tip the scale. He desperately wanted to give her that. Over and over again. When she braced a hand on his chest, the touch seared through him like iron from a forge, and he lost it completely.

He gave the bindings a hard yank and gave Fate a pleading look. "Please...I need—" His brain had checked out the minute she'd started riding him, and he couldn't even finish his sentence. Someone must have heard him though, because the tension on his wrists and ankles abruptly eased, and he was able to move.

She paused and regarded him with a direct stare before speaking in a husky voice. "Touch me."

Didn't have to tell him twice. He raised his hand, aware of the ropes still knotted tightly, but untied from the bed. *She never moved—must have broken them myself. Don't care*, he thought as he filled his hands with her perfectly formed breasts.

She shuddered as he scraped his thumbs across her dark pink nipples, and then surged up to take one in his mouth. It was hell on the abs, but so goddamn worth it. She gasped out a shocked cry as he pulled the sensitive bud in between his teeth.

Matthieu's greedy hands roamed all over her and finally settled with a tight grip on her hips, gently raising and lowering her. He bent his knee to get a better angle, thrusting into her from below. Releasing the white-knuckle grip of one of his hands, he brought it between her legs to stroke her just above where they were joined.

There wasn't anything more beautiful than that moment when she threw her head back, face partially obscured by the fall of sweat-dampened blond waves. Her release came on a keening wail as her body clutched at him tight enough for him to see spots across his vision

He slowed his roll as she came back down, her eyes wide and her full lips parted in surprise. "That was...I never knew..."

Matthieu raised himself up again, unable to resist the need to kiss her. He began with a gentle nibble, still sheathed deep inside her, and moved on to delve into the depths of her sinful mouth.

When he felt her breath begin to hitch and stutter once again, he lost his battle with patience. Hoping he'd shown her enough tenderness, he banded his arms around her slender waist and rolled her onto her back.

His arms shook as he held his weigh off of her, surging his hips in a demanding rhythm. Instead of looking scared, Fate pulled her lower lip between her teeth as was her habit, and stared directly at his mouth.

It was a look of invitation that caused his stomach to flip-flop, and the hairs on the back of his neck to rise. With a possessive growl, he hiked her leg higher on his hip to get deeper still, and swooped down to capture her mouth again.

From that moment, Matthieu was lost to the world, pulled under by the sensual fever his woman created in him. His hands tangled in her hair, he gave her everything, hips undulating with a power and force that he'd always been too afraid to let loose.

But she took it with greed, clawing at his back, asking for more. When she reached back and dug her nails deep into the hard muscle of his ass, he went off. The bed shook as the flood of release overtook him, the most powerful one he'd ever felt, and she was right with him, falling over the edge.

Truly spent, Matthieu collapsed half on top of her, struggling to catch his breath and calm the wild pounding of his heart. With a grunt, he tried to shift some of his bulk off of her, but she stopped him with a grip on the back of his neck, her legs tangling with his.

Fate's hand slid up and burrowed into his too-long-for-a-fucking-soldier hair, and the light scrape of her nails on his scalp made him shiver. The hypnotizing stroke of fingers in his hair and the lazy caress of her other hand, up and down his spine, made him forget to panic as he surrendered unto the perilous void of sleep.

CHAPTER NINETEEN

IT WAS THE SILENCE THAT STARTLED MATTHIEU AWAKE. He blinked into the darkness, but when his eyes adjusted, he saw that the diffuse glow of dawn had begun to seep in from behind the drapes. He was confused and disoriented, not having woken to silence—or to anything other than visions of pain and death—since before his father died.

He struggled to clear his head of sleep, to remember where he was and why he was pinned down by a warm weight. Shifting to get his bearings, Matthieu looked down as the unfamiliar weight grumbled faintly and tightened its grip.

Then he remembered—the hit, the fishing shack, the woman—Fate, in his bed. He must have passed out shortly after their lovemaking, and then they'd shifted positions sometime during the night. Fate lay across him, much like how they'd started, with her head pillowed in the crook of his neck and one leg pinning him down between his.

The slow rise and fall of her shoulders told him that she was still asleep, and he hated to wake her. Of course he knew that once they got up to face the coming day, they'd have to move on from this. This absolutely, beyond a shadow of a doubt, could not happen again. It was too dangerous, and he was still much too messed up to be of use to anyone.

Matthieu knew he should get up, get back to the business of keeping the two of them alive. But for once, the demons had receded far into the back of his consciousness, and he could *almost* pretend like everything was normal.

As blissful as the silence was, Matthieu had to find a way to get back the professional distance he'd held her at before—and he preferred to do it without hurting her. Even the mere thought of it burned like a hot coal in his gut.

In an absent motion, he lifted his wrist to examine the damage from the rope knotted around it. As he'd suspected, the skin underneath the rope was chafed and abraded from his struggles but, of course, he didn't regret a moment of it.

His eyes followed the line of rope from the intact knots at his wrist to the ends that had been tied to the headboard. Frowning, he examined the free ends that fell loosely against his forearm. He'd assumed he must have broken the rope, but nothing was torn or frayed. The rope was in perfect condition as if it had simply been untied—which was, of course, impossible since neither of them had touched the ropes. *The fuck?* he thought.

"Stop thinking so loud," Fate mumbled against his chest, breaking his puzzled concentration. "You're keeping me from my beauty sleep."

Matthieu felt his lips unwittingly wanting to curl into a smile and his arms wanting to cuddle her closer. Instead, he stretched out his big body in an effort to dislodge her hold on him. "Like you need any of that."

All he got in answer was a noncommittal grunt, and she didn't move an inch. *Stubborn wench*, he thought with a smile on the inside. "Sorry to wake you. We've got a lot to do today...got things on my mind."

Fate heaved a put upon sigh as she finally sat up, and Matthieu immediately mourned her warmth and softness. And he had to bite back a lustful groan as she stretched like a cat, unashamed of her nakedness. "All right, have it your way."

Crawling over him, and torturing several traitorous body parts along the way, she hopped off the bed and slipped into her underwear. But instead of putting her sleep clothes on, she dug through his duffel and pulled out one of his t-shirts.

It was his old Army Strong t-shirt that he'd gotten in Basic, well used and softened from wear. She put it on and it swallowed her, the hem just brushing her upper thighs. Rubbing her face against the soft material, she turned and smiled at him. "Smells like you."

With a wink, she sauntered out of the room with a soft roll of her hips. Matthieu had to seriously fight back the urge to follow behind her like an errant duckling, and the rush of possessive pride that rose up from seeing her in his clothing.

When he finally pulled himself together and made it out to the kitchen, the room was empty. He could hear the water running in the bathroom and figured Fate was getting ready for the day, so he decided to make himself useful and brew a pot of coffee.

When Fate emerged from the bathroom, she felt refreshed from her shower, though her body was deliciously achy from the night's festivities. She'd bound her damp hair into a long braid over one shoulder, and she still wore Matthieu's shirt. She knew it was sappy, but wearing it was a reminder of the night they'd had.

Smelling coffee—nectar of the gods—she made her way into the kitchen. There, she found Matthieu sitting at the bar, glaring at his mug as if it had pissed in his...well, coffee. She walked past him to fill her own mug and rolled her eyes at the back of his head.

"Don't start that."

"Start what?" he growled back at her.

She leaned over the breakfast bar so she could look him in the eye. "You know, we haven't known each other that long, but I understand the way you think. Stop thinking of reasons why last night should never have happened, and how you're too dangerous for me. You'd never hurt me, Matthieu."

"You don't know what you're talking about," he said as he continued to snarl at his primo Guatemalan. "Even if I was thinking that, I wouldn't be wrong."

"You forget, I've seen all of the skeletons in your closet that you hide from the world...and I'm still here. Do I look afraid to you?"

His dark eyes flicked up to her face, and back down to his mug. "You haven't seen everything. But since you brought it up...we need to talk about last night. Uh, not the sex. The before."

Fate's heart lurched as the moment she'd been dreading was upon her. She hadn't told anyone the whole truth about her *visions* except her mother, and that hadn't gone well at all. Here was the moment when he would call her a freak, accuse her of spying on him—maybe he'd say to hell with her and leave her at the mercy of Eli and his business partner.

She went to sit on the couch and motioned for him to join her. If she was going to lay herself bare, she might as well get comfortable. Once Matthieu had settled in on the cushion next to her, he turned an expectant look towards her.

Sighing, she took a sip of her coffee...and stalled. "What is it that you want to know?" she asked, although she very well knew.

He snorted and set his mug on the coffee table to turn his full attention on her. "That's a loaded question, but how about we start with the dreams? Twice now, you've woken me from my nightmares and known what I'd been seeing. Plus, I saw you there too. So...what's up with that?"

Fate gave the end of her braid a nervous tug, and thought about how she might phrase her reply so as not to come off as a complete nut job. There really wasn't anything for it. "I have this sort of ability, where if I touch something, I can get a sense of its history—sometimes even flashes of it."

"Before I learned to control it, it got to be kind of debilitating. Every object, living or inanimate, has a physical history. Imagine being assailed with images from every single thing you came in contact with. It's enough to drive you crazy."

"I could see that," he agreed, betraying nothing in his voice or expression.

Wetting her lips again, Fate willed her pulse to calm so she could continue. "I slowly learned to desensitize myself to much of the visions—especially with things I have to touch and use regularly, but there are times when I can't hold them back. It's why I won't let strangers touch me, and it's why I was so concerned with what the Glock had been used for when you gave it to me."

Matthieu nodded, as if it all made perfect sense to him, which just had Fate feeling even crazier. "And the dreams?" he prompted.

"That's actually never happened before." He quirked a brow at her which clearly said *'explain'*. "I've picked up on people's memories before, sure, and flashes of their lives. But I've never, ever been pulled in like that. It seems as though my visions are stronger where you're concerned—or you affect my ability to control them. Everything seems more volatile around you."

She stopped and waited for him to respond, but he kept quiet. His eyes were focused on a point beyond her as if he were thinking very hard about what she'd told him. She had no idea why, but that suddenly made her feel defensive.

"I'm not sorry, though," she said, disliking the petulant tone of her own voice. "I helped you."

"Did you?" She thought his lips might have twitched just the slightest bit, and she somehow got the idea that he teasing her.

When she just scowled at him, his expression once again grew serious—relatively, of course. "You did help me...I could have been trapped till dawn...or whenever they decided to release me."

He mumbled the last part, and she wasn't exactly sure if she'd heard what thought she heard. "Who was that man, Matthieu?"

He blinked at her a few times, and she thought he might pretend he didn't know who she meant. Eventually he lowered his eyes to the cooling coffee in his hands, long inky lashes brushing his cheeks, and his big shoulders heaved with a deep breath.

"I don't know." His voice was gritty from the acrid smoke of long ago explosions and freshly exhumed pain. "But I've never been able to get him out of my head."

Fate fingered the leather cuff she almost always wore on her left wrist. Somehow, she was connected to Matthieu and the man from his dream, and she was terrified of what he might think when she told him. "What I've got to show you is only going to make it worse."

He looked at her with a question in his eyes, but silently waited for her to get on with it. It was ridiculous to feel exposed just from uncovering her wrist, but it was a part of her past that she preferred to keep buried.

With shaking fingers, she unsnapped the cuff and twisted her arm so that he could see the inside of her wrist. His mug was on its way to his lips when he looked down, and he'd just taken a sip when the connection was made.

His eyes widened and he appeared to inhale a lungful of coffee. When he dissolved into a fit of rib-cracking coughs, Fate jumped up to pound him on the back. "Christ almighty," he croaked out between lingering coughs.

He seemed to be able to breathe again, so she sank back down on the couch, still watching him carefully. With a surprising gentleness, he took her wrist in his hand and pulled it into his lap.

When he looked back at her, his expression was disbeliev ng and not a little accusing. "Why would you get this tattoo?" There was pain underneath the grit as he questioned her, as if he felt she'd somehow betrayed him.

Looking down at the skin on her wrist, she tried to imagine what he saw. The skin was thin there—so thin that the blue veins that crisscrossed at her pulse point could be scene. But scored into the flesh was a symbol—one that she'd never known the meaning of, and one that she despised with everything in her.

Three nested circles, with three perpendicular slashes that were at the vertices of an invisible triangle. While it seemed innocuous enough, she knew it was the image inside the smallest circle that had no doubt caused Matthieu's sudden coughing attack.

Yes, it was the crude glyph of a snarling jackal imprinted into her skin that was causing him to look at her as if she was a stranger—the same glyph that had been on the forehead of the man in Matthieu's dream.... *Draconus.*

"It's not a tattoo."

He gave her a dubious look, but he swiped his thumb across the mark, making her shiver despite the situation. "You probably won't believe me, but I've no reason to lie to you. This appeared on my wrist on the day after my seventh birthday."

His eyes snapped to her face and raised his brows. "What do you mean *appeared*?"

"Just that. It wasn't there one day, and it was there the next. For the first two days I had it, it felt like I'd raked my arm across hot coals. The burn eventually faded, but the mark didn't. I didn't know what it was or how it got there, but I knew one thing. If my society matron of a mother ever saw it, there would be hell to pay—I knew that with certainty even at such a young age. So I took to covering it, and have ever since."

Matthieu opened his mouth to speak, then closed it, and then opened it again, gaping like a fish. "Did you ever try to find out what it was?"

Fate shook her head, feeling her face heat from shame. "I was too afraid. I was worried that I'd find out something crazy, like I was the spawn of Satan or the get of some visiting alien species. I was *seven*," she emphasized when he gave her a skeptical look.

"I carried that fear with me until I was so paralyzed by it; I never wanted to look at that mark again. But now, somehow, it's connecting me with you—and the man you think killed your father—and I have no idea how to find out why."

"There's only one person I know of that may be able to figure it out, and I sure as fucking hell don't want to ask him," Matthieu said, shoving impatient hands into his hair.

"Who?"

"My brother."

CHAPTER TWENTY

MATTHIEU SAT IN STONY SILENCE AS FATE GAPED at him, probably wondering why the hell he wasn't already on the phone with Jeremiah. Well, that shit was *much* more complicated than it looked. He'd basically shunned his whole family and lit out as soon as he could. And before that, he'd been pretty distant, blaming himself for his father's death.

He'd known Isla wouldn't have let Jeremiah turn them away when Ridley needed a safe place to stay, but if there wasn't a child involved...he wasn't sure his brother'd spit on him if he was on fire. Couldn't say he'd blame the guy, either.

"Wait. Your *brother*?" Fate asked, pinching the bridge of her nose. "You mean that nice man with the sweet young wife who's looking after my daughter. *That* brother?"

Matthieu only nodded, feeling the onset of a monstrous headache tickling the back of his skull. "That'd be the one."

"How could he possibly know anything about this symbol?"

"He probably doesn't, but he'd figure it out. Jeremiah has a doctorate in parapsychology. The study of paranormal phenomena," he clarified, when she just stared at him.

"Paranormal?" Her voice rose about an octave and Matthieu almost laughed.

"Well what would you call dream-walking and mysterious tattoos appearing out of thin air, if not paranormal?" When Fate merely shrugged, he went on.

"Basically, my brother makes a living traveling all over and researching all of the weird, unexplained shit in the world. If anyone could figure out the meaning of that mark and the connection between us, it would be Dr. Jeremiah Rousseau, PhD."

Fate's eyebrows raised and she actually smiled at him. "Well, what are you waiting for? Let's call him."

"I can't...not yet. There's just a lot of history there. He may or may not agree to help us but, one way or another, he's gonna take a bite out of my hide when I come to him with my tail between my legs."

He'd expected her to argue but instead, she just patted his knee. "Believe me, I totally understand the concept of being the family disappointment. We'll figure it out somehow, with or without your brother's help."

She was so incredible. It was like she just...got him. No matter how hard he tried to push her away, to scare her, or hold her at arm's length—she just took it all, and understood. "Thanks," he said, barely a whisper.

He'd decided to wait to tell her that this Draconus and the mysterious Drake Maxwell might be one and the same. He felt bad for hiding things from her, but he didn't want to worry her until he was sure.

"There is one more strange thing, though."

Something flashed in her eyes when he spoke—something like wariness...or guilt. "What?"

"Last night, when you untied me—"

"I didn't untie you! I assumed you broke the ropes," she said, her cheeks pinking up from embarrassment.

"Exactly. But I didn't. The ropes were completely intact, as if somehow they'd come untied—even though they'd been holding me still all night long."

Her wide, rosy lips parted on a gasp. "One more thing to ask your brother about, I guess. Assuming he helps us," she said. She couldn't seem to meet his eyes all of a sudden, and Matthieu's bullshit meter cranked up.

Tipping his head all the way to the side the way he did when he was trying to figure something out, he narrowed his eyes at her and watched her grow increasingly uncomfortable. He didn't need his military intelligence training to know that she was hiding something.

She opened her mouth to speak and he was sure she would tell him but, instead, she turned the tables on him. "You said full disclosure, right?"

"Yes," he answered, giving her a wary look, and wondered where she was leading with her question.

"Tell me about Lieutenant Ward. Why do you work for him, and how much is he involved with the men who are after us?"

Matthieu sighed, running both hands through his hair. Of course she would go there. She inevitably did the exact opposite of what he wanted her to do. Ironically, it was one of the things he loved about her. *Whoa.* Where had that thought come from?

Oh, fuck it. What would she do with the information anyway? Blackmail him? Turn him into the Feds? He doubted it. Turning to her, he saw nothing but naked curiosity reflected in those stormy eyes.

"Shortly after I enlisted, I was recruited by Lt. Ward for an elite special forces team called G9X Ops."

"Never heard of it."

"Yeah, that was the idea. I guess I was recruited because I had a special skill set that Ward found *desirable*." Matthieu was unable to keep the sneer from his face and the sarcasm out of his voice when he spoke of his former lieutenant.

"Which is?"

Matthieu scratched the scruff on his jaw and thought absently that he needed a shave. "Ah, well, I guess it probably had a lot to do with my expertise in engineering and programming. Don't get me wrong, my brother's the only one in the family a fancy degree—unless you count Drew."

Matthieu rolled his eyes at her questioning look. The more he talked about his family, the more he was going to seem like an abject failure. "My brother's best friend. He lived with us for a while growing up. *Dr. Andrew Deveraux, PhD.*"

He waived it away. "Not important. Anyway, I've always been good at building things. If I couldn't find a gadget I needed, I built one. Once technology began to be more of a factor, I started studying programming as well." Fate gaped at him, and he felt his face began to burn with self-consciousness. "I'm a quick study," he said with an uncomfortable jerk of his shoulders.

"Clearly. So what else did Ward see in you?"

"Well, I'm an expert marksman—a sharpshooter I guess some would say. And I'm what the unit called a *finder,* really good at tracking down information—or extracting it," he paused, letting that sink in. "But I'm sure the biggest attraction for Ward was my uncanny ability not to give a fuck about anyone or anything."

Fate's head jerked back, staring at him in shock. "Pardon? Explain..."

Matthieu rubbed tired eyes, aware that he was revealing more about himself than he'd ever told another soul. The only reason Ward and the boys knew was because they were there. He was *so* fucked. When he looked back at her, the guarded expression on her face nearly undid him. When had he begun to rely so heavily on her misplaced faith in him?

"I've been so screwed up ever since the thing with my father that I didn't really care what happened to me. I suppose I didn't care about anything—I didn't want to feel anything anymore. I was so tired of the guilt, the pain...other stuff. I guess that's why I enlisted."

He could have sworn her eyes began to brim with tears, but he didn't want her pity, didn't deserve her affection. Clearing his throat, he continued his sordid story, knowing she'd feel anything but affection after she heard the whole of it.

"G9X was sort of an unsanctioned team. As far as most of the military and government officials were concerned, we were just another Special Ops unit. But the reality was, we handled the missions that the Army couldn't get the green light on from the Joint Chiefs—raids on enemy territory, assassinations, that kind of thing. Only a few of the higher ups in the Administration were aware of what we were doing—but a lot of our missions came from the ones who did."

"So it was illegal operation?"

"Yes and no. Our orders did come from the Federal Government; they just weren't necessarily all privy to it. We had to be flawless, though, because if we failed, they didn't know us— plausible deniability and all that. We'd take the fall."

"That's horrible," she said. She seemed shocked—not *by* him, but *for* him, and it caused his heart to speed up.

"Yeah, well, we didn't screw up, so... Came close in Kandahar, so we were disbanded shortly after that. I was given a medical discharge and forced into early retirement."

"Do you miss it?"

Matthieu started to answer automatically, but stopped short, considering. No one had ever asked him that before. "Sometimes. I don't miss it for the reasons I enlisted originally, but I do miss being part of that team. I guess when you can't trust yourself; it can be nice to have others trust you for a change."

Fate made a *hmm* sound, as if she understood. "What happened after? Why did you choose to, um...*work* for Ward?"

Cursing under his breath, Matthieu knew that when she said *work*, she really meant *hunt and kill people*. His voice came out as barely a whisper. "It wasn't a choice."

She cocked her head just a bit, and her brows pulled low over her eyes. "How so?"

"Ward has a file on each member of the team—those who came home alive, that is. "He contacted me after I'd been stateside for about three months, said if I didn't agree to work for him, he'd send my file to the authorities, and I'd be prosecuted as a rogue assassin."

"He blackmailed you? Bastard," she breathed after Matthieu nodded. He couldn't help it—he felt a smile tug at his lips at her outrage on his behalf.

"That's how Ward's connected to the hit on us. I don't get the feeling Farrell and Maxwell are anything more to him than another job." Considering the exchange he'd seen on the video feed, Matthieu wasn't so sure that they wouldn't turn on Ward in the end.

"Well, now that you know all of my secrets, maybe you'll understand why I have to do what I'm going to do next," he said, gauging her reaction.

"Which is?" she asked again, raising a brow.

"I've got to find where Ward's stashed those files and destroy them. I'm sure if he can't find a way to kill me now that I've gone rogue on him, he'll turn me in as soon as he can afford the fucking postage."

"So how do we find them?"

"Um, we?" he asked, glancing at her from the corner of his eyes as he faced the back door.

"Yes, *we*. You're helping me, so I'm going to help you."

Matthieu raised a brow, wondering exactly how she thought she could help, but still touched that she'd want to. "Are you, now?"

She rolled her eyes at him, but smiled as she did it. "Do you know it drives me crazy when you answer me like that?"

"Yep," he said with a wicked grin. "I think I've got a lead on where he might be keeping the information. When I broke into Ward's financial records, I noticed that he's got property in Savannah and I'm willing to bet it's a safehouse. I'm going to drive out there tomorrow and do a little recon."

"I'm coming with you."

"You'd be safer if you stayed here."

"You need someone to watch your back. And besides, there's safety in numbers."

Matthieu gave her a dubious look, knowing she was right but not so sure he could survive another trip with her without touching her. "All right, but you need to be ready to go at oh-five-hundred."

"Matthieu, I have a seven year old. Do you really think I'm going to be scared off by a little sleep deprivation?"

Well, yes, he had thought that, mainly because he didn't want to admit, even to himself, that he wanted her with him.

Rising to gather their mugs, Matthieu made his way to the kitchen as Fate excused herself to go outside. She stopped at the door and tossed a smile at him over her shoulder—a sweet one, tinged with a little wickedness, just around the edges—and Matthieu had to grip the rim of the counter to keep himself upright.

Luckily, Fate had already stepped out when his mini-meltdown came over him, as the impact of that smile slammed into him. He was *oh, so* royally fucked. He didn't want to want her, and he sure as hell *couldn't* start to goddamn need her.

He laughed at himself, cruelly, because the fuck if it hadn't already started to happen. Matthieu pulled in deep, shaking breaths because he suddenly couldn't get enough oxygen to his brain, and his vision started to waver.

SFC Matthieu Rousseau was a dead man walking—had been since he was seven years old. He knew it for damn sure, and the demons knew it too. He had nothing to give anyone because he was a ticking time bomb.

Hell if he didn't still want her anyway, regardless of the consequences to both of them. One thing he did know was that he would hurt her, contrary to what she believed—and that was fucking gospel. He wouldn't mean it, and it would be like tearing out his own still-beating heart with his dirty, bare hands, but it would happen—sure as the sky was blue.

Cursing himself ten times a fool, Matthieu's feet began moving of their own free will—taking him outside and back into her orbit.

CHAPTER TWENTY·ONE

MATTHIEU SMACKED INTO A SOLID WALL OF Louisiana humidity as he stepped out onto the deck, dodging mosquitos the size of bats. Shading his eyes with his hand, he looked around for Fate. He found her sitting on the end of the dock—and she was not alone.

She had her back to him, as did the dark haired kid sitting shoulder to shoulder with her, and they both had their feet dangling in the muddy water. Off to the side, a rusty pirogue bobbed against the rotting Styrofoam that floated the dock.

Staring at the kid's shirtless back, Matthieu tried to figure just where the hell he'd come from. As if sensing his stare, the kid turned his head and pierced Matthieu with startling gold eyes—adult eyes. He realized that he was looking at not really a kid, but rather a young man.

The stranger laid a hand on Fate's shoulder and whispered something in her ear, and she turned to look at Matthieu as well. Her expression was one of shock that turned almost immediately guilty, but he paid little attention. He'd zeroed on the familiar touch, and the proximity of the kid's lips to Fate's ear, until he could see nothing else.

Matthieu was unprepared for the demons' assault, slamming into him full force out of nowhere—though he should have known they would strike in a moment of weakness. His vision blurred around the edges, and then filled with a dark red haze. The voices scraped at the inside of his skull, screeching rather than whispering as they usually did…screeching things like *blood* and *kill* and *pain*.

They weaseled their way into his thoughts, poisoning him with images of this slender young boy with his hands all over his woman, *their* woman—touching her, *fucking* her, doing unspeakable things. And then there were images of the kid, broken and bloody at his feet.

The last thing he remembered was wondering if the demons wanted him to kill the kid as a reaction to Matthieu's own jealousy, or because they loved her too. After that, his vision grayed out completely and he knew nothing but darkness.

ᔖᑢ

Fate had been sitting alone, contemplating what on Earth had possessed her to not only agree to but insist on going on another one of Matthieu's wild escapades—possibly involving breaking and entering with a little larceny thrown in the mix, at best. She just couldn't seem to stop herself. Something about the man, broken though he was, and the way he kept trying to claw his way to the surface and keep his head above water…it just spoke to her.

And then there was the incredible night they'd had. She could tell that Matthieu was not a man who was used to relinquishing control, and yet he had, for her. And while their lovemaking had been...intense to an immeasurable degree, it had also been tender—something she hadn't been expecting at all.

But she wasn't an idiot. She didn't believe that one night with her would make Matthieu forget all of his troubles and want to live happily ever after with her and Ridley, but last night had given her hope. Hope that maybe, just maybe, she could help him heal some of his old wounds, and her own.

Her thoughts had scattered when Étienne rowed into the cove. He wore nothing but ratty camo shorts, making Fate wonder how much clothing the kid actually had. She'd already figured out that he was basically homeless, camping out in the woods and living off the land—which was a much more dangerous undertaking on the bayou.

The boy provided her with a much needed distraction as they chattered on about everything and nothing in particular and watched the lazy ripple of the swamp water. Fate settled into a comfortable lull, baking in the sun and the humid air, listening to Étienne's faintly accented voice.

She felt rather than saw Étienne turn his head and look behind them. He caught her attention with a gentle touch on her shoulder and leaned over to as if to say something. The moment he whispered, "Your friend is watching," in her ear, she felt a blast of cold energy knock into her, causing her to shiver from head to toe.

Likewise turning, Fate saw Matthieu standing on the back porch staring at them with an odd look on his face. No, not odd. Murderous.

Only it wasn't really Matthieu, was it? Sure, he looked the same as always, but it was all about the eyes. They were still brown, unlike how they'd been when she'd woken him from that terrible nightmare, but she could see the shadows flickering in them even at a distance.

Something was definitely not right. His posture was defensive, with his arms locked to his sides, hands balled into fists. His muscles rippled and bunched as if his entire body was wired to spring, and his shoulders moved with the force of his panting breaths.

He was staring at them, *through* them, because he didn't seem to see at all. Eventually, his dark brows lowered and his head turned in an eerie swivel to look directly at Étienne. She felt the boy tense, making ready, but he didn't seem to be surprised. Well, Fate sure as the hell was.

"Whatever happens, don't get in his way," Étienne said under his breath. She whipped her head around to look at him, to ask him what he meant, but stopped short. His face looked sharper somehow—intense—and in that moment, he ridiculously reminded her of the hawk that often watched her.

Étienne tensed and stood, readying himself as Matthieu strode down the pier to the dock with all the finesse of an angry bull. Still, Fate saw no fear, only resignation and that fierce focus of his. Without so much as a glance towards her, Matthieu rushed Étienne; his big, scarred hand gripped the younger man's throat.

To add insult to injury, Matthieu locked his free hand around Étienne's bicep and lifted him in the air, only to slam him back against the heavy pylon. Fate was so shocked, she could only stand and stare at those brown bare feet dangling in thin air.

Finally dragging her gaze up to the boy's face, Étienne locked eyes with her. For some reason, this seemed to anger the beast that currently inhabited Matthieu's body. With a growl, he removed his left hand from Étienne's arm and brought it up to join the right, around Étienne's throat, pressing him harder into the splintered wood.

The young man's face began to turn red, which was impressive with his toasted complexion, and Fate was sure he was no longer getting air. Snapping out of her shock, she looked around for something—anything—she could use as a weapon. She didn't want to hurt Matthieu, because she didn't think he knew what he was doing, but he looked like he was seconds away from killing Étienne.

Fate considered his nightmares, wondering if this was some kind of freak bout of narcolepsy, and that Matthieu was somehow stuck inside his own mind again. She had been able to help him before, so she had to try.

She placed one hand on Matthieu's straining shoulder, and the other on the back of his neck, where his skin felt clammy and cold, despite the humidity. She closed her eyes, and when she wasn't immediately pulled in as had been the norm with him, she pushed.

All she found was an empty void—just complete, never-ending blackness. Whatever had control over Matthieu had pushed his consciousness so far down, she couldn't even feel it anymore. Acting on instinct alone, Fate pushed her own energy into him, willing him to stop, to think.

Instantly, he dropped Étienne and was propelled backward where he landed on his back with a force that rocked the pier. Étienne slid down to the weathered boards of the dock, gasping for air and clutching his throat. Matthieu sat up and shook his head violently, blinking until his eyes shone dark brown and clear.

Fate knelt down to check on her friend while keeping wary eyes on Matthieu, where he sat, stunned and panting. "*The fuck?*" he whispered to himself, and Fate wasn't even sure he knew they were there.

She put an arm around Étienne's shoulders to help him stand, and that seemed to draw Matthieu's attention. He looked up at her with such a weary and lost expression, she ached for him, even though she was furious.

"We're going inside so I can check him out. You," she said in a clipped tone, pointing at Matthieu, "stay here and calm the hell down."

Matthieu folded his arms over his knees and laid his head on them, and Fate was sure she heard a quiet sob that he tried to cover with a cough.

∾)(∾

Fate had brought Étienne inside and seated him on the couch. She handed him a steaming cup of tea mixed with honey that would hopefully soothe his throat. The boy hadn't said a word, and Matthieu had yet to come inside, both of which made her jittery as hell.

Unable to calm her anxiety, Fate paced back and forth across the living room, tugging on her braid until her hair escaped its confines. Finally she stopped and faced Étienne, throwing her hands in the air. "Holy crap on a cracker, what *was* that?"

Étienne looked at her with the same intense expression he'd held onto throughout the whole incident. "That, *ma chérie*, was a test. You passed. We might all be just fine," he said with a cryptic smile.

"What do you mean—?"

She was cut off by the slamming of the back door as Matthieu strode in, looking ashen and scared. He had dark circles under his hollow eyes, and his shoulders were hunched as if he were mere seconds away from collapsing.

"Going to take a shower," he said without looking at them, his voice sounding like ice over gravel. He kept on walking until he disappeared into the bathroom, and the door shut with an empty click behind him.

Fate looked at Étienne but he just shrugged and flicked an uneasy glance in the direction of the bathroom. "I don't understand what's going on," she said.

With a tired sigh, Étienne set his empty mug on the coffee table. "He's going to have to tell you himself. It won't help him otherwise."

"How do you know anything about him?" Fate was getting frustrated with the speaking in riddles, and the talk of tests. Étienne shrugged again and closed his eyes—it seemed the ordeal was finally catching up to him.

Fate was just about to tell him to lie down and get some rest when they were both startled by a loud thump from the direction of the bathroom. She froze, her heart leaping into her throat when she heard a muffled wail. "Matthieu!"

CHAPTER TWENTY·TWO

FATE'S HEART WAS POUNDING IN HER EARS WHEN SHE burst into the bathroom. It was dark, with only the light from a small window illuminating it. She was stunned by the temperature change—any colder and she felt like she'd be seeing her own breath misting in front of her.

Inside the shower, the water was still running at full blast, but no other sounds came from behind the opaque green curtain. Terrified of what she might find, Fate forced herself to step up and pull back the material.

Another frigid blast of air hit her as she noted that the faucet was set all the way to cold. Matthieu sat on the floor at the other end of the shower, where the water battered his naked body full on. He was curled up with his head down, and his forehead rested on his knees in much the same posture as he'd been in when she left him on the dock.

His hand clutched an old terry washcloth, and his skin was red and abraded, as if he'd tried to scrub off the top layer of it.

Pushing back the curtain all the way, she sat on the edge of the tub and put a hand on his shoulder. It was ice cold. "Matthieu?"

The lethargic way in which he raised his face to look at her scared her almost as much as his expression. It wasn't sad, angry, or remorseful—it was resigned. Done. As if he'd given up, and she didn't even know what he was fighting.

His skin was pale, sallow, and the dark smudges under his eyes stood out in blunt contrast. There was a cut across his eyebrow that dripped a steady stream of blood, and Fate didn't know if he'd fallen, or banged his head against the wall on purpose. Perhaps the most troubling was the fact that his lips were blue, and she finally noticed that he was shivering all over.

Without any consideration for herself, Fate nudged him to slide forward and she sank down behind him, still fully clothed. She gasped when the water hit her, but it almost immediately began to warm up. She knew the first sign of hypothermia was feeling warm, but it wouldn't happen that fast—would it?

Ignoring it, she concentrated on rubbing her hands over Matthieu's arms, trying to warm him up and return some blood flow to his trembling muscles. He leaned his head back on her shoulder and took a shuddering breath that sounded like it was strained through broken glass. Moisture ran down his face, tinged pink with the blood from his cut, and Fate wondered if it was all from the shower, or if it was mingled with tears.

"That wasn't me out there," he finally said in a ravaged voice.

"I know, baby. I know." And she did. Whatever had happened out on the dock, the one thing she was sure of was that Matthieu had not been in control of his own actions. "Can you tell me what happened?"

"You knew I wouldn't want you befriending a local, yes?"

"Yes."

"And you did it anyway."

"Yes," Fate said, seeing no point in lying now. "Étienne's a harmless kid. He's homeless."

"Before, that would have made me angry—probably should have—but I trust you. Something else happened out there...something I can't explain."

"Can you try?"

He leaned heavier on her and heaved a deep sigh. "I'd never hurt that kid...or anyone else innocent. Yes, I've killed people, but never a civilian who wasn't some nasty criminal. At least...not since Afghanistan."

Fate tried to keep her voice steady, although the idea of Matthieu killing anyone was hard to swallow. She knew what he was trying to tell her. "I believe you."

"Something's inside me; something that doesn't belong. It's always there—which is one of the reasons I can't promise I'll never hurt you."

She looked down at his face where his head rested on her shoulder, and the anguish in his eyes tore through her.

"If I were a religious man, I'd almost want to say I was...possessed...by something not entirely of this world. Kind of an idiotic explanation, but it's the best I can do."

Fate thought it over, and she had a feeling he wasn't too far off the mark. And whatever it was, Étienne seemed to know something about it. She'd have her own questions for the kid once he and Matthieu recovered.

"I think it might be pretty accurate, actually." She tried to give him a stern look, but she knew it probably failed. "Mathieu, we need to call your brother."

He sighed again, but she was glad to see he was no longer shivering. "I know, okay? But I've got to follow this lead on Ward first. That's non-negotiable," he said, getting some of the power back in his voice. "I can't bring that shit to my brother's doorstep. Can you understand that?"

"Yeah. Yes, I can. Come on, let's get changed and get on the road now. The sooner we get this done, the better."

Hesitating, but moving before she could think better of it, she placed a hand on his scarred cheek and turned his face toward her. She brushed her lips over his, savoring the warmth that had replaced the bone deep cold. He let out a stunned breath across her mouth and leaned up to deepen the kiss.

They stepped out of the shower and dried off in silence. Matthieu paused while running the towel over one of his muscular legs, and looked back at her, grinning a little when he caught her staring. He quickly sobered and flicked a worried glance at the door. "What about the kid?"

"He was pretty freaked, and worn out. I imagine we won't see him for a while."

Matthieu cursed to himself as he put his clothes back on. "Didn't mean to scare him. Maybe we can hunt him down when we get back so I can apologize."

"Yeah, we should. I've got a couple of things to say to him myself."

CHAPTER TWENTY·THREE

JEREMIAH ROUSSEAU LAZILY SIPPED ON A LONGNECK AS HE
watched his wife talk on the phone. Even soft and rounded
with their child, she was stunning and never failed to stir
his blood. At the moment, however, her forehead was creased
with worry as she spoke softly into the cell phone.

"Earth to Jeremiah. Wake up, buddy," his best friend Drew
Deveraux said. He made as if to wave a hand in front of Jere's
face—which was funny, because he was sitting on the other
side of the room. "Jesus, I thought the honeymoon period would
be over by now."

Drew's wife of all of three days snorted at them from her
perch, draped across Drew's lap.

"Shut up, asshole," Jeremiah said without heat, flipping him
off. "Still can't believe you guys eloped to Vegas."

Raven raised one of the dark, slashing brows that hinted of
her Creole heritage. "Really? You can't believe it? I grew up in
Vegas, you know that."

"Not that, I just can't believe either of you could sit still long enough to tie the knot."

Drew ran his hand over one of Raven's caramel colored legs and looked up at her adoringly. "It was a near thing, but she managed to stand me for the five minutes it took to say the I-do's."

Jeremiah chuckled at their antics, knowing that the two were very much in love. They'd both struggled with the idea of commitment, having been hurt too much in the past—until a couple of life or death situations forced them to grow up.

"Guess I should fill you in on what you missed—hold on," he broke off as Isla finished her call and joined him on the couch. He noticed her troubled expression hadn't eased. If anything, it had gotten worse. "What's wrong, darlin'?"

"That was Fate. They're heading up to Savannah for another super-secret Matthieu-mission. She said it shouldn't take long, and she just wanted us to know where they'd be. She sounded off to me, though. I think something may have happened, but she wouldn't elaborate."

"What's going on? What'd we miss?" Drew asked, nudging Raven off of his lap so he could lean forward.

Jeremiah glanced to his left as Marduk shuffled into the room, fresh from another nap. The kid had been sleeping more than he was awake, ever since the incident in October—the day they lost Brynna.

"God, I don't even know where to start. My brother's gotten himself into some trouble—him and this woman, Fate."

"What, your *brother*?" Raven asked. "Your antisocial, borderline psycho, stone-cold killer brother. *That* brother?"

"Easy Raven. That *psycho* saved your father's life, remember?" Drew scolded.

"Hey, I meant it as a compliment. I fucking like the guy—he's bad-ass nasty in a good way. But I can't imagine what it would take for *him* to get into trouble he couldn't handle. What happened?" she asked. Jeremiah knew her concern was real, even though she hid it behind her customary snark.

He gave his friends the abbreviated version of how Matthieu and Fate had ended up with hits out on them, and how they were currently hiding out in a safehouse.

"Holy fuck, Matty really stepped in the shit this time," Drew said.

"Oh, there's more, *gràdhach*," Isla said, "Fate has a daughter, and she's staying with us."

As if on cue, they began to hear soft cries coming from one of the back bedrooms. Jeremiah started to rise but Isla patted his leg and got up instead. "I'll get her."

Isla was gone only a few minutes when she returned wide-eyed and ashen. When Jere saw the look on her face, he immediately stood up to guide her back to the couch. "What's happened, baby?"

Underneath her thick, black fringe of bangs her bright green eyes shone with unshed tears, and they were wide with what he thought was fear. His heart turned over as he put his hand on her rounded belly. "The baby?"

"No, no," she said immediately, trying to ease his worry. "It's Ridley. She was crying because her back was hurting her. She has a *signa*, Jeremiah. She's a *praeda*."

"Oh, *fuck*," he whispered as he heard the shocked gasps from the others in the room. "I'm sure Fate has no idea."

"What about Matty?" Drew asked.

Jeremiah shook his head. "I haven't told him anything about the *Vigilati*. It's hard enough to track him down to begin with—

and if I began regaling him with tales of witches, I'd probably never hear from him again."

Isla cast a worried glance around the room. "We've got to tell them."

The *Vigilati* was a sect of witches who were born to protect the world from the *Lochrim*; demons intent on destroying all things human. Isla was a *Vigile* and so was Raven, and they both had the brands etched into their skin to prove it.

Jeremiah wrapped Isla up in his arms and pulled her to him. "We will, as soon as they get back from Savannah. I don't want to distract him while he's dealing with whatever danger he's caught up in."

"In the meantime," Drew spoke up, "we could look up her *signa* in the book of shadows, see what we're dealing with."

"Good plan," Jeremiah agreed. Drew had uncovered the book at an archaeological dig last fall, and it had become invaluable to them. It contained every *seal* of every *Lochrim* that its author had been able to compile.

Jeremiah now kept the book, along with the one he'd found in Rome that detailed what little was known about the *Vigilati* in his home safe. He got up and spun the combination, pulling out the thin, leather bound volume. "Isla?" he prompted, handing the book to his wife.

She thumbed through it with care for a few moments before stopping on a page in the middle. "This is it," she said, pointing to a crudely drawn symbol.

When Jeremiah saw which one she was indicating, he cursed under his breath as his blood ran cold. He'd seen that *seal* before—on the bad motherfucker who'd tried to take him when he as twelve. Isla gave him a wary look, but he just shook his head. He'd talk it out with his wife when they were alone.

"What's it say? he asked Drew, who was not only an expert in antiquated languages, but also fluent in French.

Drew scanned the page when Isla passed him the book. "This *seal* belongs to the demon Eligos, and the symbol seems to be a specific one. It's called the *totem rune*, and it means death."

Raven peeked at the book in Drew's lap before uttering a soft curse. "We're going to have to help this little girl and her mother. This is going to be a lot to take in, especially for the mother. She's not going to understand what her daughter will someday have to do."

"I can't believe none of you witches and PhD-types have figured out the connection yet," Marduk said from his spot at Isla's feet.

Jeremiah nudged the kid with his foot, trying to at least get a smile out of him. He didn't think he'd seen the *feradux* smile since Brynna had disappeared. "You got a theory, fur-ball? Let's hear it."

"I think Ridley isn't just a *praeda*. She's the *brevé*. The *Vigilati* bloodline is no longer skipping a generation."

Isla turned confused eyes toward Marduk. "But her mother isn't a *Vigile*."

"Isn't she?" Marduk asked with a sneer. "Do none of you remember what Leora said to us about winning the war?" Leora was the *Bruixi* goddess of fire, who'd been known to appear when they needed help.

"Oh, gee, did you mean the cryptic riddle or the *other* cryptic riddle?" Jeremiah asked.

Marduk rolled his eyes at the sarcasm and raised a brow until Jeremiah waved at him to continue.

"You said this woman's name is Fate, yes?" Isla nodded. Marduk then turned to Jeremiah again.

"Jeremiah, what was your brother's nickname thing in the army again?"

"Codename. It was Cobra."

Marduk looked around the room in exasperation. "Still nothing?"

Drew smacked him in the head with a pillow while Raven cackled. "Get to the point, *ma bon loup*."

Trying and failing to look offended, Marduk chucked the pillow back. "Okay, *professor*. I believe Leora's exact words were 'in order to survive, you must find the Serpent's Fate,' were they not?"

"Fuck me," Jeremiah said as he rose to pace. "Serpent. Cobra. Fate is Leora's third descendant...which means that Ridley is the first consecutive generation *Vigile*. Somehow, Matty's mixed up in all of it as well—and neither of them has any clue what's going on. Shit. *Shit!*"

Isla stood up to wrap her arms around him from behind and laid her head between his tense shoulder blades. "They'll be okay, *a ghràidh*. If anyone can handle crazy things being thrown at him, it'd be Matthieu. As soon as they get back from Savannah, we'll meet up with them and talk it out."

"Don't hold your breath. Matthieu won't want anything to do with us."

"You forget, I've got Fate in my pocket. She'll trick him if she has to do. I don't know her that well, but I know that woman will do anything to protect her daughter."

CHAPTER TWENTY·FOUR

THE DRIVE INTO SAVANNAH HAD TAKEN LESS TIME than Matthieu had expected. The sooner they got this done and got back, the better. Fate had been quiet and pensive for most of the trip—probably ruminating on his little Jekyll-and-Hyde from earlier.

God, that must have scared the shit out of her, because it sure as hell scared him. The demons had never taken over like that before, completely wiping him out. They were escalating— of that, he was positive.

But the craziest thing of all was the fact that she was still sticking by him. True, he was helping her escape the hit, but she'd seen him go bat shit crazy right in front of her and she hadn't panicked. She'd been...amazing. He still didn't know how she pulled him out of it—and he knew she'd done something— but he knew he may not have come out of it without her.

Looking over at her, he watched her animated face as she took in the sights through the window. She'd said it was her first time in Savannah, and he had to admit that the city did have a sort of out-of-time magic about it.

She brushed her hair away from her face and back to where it fell in soft waves down her back. Then she turned and caught him looking, and gave him a genuinely happy smile. His heart tripped over itself a little before he turned his eyes back to the road.

Holy Christ, Rousseau, what are you doing? He so could not fall for this woman—the same way he most definitely couldn't fall for her charming daughter—but he couldn't seem to keep himself from sliding in a little deeper each time she looked at him.

To distract himself from the turn his thoughts were taking, he tried to strike up a conversation. "So, singing, huh?"

Fate blinked at him as if she was trying to tune back into the present. "What?"

"Your career. Singing? You were singing in a club when we met…plus the whole Juilliard thing." Matthieu fumbled for words—men like him weren't often skilled in small talk. "Is that what you want to be when you grow up? A singer?"

Her lips tipped up in a wistful smile, and she turned back to the window. "Not really. Not enough, anyway. I entertained the notion for half a second while I was at Juilliard, and again when I was with Eli. I honestly didn't want it bad enough to live the kind of life, to have the kind of discipline I would need to make it as a recording artist. And I don't want that kind of childhood for Ridley.

"Besides, I'm an introvert at heart. I'd never get used to constantly being on display…being judged like that. On top of that, the industry isn't very forgiving when it comes to looks. I was always told that there aren't a lot of curvy performers out there—and the ones who are successful enough to not be questioned about it." Her smile turned slightly sad, and she sighed. "I don't want to spend the rest of my life starving myself. I am what I am."

"You're stunning," he said without hesitation. He had to fight not to clench his teeth when he thought of people telling her she wasn't good enough; wasn't pretty enough; wasn't skinny enough.

Her head whipped around and she stared at him, open-mouthed. "You really believe that, don't you?"

"It's not a matter of belief. It's about vision. All I have to do is look at you."

She just looked at him while his gaze bounced back and forth between her and the road. He could have been wrong, but he thought it looked like she was blinking back tears. "Thank you," she whispered.

He knew she meant well, but her thanking him for simply telling the truth kind of pissed him off a little. "You don't have to thank me for calling it like I see it," he said, maybe a bit too harshly.

It didn't seem to bother her, though, because she gave him a genuine smile and turned back to the window.

"So why sing in clubs, then?" he asked, bringing them back to the subject at hand.

"What I really want to do is write. Problem is, no one is going to hire a songwriter they've never heard of, so I've got to go out there and perform—both covers and my own stuff—and hope someone's interested."

"Wow, I never knew it was such a complicated an industry."

"Yeah, it's all about making a name for yourself." She chuckled softly. "I can't wait until I'm well-known enough to sit around in my living room, writing music and collecting checks. That's the dream."

He laughed with her, and they didn't speak again for a while. His thoughts began to drift again, circling around to Fate and Ridley in that living room, and him sitting right there with them. *What a ridiculous fantasy*, he thought. As if he'd ever have a house and a wife, or a child. Trying to pull his mind back to the job at hand, he turned on his GPS and called up a search for hotels. "I'll book us a room so that you'll have somewhere to hang out while I'm gone. No call for you to sit in the car—it could take a couple of hours."

She shook her head and waved him off. "Don't bother. I'm coming with you."

"Like hell," he growled.

She gave him a quelling look that clearly told him where he could stick his controlling attitude, but he wasn't backing down—it wasn't goddamn safe for her.

"I would think that today's events would have shown you that you are not an island, Matthieu. I may not be a big shot super-soldier like you, but I've got eyes and I've got instincts."

"Fate—"

"No. Listen, you need someone to watch your back. It was a close call last time you went after Ward."

"I wouldn't say—"

"If you dump me at some hotel, I'm just going to follow you on my own," she blurted.

Matthieu saw the determination in her eyes and knew it was the truth. With a deep sigh, he thumped his head on the driver's side window of the Jeep.

"Fine, but you have to do exactly as I say once we get there. No. Arguments. Deal?"

"Deal," she said, flashing him another smile that made him feel like the solid ground beneath his feet had suddenly disappeared.

He drove through the city on Main Street, allowing Fate to get a good look at the gorgeous riverfront houses, the charming shops, and the well groomed streets lined with Southern oaks and draped with Spanish moss. She rolled down the window to get a better view when he drove her past the Colonial Cemetery. The look on her face made him wish he was bringing her here for pleasure rather than business.

They continued to roll through the city proper until they made it to the outskirts of town, where the buildings had less of a luster, and the streets were darker, especially now that the sun was sinking below the horizon. Matthieu pointed out a waterfront shipping warehouse as they drove past it.

"That's Ward's safehouse."

"Aren't we going to stop?"

He gave her a look that he hoped shouted *amateur* very clearly as he shook his head. "I'm going to drive to the next block and park somewhere out of the way. If Ward has someone watching the place, I don't want him to see us drive up."

"Oh."

"Yeah, *oh*," he said with a wink, finding that he enjoyed teasing her. This was so far removed from her lifestyle, he didn't expect her to know what she was doing, but that didn't stop him from giving her a gentle ribbing.

Signaling a turn, Matthieu maneuvered the jeep into the parking lot of an abandoned building and cut the engine. He climbed out of the SUV and lifted the hatch in the back. He pulled out a black back pack that blended in with his black t-shirt and fatigues, and he shrugged it on. He wasn't sure if the G9X files would be digital or hard copy, but he wanted to make sure he could carry them. Since he didn't know how much he'd have to carry, he wore his gear on a utility belt that rode low on his hips.

He had forgone the shoulder holster and SIGs because wearing a jacket to conceal them in this heat would be impossible. His belt had a holster for his favorite sidearm, a Walther PPK. His backup piece, a Kimber SOLO, was strapped to his ankle.

Fate came up behind him and laid a hand on his shoulder, and he could feel her heat seeping through his skin. *God, this is such a bad idea. Fucking distraction.* But he knew it would be a bigger distraction to be worry about her sneaking out of the hotel.

"So what's the plan?" she asked without a hint of nervousness. Either she had some serious *cajones*, or she just trusted him to make everything all right. He hoped it was the former.

"I wasn't able to track down a floor plan, so I'm going in blind. You stick close to me until we get inside and I can find a place for you to keep a lookout."

"You got it, Boss."

ഔൠ

Instead of walking up the street, they followed the riverbank to the back of the old warehouse. Skirting around the corner of the building with Fate practically molded to his back, Matthieu located a side door. It had a simple door handle with a single lock, and it definitely wasn't protecting any of Ward's secrets. But it was only the first gate of Matthieu's personal hell.

His skin was buzzing all over, and not from the beautiful woman almost climbing inside him. No, he was ramped up because he *knew*. Ward had something here, he could goddamn feel it.

Taking out his kit, he quickly jimmied the lock and eased the door open with caution. The warehouse was dark, but enough light drifted in from the high, barred windows that he could see enough to get by.

Ushering Fate inside, he quickly closed the door behind them and scanned the perimeter. The large open space was stacked high with industrial containers, from China by the looks of it, and it was dead silent.

Many shipping warehouses had internal structures built—completely walled in and insulated—that served as offices or meeting rooms. This one was no different. Matthieu quickly located the structure, and instinctively knew that was where the security would be.

Weaving through the towers of containers, holding Fate's hand, he located the door. He had no idea what he'd find on the other side, so he knew that he would have to find a spot to stash her.

Matthieu pulled her over to a tower of blue industrial boxes and positioned her behind it. From there, she could see the side door from which they entered, the front door, and the entrance to the inner room. Perfect.

"I need you to stay here," he whispered, giving her a stern look so that she would see he was serious. "Keep out of sight, but watch the doors. If you see anything or hear anything, text me and hide. Got it?"

She kept her lips tightly clenched but nodded. As he watched, her tongue snaked out to moisten her lower lip. Before he could think better of it, he sank a hand into her hair, and pulled her to him, taking her mouth in a desperate kiss.

Hesitating out of surprise, she went still for a moment before grasping his arms and kneading his muscles like a cat. Drowning in her, he slid his tongue inside to duel with hers, and swallowed her soft gasp.

They were both breathing hard when he finally managed to pull back. Fate looked at him with wide, stormy eyes and raised a hand to touch her lips. "What was that for?"

Shrugging, Matthieu struggled to find an answer because he didn't really have one. "I don't know, luck?"

Fate just smiled at him and backed up into the shadows. *Right, time to go to work.* Something felt off as he approached the door to the interior building, and his hackles rose immediately. He reached out to give the door a gentle push and it swung open wide, the lock clearly broken.

So he wasn't the first one to figure out where Ward kept his secrets. He just wondered if it was one of the G9X boys or Maxwell and Farrell who'd tracked him down. Not taking any chances, Matthieu drew his sidearm and traveled the perimeter, melting into the walls.

Instead of the office building like he'd first thought, he realized he was standing in a fully kitted out apartment, complete with kitchen, living room, bedroom, and office. And another thing quickly became apparent—the place had been tossed.

Chairs were overturned, cabinets were opened and the contents strewn about the room. All of the upholstered furniture had been slashed and gutted. Matthieu slipped into Ward's office and found much the same. Papers littered the room, as all of the drawers in the desk and file cabinets had been pulled out and dumped.

Whoever it was had been thorough, if not a little reckless. As Matthieu checked the room, his foot hit something solid. He nudged the busted MacBook with the steel toe of his combat boot. *Idiots*, he thought. That ruled out any of his fellow operatives. They would have come in with purpose, and taken anything that could have contained their personnel files.

With as much speed as he could manage the delicate work, Matthieu used his tools to remove the hard drive from the computer and tucked it into the pack. Just in case. But the files wouldn't be in here. Too obvious. There'd be a hidden safe, or another computer stashed somewhere. Something.

When he made his way into the bedroom, he holstered his weapon and pulled out his tiny Maglite to sweep the room. The standard issue, Spartan bedroom furniture had been left intact but he had no doubt it'd been checked. As he shone the flashlight around the room, his attention was caught by an enormous dresser.

Or so it had been created to appear. Approaching the massive piece of furniture, Matthieu felt along the sides until he found what he was looking for—a hidden lock panel, which he quickly went to work on. When the tumblers finally clicked into place, he opened one of the cherry wood veneer drawers to find what he'd thought he would. Rows and rows of files.

Matthieu checked in the R's and M's but found nothing, as he suspected. He began sifting through the files more carefully, looking for any references to G9X. He almost yelled out loud when his fingers lit on a manila folder that was labeled COBRA. It was as thick as two of his fucking fingers, and it probably had every piece of information that existed about him in it.

But what really got him excited was the portable flash drive that was taped to the inside of the folder. This was it, he knew it. Not wanting to linger any longer than was necessary, Matthieu stuffed the folder into his pack and started for the door, only to be stopped by the buzzing of his phone.

It was a text from Fate that ratcheted his adrenaline up to a dangerous level. *Got company.* Keeping in the shadows, Matthieu crept back into the main room and did his best to fade into the background. He watched from his vantage point as the door opened and closed behind a figure.

A hiss of a breath was the only reaction to the sight of the place, turned over as it was, but it was enough. Matthieu knew it was Ward. The former lieutenant was shorter than him, but bulkier, with a meticulously maintained crew cut and a stubborn jaw. He was currently muttering to himself as he beat a hasty path to his office.

"Sonofa*bitch!*" Ward came rushing back out and into the bedroom where he yanked a large service issue duffel out from under his bed, and began stuffing it with clothes. The man's intentions were clear—he was ghosting.

Well, it's now or never, Rousseau. Pushing off the wall, Matthieu slipped into the bedroom behind Ward. He slowly eased the door closed but let it shut with an audible click. The older man froze, his shoulders stiffening.

"Sergeant," he said with resignation before turning to face Matthieu, careful to keep both of his hands visible. Now that Matthieu got a good look at the man, he was shocked at the differences he noted. Short and stocky, he was still built like a brick wall, but there were hollows under his cheeks and bags under his eyes, and his hair had grayed significantly. He looked defeated.

Matthieu stroked his index finger along the barrel of his sidearm, which he'd drawn but kept aimed at the floor. He raised a brow at the sad state of his former commander. "Give me one good reason why I shouldn't shoot your ass."

"Wouldn't do you a damn bit of good," he answered, his Southern Alabama drawl accentuating the vowels. "I'm no threat to you anymore. I assume you found the file."

He waited for Matthieu's nod before he began speaking again. "I've already messengered files to Dodge, Six, Tango 'n Bull. Destroyed the ones on Striker and Banjo, before you ask. I just want out, so if you're gonna kill me, do it now—otherwise, get the hell outta my way."

Matthieu sighed and re-holstered his weapon as all the fight bled out of him. "Arlen," he said, waiting for the older man to look at him, and then waved a hand in the direction of the trashed apartment. "You're so deep in the shit, you don't know your ass from your elbow right now. What are you going to do?"

"These guys that are after you, Cobra, are some kind of crazy. Like nothing I've ever seen before—and you know that's sayin' something." Matthieu acknowledged this with a nod, because he did know. Ward had been in the trenches with them in Afghanistan and before that, he'd served in Desert Storm. "They're turnin' on me now, thinking I'm holdin' out on 'em. What am I gonna do? I'm gonna get the hell outta dodge before I get myself bagged and tagged—and I suggest you do the same."

Matthieu considered him for a moment—considered just putting a bullet between his eyes for all the trouble he'd caused over the years. But revenge wasn't his priority anymore. Keeping Fate and Ridley safe was. That thought made him stop and blink. *What the hell?* When had that happened?

Finally he stepped away from the door, allowing Ward to pass through. "Lieutenant."

Ward turned just inside the door frame and looked back at him. "Sergeant?"

"Mind your six."

"Always." Ward nodded, threw him a hasty salute, and disappeared into the darkness. Moments later, Matthieu heard the main door shut. He expected Fate to come running in when she saw that Ward had escaped without a bullet in him, and Matthieu had yet to come out. When she didn't, he couldn't help but feel a little bit offended—until the back of his neck started to prickle. His skin heated and tightened, and the scar on his cheek began to pulse.

He felt the same kind of black stain that ran through his veins sink into the atmosphere of the old warehouse. Matthieu had a terrible feeling Ward had just been bait—and something was very, very wrong.

ဆာ)ભ

Fate had dropped out of sight when she'd heard a key turn in the front door of the warehouse. After sending Matthieu a quick text with shaky hands, she squeezed herself into a tiny alley between two tall stacks of containers.

Stuffing her borrowed phone back into her purse, and watched the door swing open. The figure of a man was backlit by the dim streetlight behind him, so she couldn't see his face. Since the man had a key, she figured it had to be Ward.

She hoped like hell Matthieu had gotten her text and wasn't going to end up getting shot in the back. Keeping well into the shadow of the containers, Fate felt rather than heard her phone vibrate. Her heart leapt when she assumed it would be a return text from Matthieu.

Retrieving the phone, she frowned at it when she saw it was from Isla instead.

Need 2 get 2gether when ur back in NOLA.

Boy, do we ever, she thought to herself. Hearing Ward open the door of the internal building, she quickly sent off a return message.

Sounds good, will call. Gotta run.

She heard no signs of a struggle from inside the building, so she had to assume that either Matthieu was hiding, or he was actually talking to Ward—although the idea of Matthieu having a discussion before putting a bullet in someone seemed a little implausible.

Even as Fate made the decision to slink a little closer to the door to be able to hear, an arm snaked around from behind her and a sweaty palm slapped over her mouth. She whimpered when an unfamiliar body pressed against her back.

She'd often asked herself what she would do differently if she were ever attacked again, and in that moment, as time slowed, she knew. Everything.

Her heart beat painfully as adrenaline pumped through her system, and she fought through narrowing vision to stay conscious as the man's hand tried to cut off her airway. She forced her body to relax and go pliant, which caused her attacker to loosen his grip just enough for her to breathe. She let her things slip from her hands as she grabbed onto his forearm and twisted her body violently, elbowing him in the ribs. The man heaved a satisfying grunt when she made contact. Fate continued to struggle until she felt his other arm wrap around her ribcage, just below her breasts, and squeeze until things began to pop.

"Easy, kitten," he said in a hoarse whisper, too quiet for her to identify his voice. As she lost her breath again, she had to stop struggling, but he only squeezed tighter. She could hear and feel his own hot breath rasping near her ear—and that, coupled with the feel of him against her, bending her forward, triggered an unwanted memory.

They had been in that position before, him and her. This was her attacker, come to finish the job he'd left undone. It was impossible and yet, here they were. The realization struck new fear in her heart as she imagined her daughter growing up without her...and imagined Matthieu coming out to find her broken and bloody, with no one to pull him back from the void.

No. Just, no. Fate went wild, twisting and jerking, throwing her weight to try and knock him off balance. As the final *coup de grâce*, she bit down hard on the hand covering her mouth until she tasted blood.

She received some gratification from his hiss of pain, until the bloody hand was quickly replaced by another, covered in cloth and an acrid, sweet smell that could only be chloroform. She made a valiant effort to hold her breath and it worked, for a moment, until he jabbed her in the ribs and forced her to suck in a lungful of polluted air.

The last thing she heard before her eyes rolled back and she reluctantly surrendered to unconsciousness was his amused—and familiar—voice.

"Let's go, kitten. Time to play."

CHAPTER TWENTY·FIVE

MATTHIEU BURST THROUGH THE DOOR OF THE interior room, and cast worried eyes around the dark warehouse. He saw no sign of Fate, and he was unable to hear anything but the frantic pounding of his own heartbeat.

She could just be hiding, he rationalized, although his gut was telling him differently. Yanking his phone out of his pocket, he brought up the tracking app he'd created. According to the coordinates, Fate was still in the building—or at least, her phone was.

He moved through the stacks to inspect the area where he'd told her to keep watch, but he found no sign of her. He tried to put himself in her shoes, thought about where she'd have hidden when Ward came in. Rounding the corner of another stack of containers, Matthieu's foot nudged something soft.

He dropped into a crouch for a closer inspection, and he saw that it was Fate's brown leather bag. A few feet away, he noticed her phone lying on the concrete floor as well, where it had apparently been dropped.

Matthieu shot to his feet to pace, shoving hands through his hair. "Jesus, *fuck*!" She was gone. Someone had to have taken her, while he'd been focused on saving his hide from Ward. Matthieu knew he was a selfish bastard, but as far as he knew, it'd never cost anyone their life. But it may have done so for the woman he—no, he wasn't going there.

With sudden purpose, he strode for the front door, flinging it open as if he expected to find Fate and her abductor still there. Looking down, he noticed a couple of dark stains on the sidewalk and bent down to check them out.

Blood. Unmistakable. Matthieu ground his teeth as he was swamped with an impotent rage, so much so that his vision dimmed to a narrow tunnel of red. He had no concrete proof, but it was Farrell—he knew it like he knew his own goddamned name.

Hearing the almost imperceptible scrape of a shoe on the pavement and acting on pure instinct, Matthieu grabbed the SOLO from his ankle holster and rose up to put the intruder within his sights in one fluid motion. As he tried to sharpen his vision, he slowly brought his quarry into focus.

Cursing viciously, Matthieu saw the giant gold eyes of Étienne blinking up at the silver barrel that rested between them. He had to hand it to the kid—after the second time Matthieu almost killed him, he still showed no fear, only a slight wariness.

Sighing, he lowered the gun, replaced it, and raised his head back up to scowl at Étienne. "What the hell are you doing here? How did you find us?"

"Followed you," he said before raising his chin a fraction. "After yesterday, wasn't sure she was safe with you."

Matthieu bit back the scathing reply that came to mind because the kid had a point, so he gave a curt nod instead. "Turns out you were right. Someone took her right out from under me."

With a sad smile, Étienne shook his head. "Not what I meant. But I know someone took her—know where they went too. It's not far."

Matthieu's head snapped back as if he'd been struck. "How the fuck do you know that?"

"Again, I followed them. I didn't feel like I would be doing her any good by trying to intervene without backup," he said with a rueful gesture at his wiry frame. "I can take you—"

Before he could even finish the sentence, Matthieu had grabbed his arm in a brutal grip and hustled him down the street, leaving the door to the warehouse standing wide open. "Where are we going?" Étienne asked, digging in his heels to stop the progress.

"To the Jeep, unless you've got a better way to travel." The boy just gave him an unreadable quirk of his lips, and Matthieu pulled him forward with a growl.

Once locked inside the Jeep, Matthieu glanced over at the kid in the passenger seat before turning his eyes to the dark road. "How far?"

"Couple of miles, as the hawk flies."

Matthieu gave him a weird look and shook his head, as the kid chuckled to himself. He wasn't so sure they weren't both a couple tacos short of a fiesta platter. "Just tell me which way," he said through clenched teeth.

Fate regained consciousness slowly, with the presence of mind to get a feel for her surroundings before projecting her awareness. Looking through her lowered lashes, she could tell she was in a dimly lit room. She was lying on her back on a scratchy comforter that covered a lumpy mattress. Hotel, most likely, and not a nice one.

Her head felt as if it was stuffed with cotton and her throat was so sore, she could have swallowed a desert's worth of sand for all she knew. It was like a hangover, without the fun parts leading up to it. But, thank God, she still had all of her clothes on.

With subtle movements, she tested her limbs to see if anything was broken. It wasn't, but she realized her ankles were tied together, as were her wrists, and there was a long line that traveled from the bonds at her wrists to the headboard. It was long enough to give her room to move, but still able to keep her from leaving.

A man sat in a chair that faced the bed, silent and unmoving. Fate could only discern an outline in the mostly dark room, but she didn't need to see his face to know that it was Eli. *Bastard.* She knew she should be scared—terrified even—but she wasn't. She was pissed.

Maybe it was some sort of shock thing, because rather than thinking about being at this man's mercy, all she could think of was getting free so she could wring his pasty neck.

"I know you're awake, darling," he said, startling her. It was Eli, all right, but his voice sounded strange to her ears. It was sort of like a B movie *Dracula* trying to talk through a mouthful of plastic teeth—all hollow and muffled.

She heard his expensive clothing rustle as he rose from the chair to come stand by the bed. Knowing she was caught, she opened her eyes to glare at him. He was still as slick as a snake oil salesman—but Fate wondered why she never noticed the filmy layer of slime over the polish. It was so glaringly obvious now; she was ashamed to have been so naïve.

A hundred different things ran through her mind when she tried to think of something to say, but she kept circling back to just one. "Why, Eli?"

To his credit, he didn't try to feign ignorance. He merely cocked his head as he thought about his answer. "At first, you were just an amusement—a delightful one, mind you, but still... And then I found out about your unfortunate mistake."

"Mistake?" she asked, raising a brow at him. She figured if looks could kill, Eli ought to be bleeding internally by then.

"Yes, the child," he said, as if it would be obvious to anyone with half a brain. "A child would be somewhat of a...detriment to me, especially in lieu of more recent events. I needed to keep an eye on you both."

Fate was so mad, her entire body trembled, and she felt tears streaming down her cheeks. They weren't tears of sorrow or fear—even though she had a right to them. They were tears of bone deep hatred. She knew if she hadn't been tied, she would have clawed his freaky eyes out with her bare hands.

What the hell was wrong with his eyes, anyway? Before she could think further on it, he reached out a hand and caressed her cheek with the backs of his long, thin fingers. The metal of the heavy signet ring he wore on his middle finger was cool against her heated skin.

"So beautiful," he murmured as she jerked away from him. She felt bile rising in her throat and she could think of nothing but lashing out, so she reared back and spit in his face.

Without hesitation, he backhanded her across the mouth before yanking out his silk handkerchief to wipe his face. The ring had smashed her lip against her teeth, splitting it, and Fate tasted blood for the second time that night—this time her own, mingled with his.

"So what's the plan, Eli?" she asked, her snarl causing her lip to bleed more, and she felt it roll down her chin. "Going to beat on me some more? How about rape me again? That's a bit old hat, don't you think? Even for you. Just like old times, I guess."

Fate couldn't stop the words from tumbling out of her mouth. She was pretty sure the number one rule in a hostage situation was not to antagonize your captor, but she couldn't help it. She was sick and damned tired of being that man's victim.

His eyes narrowed on her, and his lip curled into a closed mouth sneer, but he kept his cool. "The plan is for you to tell me where the child is. *Our* child. Then I'll decide what I'm going to do with you."

Snarling at him again, Fate leaned back on the bed as if making herself comfortable. "Well, we're going to be here for a long time, because I'm not telling you anything."

Eli paced back and forth alongside the bed, considering her. "Waiting for your idiot watchdog to come find you? I assure you, he won't. By the way, how *are* you paying him for his services?"

Fate clamped her jaw on the instinct to defend first Matthieu, then herself—but she realized Matthieu wouldn't give two shits what Eli thought, and neither should she. She had to focus on the matter at hand—Eli wanted her daughter, and she needed to find out why.

"What do you want with my daughter?"

"Let's just say something has been set in motion, and I intend to stop it." Eli bounced on the balls of his feet and she could tell he was enjoying it, this little cat-and-mouse game.

Closing her eyes with a deep sigh, Fate gave him the only possible answer. "I'd die before telling you where she is," she said, suddenly pinning him with a furtive stare. "I'm not afraid."

She couldn't help but remember when Matthieu had said the same words to her under very different circumstances. It gave her strength, thinking of him, and she really *wasn't* afraid. And she thought it was because, deep down, she really did think he'd find her in time.

Eli's tetchy movements halted by her head at the bed, startling her, and she thought she may have heard a soft snort. He stretched out a hand as if he would touch her again, but obviously thought better of it.

"Oh, kitten, it's as if you don't think I can make you talk." He said it so casually that it caused a chill to scurry down her spine. Okay, maybe she was a little afraid. As she stared up at him, she noticed subtle differences about his facial features that hadn't been there before.

His cheekbones seemed sharper and more pronounced, and his brow seemed more prominent. And his eyes...they weren't his eyes anymore. While she watched, they changed from a shadowy blue to almost crystal clear, translucent orbs. She'd seen this before—in Draconus, the man who'd killed Matthieu's father, and in Matthieu himself.

She wasn't surprised at all when the shadows emerged and began to writhe. She wasn't even that surprised when a symbol appeared on his forehead, resembling a peace sign without the circle.

She may not have been surprised when he opened his mouth to sneer at her, and she got full view of a nasty set of serrated fangs. Not surprised, no—horrified. "Eli? What—"

Her panicked questioning was cut off as he shot out a hand to cover her face, and she could feel razor sharp nails digging into her flesh. He climbed beside her on the bed and leaned over her, squeezing her jaw in a vice-like grip to force her to look up at him.

Eli snorted again, and those bewitching eyes sparkled with relish. "There's more than one way to get information from you, kitten," he drawled, and leaned closer to whisper in her ear. "And, by all means, fight—I'll enjoy it more."

Fate immediately felt her muscles go slack, beyond her control, and her mind grew fuzzy around the edges. It was a familiar sinking feeling, much like the one she got when she was pulled into Matthieu's dreams—but the only thing that waited for her on the other side was blackness.

CHAPTER TWENTY·SIX

MATTHIEU'S LEFT LEG BOUNCED ANXIOUSLY AS HE maneuvered the Jeep according to Étienne's directions. While he should have felt relief that he'd been presented a fortuitous way to track down Fate and her attacker, he was nothing but a giant ball of nervous energy. The closer they got to their destination, the twitchier he became. It wasn't just him, either—the demons were riled. He could feel their shivering energy sliding underneath his skin.

And worse yet, he was beginning to feel the pull of a flash-back curling around the edges of his consciousness—and now was *so* not the time. Before Afghanistan, he and the team had done scores of smash and grab, POW rescues in Iraq, from enemy camps to shitty hotels like the one up ahead. Matthieu could feel the lines being blurred in his head already, but all he could do was his best to keep it together.

"There!" Étienne shouted as he pointed to a shabby sign that announced the presence of the *Riverside Resort*. Matthieu coughed out a laugh. If that place was a resort, then he was Mary fucking Poppins.

"Hang on to your balls," he muttered as he whipped the Jeep into a screeching turn from the center lane, not bothering with the left turn lane. Despite the seatbelt, Étienne crashed into the passenger side window with a yelp.

"Warned you," Matthieu said when he caught the kid's glare in his periphery.

Pulling up close to the lobby of the dilapidated building, he parked sideways over several parking slots and killed the engine. "Room?" he asked, although he figured if the kid knew, he'd have said so already.

Étienne shook his head with an apologetic frown. "Once I saw where they were going, I figured I shouldn't let too much time pass before I came back to get you."

Matthieu nodded, accepting the answer as the best possible action under the circumstances. Drawing his PPK, he dug out a suppressor and screwed it into the barrel. "I'll just have to get creative in convincing the night clerk to tell me what I need to know," Matthieu said, glaring at the young man through the cloudy lobby window, and the shiver of anticipation he felt reminded him a little too much of Baghdad. Étienne rolled his eyes and placed a slender hand over the gun barrel, forcing Matthieu to lower it.

"How about you let me try? I can be pretty persuasive when I need to be. Just wait for me, and if I can't get it then you can go all *Dirty Harry* on him."

Matthieu merely grunted in response, but he lowered his gun. "Five minutes," he growled, and the kid was out of the car before he'd even finished the words. Kid had guts—that was something Matthieu could almost respect, if that was an emotion was even able to feel towards anyone other than his 'band of brothers.'

He watched Étienne enter the lobby and took a moment to really look at the young man. He was wearing artfully torn jeans slung low on his slender hips, and a fitted graphic t-shirt. In fact, he was wearing a lot more clothing than he had been when Matthieu had first seen him.

Matthieu supposed he was an attractive enough kid—if you liked that kind of thing—even if it looked like he'd cut his own hair with a dull Swiss Army knife.

He raised a brow as he watched the kid saunter—because there really wasn't any other word for it—across the lobby, toward the desk clerk. There was a swing in his hips that accentuated the strip of tanned midriff that peeked out below the shirt that was almost...flirtatious.

Then, just as Matthieu had seen countless women do when they saw him and his boys out at a bar, Étienne caught the poor clerk's eye—and he watched as the guy did a double take. *Oh.* So it was like that. Well, if it worked to their advantage, Matthieu sure as hell wasn't going to complain.

Étienne sidled up to the counter and leaned over it on his elbows, as if he owned the place. Matthieu knew he must be hitting the clerk with a puppy dog look from those freaky golden eyes, and he almost felt for the guy—he didn't stand a chance.

They chatted for a few moments, blatantly flirting, before Étienne pulled out his phone and showed it to the clerk. Matthieu figured it was most likely a picture of Fate. The clerk said a few more words before sliding a piece of paper across the counter, on which Étienne scribbled something, only to pass it back.

Mission accomplished, Matthieu hoped, because the kid was practically bouncing as he headed out the door. Étienne gave him a smug look as he hopped back into the Jeep. "Room thirteen, on the back side."

"Of course it is," Matthieu grumbled. "Wonder if Farrell paid extra for that."

"Farrell?"

"Never mind. We're going."

As Matthieu maneuvered the Jeep around to the unlit backside of the motel, he had to blink to clear his vision as things began to blur even more. One specific mission kept trying to creep in—G9X had been dispatched to rescue some civilian American reporters who were being held prisoner by Iraqi forces.

They had intel that the civvies were being kept in some fleabag hotel on the outskirts of Baghdad and their orders were to rescue them as quietly as possible, with limited enemy casualties. Matthieu had driven the rescue vehicle that night as well.

He scrubbed a hand over his face as it became harder and harder to keep his grasp on reality. The Iraqi mission was superimposed on top of his reality like a double-exposed photograph, until Matthieu could no longer trust what he was seeing. It was like falling backwards off a cliff—losing himself, losing control.

Backing the Jeep up to room thirteen, he parked it diagonally across two spaces, both to give them an easy getaway and to provide a little bit of a cushion if things got hairy. Matthieu had a brief but horrific moment of darkness, in which he thought the demons might take over again. He gripped the steering wheel and squeezed his eyes shut.

He breathed a sigh of relief when he opened them back up. He was exactly where he was supposed to be—at the hotel in Baghdad. Matthieu's eyes slid to the rookie in the passenger seat and spared a moment to wonder why the hell it wasn't Striker, his long-time ops partner, sitting there. *Must have had too damn much to drink the night before and lost the bet over who'd have to break in the newb.*

"Get out. Come around to my side," he grunted at the rookie, who scrambled to comply. Christ, where were they getting these kids these days? This one looked like he could be knocked over with a feather.

Once the kid came around in the darkness, Matthieu stepped out and eyed the position of the vehicle relative to the room, nodding. "Listen up," he said to the kid in a harsh whisper. "While I'm neutralizing the subject, you need to get the civilian out of that room. Get in and out quick, and keep both of your heads down. You copy, soldier?"

The rookie was looking at him like he'd lost all of his marbles and the bag they came in. Matthieu rolled his eyes and pinched the bridge of his nose. "Fuck, okay, how 'bout gimme a nod for yes, shake your head for no, cool?"

Nod.

"Did you understand what I said to you about getting the victim out?"

Nod.

"You got a knife on you?"

Shake.

With a heavy sigh, Matthieu unclipped a folding combat knife and handed it to him. When the kid just stared at it with his eyebrow raised, Matthieu grabbed his hand and pressed the knife into it. "Victim could be restrained."

Nod.

Oh, this was *not* going to go well. The fuck was the kid's name? Screw that, they were going to have to give him a com name anyway. Matthieu looked the kid over, from his slender body and sharp features, to those piercing eyes. He was sharp—maybe he'd turn out to be a deadeye with some training.

Matthieu sneered as he remembered a character from his childhood comic book days. "Okay, Hawkeye, just stay behind me and try not to get dead."

The kid's eyes widened and he choked a little when he heard that. Whether it was the name or the dead part that churned his butter, Matthieu just hoped he wouldn't hurl. That was always the icing on the cake with a rookie onboard.

"I go high, you go low. You ready?" Matthieu asked, knowing the answer was 'hell, no.'

Gulp. Nod.

Matthieu walked up to the door of room thirteen, assessing how much force it would take to kick it in. He could hear no sounds that would give him an idea of the location of the occupants, and the drapes were drawn shut. He was going in blind. With a rookie. *Fuck.*

He holstered his suppressed pistol but kept it at ready access. He wasn't going to go in shooting without a ten-twenty on the victim. With a glance behind him to see that Hawkeye hadn't passed out, Matthieu backed up a few steps to get a running start, and hit the door with a heavy mid-rear round kick.

The door flew open and bounced against the inside wall, no doubt startling the occupants and giving Matthieu a split second to assess the situation. Two occupants. Woman restrained on the bed, assailant leaning over her with a hand on her face.

Something about them, though...especially the woman. His mind was trying to tell him that something was different about her, about this mission—she was special. It pecked at him like a memory that he couldn't quite get into focus.

But what he knew for sure, was the sight of the scrawny ass man who had the nerve to threaten her, to put his hands on her, caused Matthieu to see red. Luckily for everyone involved, his deeply ingrained training took over, and he leapt high, tackled the man, and rolled with him across the bed and onto the floor.

He hoped like hell the rookie had followed his instructions, gone in low and gotten the woman to safety…because the little bastard he was grappling with had a wiry sort of strength, and was doing his best to get the upper hand.

Pinning the man with a knee, Matthieu lifted his head so he could see over the bed and noted the empty room. Good. Now he didn't have to hold back. Reaching down, he grabbed the assailant by the collar and stood, lifting the guy off the ground and throwing him across the bed where he landed in a heap.

Keep it quiet, minimize fatalities. The team leader's orders echoed in Matthieu's head as he advanced on the enemy soldier, who was already climbing to his feet. Matthieu could make it quiet, sure—but he could also make it painful. Rearing back, he planted the guy's jaw with a vicious haymaker, sending him sprawling backward into a dingy armchair.

Neutralize. Subdue. Lieutenant Ward's voice barked in his ear, which baffled him because he wasn't wearing a com. Why wasn't he wearing a fucking com? *Bleed. Maim. Kill. Destroy.* Another insidious voiced hissed at him over his commander's orders. And then there was the overwhelming, sick feeling that neither was the voice he was supposed to be listening to.

As he stared at the guy slumped in the chair, wiping the back of his hand over his bloody mouth and panting, Matthieu didn't feel the rush of victory from a mission completed, like he usually would. He felt nauseated, disoriented; his skin grew clammy and he broke out in a cold sweat.

Something wasn't right about this scene, something big. When he looked down at his adversary, the man seemed to be in no hurry to get away from the big, hulking wall of soldier that might be one sneeze away from planting brass in his gut.

No, the guy didn't look scared at all. In fact, he looked slightly amused...and maybe a little bit bored. He just stared back at Matthieu with eyes that just couldn't be right, and leaned his head back to bare his teeth in a bloody sneer—only they weren't teeth. Nope, they were...something else entirely.

Matthieu wasn't proud of taking a step back, but he sure as hell did it. He may have been several feet away from the man, but the physical anomalies were unmistakable. Crazy Eyes treated him to a snort and a half-hearted chuckle, before jerking his chin at Matthieu.

"You got here faster than I gave you credit for, watchdog. Whatever she's paying you, you should ask for more."

Cocking his head sideways to study the man, Matthieu tried to puzzle out what he was babbling on about, but he just kept talking. "Too bad you won't be around long enough to ask for that raise."

As the meaning of those words registered, Crazy Eyes was already reaching underneath the lapel of his jacket. Before he could even finish the movement, Matthieu drew his sidearm and put a bullet between his eyes.

Matthieu barely had time to notice the double barreled Derringer as it clattered to the ground before he was thrown backward by a blast of sulfur and smoke, a spit of fire and a loud pop. He rolled into an automatic duck and cover position, but not before he noted the empty space where the body should have been, and the oily black mark left on the wall behind it.

The small explosion brought back the ever present nightmares of Kandahar—the bomb, the torture, the death. Matthieu felt himself slipping under the cloud of black smoke, as he heard the familiar ringing in his ears and burn in his throat.

That's why Striker wasn't partnering him on this mission, he thought as he groped around blindly to get his bearings—not knowing which way was up. Striker was dead, so he obviously had a new partner—a goddamn rookie.

Matthieu's head pounded as the confusion hit him hard. Kandahar had been their last mission before they disbanded, so why were he and Hawkeye rescuing civvies in Iraq?

Stumbling to his feet, Matthieu made a drunken lurch toward where he thought the door was because he still couldn't see, and realized too late that it was already open.

He pitched forward, tripped over a curb or something, and went down like a sack of potatoes. He let out a loud curse when he smacked his head on something hard. He lay there panting for minutes, or maybe hours before his vision cleared long enough to notice that he was sprawled on his side in a dark parking lot. It looked like he'd cracked his noggin on one of the concrete wheel blocks.

Groaning, Matthieu flopped onto his back, but the motion proved to be too much for his fevered mind and churning stomach. He rolled over just quick enough to avoid making a mess of his clothes as he retched up his last meal.

Matthieu had no clue if he was in Baghdad, Kandahar, or the godforsaken shack in the bayou. He didn't even know if he had all of his parts in tact—and he sure as the hell didn't know what had happened to the guy who'd ended up on the wrong end of his PPK.

When his head stopped spinning enough, he hefted himself up to sit on the curb, and tried to remember what he was supposed to do. He thought he was supposed to call Hawkeye for a pick up, but with where his head was at in that moment,

Matthieu wasn't sure the kid even existed. But he really didn't have any other ideas.

Digging in his pocket for a pack of gum, something he'd taken to keeping on him ever since he'd quit smoking, he popped in a piece and yanked his phone off his belt. Scrolling through his contacts, he found Hawkeye which gave him a momentarily wave of relief. That part, at least, had been real.

Deciding against calling because he still wasn't sure if he'd been in an explosion and if he could even speak, Matthieu dashed off a quick text.

All clear. -Cobra

He hoped the kid would get the picture, because he didn't have any idea what else to say. With a ragged sigh, Matthieu hit send and leaned back on his hands to wait it out.

CHAPTER TWENTY·SEVEN

WHEN FATE EMERGED FROM THE DARKNESS, SHE was falling—or rather rolling—until she landed in an ungraceful heap beneath another body. Thinking Eli must have tackled her, she began flailing her arms, trying to land a blow. In seconds, strong but lean arms banded around her to pin her own to her body.

"Calm down," whispered a familiar accented voice. Fate closed her eyes as the rush of relief made her light headed. *Étienne*. She nodded against his shoulder to let him know she understood.

"Keep your head down and stay with me. We're going to try for the door."

She could hear sounds of a brutal fight going on behind her, but Étienne kept a protective arm around her shoulders as they crawled, so she couldn't turn and look. Once they crossed the threshold, he hauled her to her feet and dragged her towards the waiting Jeep, double parked in front of the motel room.

"Get in," he commanded, and being still too disoriented to know any better, Fate complied. She'd barely had time to fasten her seatbelt before he cranked the Jeep and peeled out of the lot. She turned to look behind them at the wide open door of the room, and it dawned on her that someone was still there.

"Wait! What happened to Eli? Where's Matthieu?" Her frantic questioning was met with stony silence, as Étienne seemed determined not to speak to her or make eye contact. In fact, he seemed rather freakishly focused on the task of driving.

He pulled into a well-lit gas station, cut the engine and buried his face in his hands. Even from across the cab, Fate could tell he was trembling. "You okay?" he asked, his voice muffled by his hands.

"I'm fine, I think," she answered, doing a cursory check for any aches and pains. "What about you? Please tell me what happened. Where's Matthieu?"

"Oh, back at the motel. *Neutralizing the subject*," he said with an edge to his voice.

"I don't understand what that means."

"Yeah, I didn't either," he muttered. "He's dealing with the guy..."

"Eli."

"Right. He's taking care of him. I'm under strict orders to get you somewhere safe and wait for his call."

"Oh, God. What if he doesn't call?"

"Then I'm to get you back to the house in Theriot."

Fate's heart constricted when she thought of Matthieu facing Eli alone. Even though she knew Matthieu could handle himself in a confrontation, Eli fought dirty.

Suddenly her mind latched onto part of what Étienne had said. "Wait a minute...orders?"

Étienne finally turned his golden eyes to look at her, and winced. "Yeah, that's the thing. I think he's locked in some sort of flashback. Was he military?"

"Army, Special Forces. What sort of flashback?"

"Like, I think he thought we were at war. He kept talking about rescuing civilians, meaning you. He even gave me a nickname. Called me Hawkeye."

Fate was unable to suppress a snort at that, because she saw how fitting it was. But she quickly sobered. She'd only seen Matthieu have flashbacks in dreams—and she didn't know if he'd ever lost touch with reality before.

"We have to go back to help him!"

"But the orders—"

"Screw the orders! This isn't Afghanistan. And if Matthieu doesn't know where he is, then he's in danger. Switch places with me and I'll drive. You can tell him I kidnapped you."

Étienne gave her a dubious look but did as she asked, climbing into the passenger seat.

They pulled into the darkened back lot of the strip motel, and Fate's stomach turned as she imagined what they might find. Would Matthieu be hurt, or worse? Would Eli be dead? What if they found nothing at all? She couldn't stand the thought of Matthieu wandering the streets of an unfamiliar city with his mind held hostage by torturous memories.

She breathed a momentary sigh of relief when she caught sight of him, illuminated by the dull glow of the Jeep's headlights. He was standing with one shoulder propped against a useless light post—its bulbs having long since burned out and never been replaced.

Her heart sank when she took in his posture, his demeanor. Something was wrong. He'd curled in on himself as she'd seen him do after coming out of one of his dreams. His hands were stuffed in the pockets of his fatigues and his shoulders slumped forward. His head was bowed so low that his chin rested on his chest, and the only movement she could see was the too rapid rise and fall of his chest as he breathed.

"Well, at least he's breathing," she muttered, turning off the car. Looking at Étienne, she made a split second decision. "You need to stay here. After that last incident, I can't be sure he won't go after you."

"I don't know if that's a good idea. What if he hurts you?"

"He won't." Without waiting for an answer, she hopped out of the Jeep and shut the door. She couldn't miss the sound of the locks engaging behind her. She approached Matthieu with caution, knowing he wouldn't hurt her, but if he didn't know who she was, all bets were off—and Fate didn't have a death wish.

As she came closer, she noted his sickly pallor. He was pale, in contrast to his usual toasted complexion, and his skin was slick with perspiration. From this close, she could see his muscles contracting at intervals as he was periodically wracked with convulsions.

His eyes were lowered and shaded by thick black lashes, so she couldn't see if they were normal or...not. He didn't seem to register her presence as she approached. Fate noted with relief that his sidearm was in place at his hip, and he didn't seem to have any blood on him. She did find it odd that his dog tags were hanging out and proud, fully visible to anyone—the only time she'd ever seen them out was the day she'd tried to touch them.

"Matthieu?" She spoke in a quiet voice so as not to startle him, but he gave no indication that he'd heard her at all.

She placed both hands on either side of his face, but almost snatched them back at the feel of his skin, so clammy and cold.

Summoning her resolve, she forced him to raise his head, but his eyes remained downcast.

"Hey, come back to me," she said, stroking his shivering skin. "Matthieu," she repeated with more force, giving his scarred cheek a light smack. While this at least got him to meet her eyes, his face was still expressionless and there was no spark of recognition. She was relieved to see that his eyes were dark brown, however dull and unfocused.

"Do you know who I am?" she asked, and hesitantly touched his face. Finally, he began to blink and a frown line appeared between his brows.

"Fate?" he asked, before having to swallow to clear some of the grittiness from his voice. He turned his head and squinted at Étienne, who was sitting in the jeep. He looked back at Fate, confused. "What—? He was supposed to have gotten you out of here."

"He did. I came back. I wasn't going to leave you."

Heaving a shuddering sigh, he leaned his forehead against hers and gripped the back of her neck. "I'm so confused," he admitted, which scared her more than anything. "Are we—"

"We're in Savannah."

She felt rather than saw him nod against her forehead. "Good...We need to get out of here—out of goddamn Georgia. Time to call Jeremiah."

Fate closed her eyes and breathed a deep sigh of relief as she clutched his shirt. "Thank God. Matthieu, what happened to Eli?"

She leaned back to look in his eyes, just in time to catch the shutters being drawn. He was planning to stonewall her again. "Gone."

"Dead?" she asked, afraid to hear the answer. Should she really care what happens to the man who'd raped her and then tricked her into marrying him? Still, the idea that he was dead gave her a sick feeling in the pit of her stomach.

"Don't know. I think so...Look, we need to get away from here. We can compare notes later."

She clamped down her jaw against the need to say more, to ask more, and conceded that he was probably right. She jerked her chin in a nod and started to head for the Jeep. He made to follow her but nearly dropped when his knees buckled.

Rushing back, Fate insinuated herself under one of Matthieu's arms to take some of his weight. She was startled when Étienne appeared on Matthieu's other side—she hadn't even heard him leave the car. Together, they were able to get him settled across the backseat of the Jeep.

With a wary look back at the darkened motel, Fate pulled out of the lot and drove off into the night.

ॐ

Matthieu had taken the wheel, but he'd yet to start the engine. He sat facing forward, hands gripping the steering wheel. Fate could see the muscles bunching in his jaw as he ground his teeth. Sighing, she sat back in her seat, knowing she could hurt herself if she sat there for too long trying to figure out what was rattling around in his head.

They'd returned to the parking lot of the abandoned warehouse they had used to stash the Jeep before searching Ward's safe-house. Matthieu had wanted to make sure Ward hadn't come back—though Fate thought that may have been an excuse to give him some time to pull himself together.

Étienne had insisted he had his own transportation, so they'd separated and agreed to meet back at the bayou house. *Maybe*, Fate thought, *if Matthieu would ever start the car.*

"Ready to go?" she asked, hoping to break the uncomfortable silence that clung to the air in the stuffy SUV cab.

His fingers squeezed the steering wheel so hard that she thought he'd snap it, before he removed his hands to shove them through his hair. "Never should have brought you with me," he said, and she couldn't fight back the shiver as the rough timbre of his voice rolled over her, even as she balked at what he was saying.

"My judgment is compromised—and now, so's my mind. I'm compromised. I shouldn't have let myself be talked into this. You could've been killed. If H—Étienne hadn't decided to follow us—"

"I didn't give you a choice. I *would* have followed you. And besides, I'm here. You saved me, even if you weren't entirely yourself."

"Étienne saved you," he insisted.

"We both know he wouldn't have been able to overpower Eli by himself. I knew you'd come. Even if you didn't know where to start, you'd have found me."

He turned to look at her then, his chocolate eyes as haunted as ever, full of guilt and self-reproach, and she knew the words he'd left unspoken. *Not in time.*

For the hundredth time her heart broke for him, and she'd have done anything to lighten the mood—to put a spark back in his eyes. She leaned over and lightly punched his shoulder. "Learn how to take a compliment, will ya? I'm saying thanks."

Sighing, he dropped his head back against the headrest. "Okay, you win. You're welcome, m'lady."

Absurdly pleased, she gave him her biggest smile. If he could play with her, then maybe he was going to be okay. "I am in your debt, kind sir," she said with a wink.

He snorted and looked at her out of the corner of his eye, a small smile playing over his lips—one that was just a little too mischievous to be safe. "You know...words are good, but...hands are better," he said, his teeth flashing in the otherwise dark vehicle.

Better, she thought. She knew he was teasing her, but she decided to call his bluff. His smile disappeared as she leaned halfway over him and slid her left hand through the hair at the nape of his neck. She winked at him when she saw the wary look he gave her, just before she crushed her lips to his.

All of her fear that she'd tried to keep at bay while being held hostage bubbled up to the surface, along with gratitude for being saved—and simply being alive. She poured it all into the kiss as she swiped her tongue over his lower lip to tease his mouth open.

He slipped his arm behind her shoulders to bury his fingers in her hair, groaning as he pulled her closer. She broke away from his mouth long enough to trail kisses over his chin and jaw, before scraping her teeth down the line of his neck and soothing it with her tongue on the way back up.

Matthieu hissed out a breath and Fate heard his head thunk against the headrest of the driver's seat. *Good to know*, she thought as she decided up the ante. With the hand that wasn't gripping his hair, she followed the trail of hard planes of muscle down his chest and abdomen.

"We probably shouldn't be doing this," Matthieu ground out, but lifted his chin to give her better access. "Don't they say that you shouldn't engage in situations like this so soon after a traumatic experience?"

She pulled back to look at him, taking in his dilated eyes and parted lips as his breaths came out in pants. He wanted her, she could tell, but he was still trying to protect her. It touched her that he would do so—but it also made her determined to break his resolve.

Biting down on his earlobe, she whispered in his ear. "Don't know who *they* are. Don't care what they say."

Before he had a chance to answer her, she captured his mouth again, enjoying the rasp of his stubbled chin against her skin. He smelled of sweat and spice, a scent that was masculine and powerful, and completely Matthieu.

Fate skimmed her fingers down the line of his inseam, and his chest stopped moving as he held his breath, waiting for her next move. She'd never considered herself particularly bold, especially when it came to sexual relationships, but something about Matthieu always brought her walls crashing down.

With trembling fingers, she pressed her hand against the hardness behind his zipper, marveling at the fact that she could feel his heat through the thick fatigues. He groaned into her mouth as she stroked him, her hand mirroring the action of her tongue.

Eventually, he broke away with a groan, his breath coming in rasps. "It's been a long night for you." his voice was like gravel as he seemed to be trying to access the rational part of his brain when all the blood was rushing south.

"We shouldn't be doing this," he repeated, although the subtle roll of his hips pressing his erection harder into her grip called him a liar.

"Matthieu," she said, keeping up a steady rhythm of strokes. "I could have died tonight—I was probably minutes from it when you found me."

She removed her hand to turn his chin to look at her. She needed him to really hear her. "I want to *live*."

He licked his perfect lips as he studied her, looking for the truth in her eyes. After a long moment, he nodded once and reached out to turn on the ignition. "All right then. We'll celebrate being alive," he said before throwing the Jeep into gear. "Let's go on home. We'll do it right."

CHAPTER TWENTY·EIGHT

WHEN THEY RETURNED TO THE BAYOU HOUSE, Étienne was waiting on the front porch looking haggard and exhausted. Matthieu surprised Fate by clapping a hand on his neck and urging him forward. "C'mon, Hawkeye, come inside and take a load off. You look like roadkill."

He gave her a wary look from over Matthieu's shoulder, but she just smiled and shook her head as she unlocked the door. Matthieu dropped his hand and shifted the grocery bags he carried to distribute the weight.

Taking a turn into the kitchen, he took out the large bottle of Cuervo they'd bought onto the counter, followed by the beer, margarita mix, and then the scotch. Fate snorted when she eyed their collection, and Matthieu shot her a look. "What? You wanted to celebrate."

Laughing, she took the bags from him and put them away. "So I did...although I'm not sure I'd celebrate life by being unconscious."

Matthieu had confessed to her on the long drive back to Louisiana that he rarely drank, because it sort of defeated the purpose of the whole avoiding sleep thing—but that he was starting to feel safe to sleep around her. To most, it would seem like such a simple thing, but she knew that for him to let his guard down in that way was nothing short of monumental.

She was still smiling to herself as she grabbed three bottles of Turbodog and headed for the couch. She handed one to Étienne, who was curled up in the recliner as if he belonged there, and Matthieu reached out to take one for himself.

He popped the top and tipped his head back for a deep swallow. "Thanks. You guys start without me, I'm going to take a shower." He turned toward the bathroom holding his beer in one hand, and pulling off his shirt with the other.

Fate couldn't help but staring at the back of him as he disappeared down the hall. She'd never met anyone who looked like him—lean but heavily muscled, his strength born of hard work and service rather than hours at the gym. The effect was nothing less than stunning.

Étienne cleared his throat behind her and she knew she'd been caught staring. A hot blush crept up her neck as she turned back to him. Trying for nonchalance, she shrugged and sipped her beer.

Étienne's own beer sat untouched on the coffee table as he yawned. She knew she should let him get some rest but, as much as she liked the kid, he had some things to answer for. When she looked again, though, she saw the strain of their *adventure* had worn on him—his eyes were tired, ringed with shadows that dulled their normally striking gold color, and he had to stifle a yawn every few minutes.

Fate figured that her questions could wait until they were all rested. Instead, she just watched him until he raised his eyes to meet her gaze. "You know we'll have to talk eventually."

It was a statement, not a question, and he nodded, clearly understanding the distinction. "I don't think meeting you was a coincidence," she continued while watching his unreadable expression. "I think you know more about me, and maybe even Matthieu, than you're saying. But right now, I'm tired, and the only thing I want to worry about is seeing the bottom of my beer bottle."

Étienne gave her a weak smile and finally took a sip of his beer, wincing slightly as the bitter taste of the dark ale hit his tongue. Fate finished off her own bottle and got up for another, on a whim, grabbing a second for Matthieu as well. She was just sitting back down when she heard the bathroom door open, and saw steam puff out into the hallway.

Dangling his now empty bottle from his thumb and forefinger, Matthieu emerged wearing nothing but a towel slung low over his hips. The water he hadn't bothered to dry off traveled in rivers over his chiseled chest and abdomen, disappearing into the vee of his towel.

Biting her lip, Fate looked her fill and then her gaze slingshot back to Étienne—because it seemed this time, she wasn't the only one caught staring. Evidently oblivious to the picture he made, and the affect it had on the others in the room, Matthieu crossed to the coffee table to grab his fresh beer.

Taking a deep pull, his gaze drifted to Fate and then to Étienne, taking in the kid's wide-eyed stare. Fate inwardly cringed, thinking that Matthieu wasn't the type of man who would be comfortable being ogled by another guy. However, he surprised her by merely giving Étienne a wink before strolling off to the bedroom.

She suppressed a chuckle when Étienne choked on his mouthful, and she had to lean over to pound on his back. When Matthieu returned, he was wearing the old Army t-shirt that she had borrowed earlier and a pair of flannel pajama bottoms. Instead of joining them in the living room, he went to the kitchen to get out three shot glasses, and filled each with a slug of tequila.

He handed one to Fate, and tried to give another to Étienne, but the boy just eyed the shot warily. "I've never had one before," he said.

Surprisingly, Matthieu smiled and patted him on the shoulder before thrusting the glass into his hand. "No time like the present. Pony up, Hawkeye."

Fate and Matthieu both burst out laughing when Étienne glared at him, irritated by the nickname. When Matthieu sat down beside her, Fate bumped shoulders with him and raised her glass. "Here's to being alive."

The three of them clinked their glasses together and took the shots. Matthieu and Fate laughed again as Étienne came up sputtering, tears leaking out of his eyes from the burn of the alcohol. Fate relished the burn for a few moments before chasing it with her beer.

"I thought we were making margaritas," she said.

Matthieu shrugged and jumped up to grab the bottle of tequila to refill their glasses. "This is easier."

She couldn't argue with that, Fate thought as she took her second shot. A pleasant warmth began to creep into her muscles, and she was finally able to relax for the first time in days. She couldn't remember the last time she'd been able to just hang out with friends. They were all friends, weren't they?

Of a sort, anyway. A motley crew brought together by a set of strange and ridiculous circumstances.

Realizing she'd zoned out, she tried to focus on the conversation between Matthieu and Étienne, stilted though it was—and promptly wish she hadn't. "...so are you really homeless?" Matthieu was asking, and he grunted when Fate elbowed him in the ribs.

"What? It's an honest question," he countered, frowning into his empty shot glass. She supposed it was—one that Étienne apparently found hilarious. It was a few seconds before he could pull himself together enough to answer.

"Not homeless, no," he said in that voice tinged with French. "I like to live simply. I don't need a lot of things."

Matthieu gave a sage nod, sipped his beer. "I get that."

Fate looked at him sharply. "You do?"

"Hell, yes. There were times when I was on mission with nothing but a map and the clothes on my back," he said, leaning his head back against the back of the couch and closing his eyes. Whether he was in the desert or somewhere else, Fate knew he was far away. "You make it work. It tests you, living off the land. There's nothing like it. Isn't that right, Hawkeye?"

"Sir, yes sir!" Étienne answered with a sloppy salute.

Matthieu reopened his eyes and shared a smile of camaraderie with the younger man. "You're all right, kid," he said, unaware of the *kid's* cheeks pinking up at the praise. "Drunk, but all right. Leaning over the coffee table, he poured them each another round.

They continued that way for God knew how long—talking, drinking, laughing, and drinking some more—until Fate was pleasantly buzzed, and she was sure the others were too. The fear, anger, and desperation of the last twenty-four hours dissipated into the blur of a hazy memory, while the languid warmth from the drink flowed through her.

It was wonderful, she thought, just for one night to let it all go. Especially after the crazy turn her ordeal with Eli had taken towards the end. *Just let it go*, she told herself. *We'll deal with it all tomorrow.*

A giggle escaped her as the room spun slightly. Matthieu turned to look at her with a heavy lidded gaze and gave her an easy grin. She loved that when he was tired, turned on—or drunk, apparently—he forgot to hide. His emotions played over his face as easily as any other person's, and the warmth she found there stole her breath.

"What's so funny?"

Fate found that she couldn't contain her giggling hysteria over the events of the night. "He had...fangs," she managed between spurts of laughter and gasps for breath. "Eli, I mean."

"That's nothing," Matthieu answered, chugging the last of his beer and wiping his mouth with the back of his hand. "When I shot him, he exploded, and then disappeared." He made an explosive gesture with his hands and mouthed a silent *'boom.'* He kept a straight face for about half a second before busting a gut.

"Oh yeah?" Étienne asked, not willing to be left out. "Guess how I got to Savannah."

"How?" Fate and Matthieu asked at the same time.

"I flew there! I can fly!" he said, stretching out his arms in a drunken pantomime of a bird in flight. That had been the last straw, because the three of them dissolved into raucous laughter before settling down into sleepy, alcohol dazed contentment.

Fate finally noticed Étienne's eyelids drooping, his beer threatening to slip out of his grip. Getting up, she wavered only a little before liberating the bottle, and hauling the kid to his feet. "I think you need to crash," she said, and his answer was a yawn wide enough to pop his jaw.

She felt Matthieu's heated gaze following her as she led Étienne down the hall to her room. She told him to make himself comfortable, and shut the door behind her. As she walked away, she heard the lock engage behind her. That made her pause for a moment, frowning, but she shrugged it off to return to the living room—and Matthieu.

₭₨

Matthieu allowed his eyes to rove over Fate as she returned to him. She was dressed simply in shorts and a tank top, her honey colored hair tumbling over her shoulders. Although his vision swam slightly, the hungry look in her gray eyes was clear. His woman wasn't finished celebrating.

When she reached him, she didn't stop—instead she climbed over him to straddle his hips where he sat on the couch. Instinctively, his hands went to her hips and his fingers flexed there as he fought the urge to pull her down on him. Her Cupid's bow lips curved up in a sultry smile and she did the job for him, pressing closer until there was nothing but clothes between them.

"You gave up your room. Gonna have to find somewhere else to sleep, I guess."

She nuzzled her nose against his cheek, breathing deep. "Guess so."

This time when she tunneled her fingers into his hair and captured his lips with hers, he had no defenses—all of them lost to exhaustion and expensive tequila. He could do nothing but ride the wave of her intoxicating flavor.

Her mouth was exquisite, silky warmth as she drew his tongue inside, sucking gently until he groaned. He was breathing hard when she released him to attack his neck—his biggest weakness—and his head spun from the sensation of her dragging her tongue over his pulse.

His throat worked as he tried to speak, drawing her attention. "You're drunk. I shouldn't be taking advantage of you."

Her warm breath across his ear made him shiver, and her sexy laughter rolled over him. "You're drunk too. It appears as though I might be the one taking advantage," she said, gesturing to their positions.

"Fair point," he agreed, before grabbing thick handfuls of her hair and guiding her back to his mouth. This time he took control, holding her still as he explored her mouth, breaking away with a curse when she writhed against him.

"Christ, woman, you're killing me."

Fate, who appeared wholly unapologetic, tossed her hair back over her shoulders and leaned back to look at him with eyes full of sensual promise. A man could really only take so much. Surging forward, he untangled his hands from her hair, placed them on her curvy backside and lifted.

As he struggled to stand, she obliged him by wrapping her legs around his waist and holding on. He grunted his appreciation and he made his wobbly way into his bedroom, kicking the door shut behind him.

Inside the room, he turned and let her slide down his body, feeling every supple curve along the way. Then he immediately crowded her up against the door, invaded her space and attacked her mouth.

He ran his hands over her, tracing her shape, absorbing the little shivers that rippled through her as he swallowed her throaty moans. He'd given her complete control the last time, to try and give her back a little piece of her confidence. This time, he knew he hadn't the patience for it.

Needing a moment to slow his hammering heart, Matthieu stepped back and set her away from him. He reached out to slide his hands along her ribcage, raising the hem of her tank top along the way, until she raised her arms and allowed him to pull it off.

Next came the shorts, and finally she was standing before him in nothing but her simple cotton bra and panties. That was enough for now, he thought, or this would be over a lot quicker than he intended.

Cocking his head as he stared at her, Matthieu decided to test her limits. She'd gained back a good bit of what she'd lost during their gentle Dominant-submissive play, and he had no desire to dominate her, but there was a certain amount of power to be gained by letting someone else take control—by trusting them to do so.

Her only movement as he studied her was her hands stroking a thick hank of her hair. She wasn't shy or embarrassed—she was simply awaiting his next move. Well, it's now or never, he told himself.

He drew himself up to his full height, took a small step forward and tipped his chin in the direction of the bed. "Get on the bed. On your knees." It wasn't harsh, or loud—in fact, he could hardly be heard over the nighttime noises of the bayou drifting through the open window— but it was an undeniable command. Matthieu held his breath as he waited for her reaction.

He saw a fleeting spark of fear in her eyes, as he'd known he would, but it was quickly dissolved as a flush of anger crept into her skin. For a moment, it looked as if she might tell him *fuck-you-very-much, goodnight,* but then he saw what he was looking for. Her gaze turned dark and her tongue shot out to moisten her lips. Her eyes flickered between his face and the bed, and back again, and an entirely different emotion was signified by the quickening of her breath. Desire.

Without a word, she climbed up onto the middle of the bed with her back to him. Kneeling, her spine straight as it disappeared into the gentle curve of her backside, she tossed a defiant look at him over her shoulder.

Well done, Matthieu thought. *Well done.*

With a series of sloppy movements, Matthieu divested himself of his own clothing before joining Fate on the bed. He was grateful for the inconsequential scrap of cotton that separated him from her—he needed to be reminded to take his time. On his knees as well, he pressed himself up against her back, and used a calloused hand to sweep her hair off her shoulder. He nuzzled her neck, fanning his breath over the sensitive skin below her ear, and watched chill bumps break out across her softness.

He placed his hands on her hips and pulled her back against him, so that they were flush, chest to back, thighs to thighs. His eyes rolled back as the lush softness of her curves pressed against his already straining erection. Unable to help the gentle undulating of his hips, he began a torturous exploration of her body.

He'd never seen anything more beautiful than her. That was what went through his mind as he stroked his hands over her fluttering belly and ran them over her flawless breasts. He teased them through the cotton shroud, rasping his knuckles over her nipples before filling his hands with her.

His gut clenched as his own need began to rise. No woman had ever made him feel this much—this desperate clawing ache. Sliding a hand up over her neck, he tilted her head to the side so that he could feast on her, nipping along the taut tendons there before biting down on her earlobe.

She gasped at the sensation, arching her back like a cat until her long, graceful neck lay back on his shoulder, and she turned her head for a lazy over-the-shoulder kiss. Matthieu had to bite the inside of his cheek to keep from throwing her down on the bed and slaking his own need, when she reached around behind her to dig her blunt nails into his ass. "Matthieu…" she said in a pained whisper, sending delicious shivers down his spine, "…I need you."

And, just like that, he was lost.

CHAPTER TWENTY·NINE

F ATE PROBABLY SHOULD HAVE BEEN PISSED—AFTER
all she'd been through, she normally wouldn't have
been able to take someone ordering her around. And
yet, she understood why he was doing it. In his crazy Matthieu
way, he was showing her that giving up control to someone she
trusted was so entirely different than being abused.

After she'd gotten over her initial reaction to his command,
she'd grown all sorts of melty inside, with heat coiling in her
belly and traveling lower. Something about his soldier-voice just
got to her.

So there she was, kneeling in the middle of the king-size
bed, with her sexy, battle-scarred hero molded to her back. She
was just beginning to learn to associate sex with pleasure
instead of pain, and she was suddenly immersed in more
pleasure than she'd ever thought possible.

Closing her eyes, Fate allowed herself to just feel; to
Matthieu's hard muscles rippling as he continued to explore her

body; to feel his breath rasping across her skin and his lips, tongue and teeth as they burned a trail down her neck to her shoulder.

One of his hands traveled down to dip inside her bikini briefs, stroking and teasing until she was unable to hold back a moan. She slid her own hand up into his hair while rocking her hips back to rub herself against him. She was rewarded with a hiss and a growl, before he dropped his head onto her shoulder.

It made her smile—his reaction—and knowing that even when he was taking the lead, she still had power over him. Power over this dark, brooding soldier who'd turned her world upside down—whose smile felt like a gift because it was as if he saved it only for her.

His gentle touches and barely held control were driving her crazy, her head spinning from alcohol and lust until she had to repeat her whispered request. "Matthieu, please."

Matthieu's entire body tensed for a suspended moment before he was spurred into action. Leaning back, he flicked open the clasp of her bra and she allowed it to slip down her arms. He started to tug down her panties but seemed to think better of it, instead grasping the material in both hands and ripping it in two.

While she was still reeling from the fact that, *holy cow*, she'd literally just had her underwear ripped off of her, Matthieu nudged her legs wider apart with his knee, and sank into her with a powerful jerk of his hips.

All Fate could really do was hang on for the ride, and lose herself in it as he surged into her relentlessly, all the while making little growling noises that caused her stomach to clench with unspent desire.

His hands were everywhere, burying in her hair one minute, sliding over her breasts and belly to grip her hips the next. But it was when he reached down to stroke her in time with his thrusts, and sank his teeth into the fleshy part of her shoulder, that she broke apart, crying out as she was consumed by her release.

Matthieu sucked in a breath as her body gripped him while the tremors rippled through her. When she grew boneless, he gently guided her forward until her head rested on her arms on the bed while he still moved within her. He braced his hands on her hips so tightly that she knew she'd be bruised, but she couldn't bring herself to care—she'd take those kinds of bruises any day.

His breath was coming in short sawing gasps from behind her and his thrusts were becoming erratic. She could feel beads of sweat dripping from his hair onto her back, to mingle with her own. Finally, he bent over to press kisses along her spine and neck as he snapped his hips. Fate could feel the beginnings of another orgasm curling in the pit of her stomach.

When he froze over her, muscles straining with the force of his release, he whispered her name against her ear, and it was the only sound he made. But it was enough. When his warmth filled her, she lost herself again in the sensation of having Matthieu come apart for her.

They both collapsed in a heap on the bed, rolling to their sides to face each other while they caught their breath. Fate couldn't help but watch his face, with its imperfect beauty, as he came back down to earth. His eyes finally focused on her, and there was that smile—the one that crinkled his eyes at the corners.

That smile was just for Fate, as if the sun rose and set with her. Her heart stuttered in her chest as she saw the raw, naked emotion in his expression before he caught himself and closed his eyes. Well, how about that, she thought. She lay there contemplating what that could possibly mean long after his breathing had evened out with sleep.

Deciding there was really no way to know until he told her, Fate chose to savor the moment and snuggled up to him. Even in sleep he sought her out, his arm curling around her to pull her close. Unable to help herself, Fate drifted to sleep with a smile on her face, thinking things would look decidedly brighter in the morning.

CHAPTER THIRTY

IT WAS THE HEAT THAT WOKE HER. BEFORE SHE'D EVEN
opened her eyes, she was consumed by it.   A raging
inferno, it surrounded her, vibrating through her body, and
the bed. When Fate opened her eyes, she fully expected to be
surrounded by a wall of flame and smoke.

But the room was the same as when she'd fallen asleep,
except for the hazy light of morning filtering in through the
window. Even so, the heat still surrounded her, suffocating her,
and the bed really was shaking. Sitting upright, she looked
around the room to find the problem. Matthieu had gotten up
sometime during the night to close the window, so the humid
swamp air wasn't the source of the heat.

She turned to ask Matthieu if he felt it, but stopped short.
Something was wrong. The tremors were coming from him. The
heat was coming from him—it was pumping off of him in waves.
She leaned over to feel his forehead for fever, and simultane-
ously touch his mind like she'd done in the past.

His skin was burning up, and her mind was assaulted with images of smoke and flame. Something was blocking her. "Matthieu?" she whispered, giving him a light shake. An anguished groan tore from his throat before he began thrashing, convulsing.

After dodging a few blows, Fate made a decision that she knew Matthieu would have made if he were conscious. Reaching under the bed, she pulled out the ropes she'd used to tie him up the first time. Grabbing one flailing wrist, she secured it to the headboard, and then tied the other.

It would have to be enough, because she wasn't getting near his legs as a kick from him would probably knock her out cold. The thrashing calmed a bit after he was restrained, although he was still shivering with fever.

Fate lifted one of his eyelids, only to jerk back, cursing. They were those translucent orbs filled with writhing shadows—just like Draconus. Just like Eli.

She was startled when Matthieu's body bowed up off the bed, muscles straining, and he let out a roar. His veins appeared darker, crisscrossing under his skin, and something flickered on his forehead—an image trying to form.

"Oh God," she moaned, hugging her arms to her body, "this is bad. Bad, bad, bad. What is happening?" Whatever it was, she was going to need help. She remembered Étienne in the next room, and though she didn't know how he could help, she didn't want to be alone with this.

So she ran. Flinging the bedroom door open, she careened around the corner and down the hall to her room. She turned the handle, but nothing happened. It was still locked. She knocked, but there was no answer, no sound from inside. "Damn it," she whispered, "Étienne, where are you?"

A hand clamped down on her shoulder and she whirled around with a scream, nearly punching Étienne in the face.

"You called?" he said.

Fate clutched a hand over her racing heart. "Mother of God, don't sneak up on me like that. Something's wrong with Matthieu. He's...sick. I don't know what to do."

The young man frowned, his eyes flicking warily to Matthieu's room. "Let's go see."

She wasn't proud of the way she stayed behind Étienne as she followed him. She knew Matthieu would never hurt her, but she wasn't entirely sure that was Matthieu anymore—and wasn't that just a little bit insane?

When Étienne first saw Matthieu, he stopped short, and Fate nearly slammed into his back. He barely made a sound as he approached Matthieu's side of the bed and repeated what Fate had done, feeling his forehead. When he lifted one of Matthieu's eyelids, he showed no reaction other than growing very still. As if sensing Étienne's presence, Matthieu lunged against the ropes, letting out a howl that caused the boy to jump back.

His eyes were wild when he looked back at Fate.

"What do you think?" she asked.

He shook his head, backing away from the bed slowly, as if he were afraid to leave his back unguarded. "I've never seen anything like it. He's...infected," he whispered.

"Infected? With what?"

"That I'm not sure of. I need to make a call—I know someone who may have a clue what's going on."

"All right," Fate said on a shaky breath. "I need to call Matthieu's brother. He's a doctor." She didn't mention exactly what kind of doctor Jeremiah was, but he needed to know about this. They may not know what's going on, but there seemed to be an unspoken agreement that whatever it was couldn't be handled by calling an ambulance.

ॐ

Jeremiah and Isla were having a mid-morning cup of coffee when the call came. Ridley was outside playing with the cats, and Marduk was watching television in his PJ's, as per usual. The minute the phone rang, Jeremiah felt a fissure of unease rippled through the air. One glance at Isla told him that she'd felt the same. As she answered, Jeremiah could hear Marduk's phone ringing as well, and that didn't bode well.

"Hello?" Isla answered. "Oh, hey...what? Okay, just a sec." Jeremiah frowned when Isla held the phone out to him. "It's Fate. She says she needs to talk to you."

Jere rolled his eyes, imagining all of the trouble his little brother could have gotten that woman into. "For chrissakes, what's he done now?"

He could hear a murmured conversation coming from the other room as he reached for the phone. "Hey Fate, what's goin' on?"

The voice that came on the line was halting and shaky. "Hi, Jeremiah. Listen...we were planning on calling you when we got back from Savannah because some...weird things have been going on lately, and Matthieu said that they may be in your...area of expertise. But now...something's wrong with Matthieu."

A bolt of fear shot through Jeremiah's gut when he heard that. He took a deep breath and tried to keep his voice calm to keep Fate from panicking. "What do you mean? What's wrong?"

"Everything was fine when we went to bed but this morning he's—he's unconscious and burning up. He's having convulsions and thrashing around...I had to restrain him."

For the life of him, Jeremiah couldn't fathom why she was on the phone with him, rather than 911. "For cryin' out loud, call an ambulance!"

"No! It's not like that. It's—he's got something on his forehead, and his eyes—"

"Fuck. Okay, we're going to drop Ridley off at my mom's. Hang tight, we're on our way."

Jeremiah didn't wait for a reply. He rang off and met his wife's wild eyed look with one of his own. "I don't know how, but they've gotten to Matthieu. We've got to get down there."

Before he'd even finished the sentence, Marduk charged into the kitchen looking grim. "I've just gotten a call from a *feradux* in Theriot. They've got trouble, and his *domina* doesn't know about him yet. I'm wondering if this might have something to do with your brother and his girl."

"Let's roll," Jeremiah said.

CHAPTER THIRTY·ONE

F ATE WAS CURLED UP NEXT TO MATTHIEU, STROKING his hair and trying to calm some of his fitful movements, when a loud pounding at the front door made her jump. "That'll be Jeremiah," she told him, talking to him as if he were a coma patient, assuming he may be able to hear her. "He'll know what to do.

She shivered as she left Matthieu's room, huddling into her favorite oversized sweatshirt. She'd set the thermostat on arctic to try and combat some of his infernal heat. When she flung the door open, she exhaled a shaky breath she hadn't known she'd been holding. Reinforcements, finally.

A grim-faced Jeremiah stood on the doorstep with an arm around a worried looking, and very pregnant Isla. The tall young man who lived with them—Fate couldn't recall his name—stood behind them, looking as gloomy as the last time she'd seen him.

"Thank God you're here. Please, come in," she said, realizing how ridiculous that was, considering Jeremiah's family owned the place.

When the three of them came inside, they all immediately shivered. "Why is it so bloody cold in here?" Isla asked.

"You'll understand once you see Matthieu. He's in the back bedroom." Fate beckoned for them to follow her.

Upon entering the room, she was blasted in the face by the wall of heat that surrounded the room, and she heard her visitors gasp behind her when they felt it too. Jeremiah walked around her to the edge of the bed, staring down at his brother. Isla and Marduk—she finally remembered—came up behind him, a silent wall of support.

Jeremiah's head whipped around and he pegged her with an accusing glare. "Why is he tied up?"

Fate lifted her chin a fraction and returned his glare with a cool one of her own. "His convulsions were becoming...violent. I can tell you that this is what he would want me to do. We've even discussed it before—he'd never forgive himself if he hurt someone while in this condition."

He considered her words for a tense moment before nodding and turning back around. "I'd like a moment alone with my brother, please," he said to no one in particular.

Isla and Marduk turned to leave, and Isla grabbed Fate's hand to tug her along. "He's in good hands," Isla whispered. Fate could only give her a weak nod.

When they returned to the great room, Fate heard light tapping on the back door. "That'll be our friend Étienne," she told them, frowning at the look that was shared between Isla and Marduk.

Crossing to the door, Fate let him in, but he froze when he saw that they weren't alone. "Étienne, this is Matthieu's sister-in-law Isla, and her friend Marduk. Jeremiah is in with Matthieu now."

"Good to meet you." He nodded to Isla and bowed his head to Marduk. It was odd, Fate thought, how he waited for Marduk to return the gesture before straightening up.

Isla stepped forward and took her hand again. "Why don't we all have a seat and you can tell us what happened, shall we?"

Grateful for something to do, Fate allowed herself to be led to a seat. Isla was face was kind, welcoming, which was a stark contrast to the tension Jeremiah had been giving off. The tiny woman with riotous black curls smiled at her companion. "Marduk, why don't you make tea?"

Étienne nearly knocked himself off of his perch on the arm of the couch as he scrambled toward the kitchen. "No, no, I'll do it. You all just sit." Fate just stared after him, unable to figure out his peculiar behavior. *Oh well, I've got bigger things to worry about than a nervous Hawkeye.*

"Fate, when you talked to Jeremiah, you said that you and Matthieu had already decided to call us before this lat-est...event. So that would mean that things were going on before that you were worried about. Can you tell me about it?"

Fate studied her hands as she tried to decide how much to share. A lot of the things that had happened were related to Matthieu and his secrets—ones she knew he wouldn't thank her for sharing. But if his life depended on it...

"Matthieu has dreams—nightmares really. In fact, I'd call them night terrors, but I know he'd object to the term."

"About the war."

"Some, yes. There are other things...but we'll get to that. Anyway, the dreams had gotten so bad that he was avoiding sleep—literally going until he collapsed and had to sleep. That's the kind of state he was in when we met."

"How awful for him," Isla said with a pained expression.

"As for me, I've always had this...ability, where I'm able to touch something—an object, a person, animal—anything, and get a vision of its history. Growing up, I learned to control it and even suppress it to an extent. It was necessary because that kind of 'psychic hoo-doo nonsense just wasn't the thing' in my mother's garden party world. That's a direct quote by the way, but I digress. With Matthieu in particular, however, I can't control it. When he's having these dreams, I touch him and I'm right there in the middle of it—seeing what he's seeing."

"Psychometry." Jeremiah spoke from behind them, before rounding the couch to join his wife.

"Pardon?" Fate said, confused.

"That's what it's called. A phenomenon in which one can touch an object or person to divine facts about its history. Although I think you may have some kind of mutation of it, as I've never heard of dream walking or being able to read actual people, rather than objects."

"Mutation. Lovely."

"How's Matthieu?" Isla interrupted.

"My brother seems to be having a crisis of identity."

"What does that mean?" Fate asked.

Jeremiah sighed and scrubbed both hands over his face, in a gesture so like Matthieu, it made Fate's heart hurt. When he looked over at her, his eyes were sad but his jaw was set with stubborn intent. "Look, we're going to have to dump a whole lot of information on you in very little time—most of it you're not going to want to believe. You'll have to forgive me, but I don't have time to hold your hand. My brother's life may be at stake here."

Isla sucked in a sharp breath and Fate nearly winced at the terse tone, but she knew it was worry for Matthieu driving it.

She took a deep breath and gave him a jerky nod. "I'm a big girl. I can handle it. Besides, I think I'll surprise you with how much I believe."

A look of grudging respect came over his face, and Fate thought maybe they would be okay. "Crisis of identity...what made you put it like that?" she asked.

Jeremiah leveled narrowed eyes at her. "Why? That mean something to you?"

"Possibly. When Matthieu—I can't describe his dreams to you. I won't. But lately, Matthieu seemed to be under the impression that he wasn't entirely himself. Like he wasn't alone in his own skin, if that makes any sense."

"Yeah, it does, actually," he said, before turning to Isla. "I think one of those bastards marked him. Invaded him. I think we're going to need backup."

"Raven?" Isla asked.

Jeremiah shook his head. "I was thinking Leora."

"What bastards? Who's Leora?" Fate was beginning to feel like the village idiot in this situation and it was annoying her.

Jeremiah leaned forward and braced his hands on his knees. "Okay, crash course. You have a marking somewhere on your body—you know what I'm talking about. Show it to me."

"I don't—"

"My love," he said to Isla, "if you'd be so kind."

Isla turned her back on Fate and lifted her heavy mass of hair, revealing a brand very similar to Fate's own, on the back of her neck.

"Fate...please," Jeremiah said.

Her belly clenched with nerves as she rolled up her sleeve and unsnapped the leather cuff she always wore. Holding out her arm, she presented them with the inside of her wrist.

"Do you have any idea what this represents?"

"Not a clue."

"I see. I think it's best if I let Isla explain, since she's in the same boat."

Fate frowned at him. This whole being on the fringe deal was not working for her. Somebody had better cough up some explanations, like yesterday.

"I'm a witch," Isla said without preamble.

"I beg your pardon?" Fate said as her eyebrows rose to her hairline. Matthieu hadn't mentioned his sister-in-law being touched in the head, but Fate was pretty sure she heard what she thought she heard.

Isla sighed, as if she were gearing up for a long story. "It's not a religion or anything; it's the way I was born. With...powers—kind of like your psychometry. Jeremiah and I started researching my background and it turns out I come from an ancient race of witches called *Bruixi*, and actually so do you. We're distantly related, which could explain the whole psychometry thing."

Fate resisted the urge to squirm under Jeremiah and Isla's unrelenting stares. They watched her closely for her reaction. "Okay. Assuming I buy that—not saying I do, but admittedly, there've been a lot of strange things going on lately—what makes you think that I'm one of these *Bruixi* people?"

"Fair question," Jeremiah said. "We were tipped off about Isla and Raven's third distant relative by a sort of prophesy. Raven is Drew's wife, by the way. Anyway, that mark is what tells us we're right."

Isla jumped back in, the two of them a perfect tag-team. "The mark signifies a particular bloodline within the race called the *Vigilati*. Bear with me, love...here's where it starts to get a little dodgy. The *Vigilati* were bred for a specific purpose—keepin' evil in the spirit world where it belongs. With me so far?"

"Theoretically," Fate said. She wasn't sure where Isla was going with this fairy tale, but she did want to hear it.

"Good. So all over the world, there are access points where the veil between the spirit world and the living is thin. We call them *locuses*. On pinnacle days during the year, especially Samhain and Beltane, it's said that the veil lifts so that what was contained has a chance to roam free.

"During these times the *Lochrim*—the demon who lives within the locus—will attempt to gain access to the human world. That is what the *Vigilati* live to prevent. Up until recently, the trait skipped a generation, but now we've reason to believe that it's happening more often."

Isla reached out and grabbed Fate's wrist, looking at the symbol there. "The three circles represent the spirit world, the world of the living, and the veil that separates them," she said. "The perpendicular slashes represent the *locus* itself—it's modeled after ancient standing stones, which were often present at locuses in the past."

Fate waited for Isla to explain the rest, but she remained silent, contemplative. "What about the thing in the middle?"

"Ah yes, that's a bit more complicated. I won't burden you with that part just yet."

She wasn't having that. Fate scrunched her brows and pinned Isla with a hard stare. "If you say I'm a part of this, I need to know it all. Besides, I know this is the important part," she said, pointing at the image inside the circle. "This is the part that involves Matthieu."

Husband and wife shared a concerned look before Isla drew a deep breath to continue. "From our research and…experience over the last year and a half, we've managed to prove a phenomenon that was only legend for the *Bruixi* before now. Through possession, manipulation, glamor—whatever means necessary—*Lochrim* have the ability to sire a *Vigilati* child. Those children could either grow up to be the death of the demon, or a boon that could possibly win the battle for him. The children are called *Praedos*. The symbol in the center of the circle is the *seal* of the *Lochrim* who fathered the *Praeda.* What do you know about your father, Fate?"

Fate blinked several times, trying to comprehend all that Isla was implying—no, outright stating. "Absolutely nothing. My only father figures growing up were my mother's few husbands, but she's never been willing to talk about my father." Isla nodded as if it made perfect sense to her, and Fate wished she'd damn well explain it to *her.*

A hand landed on Fate's shoulder, causing her to jump a foot out of her chair. "Oh, my God!" she yelped, before realizing it was just Etienne bringing her tea. "Gonna have to put a bell on you." This got a snort from Marduk, which is the most interest he'd shown since they showed up.

Etienne merely smiled and took a seat on the floor next to Fate's feet, much in the same manner as Marduk did with Isla.

"And then there are the *feradux*," Isla said, her eyes sparkling.

"The who now?"

"*Feradux*," Jeremiah repeated. "Whiny, sulky, bratty animal guides."

Marduk gnashed his teeth at Jeremiah—teeth that looked a little too long for Fate's comfort—before Isla petted his head. "Wiccans believe in *familiars*—an animal with whom a witch has a magical connection. With the *Vigilati,* each *Vigile* has an animal spirit guide to help her in the fight against these demons. Marduk is mine. Looks like Étienne is yours."

Étienne tilted his head back to give Fate a shy smile, but she just stared back in confusion. "Okay, but I don't get the animal part."

"They're shapeshifters," Jeremiah said. "Marduk is a flea bitten mutt—"

"A wolf," Isla said. "And Étienne is...?"

"Hawk," he answered quietly.

Fate stared down at him in open-mouthed shock. "I've seen you! Always out there watching me. No wonder you said you live off the land. Hawkeye," she said with a snort. She felt that if she didn't laugh, she might burst into hysterical tears. "I'm definitely going to have more questions about this later. Like, a lot of questions. But what's all this got to do with what's wrong with Matthieu?"

Jeremiah rubbed his eyes before turning a sad glance toward the back bedroom. "What's going on with him is similar to what we've seen in the past with *Lochrim* possession. Similar, but not exact."

"What's different about Matthieu?" Fate's brow furrowed as she tried to make sense of the overwhelming rush of information.

"It's difficult for me to explain when you haven't seen it. A human possessed by a *Lochrim* is still fully functional, only their mind is completely under the control of the demon. Matthieu is, for all intents and purposes, catatonic. It's not the *Lochrim's* usual M.O."

"How would you normally help someone who was possessed?"

Fate's attention was pulled back to Isla when she shared a troubled look with Marduk, before turning back. "Normally, I can use my powers to isolate the *Lochrim's* energy and push him out."

"So do that!"

"I've tried already. Matthieu's situation is...complicated. I can't seem to be able to differentiate between the two different energy sources. It's like Matthieu's been integrated with whatever entity is holding him hostage."

Shooting out of her seat, Fate began to pace around the room. "So what are we going to do? How do we help him?"

"This leads me back to the one person who can help us," Jeremiah said. "I'm sorry Fate, but the explanation will probably blow your mind. What's left of it, anyway. Leora, the woman I mentioned before, is a *Bruixi* goddess, and she's sort of our ace in the hole. We summon her when things get rough and she helps us as much as she can."

Fate wanted to laugh, to scream, to throw things. A goddess? What next, mermaids? Honestly it was as believable as all the other crap they'd thrown at her, and she didn't have time to let it marinate. She just wanted Matthieu to be okay.

"Fine. What are you waiting for? Call her."

"Not call, summon," Jeremiah said, his patient tone grating.

"What*ever*! I don't care if you have to get in your special spaceship and fly to the moon to find her. Just help Matthieu."

Jeremiah stared at her for several tense moments before his mouth quirked up in a half smile. "Yes ma'am." He turned to his wife and handed her another book that he'd pulled out of a serious looking briefcase. "We should call Raven. We need her power to help Leora to manifest."

"Oh, bugger that. We don't have time. I'm stronger now. Marduk and I can handle it," Isla said fiercely.

Jeremiah raised his hands in a capitulating gesture. Clearly it was an old argument, and he was picking his battles. "Let's do it, then."

CHAPTER THIRTY·TWO

FATE WATCHED, FEELING A LITTLE BIT HELPLESS, AS Isla and Marduk knelt down on the floor and joined hands. She took long, slow breaths to control her nerves. She was trying desperately to keep it together. She knew she hadn't processed all the crazy they had just dumped on her, and she was probably due for a giant meltdown when all was said and done.

But not right now...now was about Matthieu. She straightened her spine and pulled her resolve around her like a warm blanket. She would handle this, as she'd handled all of the other what-the-fuckery in her life—head on.

Isla turned kind and patient eyes up to her. "I know it hasn't all sunk in yet, dearling, but we could use your help. Whether you knew about it or not, there's power in you. It takes all we've got to summon a goddess." She motioned for Fate to kneel and take her other hand.

Fate swallowed down her trepidations as she lowered herself to the floor and clasped Isla's hand. She was shocked by the immediate sensation of energy shimmering under her skin from the contact.

Isla gave her hand a reassuring squeeze when Fate would have tried to pull away. "It's a good thing," she said. "We make each other stronger." She then nodded her dark head at Étienne, who immediately dropped to Fate's other side and took her hand.

"What now?" Fate asked, not proud of the way her voice trembled.

"We close our eyes, speak the words, and hope she hears them."

Her three companions closed their eyes, and Fate reluctantly followed suit. A shiver ran down her spine as Isla began to speak.

"*Vetera novis per loqui et respondere moment.* Mother Goddess, come to us. We need you now more than ever. *Matre dea nobis veniat.*"

There were a few moments of silence before Isla broke her handholds and stood up. Fate looked around the room, and felt foolish for having expected something to happen. "Um, so…where is she?"

Jeremiah gave her a wry smile. "Leora always does things on her own damn terms. No telling when—"

"Or where," Drew interrupted.

"—she'll show up." Jeremiah got up and crossed the room, unlocking and cracking the back door.

Seriously? He thought she was just going to walk in the back door, Fate thought. She flinched as a headache began to throb between her eyes. "So we just wait? Does Matthieu have time for that?" she asked, sounding a little desperate, even to her own ears.

Any reply Jeremiah would have made was cut off when a gust of cool wind blasted through the back door, sliding it the rest of the way open. Fate knew that the bayou was as hot and muggy as ever, without a cloud in the sky, so she had no explanation for the sudden gale.

All eyes watched the door as a tiny woman glided through it. Literally glided—as in her feet didn't touch the floor. The woman wore a gauzy white gown and her dark hair fell in glossy ropes down to her hips. Fate's gaze was quickly drawn to her milky white, unseeing eyes.

This woman was magick personified. She was ethereal, haunting. And she was familiar. Fate was unable to stifle a gasp as she recognized the woman as her 'guardian angel'—the one who'd visited her during difficult times throughout her life.

Fate stood up so fast that her head spun, and she had to grab onto Étienne to steady herself.

The woman's sightless stare focused on the movement, and she smiled. "It's good to finally meet you, *ma petit lumière*. I am Leora." She turned to Isla. "Hello again, daughter. I see you've found your light."

As Isla nodded, Jeremiah stepped forward, his mouth held in a grim line. "Beg your pardon…I know we'd all love to hang out and catch up, but we summoned you because we have an emergency. We need help."

Leora's delicate brow furrowed as she listened. "Of course, young one. What has happened?"

"It's my brother."

"Ah, I knew he would be a difficult egg to crack, no? Is he resisting his role in the battle to come?" she asked.

The conversation was completely lost on Fate, so she stood back and let Jeremiah handle things. Apparently Matthieu had some kind of part to play in all this madness.

"We never got that far," Jeremiah answered. "Something's gotten to him. He's...it's like nothing I've ever seen before. We don't know what to do."

Leora frowned. It was an expression that looked out of place on her usually tranquil face. "Take me to him," she commanded.

The mood of the group was somber as they filed into Matthieu's room. Fate climbed onto the bed next to Matthieu, while Jeremiah, Isla, Marduk, and Étienne surrounded the bed. Leora sailed in around them and went to the opposite side of the bed.

Matthieu had calmed into a catatonic state, but when Leora's presence filled the room, he began to writhe and scream again.

With lines etched in her face that hadn't been there moments before, Leora stepped forward and placed a hand on his forehead. *"Non. Paix."* Peace.

Instantly, his thrashing movements calmed, but Leora didn't remove her hand. Instead, she slid it down to the scar on Matthieu's stubbly cheek. She jerked back with a hiss, and the large *signa* on her face began to rotate.

"This is...most unusual," she said, her voice quivering just a bit.

Well that was reassuring, Fate thought. "What is it?" she asked.

Leora shared a tense look with Fate before turning to Jeremiah. "He's been touched. Marked by the blood of a *Lochrim*. He has been living with a piece of it inside him, but fighting it—until now. The battle is slipping out of his favor."

Jeremiah paled and sank down onto the end of the bed. Running a shaky hand through his unruly brown hair, he turned anguished eyes to the goddess. "How can we help him? There's got to be something."

Horrified by what Leora was suggesting, and what she might say next, Fate suddenly wanted to shield Matthieu from any negativity. If Leora was going to say there's nothing to be done, she didn't want him to hear it.

"Why don't we let Matthieu rest? We can talk about it in the other room." She placed a kiss on his forehead, climbed off the bed and left the room. The others followed shortly after, looking shell shocked.

Five faces turned to Leora expectantly. The dainty woman eased herself down on the couch and folded her hands in her lap. "Being a line of natural witches, the *Bruixi* rarely have to rely on spells, but in certain dire cases we must utilize them. You have to perform a ceremony to break the demon's hold on the boy."

"Like an exorcism?" Jeremiah asked, looking a bit scandalized.

"Not exactly," Leora said. "An exorcism is performed to try and expel an evil spirit from an inflicted person's body. The *Lochrim* cannot be expelled. He must be destroyed in order for the hold to be broken completely."

"So what would this ceremony do?" Isla questioned.

"You would have to cast a circle and combine your power to perform a dispossession—a ritual that would temporarily break the demon's hold on Matthieu so that he could fight it once again. I fear it is a short-lived solution. Eventually the demon will pull him under again—or keep trying until it finally breaks him."

Fate's throat closed up around her protest before it could burst out. The thought of her strong, virulent soldier succumbing to the will of that…creature, well, it was just too much. It didn't bear thinking about. So she wouldn't.

"What do we need? How do we do it? I'd imagine that the longer we leave him like this," she gestured toward the bedroom, "the less likely he is to come out of it." She turned to Leora and prayed for her to say she was wrong.

"I would imagine that you are correct," she said instead. She turned to Jeremiah and Isla when she next spoke. "You still have my Book of Shadows."

Jeremiah nodded. "It's locked up in my briefcase, along with the Grimoire." Fate had learned that the Grimoire was a book of *Bruixi* history that Jeremiah had found in Rome, and it eventually led him to Isla.

"In the back of that book are a few spells and rituals that I have learned of and even created over the years. Most of them are in French, but some have yet to be transcribed from the original *Bruixi* Latin. I believe you'll need the help of young Dr. Deveraux."

Jeremiah's brows dipped low over his hazel eyes. "But you—"

"I cannot help you in this. I can only guide your way. You know this, young one."

Isla placed a comforting hand on her husband's knee. "We can do this, love. Leora will tell us what we need."

"You need, of course, the three sisters—the dark, the light, and the in-between. The mates should be there as well, to strengthen their power," Leora answered.

"Sisters?" Fate asked. This was all going just a bit over her head.

Isla took pity on her and gave her a small smile. "She means us, dear. You, myself, and Raven. We're all three of us descended from Leora, so she calls us sisters."

Leora nodded, continued. "The wolf and the hawk should be present as well. Would that we still had the cougar, but we shall make do with her in our hearts."

Fate gasped as she suddenly felt the mood in the room turn cold. Isla discreetly wiped away a tear, and Marduk surged to his feet to pace. Fate was sure there was a story behind the disappearance of Raven's *feradux* and she'd find out eventually, but she only had thoughts for Matthieu in the present moment.

"Follow the spell to the letter," Leora said. "Follow it and pray that it works."

ഇ⊃യ

Fate huddled in the plush La-Z-Boy, wrapped in an oversized sweater to ward off the frigid temperature of the living room. She still had the air conditioner cranked up high to offset the cloud of heat in Matthieu's room.

She continued to sit silently, observing as the newcomers trickled in. Her skin prickled with anxiety and she felt over-whelmed by the growing crowd. It was funny that she could deal with stories of demons, witches, and goddesses seemingly much better than she could a room full of strangers. Not that she was particularly dealing with any of it but, positive thinking and all that.

Étienne had given up on the tea and brought her a steaming mug of coffee, God bless the boy. Her eyes rolled back in her head as she took her first gulp of the rich beverage and let the aroma surround her. Feeling more settled with coffee in hand and Étienne at her feet, Fate turned to survey their visitors with a little more interest.

She had to admit, they were quite an unusual pair. The first to enter had been a tall man with a headful of honey blonde curls and sparkling blue eyes that crinkled at the corners. He had the tanned skin, square jaw, and dimples that bespoke a classic American boy. Although, as he and Jeremiah conversed with their heads together, Fate heard a faint accent, much like a watered down version of Étienne's French-Cajun.

The woman who'd come in after him seemed to be his complete opposite in every way Fate could see. She was tiny—even shorter than Isla, barely topping five feet—but her presence seemed to fill the room. There was some kind of mixed heritage there, Native American maybe, or Creole in this area—it read in her burnished copper skin, sharp jaw, and thick, dark brows.

Must be Raven, Fate thought. She had long, dark brown hair pulled back in a sleek tail, with cornrows at her temples that gave it a Mohawk effect. Dressed simply in a white t-shirt and ratty jeans, Raven maintained an air of indifference, but Fate could see her shrewd amber eyes bouncing around the room.

She moved with lithe grace as she sauntered through the living room and plopped down on the couch. "God, it's colder than a witch's titty in here!"

"Pun intended?" Jeremiah asked, lifting his head up and raising a brow.

Raven merely flipped him off over her shoulder and turned in Fate's direction. She cocked her head in a curious manner that made Fate ache for Matthieu again.

"So you're the third, eh?"

Fate's head was spinning, on information overload, and she felt like she was headed for a crash. Trying to avoid losing it completely, she shrugged and looked down at her hands. "Apparently."

"Leave 'er alone, Rave," Isla said gently. "She's had a long day. We've got to focus on helping Matthieu just now, then we'll deal with all the rest." She sat down next to Raven and gave the other woman a sharp stare. "Remember, sweeting, you owe him."

Her jaw tightened but she nodded. "I know. That's why I brought my luscious, adorable, brainy husband to translate shit for Sergeant Cobra in there."

"Thank you," Fate croaked, then cleared her throat and tried again. "Thank you."

Raven nodded and looked over her shoulder at Drew and Jeremiah. "Boys, come on over, we haven't got all day."

"Yes, Mother," Jeremiah mumbled as he came over to sit by his wife, and Drew did the same.

Isla smiled at Fate and an unexpected calm washed over her, as if Isla knew exactly what she was feeling and understood.

"Fate, this is Jeremiah's best friend, Dr. Andrew Deveraux, and you met his wife, Raven."

When Drew reached out a hand for her to shake, Fate took it. "Drew, please," he said. "Let's get down to business, shall we?"

God, yes. Please, let's. She thought it, but all she really managed was a weak nod. Apparently Drew needed no further encouragement.

Jeremiah lugged his locking briefcase onto the coffee table and popped the combo. He first took out a thick, ancient-looking book. It was leather bound with a *Vigilati signa* embossed in the hide of the cover. Next, he took out a much thinner volume, also leather bound but obviously much newer. The *signa* was crudely burned into its cover.

"This is Leora's Book of Shadows," Drew explained for Fate's benefit as he gently lifted the newer book. "It's basically part spellbook, part journal. There's a section in the back here that's marked Rituals. It has all kinds of stuff—blessings, summoning, invocations, dispossessions...extractions."

"Dispossession," Jeremiah said, stopping Drew's rambling. "That's what Leora said we had to do. Will you be able to translate it?"

Drew donned a pair of wire-rimmed reading glasses and scanned the page. "It's written in a mixture of French and *Bruixi* Latin. Give me a few minutes and I should be able to figure it out."

He studied the book where it rested in his lap, one hand turning the page while the other rested on his wife's leg and slid into a hole in her jeans. Fate found it fascinating to watch, really, as he mumbled and hummed to himself while absently stroking Raven's skin. It was such an intimate gesture that she almost felt like looking away. Almost.

Drew's brow furrowed and he frowned down at the page. Abruptly, he snapped his fingers at Jeremiah without looking up. "Got a notebook? Pen?"

Jeremiah dug out the requested items from his briefcase and passed them over. Drew pushed his glasses up on his nose and began scribbling furiously, grumbling and chewing on the pen whenever he paused.

The tension built in the room as they all waited. No one made a sound; no one dared interrupt Drew's train of thought. Fate thought she might explode from the waiting, anticipating the outcome that would decide Matthieu's fate.

His face darkened briefly before he took his glasses off to rub his eyes. Fate sat forward, wanting so much to fire off a hundred questions, but Étienne placed a staying hand on her back.

"What've you got, brother?" Jeremiah asked. "Tell me we can pull this off. Please."

Drew cleared his throat as his face settled into hard lines. "We have a shot to pull this off. But...shit, man, it's fucking dangerous."

"Dangerous for Matthieu?" Fate asked, eyes wide.

"For all of us."

Jeremiah bared his teeth, flashed his overlong canines. "Don't care. We're doing it. Anyone doesn't want to risk it, there's the door. No harm, no foul."

Not a one of them moved. Fate was finally able to let out the breath she'd been holding. It felt like she'd been holding it forever, waiting for an answer. They were here. They would help. "What's the plan?"

"First, you all need to understand what we're risking here," Drew said. "This dispossession, it ain't no joke. We have to temporarily disable the barrier between us and the *Lochrim*. Essentially, by casting a circle, we'll be creating our own *locus*—and then busting it wide open like it was the witching hour on Samhain." Drew looked around, making eye contact with each of them, communicating the seriousness of the situation. "This could go fuck-all to hell really quickly. Especially since we don't know how the *Lochrim* got to him in the first place."

Oh, hell, Fate thought. She'd hoped it wouldn't come to this. Could she break Matthieu's confidence if it meant saving his life? He may be grateful in the end. He may never forgive her. "Would that matter?" she asked. "Knowing how."

Drew stared at her for a few seconds before shrugging. "No way to tell without knowing. Got something you need to say, Fate?"

Fate looked down at her shaking hands, twisting in her lap, before heaving a deep sigh. "I was reluctant to say anything because I didn't exactly obtain the information from Matthieu...willingly. It was a dream—or a memory...whatever. We talked about it after, so he knows I know."

She stopped, throat closing up, feeling betrayal burn in her gut. She wanted to be someone Matthieu could trust. Lord knew he had precious little of that in his life. But, even after such a short time, Fate wasn't ready to face a world without him in it—even if he hated her.

Isla gave her a sympathetic look and squeezed her knee. "I know you feel uncomfortable telling Matthieu's secrets. You wouldn't be a good friend if you didn't. But if it could help save his life..."

"I know," Fate answered miserably. Before she could lose her nerve, she looked directly into Jeremiah's eyes, knowing what she was about to say would affect him the most. "It was a blood exchange. The man—demon cut himself with a claw, and then cut Matthieu."

Jeremiah closed his eyes and cursed. "When?"

"It was the day your father died," she answered, and he sure as hell didn't have anything to say after that revelation.

"The *Lochrim*—did you see anything on his forehead? His *seal*?" Drew asked, giving his friend a moment to recover.

Fate nodded, held out her wrist and tapped it. "This one. The Jackal."

"It's that goddamned scar on his face, isn't it?" Jeremiah barked out of the blue, startling her. "The one that never healed right and he would never tell us where he fucking got it."

Still breathing hard, she jerked her head in acknowledgement. "That's all I really feel comfortable saying without his permission. Do you think this could help him, Drew?"

Fate's stomach lurched when Drew sighed and scrubbed a hand over his face. "No. It may make the dispossession even harder to pull off. But knowing this, I'm certain now that he won't be completely free until we've destroyed—"

"Draconus. That's his name. In the dream—memory—it seemed like he was under the impression that Matthieu would bring his daughter to him. I guess that means me, according to you all," she said with a delicate shudder.

Her head whipped around as another roar rent the air, and Matthieu's bedframe began to creak. "Whatever the risks, we need to do this now."

Jeremiah nodded, still looking pale and shaken from the news of his brother's encounter with the demon. He looked at Drew, his face hollowed out and blank. "What do we need to do?"

"I'm going to need a few more minutes to work out the translation for the actual spell. Don't want to run the risk of getting something wrong. Meantime, we're going to need some supplies. There any kind of store in this godforsaken swamp?"

"Yeah, there's a general store up the road a ways," Jeremiah answered, finally tuned back into the conversation. "Give us the list, Drew."

"Ah, okay. Some of it's pretty basic—chalk, salt, candles. Then it gets a little weird. We'll need an *athame*, a chalice, some sage and a feather for cleansing."

"What's an *athame*?" Fate interjected.

"It's a ceremonial knife or dagger, usually double-edged," Drew answered absently, distracted by his translations.

Fate jumped up and headed to Matthieu's room. "I have an idea," she called over her shoulder. Quickly locating Matthieu's scuffed combat boots, she grabbed what she was looking for and hurried back out to the living room. She handed Drew one of Matthieu's folding combat knives, a wicked looking, half-serrated, double edged weapon. "I thought maybe it would help if it was something connected to Matthieu. Will this work?"

Drew turned it over in his hands before unfolding the blade to examine it. "Yeah, I don't see why not. Good thinking," he told her with a smile. "Jere, why don't you, Isla, and Étienne go to the store to look for this shit? Everyone else can stay here and look after Matthieu while I finish translating."

"Sounds like a plan."

Isla gave her husband a sympathetic look. "Love, I don't think we can find those things at a general store in the middle of the swamp."

Jeremiah just winked at her and grinned. "We can if the owner of said store is the local voodoo priestess who might happen to owe yours truly a favor or two. We just need to visit *Madame* Amara's back room and we'll be all set."

"And I know where we can get a feather," Étienne dead-panned, surprising a laugh out of Jeremiah.

"Kid's funny," he said to Fate. Then he turned to his wife and her *feradux*. "Let's get going. Deveraux will most assuredly have those passages translated by the time we get back."

Drew flipped him off without looking up from his notebook.

Fate chewed at her nails while she watched the three of them leave. She suddenly felt very alone, sitting in a shack with a possessed Matthieu, a shapeshifter, and two virtual strangers.

CHAPTER THIRTY·THREE

MADAME AMARA LEFLEUR WAS AS STUNNING AS she was terrifying. The proprietress of LeFleur's General Store was a statuesque woman of indeterminate age. To Jeremiah's discerning eye, she didn't look much older than him, but he remembered her from his trips to Theriot as a boy—and she'd looked like a full grown woman even back then.

Maybe she'd stumbled on some kind of voodoo fountain of youth. She was of mixed heritage, although no one could quite pin down what the mix consisted of. She had coffee-colored skin just a shade darker than Raven's, and her hair fell down her back in a mass of thin dreadlocks adorned will all manner of shells, feathers, crystals, and other talismans.

Her eyes were a startling light green against her dark skin and lashes, although the left one was now filmed over with a cataract. Jeremiah doubted she could see through it but, much like Leora, Amara had always seen much more than anyone else.

LeFleur's General Store was housed in an old fishing shack similar to Paul Rousseau's, except the fact that half of the building was suspended over the swamp on hefty pylons. The inside was all unfinished wood paneling, and a lot of the wares were piled in halves of old liquor barrels. It was innocuous enough—unless you went to the back room.

As a parapsychologist and a native Orleanian, Jeremiah had learned a healthy respect for the voodoo community. A few years back, Amara had fallen on hard times and he'd been in a position to help her. Since he was known for investigating the validity of paranormal phenomena and writing both fiction and nonfiction books about his findings, he'd suggested doing a piece on voodoo to his editor. The project had actually turned into a documentary series about the local witchcraft and folklore, and the money Amara had been paid to share a few of her secrets on film had allowed her to keep her store running.

Jeremiah gestured for his wife and Marduk to explore the store while Amara was helping a customer. No one had ever been able to figure out Amara's accent either. It was pure Cajun laced with something that sounded possibly Caribbean, or even West-Indian. Jeremiah had always thought Haitian, but he didn't think he'd ever know.

Isla and Marduk wandered off to look at the variety of wares in the rustic store, while Jeremiah leaned against the counter, studying its contents and discreetly eavesdropping on the conversation.

The woman speaking in hushed tones to Amara struck him as pretty ridiculous, almost a caricature of what women were told men were supposed to want. She was model thin and her spindly legs were covered in garish hot pink skinny pants, and she teetered on absurdly high heels. The face that was framed by over-processed brownish-blond hair may have looked pretty from a distance, but up close, it was decidedly masculine.

Jeremiah listened with detached amusement as Amara handled her customer.

"So y'say ya wan' a love spell for yer boyfrien'?" Amara asked, her lip curling slightly.

He knew the priestess detested weak willed women, but those were usually the ones that sought her particular brand of help.

Skinny Jeans' brow furrowed before she shook her head. "I don't care about love," the woman said in a haughty voice that grated on Jeremiah's nerves. "I just don't want him to leave me. I think he might be cheating, but we've just bought a house together and if he leaves, there's no way I can afford it. I need something to keep him with me."

Jere rolled his eyes and tried unsuccessfully to suppress a snort. Amara heard and flicked her eyes towards him and winked, before turning back to her customer.

"Are ya sure 'bout dis? Dese t'ings don' always work out how ya wan' dem to. Even I can't control da universe."

"Yes, yes, whatever. Do you have something to help me or not?"

"Oh, dontcha warry now. *Madame* Amara's got somet'in' far ya." Amara excused herself and disappeared into the back room.

The customer noticed Jeremiah watching, and went out of her way to look down her nose at him, even though she was barely pushing five feet tall. She looked him up and down until he got the impression that he'd been judged and found lacking.

Amara returned carrying a small burlap sachet with unidentifiable symbols painted on it in a substance that looked a little too much like blood. "Ya take a lock a yer hair and one 'a his, braid dem togedah, an' tie it aroun' da sachet. Keep it under 'is pillow far one mont' and he'll be bound ta ya."

The young woman happily paid a small fortune for the sachet and hightailed it out of the shop, probably to head back to the city before she was seen slumming. Amara turned to Jeremiah with a smile in her eyes.

"Well if it isn't the eldah Rousseau, come back t' the sticks. Still gettin' in the same kinds 'a trouble, I'd bet. What brings ya t' Miss Amara's?"

"Just needed to pick up a few things," he said, waving Isla and Marduk over. "Amara, this is my wife, Isla, and our friend, Marduk."

"Good to meet you," Isla said with a wink, and set her basket on the counter. Marduk just nodded stonily.

Amara nodded back before taking a look inside the basket. "Yer gon' be needin' more dan dat, I t'ink."

"Definitely. I think we need to visit the back room," Jeremiah said quietly.

The priestess turned and pinned him with a stare that Jeremiah would swear he felt tickle his soul. "Dat Jackal-mon, he gatcher bradah. You g'wan take care 'a dat?"

"That's the plan, we just need a few supplies," he answered, not really surprised that, again, Amara knew things she couldn't have known.

"Good," Amara said, eyes burning with what looked like hatred. "Amara an' da Jackal-mon 'ad words more dan once. Be glad t' see tha back 'a him. Follah me."

She disappeared through a bead curtain behind the counter, and Jeremiah motioned for Isla to follow him.

"How did she know about that?" Isla whispered.

"If there's one thing I've learned throughout my career, it's don't question a voodoo priestess. Just be glad she's willing to help us."

₨₩₢

Fate was crawling out of her skin while she waited for the others to get back from the store. After she'd stared at Dr. Deveraux doing his translations for as long as she could without looking creepy, she had sneaked away to check in on Ridley.

Jeremiah had asked that she not mention Matthieu to his mother, and she agreed. No use getting the poor woman all worked up before they knew what was happening. She found Mrs. Rousseau—*Esme, please, dear*—to be a delightful woman, warm and funny. She had much more in common with her eldest son than her quiet, brooding younger one.

After a brief conversation with Esme, she was able to talk to Ridley for a while, and hoped that her daughter wasn't able to hear the tears in her voice. It seemed as though Ridley and Esme were equally smitten with each other, and Ridley was having a wonderful time. While Fate was a bit sad that her daughter didn't seem to miss her that much, she was glad that Ridley was getting to spend some time with someone who was like a grandmother. Lord knew Fate's own mother wasn't interested.

Fate shook off her depressing thoughts and returned to the living room to find everyone in much the same position as when she'd left. "Would anyone like anything to drink?" she asked, desperate to break the oppressive silence.

"A beer would be great," Drew mumbled without looking up.

"Make it two," Raven said.

Étienne gave Fate a nod when she raised a brow at him. She disappeared into the kitchen and returned with three cold bottles. After she passed them out, she sank back down into the recliner and went back to trying not to beat her head against the table.

Raven took a long swallow of her beer, then narrowed her eyes at Étienne. "So what'd you do, kid?"

"What do you mean, what did he do?" Fate asked

"*Raven*. Seriously?" Drew scolded, though he couldn't keep the smile from tugging at his lips.

Raven ignored him completely. "When a *feradux* is called into service, it's because he commits some kind of crime. I know it's none of my beeswax and all that, but... well?"

A muscle twitched in Étienne's jaw as he looked down at his beer, twirling the neck between his fingers. "I nearly killed someone while trying to protect my lover."

Raven at least had the grace to look a little sheepish. "Well, shit. That doesn't seem to be bad enough to be punished for. Is she okay?"

"He," Étienne replied raising blazing golden eyes to face the group. "He ended up being all right, but was whisked away to parts unknown. Some didn't take to kindly to my *corruptive* ways, either. Influential someones. So here I am."

"Oh." Raven clamped her mouth shut but gave him a look that clearly said that they'd talk about it again eventually. "Well, fuck 'em," she said, and that was that.

They continued to drink in agonized silence until they heard the front door open. Fate shot to her feet when Jeremiah stepped inside. "Did you get everything?" she asked, not even trying to hide her anxiety.

He gave her a fleeting smile and nodded. He walked over to the couch and flopped down beside Drew, pulling his wife down beside him. "Tell me you've got something, Deveraux."

Drew carefully set his notebook aside, pulled off his reading glasses and folded them neatly. "Yeah, I think I got it. We're going to have to improvise a little to tailor the ritual to Matthieu's situation. I figure we should do the whole thing in English. While I'm getting better at translating *Bruixi* Latin, I don't want to bet my life on being able to transcribe it on the fly."

"Let's get started then," Jeremiah said, rubbing his palms on his denim covered thighs. "You can instruct us as we go."

"All right, first we need to move all of this furniture out of the way. We need space on the floor."

Jeremiah handed his bags from the general store off to Fate, and she moved to the kitchen to put them with Isla's bags. The three women went about unloading the items onto the kitchen counter, while the men made quick work of moving the furniture.

When the hardwood floor was clear of furniture, Drew called over to Raven. "Babe, can you bring me the chalk and the salt, please?"

"Sure thing." She grabbed what they needed and brought it to him, and Fate followed along behind.

"We need to draw three nested circles on the floor with the chalk, just like the *Vigilati signa*. Only the smallest circle will have to be big enough to fit a man—namely Matty—inside without touching the chalk." He raised his eyebrows and looked around the group. "Who's got a steady hand?"

Jeremiah stepped up and took the chalk from Raven's hands. "He's my brother. I'll do it."

He drew the three circles surprisingly well. When he was finished he gestured to the kitchen. "Hey, love, will you grab the sachets for me and put them on the door knobs?"

Fate gave him a confused look as Isla hurried to tie small burlap sachets to the knobs of the front and back door. "What are those for?"

"Just a little protection spell from the local voodoo priestess, who happens to share our dislike of the 'Jackal-man' as she puts it," he said with a shrug. "I figure we could use all the help we can get."

Drew went to the kitchen for the bundle of sage and the feather Étienne had generously provided. "This wasn't part of the spell, but I think we ought to smudge the room." He held the items out in Fate's direction. "In fact, Fate, I think you should do it, since you've spent the most time here with Matty."

With shaking hands, Fate took the feather and the small bundle of dried sage. "How do I do it?"

Drew lit the sage for her, until it began to puff out a steady stream of dense blue smoke. "You just walk around, letting the smoke permeate the room, and spread it with the feather. Pay particular attention to the doors." He turned to the rest of the group. "Everyone try to clear your minds as much as possible and visualize a safe space."

Fate wandered around the room, doing as Drew had told her, and tried not to feel silly. She'd never really believed in such things as spirits and demons, regardless of her visions. Now, all of a sudden, it seemed as though she was being thrust into some kind of *Rocky Horror* nightmare. What next, she wondered. Vampires? Werewolves? *Oh, wait.* She stopped that train of thought and cast a wary look at Marduk.

When she finished "smudging," Drew took the sage and placed it in a heavy ashtray that Jeremiah had found in the cupboard, and let it burn. "Perfect," he told her with a distracted smile. "Now we need to draw the points of the triangle. The slashes will be at North, Southeast, and Southwest points. They'll be perpendicular slashes, again, just like the *signa*."

He dug his iPhone out of his pocket and consulted the compass app, then indicated with his foot where Jeremiah should draw the line. "Here. Fate, this will be your spot. This is the position of the water element, and through the process of elimination, I think that's you."

Isla, fire, was given the Southwest point, and Raven, air and space, would take the Southeast spot.

Fate didn't know much about witches, but she'd seen enough movies. "Aren't there supposed to be four elements? Four directions?"

Drew nodded and didn't seem to be annoyed by her questioning him. "In Wicca, yes. But the *Bruixi* are…different. Not so much a religion as a people. And these weren't so much rituals to them as ways of life. So things will be slightly different. In the *Bruixi* beliefs, earth is always a part of their ceremonies as it is the element that holds us all. Earth is a force that man cannot begin to control."

"And while the four directions make up four corners in Wicca, most of *Bruixi* imagery is based on triangles and circles."

"One of these days, when lives aren't on the line anymore, I'm going to want to hear more about this," Fate said with a quick smile.

"Absolutely." Drew winked at her, but then his expression sobered. "Matthieu will need to be inside the circle for the rest of the setup. Jere, Marduk, let's go get our boy."

They disappeared into the bedroom and returned carrying a prone Matthieu between the three of them. Matthieu's hands and feet were bound, and his head lolled on his shoulders. As the men moved him toward the circle, he let out a ragged groan that ended in more of a growl, and his eyes rolled back until only the whites showed.

Fate wasn't proud of it, but she sort of braced herself for pea soup. As they approached the circle, Matthieu began to struggle. His body convulsed and contorted, trying to break the grip of his captors. It broke Fate's heart to see, but she imagined that it was a good sign that whatever had a hold of him did not want to be in that circle.

Finally, they were able to maneuver him over the chalk lines, and laid him down in the center of the circle. He immediately stilled, his eyes closed and he took a deep, shuddering breath.

"Now we need to hurry before the demon rallies," Drew said as he stepped into the circle. He set up a makeshift altar near Matthieu's left shoulder, using an old wooden crawfish trap covered by a sheet. On it he set the wide, silver chalice that Jeremiah had procured from Amara, which he'd filled with water. Then, he set a floating candle in the water.

"This will bring all of the elements together, and the blood will bind it," he said before placing Matthieu's knife beside the chalice. He then passed around hastily scrawled scripts so that they would all know what to say and do, and when. "Everyone ready?"

When vague nods and grumbles seemed to be all he was going to get, Drew rubbed his hands together. "Jere, take the salt and cover the center circle with it. Make sure it's one continuous line, absolutely no breaks."

Once Jeremiah had created the salt circle, Drew turned to Fate who was flanked by Isla and Raven. "Ladies, take your seats at your respective directions. Your mate should be seated on your left, if you have one, and your *feradux* on your right.

Keep in mind that these points are the only exits to the circle, so you need to follow my instructions to the letter."

Fate took her seat at the northern point of the circle, with Étienne on her right side. She worried that the holes in their circle might affect the ritual—since she had no mate, and Raven's *feradux* was gone—but she had no choice but to put her faith in Drew.

"Remember, everything is bound by blood. Y'all know what to do?" When Drew got nods from all of them, he handed Matthieu's combat knife to Isla, who was to begin the ritual, and took his seat next to Raven.

Isla opened the knife and poised it over her palm. "We call upon the elements to cast our circle," she said, then repeated the sentence while the others joined in. "By the power of fire..." She made a shallow slice across her palm and leaned forward to allow a few drops of blood to hit the water in the chalice. She then swiped her bloody thumb over the scar on Matthieu's cheek. His facial muscles twitched but he showed no other reaction.

Using nothing but the power of her mind, Isla sent the knife skittering across the floor to Raven, who deftly caught it by the handle. "By the power of air and space..." Raven repeated Isla's actions until her own hand was dripping blood. Her toss of the knife to Fate was gentler, since she could manipulate air currents, and Fate caught it easily.

With a convulsive swallow, Fate cleared her throat to say the words. "By the power of water..." She winced as the razor sharp blade sliced her flesh, but it was quickly replaced by determination. She was glad to be finally doing something, even if it that something happened to be bloodletting.

After she'd swiped her blood over the others' on Matthieu's cheek, she returned to her seat where they joined together to finish the circle chant. "And by the power of the earth beneath, that binds us all. The flame seals our circle."

Drew lit a match and touched it to the wick of the candle that floated in the chalice, and they all watched as it sparked to life. Matthieu let out a low growl and began to writhe on the floor. "Well, now that we've gotten its attention, we need to call the spirits. Fast," he said. "Isla?"

Isla jerked a nod and focused her attention on Matthieu. "Leora, Mother of Fire, surround us with your flame. Hold our circle strong."

"Anila, Mother of Air and Space, cradle us to your bosom," Raven chanted.

Fate shook visibly as she tried to remember her words. "Kallan, Father of Water, cleanse and purify us with your sacred spirit."

Together again, they spoke the last of the invocation. "Solon, Father of Earth, ground us to your body to protect us from evil.

"We invoke the spirits of our ancestors to protect and hold our circle as we banish this demon from our midst..."

A disembodied screech echoed around the room as Matthieu's tremors turned violent. He threw his bound wrists up over his head, and clawed into the hardwood floor until his nails were chipped and bleeding. His powerful body repeatedly bucked up off the floor, as if the demon was trying to throw him out of the circle with the force of his will.

"This circle, though open, shall never be unbroken. So mote it be."

THE SERPENT'S FATE

Carefully, Fate wiped away the chalk and salt at the intersection of the middle circle and her pinnacle point, opening the circle. Raven and Isla did the same. Drew had figured they would only have minutes to complete the dispossession spell and close the circle before they let something even worse out.

Together, they recited the only part of the ritual that was spoken in *Bruixi* Latin.

"Draconus, Filius Mortis, et virtutem Elementorum, virtus Dei est, proiciam vos." Jackal, Son of Death, with the power of the Elements and the strength of the Gods, we cast you out.

With an inhuman snarl, Matthieu's body bowed up off the floor and he bared his teeth, which looked no longer human. His head smacked against the floor with the motion, and his eyes flew open—only not *his* eyes. Clear, marble-like orbs filled with those wicked shadows stared out from his ravaged face.

Fate watched in horror as a ghostly specter rose up above him, as if it were attached by an invisible tether. While the creature clearly wasn't corporeal, it was no less frightening with its oozing flesh, dripping fangs and bloodshot, dead eyes. Eyes that mirrored Matthieu's exactly. It howled and lashed out at Isla, then Fate, but was stopped each time by the unseen barrier of the circle.

In retaliation, the creature stirred up a whirlwind in the room, sending papers and books flying into a maelstrom of projectiles.

"Finish it!" Drew shouted as he ducked a coffee mug that flew past his head.

"Solve teipsum ab fratrem nostrum spiritus hominis ista relinquo circuli." Unbind yourself from our brother's spirit and leave this circle.

The three women struggled against the swirling wind and the screeching, clawing demon to re-chalk and re-salt their pinnacle points, thus closing the circle.

"Fire, Air, Water, Earth, aid us in this man's new birth. Close the circle, close the gate, cast out evil, seal his fate. So mote it be," they spoke in unison.

Once the words were spoken and the physical circle was closed, the wind abruptly died. In the center, Matthieu lay very, very still. Too still.

CHAPTER THIRTY·FOUR

MATTHIEU WAS IN HELL. NOT HELL AS IN A BAD situation. Like real, honest to God, *Dante's-fucking-Inferno*, Hell. He recognized it, had been living with it in his head since he was seven. But this was different. The roles were reversed, and now he was living in *it*. Wherever *it* was.

It was dark. It was sweltering. There was no sense of time to be had. He could have been there for minutes or years for all he knew. That might have been the most terrifying part. He couldn't see anything, anyone, but he could sense them; skittering around, bouncing off the walls, the ceiling. They circled him, ever closer, until he could feel their claws dragging over his skin; until he could smell their putrid breath on his face.

But they never touched him beyond that; never hurt him. He'd wondered for half a second if he was dreaming, but even in his fugue state he knew that if it had been a dream, Fate would have been right there with him, guiding him out of it.

He hissed out a breath as Draconus' face floated into his field of vision. Matthieu couldn't be sure if the demon was actually there, or if the image was just in his head. But either way, it wasn't good. Maybe he'd finally succumbed to the pull of evil. He just hoped those around him were safe.

Matthieu wondered what would happen to Fate and Ridley now. Who would protect them? *That's none of your concern*, a voice whispered in his ear, and again he wondered if it was real. *You are right where you were always meant to be. You're mine.*

It must have been Draconus's voice. Matthieu strained to hear more, but nothing was forthcoming. Maybe the fucking demon was right. He'd killed. He'd tortured. In fact, helping Fate was probably the first time he'd been driven to do something unselfish. Maybe it had been too late. He belonged in Hell with the demons.

He was so tired. Matthieu could feel himself slipping away, but he was too tired to fight. He should just let them have him. Everyone would be better off.

His brows bunched in confusion. That couldn't be right. Could it? Would his brother be better off? His mother? Fate? He'd been trying to do better, to *be* better. And he thought he'd been succeeding.

Struggling to stay awake, Matthieu held on to the images in his head of his loved ones as he heard the faint sound of chanting fill the darkened space. The demons went mad, screeching, moaning, writhing, as if they were in physical pain from the noise. A raw curse in a deeper voice sounded in Matthieu's ear before the room, or whatever structure he was in, began to quake.

All Matthieu could do was flail around in the darkness as the demons deserted him. He felt a ripping deep inside him, as if someone was trying to pull his intestines—or perhaps his soul—out through his ears. God, it was painful, like being torn in two.

What happened next could only be described as what it must be like when a toilet flushed in Hell. All the matter around him began to swirl around him, and he could feel himself being pulled with it, down into some kind of black hole. God Almighty, was this it? Was this what death felt like?

Matthieu fought it for as long as he could; grappling with hands and feet to avoid being pulled down into the void, which somehow seemed much darker than his current prison. He fought it, but eventually he lost and went catapulting into nothingness.

Matthieu struggled to open eyelids that seemed to be strung with ten pound weights. He could feel them move, so maybe that meant he wasn't dead. Right? He hazarded a hazy look through his eyelashes and blinked to clear the blurriness from his vision. Dingy white popcorn ceiling. Rotating ceiling fan.

He tensed when his brother's scowling mug filled his sight. Oh, Jesus, what the hell was he doing here? Jeremiah's lips were moving but all Matthieu could hear was a low level buzzing in his ears.

Hands tapped his face lightly, and again with more force behind it. He slapped them away, annoyed. "G'cher hands off me," he growled. Well, that's what he tried to say at least. He wasn't sure how it came out.

Jeremiah was talking again, but Matthieu focused on a point over his brother's left shoulder. Fate's worried face had appeared behind him, her mussed blond hair forming a halo around it, and Mathieu felt himself finally relax. The buzz receded, only to be replaced by Jeremiah's frantic voice.

"...you hear me Matty? Can you at least nod or something?"

"'Course I can goddamn hear you. You're screamin'." His voice was rough, sort of like he'd been shouting at a football game. That had lasted a week. But it was there.

Jeremiah gave him a shaky smile. "There he is, the surly bastard we all know and love." The catch in his voice belied his teasing words.

As usual, Matthieu was uncomfortable with emotion so he responded the way he always did—with snark. "Aw, hell, put away your big bleedin' vagina for a second and help me up, will ya?"

"God, you're such an ass," Jeremiah retorted, but he was smiling for real now. "He's baaaaack." With a hand on Matthieu's shoulder, Jeremiah helped him into a sitting position.

The room spun sickly and his head pounded with the sudden onset of gravity. He knew he'd gotten his drink on the night before but...damn. With a careful swivel of his neck, he surveyed his surroundings. He was still in the fishing shack, only it looked like a hurricane had blown through. Literally.

He was on the living room floor, or so he thought. It was hard to tell with all of the furniture moved and debris strewn around the room. Books, papers, throw pillows—feathers?—littered the floor around him.

Chairs were toppled, the ceiling fan he originally noticed was hanging at an odd angle, and there were strange chalk markings drawn on the hardwood floor. Matthieu scanned the faces of the people surrounding him, relieved to find that most of them were familiar. He'd already seen Jeremiah and Fate and to their left, he saw Isla and her strange friend—whatever the hell his name was.

Hawkeye was at Fate's side, as if protecting her, so Matthieu gave him a weak nod. Turning to his right, he saw Drew

Deveraux and a small Native American looking woman next to him. Maybe the girlfriend? The wife? He couldn't keep it straight.

Matthieu turned back to Jeremiah and raised a brow at him. "The fuck happened in here?"

Jeremiah sighed, and the relief evident on his face made Matthieu nervous. "We'll explain everything in a minute. First we need to take care of you. Think you can get up?"

"Well, we're sure as the hell going to find out," he grumbled as Jeremiah hauled him up by his elbow. Fate made to step forward and help, but he held up a hand to still her movement. "Just gimme a minute."

As glad as he'd been to see her, he didn't want her touching him. Not only was he sweaty and probably smelling like microwaved shit, he felt like his body was covered in a thick layer of evil demon sludge. It was like he'd been rode hard and put away wet. By Satan. He felt too dirty to touch her.

Standing, Matthieu stretched his tense muscles and felt some unpleasant pops and cracks. He looked down at himself, surprised to find that he wore only his Calvin's and nothing else. He shrugged and ran a hand over his face. "I need a beer," he muttered, and padded into the kitchen to rectify that.

He pulled out one of the kitchen drawers and raised a false bottom, revealing a humidor that held Paul Rousseau's collection of Cuban cigars. "Hell, if this ain't a time for Dad's secret stash, I don't know what is."

Matthieu pulled out the small, wooden box and placed it on the counter. With practiced movements, he extracted one of the fat cigars and sliced the tip cleanly with a metal cutter shaped like a bullet. He stuck the cigar between his teeth but didn't light it. He raised a brow at Jeremiah and Drew. "Boys?"

Jeremiah smirked at him but shook his head. "Not in the house, yeah? Got the baby to think about," he said, casting a glance at his pregnant wife.

Matthieu nodded and started to close the humidor. Raven snorted, walked over and snatched the cigar from his mouth. She picked up a matchbook from the counter and sauntered toward the back door.

"We're gonna go outside anyway. Come on ladies, let's give the boys a chance to catch up. I'll stay downwind," she explained after catching a glance from Jeremiah. She seemed to pull Isla and Fate into her orbit and the three of them headed for the back deck.

Étienne glanced after them, and then at the men. Matthieu could sense the kid's indecision, knew that he'd built a special protective sort of rapport with Fate.

He nodded his head toward the door. "Go. Keep an eye on them."

Étienne gave him a grateful smile before following the girls outside.

ℝ℞

Fate and Isla stood side by side, leaning up against the deck railing, while Raven lounged on a chair and puffed her cigar. Fate glanced at Étienne who stood awkwardly between them.

They had taken refuge outside in the muggy bayou morning while Matthieu was being filled in on the details of their *situation*. "He's not going to take this well, you know," she said to nobody in particular.

She saw Isla nod out of the corner of her eye. "Accepting things you'd thought were impossible can be hard."

"No, I think between the two of us, we've seen enough in the last couple of days to make believing sort of a non-issue." She turned her head slightly and gave Isla a grim smile. "I mean the possession. He's not going to take that well. I haven't known Matthieu for all that long, but knowing that he's not entirely in control of himself, that he can't trust himself especially around the ones he loves…it's his worst nightmare."

"I can totally relate," Raven said, then blew a few smoke rings and focused her attention back out to the water.

"Do you think that might be why he is the way he is?" Isla asked. "I had originally thought it was some sort of PTSD, but Jeremiah said he's been this way since he was a kid.

Fate thought about covering for him again, but she felt that the time for keeping secrets from Matthieu's family was over. "I know it is. He's been running from this thing for most of his life. He pushes people away because he thinks it will keep them safe—but also to punish himself. He'll do it to me next," she said with a decisive nod.

"Maybe he'll let us help him this time."

Fate snorted and twisted her lips in a sardonic smile. "You think?"

"No," Isla answered with a smile. "But I'm an optimist."

Fate returned the smile with a sad one of her own and looked out across the canal. "Mark my words; he'll try to distance himself from me. I know what it's like to be different…to have a part of yourself that you feel you need to keep hidden."

Raven glanced over at Étienne, then back to where Fate stood with Isla. "Welcome to the club, sweetheart. We're all freaks of nature here," she deadpanned.

Fate winced but Isla simply nodded. "Too true, love. Once Matthieu realizes that, he'd be a fool to turn his back on us."

Raven raised a brow and stubbed out her cigar on the dilapidated deck railing. "Just remember, you said it, not me." She pushed off of the railing and turned toward the door. "Come on, ladies and birds. Let's go join the fray."

35 CHAPTER THIRTY·FIVE

"**I** know this is a lot to take in," Jeremiah said from behind Matthieu. "But unfortunately, we don't have a lot of time for you wrap your mind around it."

Matthieu ignored him. *So. Witches*, he thought. *Witches and demons and shapeshifters, oh friggin' my.* Not that he was all that surprised, considering he'd been sharing headspace with the crazy bastards since he was seven.

The part that was really getting to him wasn't this new reality of supernatural beings and mortal danger. No, that wasn't really all that new. Deep in the back of his mind, though, he'd always held out hope that his little demon mindfuck was just a product of his being completely bloody insane. It was the loss of that delusion that was really bugging him.

Why would he wish he was a total nut job? Because then he would be the only one suffering. But no. This involved his brother, his wife, and their unborn child. It involved his foster brother and *his* wife. And, maybe worst of all, it involved Fate and Ridley.

Matthieu interrupted Jeremiah's monologue, of which he hadn't heard a word. "So what's the plan," he said in a clipped tone.

"Sorry?" Jeremiah looked at him, startled.

"The plan," he said through gritted teeth. "You know, plan, strategy. *Course of action.* How do we kill the bastard?" *God, I'm such an asshole*, he thought. Maybe they would chalk it up to his demon hangover.

"We can hurt him with knives, guns, grenades, what-the-hell-ever. Those will cause some damage and slow him down, but ultimately, the only way to kill the *Lochrim* is direct contact with the blood of the *Praeda*."

"Meaning Fate," Matthieu growled.

"Yes." Jeremiah's stare was serious and unwavering.

"Simple enough. What are we waiting for? Let's weaponize that shit."

"The fuck are you talking about, Matty?" Drew snapped.

"I'm talking about military efficiency, Deveraux. Say we somehow—painlessly—obtain some of Fate's blood. I'll handload a mountain of centerfire cartridges and shotgun shells, and we'll take the son of a bitch down."

Drew cursed and rolled his eyes. The guy's attitude was getting on Matthieu's last damn nerve. "No, no it's not simple. We've learned that the manner of contact with the blood can be different with each individual *Lochrim-Praeda* pairing. Alastore—Isla's father—was killed with blood-to-blood contact, whereas Raven's mother, Azibel, had to actually ingest the blood."

"Drew's right," Jeremiah said. "But you may be onto something with the bullets. It's worth a shot. If we got lucky and a blood-laced bullet *would* kill Draconus, it'd be a pretty quick and efficient way to do it."

Drew nodded, and it seemed as if he may finally be on board. "Just one problem, though. How are we going to get the blood without hurting Fate or creating suspicion?"

Jeremiah stared at Matthieu for a few seconds before answering. "We could go to a red cross van, under the pretense of donating. Then Raven can work her larceny magic on the blood bag.

"Raven? The tiny biker chick? Just a frog's hair over five feet, Raven?" Matthieu asked.

Drew snorted at that. "She hears you call her a chick and she'll gut you like a fresh catch. But, yes. My wife can break into just about any-damn-where. She'll get what we need."

Sighing, Matthieu rested his elbows on his thighs and ran his hands through his hair. "How do we ask Fate to donate her blood, man? She's already been through so much—"

He broke off as the women and Étienne came back inside.

"All caught up?" Raven's voice was a sarcastic chirp as she walked up behind Drew and put her arms around his neck.

Fate stopped in the middle of the room and clapped her hands together. "So, have we figured it out yet?"

"Figured what out?" Jeremiah asked.

"How were going to get some of my blood and use it to take this son of a bitch down."

"We've got a couple of ideas about that," Jeremiah said, grinning.

Matthieu gaped at her, once again marveling at her tenacity. It almost made him forget what he had promised himself—to let her go, to keep his distance. Yes, he may have saved her life from the initial attack, but he'd done nothing but put her in danger since then.

So that was why, when she sat down next to him, he shot off the couch, mumbling some excuse about getting a drink. Instead, he just walked over and leaned against the bar that separated the kitchen from the great room.

He thought he saw Fate and Isla share a look, and he was *certain* he saw Raven roll her eyes. Fate stood and swiveled her head slowly to face him. Her expression determined, she approached him, walking around until she was behind him.

She gripped his hips and gave a subtle tug to get him to turn. He briefly thought about refusing, but that would have been childish even by his standards. Jerking a little harder, she brought him closer to her and pinned him with a hard stare. He couldn't shake the feeling that he'd disappointed her somehow.

"You're not giving me enough credit."

When he gave a noncommittal grunt, she leaned forward and brushed her lips against his ear. Their bodies were angled in such a way that the others wouldn't be able to see or hear. "I'm stronger than you think," she whispered. "I've been raped, beaten, and kidnapped by a demon—all of which I've survived. I can handle your baggage. I can handle you, Matthieu."

She took advantage of his moment of stunned silence and licked trail up his neck over his pounding pulse, then lightly smacked his unscarred cheek. "So, do we need to discuss this matter further?"

In a daze, he shook his head and had the absurd thought that she sounded like a schoolteacher. Even more absurd was how much that actually turned him on. Gathering his wits and trying to control his body's reaction to her, he slowly met her eyes.

"You win." He sighed and rubbed a hand over the back of his neck. "I'll quit trying to push you away. But I think we can both agree that close physical proximity to me comes with very real danger. So I will put physical distance between us whenever I see fit."

It would have been more convincing if his voice hadn't been shaking. Fate stepped back and gave him a serene smile. "We'll see."

Matthieu swallowed and tried to get his rapid breathing under control. He'd been to war. He'd been to...hell. But he didn't have a fraction of the strength that Fate had. Humbled beyond reason, he kept quiet and rejoined the group.

Jeremiah began to fill the women in on the plan they had so far. "Fate, if we can have some of your blood extracted, Matty thinks that he may be able to lace some bullets with it. No guarantee they'll kill Draconus, but it's worth a shot."

"And just how did you plan on gettin' the blood?" Isla asked.

"Easy. Blood bank," Jeremiah answered.

Isla's dark brows shot up beneath her thick bangs. "You think they're just going to let us waltz in there, pull a pint, and stroll out with it?"

"'Course not," Drew said, eyes twinkling. "Raven will five-finger it, no muss, no fuss." He smiled indulgently at his wife.

"So, not only are we blood-letting Fate, but we're going to have Raven commit a felony? No. Just...no," Isla said.

Fate laid a calming hand on Isla's shoulder before returning to her seat beside Matthieu. "Do you trust her, Jeremiah?" she asked.

"I do."

"That's good enough for me. We'll go first thing tomorrow."

"Fate, you don't have to—," Isla began.

Fate cut her off with a raise of her hand. "Of course I do. You and Raven know that better than anyone. I can handle it."

"Good, it's settled then," Jeremiah said. "Now, Matty, you need to tell us everything you know about this Draconus."

J.K. HOGAN

His brother looked at him steadily, his brows drawn low over hazel eyes. He was looking at him as if he was waiting for Matthieu to say something profound. Like he thought Matthieu was holding out on him.

"I can do you one better. I'll show you." Matthieu got out his laptop and pulled up his homemade surveillance program. "When Fate and I went to New York, I broke into the office of one Lieutenant Arlen Ward. Ward was my commander in the Army...and my handler on the outside."

"Handler," Jeremiah said. Matthieu knew he didn't have to explain the implications to his brother.

"Yes. He was the one who handed out all of the mercenary jobs. He controlled me and the other members of my unit with information he had on us from our time in the service."

"He blackmailed you," Jeremiah said through a clenched jaw.

"That he did, but that's a story for another day, brother. The important part here is that Ward was the one who was 'hired' to find Fate. He put me on the job. As you know, I was ordered to kill her and I refused, making us both targets.

"I broke into his office to place several recording and listening devices, hoping to catch a glimpse of who the client was." Matthieu pulled up the recorded feed that he'd seen after their New York trip and spun the computer around to face the others. "See for yourself," he said, and hit play.

He knew Fate hadn't seen the footage yet; she hadn't had to confront the image of Eli and what it was that he really wanted. So he placed his hand over hers and laced their fingers together.

Matthieu vaguely noticed his friends' expressions as they ran the gamut of emotions that he'd experienced while watching the clip—including the jolt of seeing Draconus look directly at the camera and show his true face.

But Fate captured the majority of his attention. She'd clamped a hand over her mouth as soon as Eli had come into the picture, and her eyes widened with shock when she realized he was talking about Ridley.

"Oh, my *God!*" she said when the clip ended. "Why? Why would Eli want to kill Ridley?"

"Who's Eli?" Jeremiah asked, his eyes sharpening on Fate.

"My abusive, psychotic rapist of an ex-husband…and Ridley's father, apparently," she said quietly.

"Don't worry about him, anyway," Matthieu said. "I killed him."

Drew snorted but Jeremiah just shook his head. "Did you, though?"

"Yeah, I'm pretty sure I did. I put a bullet in his skull." He saw Fate flinch, but there wasn't much he could do about that now. "And then…never mind."

"And then what?" Jeremiah asked.

"And then, he sort of…exploded," Matthieu mumbled.

Jeremiah and Isla nodded as if that made perfect sense, which made Matthieu's head hurt a little. "You don't seem surprised. Why?"

"Because," Fate said in a moment of sudden comprehension. "Eli's a demon too."

"Wait, how do you know that?" Matthieu asked.

"Because I saw him. When he was holding me hostage, I saw what he really looks like." She turned sad eyes to Isla. "So, that means that Ridley is like us then."

"Yes, I'm afraid it does," Isla said. "But she'll be better off than any of us ever were. She'll be raised by someone—and hopefully around others—who know what she is. She won't grow up wondering why she's different, and she will have people to ask when she is unsure."

"I guess so," Fate said, but Matthieu could feel her hand shaking.

"Let's not worry about Eli right now. We need to focus on Draconus." Jeremiah once again gave Matthieu that piercing stare. "It was good to see what he looks like, but I still need you to tell me everything. Starting from the first time you saw him."

Ah, hell. Matthieu thought about making something up, but he couldn't be sure how much Jeremiah knew. He had a feeling that if he lied now, he might lose his brother for good. It took everything he had to raise his eyes to meet Jeremiah's, but he did it. "It was the day Dad died. Or rather, the day I *let* him die."

With a heavy sigh, Matthieu closed his eyes and began to do something he'd promised himself he never would—tell his brother everything.

CHAPTER THIRTY·SIX

HE TOLD THEM EVERY LAST DETAIL, FROM THAT DAY when he was seven to the explosion in Kandahar and beyond. He even told them about Emilie. He'd talked so long, the sun was setting once he finished. By the time it was over, he was shaking, nauseated, and he couldn't meet his brother's eyes.

Matthieu was afraid of what he might see there. Disappointment maybe, shame, or worst of all, pity. Instead, he avoided it all together. Keeping his eyes averted, he walked into the kitchen and opened the humidor. "'Bout time for one of these Cubans," he mumbled and made for the back porch.

Sure, it was the coward's way, but it wasn't like he was getting out of it. Jeremiah wasn't going to let it go. He was just buying himself a few seconds to breathe. With jerky movements, he cut the cigar and lit it while taking long drags. He sighed as he breathed the fine Cuban smoke into his lungs.

Matthieu's shoulders tensed when he heard Jeremiah come out onto the deck behind him—he had no illusions that it would be anyone but his brother coming after him. He just kept on puffing on that fat Havana like it was a goddamn lifeline.

"Why didn't you tell me?" came his rough voice from the shadows.

Holding his arms wide like a criminal surrendering, Matthieu turned around and met his brother's stare. He could barely see Jeremiah's face in the darkness, but it was enough. Jeremiah's eyes flashed as he walked over to lean on the railing beside Matthieu.

Matthieu could see the barely restrained fury in the muscle ticking steadily in his brother's square jaw. That was...unexpected. "Tell you...about the day I let Dad die?"

"Stop saying that," Jeremiah hissed as he turned towards Matthieu. "How can you *say* that? You were just a little kid!"

Feeling his own anger rising, Matthieu spun around to face his brother. "Well, let's see. A..." he began, ticking off a finger as he explained, "...if he didn't have me to worry about, he might have been able to get away. B, I just stood there and let it happen."

He held up a hand when Jeremiah started to protest. "And C..." He swallowed convulsively. "And C, it was after me in the first place. Draconus realized it after Dad was already gone."

Jeremiah's eyes were wet, but his anger was still evident on his face. "None of that explains why you didn't tell me. You were so little then. I'm your big brother, and I was supposed to look out for you."

"That's exactly why the fuck I didn't tell you," Matthieu snapped. "From that point on, my life wasn't my own anymore. I didn't want to infect you with the evil that was part of me. I didn't want it anywhere near you or Mom. So I got as far away as I could, as soon as I could."

Matthieu shoved a hand through his hair and looked out over the dark water. "Am I sorry it had to be that way?" he asked, turning back to his brother. "Absolutely! Do I regret keeping y'all safe? Not for a goddamn second!"

It had been a long time since anyone had gotten the jump on him—maybe since his first few weeks of Basic—but, then again, he hadn't been expecting violence from his brother. Jeremiah reared back and socked him with a left hook in the mouth. Matthieu hit the railing, bounced off of it, and fell ass over teakettle onto the weathered wood of the deck.

His vision swam, and he lay there with a hand clamped over his mouth, trying to collect his addled wits enough to speak. His voice was a dangerous growl when he finally managed it.

"What the *hell*, Jeremiah?" He felt blood trickling down his chin so he dabbed at it with a careless hand.

Jeremiah stood over him, fists clenching and unclenching in a jerky rhythm, and Matthieu could see him trembling all over.

"I should be asking you that," he said surprisingly quietly, considering his posture and the fact that Matthieu was currently tasting his own blood. "I did *everything* I could to try and be a good brother to you. You seemed so...broken after Dad died, and I tried my best to fill his shoes for you, but nothing I did seemed to work. You just kept slipping farther and farther away."

Jeremiah hung his head and rubbed his eyes. "Broke Mom's heart. She never could figure out what we'd done to drive you away, and she never stopped hoping you'd come back. And you have the nerve to say you don't regret it? You're such a goddamned bastard!"

Matthieu was recovering from his shock—and mild-to-moderate head trauma—and was starting to get angry again. He suddenly had the urge to stand up for himself and his choices for the first time in, well, ever.

"You know what? Fuck you and the horse you rode in on, big brother! You're the perfect golden boy, living in a golden cage—perfect house, perfect wife, perfect life. You have *no* idea what it's been like, living with this! And having to do it alone..."

Matthieu's words trailed off and he blinked into the darkness. Where had that come from? His solitude was a choice—it was something he craved as much as it was necessary. Wasn't it? Confused and bewildered, he stared up at Jeremiah from where he still lay on the deck floor.

"You didn't have to be alone!" After that outburst, Jeremiah's expression softened. He sank down on his knees and got right up in Matthieu's face. "You're right. I don't know what it was like and that ends today. All this Prodigal-Son-I-am-an-island bullshit is over, Matty. Today you're going to quit blaming yourself for Dad, rejoin the living, and be the brother and son you should have had the opportunity to be."

Jeremiah gripped the back of Matthieu's neck and forced him to really look at him. "And remember I said I had contacts in the P.I. business? You ghost out again, I *will* find you and haul you back home just so I can kick your ass. Don't think I won't."

Matthieu stared at his brother for a few more seconds before breaking out into a grin. "I hear ya." He stretched his arm around as if he were going to embrace Jeremiah, but instead smacked him across the back of his head. Hard.

"Ow! The fuck?"

Swiping a hand across his mouth where it was still bleeding, Matthieu cackled. "You ask me, you got off easy. Now, are we done with our Oprah moment, or what? We need to start planning for war."

Jeremiah snorted as he got to his feet, and reached out a hand to pull Matthieu up. "Yeah, we're done. Let's go back inside."

CHAPTER THIRTY·SEVEN

FATE LOOKED OVER WHEN MATTHIEU AND JEREMIAH came back inside. Matthieu was dabbing at his lip with his sleeve while Jeremiah rubbed the back of his head. She sure as hell hoped they'd worked something out, because it just looked to her like they'd been in a bar fight.

"*Sweet Lord of the Rings*, what the hell happened to you?" Raven asked Matthieu, although it was pretty clear exactly what had happened.

"I ran into a door," Matthieu grumbled, and said something under his breath that sounded a lot like "with a fist."

Raven grunted out a laugh and rolled her eyes, something that Fate was realizing was a habit of hers. "All right, well if you and your brother are finished acting like giant douche-nozzles, can we get back to the topic of demon-killing, please?"

Jeremiah patted Matthieu on the back and took a seat beside Isla, while Matthieu stood glaring at Raven. "Deveraux, you need to put a muzzle on you your woman. She talks too damn much," he snapped.

She snorted and raised a brow at him. "Woof."

Fists clenched, Drew started to get up, but Raven put a hand on his shoulder and pressed him back down. "Settle down, Professor. I can handle Soldier Boy. Gentleman," she said, making eye contact with Matthieu, Jeremiah, and then Drew. "No need to whip your dicks out and go for the ruler. We've got bigger things to worry about. We can get back to the chest-beating later."

Surprisingly, Drew sat. Raven obviously had him completely enraptured. Fate hadn't realized that kind of focus from a man was something she longed for, she'd been alone for so long. She shook the thought off, but her heart gave a little thump when Matthieu chose the seat next to her, despite his intention to keep his distance.

"So," he began, rubbing his hands together. "What are we going to do about Draconus? What do we have to do to waste the fucker?"

"We know from legend—mostly Pagan and Wiccan lore—that the barrier between the spirit world and the living is the thinnest during the Pagan high pinnacle days," Jeremiah said. "That means primarily Samhain; but also Beltane, the spring and autumnal equinoxes, as well as the winter and summer solstices."

Drew put on his glasses and peered at Matthieu's laptop, where the image of Draconus was frozen on the screen. "He hasn't confronted any of us directly yet, nor has he sent any of his minions—called *auchrim*," he said for Fate's benefit, "so I think that has to be a good sign. It seems as though the hit out on you two was initiated by this Eli character.

"Written histories of the *Vigilati* are spotty at best, even with my translations, and the oral accounts that we know of seemed to have died with Isla's grandmother, Mhairi," he continued, giving Isla a sympathetic smile. "Beltane has more typically positive connotations in history—a celebration of light and beginning. I think he would be unlikely to make his move then, but we should scout out the surrounding areas just in case, see if we can find the *locus*. But everything we've read, and experienced so far, has put all of the action going down on All Hallows. That gives us five months."

Jeremiah looked back and forth between Marduk and Étienne. "*Feradux*, what do you think? You've been around quite a bit longer than any of us."

Étienne bowed his head at Marduk, deferring to the older *feradux*.

"I think that, if there are rules, the *Lochrim* will do everything possible to break them. We need to always have our guard up," Marduk answered.

Jeremiah nodded decisively. "Right, we'll start scouting first thing tomorrow."

"And Raven and I will head to the blood bank," Fate said.

Jeremiah swiveled Matthieu's laptop to face Raven and Drew. "In the meantime, let's see what we can learn about Mr. Drake Maxwell."

Raven began fiddling with the surveillance program, changing the angles and zooming in. Fate had learned that Raven and her business partners, Trystan Stiles and Ryder Nash, were in the private security and P.I. business. She was always on the lookout for new technology and ways to improve their operations.

"Holy crap, this is some high tech shit. Who's your supplier?" Raven asked.

"Huh?" Matthieu glanced up from where he'd been staring at his hands. "Oh, that? That's just something I put together myself. There wasn't anything on the market that was exactly what I needed so I just made something up," he answered distractedly.

Raven stared at him, open mouthed, before turning questioning eyes to Jeremiah. He just shrugged and quirked his lips in a half smile. "What can I say? My brother's a bit of a tech savant. Among other things."

Fate looked over at Matthieu, who seemed to have withdrawn into himself. His eyes were wide and unfocused, and he was visibly trembling. He'd been through a lot in the past forty-eight. He'd been possessed by some psycho demon spirit, been through a ritual to cast out said demon, laid himself bare in front of everyone, and fought with his brother. Enough was enough.

Clearing her throat, Fate stood scanned the room. "I think we should pick this up in the morning when we've all had a good night's sleep. I don't know about you all, but I'm beat."

Matthieu gave her a weary but grateful smile while the others began packing up. He looked dead on his feet, but Fate knew he was too reserved to say he needed to rest.

They'd all agreed that the five visitors would bunk at a motel in nearby Theriot, while Fate, Matthieu, and Étienne stayed in the canal house. They quickly said their goodbyes, making plans to meet at nine a.m., and then the three were alone.

The pervasive silence settled around them, mixing with the shadows to form the gloomy mantle of night. Matthieu rose off the couch like a zombie and shuffled towards his bedroom. "'m gonna go lie down," he mumbled without making eye contact.

Fate watched him disappear into the dark room and shut the door. She heard the lock engage with a click of finality. Message received. Keep out. *Got it.*

Her head whipped around as she heard a loud pop behind her. "Oh my...*hell.*" *There* was a blinding flash and a puff of smoke. When the smoke cleared, there was a beautiful red-tipped hawk perched on the back of the sofa.

A hand pressed over her racing heart, Fate stared into the familiar eyes of the hawk—of Étienne. "Alrighty then," she murmured. "Guess you won't be needing a bed."

Étienne pecked at his left wing for a moment, then tucked his head to his chest and closed those golden eyes.

"Great," Fate said to the empty room. "Now what?"

She was tired, but too keyed up to sleep. Too worried about Matthieu, and demons, and saving the world. A heavy weight settled on her shoulders, and she sighed as it pressed in on her from all sides.

She was about to let it go and head to bed, when she heard the high pitched squeal of a door on its hinges. When she looked up, Matthieu stood leaning against the door frame in nothing but his boxer briefs, looking lost and solitary. He wasn't alone in the house, yet he was isolated. Set apart from everything, everyone.

His massive chest seemed almost concave as he sagged forward, his posture wilted. He rubbed a hand up and down the arm he'd pressed against his side as if he were cold, rather than in a pleasantly warm and humid house in the swamp. He couldn't meet her eyes, just stared at the floor and continued to rub that arm while he breathed a hitching sigh.

He couldn't say it. *Wouldn't* say it. But she knew what he needed. He needed to sleep and was afraid to do it alone—afraid of himself and what could happen to him. He needed her.

Her footfalls were nearly silent as she approached him. She paused briefly, placing her own hand over his to still the restless movement, then dropped it and walked past him into the dark room.

ЅѺ℃Ѽ

Matthieu closed the door, effectively shutting out the soft glow of the moonlight and surrounding himself in welcoming darkness. He remained facing the door for a few moments, and took some calming breaths while he listened to Fate shed her clothes and slip into bed. His bed.

He shuddered, thinking of all that softness sliding up against him, something he'd not allowed himself the pleasure of until now. It hadn't been worth the risk until Fate.

Sleep. That was all he needed. He told himself he'd be good. He told himself he wouldn't touch her, that he'd just take advantage of the security of having her near while he slept. And then he called himself a liar. A good man would leave her alone. A better man would figure out how to go the fuck to sleep without a woman standing guard, witch though she was. But he wasn't a better man. Wasn't even a good one.

So when he slipped between the sheets, his body automatically reached for her, pulling her against him. Their bodies lined up perfectly. Her softness against his solidity. Her warmth against the ice in his soul. So perfect it almost burned him.

With a gentle hand on his shoulder, she pushed him down on his back and lay on her side, facing him. She just watched him for what seemed like forever, searching his face, waiting for...something. When she didn't find was she was looking for, she spoke. "Why was telling Jeremiah so hard for you?"

Matthieu couldn't find the words. He struggled against the wall of silence he'd always kept so firmly in place—old dogs, and all that.

When he failed to answer, she tried a different tack. "Why does it always have to be you, Matthieu? Why do you always have to be the one standing between everyone else and trouble?"

"Because if I don't, things like Riksa happen! Like Stryker... Things like Dad," he blurted, then clamped his mouth shut when he realized what had come out.

Fate sighed, smoothed warm fingertips over his furrowed brow. "None of those things were your fault, Matthieu. They were horrible things that happened, but you didn't cause them."

"Bullshit, they weren't my fault," he said quietly. She didn't understand. He was fucking cursed. "Death follows me everywhere. Always has, whether I caused it purposefully or not. If staying away kept them safe—Jeremiah and Drew, their wives, Mom—then I'd gladly do it again."

"Matthieu—"

"No! It's a good thing I did it. I'm sure of it, now that I know what I was protecting them from...me and my cursed blood. You can't deny that...you saw what happened to me."

"Oh, believe me, I had a front row seat," she snapped, and Matthieu immediately regretted his words.

He sat up in bed; sheets pooled around his hips, and put his head in his hands. "I know. I'm sorry."

She rubbed his tense back slowly, rhythmically. "Don't be. Like I said, wasn't your fault. Look, I don't know your brother all that well, but he seems like a pretty capable guy, yeah? And Drew, too?"

When she paused, he gave a sharp nod.

"And Isla...it seems like she's gone a few rounds with these demons, so she knows what she's talking about. True?"

Another nod.

"And to be quite frank, Raven terrifies the daylights out of me, so I'm not worried about her at all."

"What's your point?" he asked, although he had an idea where she was headed.

"The point is, they're all strong, capable adults, for heavens' sake. I'm sure they would resent the implication that you and you alone can keep them safe. Especially since it's *not true*."

"I'm a danger to everyone. I'm a draw for the demon."

"In case you weren't listening to your *paranormal investigator* of a brother, let me reiterate...we are all already in danger. And if Jeremiah and Isla are to be believed, *I'm* just as much of a draw for the demon, if not more."

Her hands went from gentle rubbing to kneading the tight muscles in his back, digging in hard enough to hurt so good. Matthieu didn't bother to suppress his groan as he let his head drop forward, chin to chest. His skin tingled when her breath tickled his nape.

"We're stronger together, all of us," she whispered. "Let us help you like you've helped all of us. Please?"

"Okay," he said on a soft exhale, his mind already moved past demons and witches and family. Turning, he pressed Fate back onto the mattress and covered her curvaceous form with his bulky one, careful not to bear too much weight down on her.

It spoke volumes about his state of mind when he'd entered the room that up until then, he hadn't registered that she was completely naked. Certainly not wanting to be left behind by that departing ship, he raised a hip and tugged down his Calvin's with little finesse.

Finally skin to skin, remarkably, he felt none of the urgency they'd had before. When a person faced eminent death and a possible eternity in hell, he kind of wanted to savor things when given a second chance.

He kissed a lazy trail up the elegant column of her neck, while she arched beneath him, tilting her chin for him. As he feasted upon that smooth expanse of skin, he kept up a languid roll of his pelvis—just a bit of pressure to stoke the fire slowly.

With a sigh and a flex of the hips, he slipped inside her—not in any hurry to get to his destination, just taking pleasure in the journey. He kept up the slow and steady routine while a sheen of perspiration formed on his skin, and her breaths began to hitch.

Her long fingers traveled through his hair, along the back of his slick neck and down to grip the muscles over his shoulder blades. Clutch and release. Clutch. Release.

He'd never done this before, made love gentle and slow. He couldn't say he'd ever *made love* at all until her. It was surprising to learn that he was just as turned on, just as urgent as ever.

At last, his own need began wrestling with his control, so he sat back and pulled her up onto his lap. Here he could hold her close, heart to heart. He could feel the long, lithe muscles of her back undulate under his hands. Her hips swiveled to meet his thrusts. She buried her face in the crook of his neck, and he brought his hands up to tunnel into her hair.

With a grip slightly tighter than was absolutely necessary, he pulled her head back and took her mouth in a searing kiss. Not violent, no. But aggressive. He wasn't sure if the slight pain over pleasure of the hair pulling was what sent her over the edge, but the sting of her teeth sinking into his lower lip was what gave him the final push.

As they lost themselves in each other, shattering and reforming, Matthieu was enveloped by an overwhelming sense of euphoria and a sweet calmness that he'd never known. If he had any kind of concept of what an angel was, she was it. Fate was the light to his dark, and he could only hope that he could keep it burning.

That night, he dreamed of death. Blood and agony. Not Afghanistan. Not his father. He dreamed of things yet to be. They all died. Tortured and bled by the demons...They. All. Died. Jeremiah, Drew, the women. The wolf and the hawk.

He couldn't save any of them. Couldn't save them because he was drowning, sinking in the murky water of the swamp, now dark red with the spilled blood of his family. He saw Draconus' eyes before him as the breath left his body in a great rush of bubbles. Those eyes were laughing.

And when he woke, screaming, shaking and clawing, Fate was there. Strong hands and power bound his wrists, held him together as he returned to himself, to the world of the living. Clasping desperately to his light, he shuddered and hung on. Those things had not yet come to pass, but they could. Would, maybe. Despite what Fate had said about strength in numbers and not having to shoulder the burden, he had to figure out a way to save them all—even if he had to sacrifice himself.

CHAPTER THIRTY·EIGHT

I N THE MORNING, THEY ATE A HEARTY BREAKFAST OF Cap'n Crunch and Twizzlers—the latter being Matthieu's side dish. Fate smirked to herself and shook her head before shoveling in a mouthful of the sickeningly sweet cereal. Matthieu was worse than her seven year old with his sweet tooth.

She'd just begun to clean up the dishes after having to fight Étienne off for the pleasure of it, when Jeremiah and his cohorts showed up. Apparently determined to get right down to business, he spread out a map on the coffee table.

"Whatcha got there, brother?" Matthieu asked around a mouthful of Crunch.

"This here's a map of Bayou Trépas and the surrounding channels. I figured first we'd ride out for a little while and see if the girls pick up any kind of woo-woo vibes. Then we can canvas the locals to find out if there've been any incidents that could have been caused by *auchrim*. We pinpoint some and it may give us a lead on the whereabouts of the *locus*. Sound good?"

"How exactly are we going to explore the canals?" Fate asked with a sinking feeling she wasn't going to like the answer.

Matthieu laughed and rubbed his big hand over the nape of her neck, two moves that didn't go unnoticed by any of the shrewd eyes in the room. And more than one pair of eyebrows were raised. "Same way everyone else does, sweetheart. In a boat." He looked at Jeremiah and jerked his chin towards the back door. "We've gotta get dressed. Why don't you go down and make sure that tub's gassed up and seaworthy."

"Sure thing."

Fate was pretty sure her rapidly pounding heart was now living somewhere above her voicebox, but she managed to croak out some words. "You want me to get on a *boat?* Not just a boat, but a freaking rattle-trap called *The Crooked Ace*?"

He looked at her, still smiling, but there was confusion in his eyes. "Well...yeah. I mean, it's not like we can fly there. Well, not all of us, anyway."

"No. Nope. Can't do it. I don't do boats. I don't do water, period."

Her revelation surprised a cackle out of Raven. "Heh. You're a water witch and you don't do water. Effing perfect."

"Has this always been a thing?" Matthieu asked

She watched him closely for any signs of mockery, something she'd had a lot of over her ridiculous fear, but there was nothing but concern. "Pretty much. When I was a little kid, my best friend drowned. I was with her."

"Shit," he hissed, the pressure of his hand on her neck steady and soothing.

"It was traumatic, yeah, but I got over it. Still never liked being in the water after that. I've gotten a little better over the years—I can be near it; even dip my toes in, but no more than that."

"Got it. Well, Hawkeye and me can stay behind with you and let the others go."

She was shaking her head before he even finished speaking. She'd be damned if she'd hold up the…investigation, as it were. "No, you all should go as planned. If you'll let me use your computer, I'll just do some internet research."

"You sure?"

"Of course. And I need to call Esme anyway, check in on Ridley. I'll be fine."

Matthieu disappeared into the bedroom for a few minutes, and then returned wearing his standard uniform of desert tacticals and a black t-shirt. Fate could clearly see the outline of his tags beneath the thin material. She couldn't help the warmth that tingled through her when he bent to give her a quick kiss on the lips.

"You sure you're all right by yourself?"

"Absolutely. I'll keep my phone on me, and yes…," she said, cutting him off when he started to speak, "I remember the rules."

He gave her a grin and a wink as he backed out the door, following the others outside.

Once they were gone, the quiet closed in on Fate like a vacuum. She took comfort in the sounds of the bayou—the chant of the cicadas, the murmur of the bullfrogs and the drone of distant motors as the fishermen went about their business. Surely life wouldn't cheerfully go on undisturbed if a psychotic demon was about to rain fire and brimstone down on all of them.

When the silence became too heavy to think through, she went outside. She hit the wall of humid air like a solid object and moisture immediately began to collect on her skin. Still, it was air and it was open, so much better than the oppressive atmosphere inside the empty house.

Bending over, she tied her thick hair into a topknot, and then made her way down to the floating dock. She didn't hate water. She liked being near it, listening to it, getting her feet wet. She just never wanted to be at its mercy the way her friend had.

She settled in and stretched out across the sun-warmed wood, eased by the gentle swaying of the dock. Smiling to herself, Fate thought she could get used to it, living in the swamp, being a part of the age old ecosystem. She closed her eyes and allowed herself a moment to daydream—she and Ridley settling here with Matthieu, helping him heal and becoming a family.

She must have spaced out for a few minutes, because she was startled out of her little Zen trip by a change in the atmosphere. Her earlier thoughts came back to haunt her as she realized the change was silence: no wind, no bugs, no birds, no gentle lapping of swamp water against the bank. Absolute dead silence.

Fate's skin prickled with unease as she scanned the secluded canal for anything, completely unsure of what she was expecting to see. She scooted her body backwards until her spine was flush with one of the heavy pylons, and slowly stood up. It was a technique she'd learned from living with an abuser—when you never knew when the next hit was coming, you didn't leave your back unguarded.

A quiet buzz surrounded her, different from the cicadas and bullfrogs. It was somewhere between a growl and a hiss, emanating from nowhere in particular. Fate looked toward the mouth of the canal, where the waterway spilled out into the main channel, and saw nothing.

The wind kicked up then, blowing its way through the trees and causing an eerie groan and clack from the Cypresses, like giant wooden windchimes. She looked the other way, down the canal, deeper into the swamp where the vegetation was so thick, it couldn't be traveled by boat. Still nothing.

Just as she began to relax, Fate heard a noise from the other direction; a gentle splash. Whipping her head around, she spotted a woman in an old pirogue—so old, it was practically rotting—paddling sluggishly toward her.

Fate swallowed hard as the hissing sound grew louder, and the trees swayed harder. Her skin crawled. The water was completely still, without even any ripples lapping the side of the pirogue to indicate that something disturbed its surface.

The dark skinned woman in the boat appeared to be paddling, but the boat barely crawled forward. Fate blinked, and then gasped when the woman was suddenly twenty feet closer. *What the hell?* Before she was even aware of moving, she pressed harder against the rough pylon, ignoring the splinters that were digging into her back.

Her eyes flicked to the back door of the cabin as she tried to judge the distance and how long it would take her to run for it. When she returned her gaze to the water, the boat was ten more feet closer. The image of woman and boat flickered like an old black-and-white television set with a faulty pair of rabbit ears. *Again, what in the hell?*

The woman had a headful of thin dreadlocks, with all kinds of tiny objects tied to them. She was slender and beautiful, except for the milky cataract over one eye.

The image wavered again, and then she was just a couple of yards from the dock. Her good eye was vacant as she rolled it upward to look at Fate. When she smiled, it was with a gold-capped glint, and creepy as all get out.

Fate's pulse jackhammered in her ears as she tried to make sense of what she was seeing. But when the woman spoke, Fate's thoughts scattered with the wind.

"Dat jackal-mon, he comin'. He comin' far ya, jus' like he come far me."

"*What?*" Fate couldn't understand who this woman was, and why she was here. Somehow, though, she knew that the 'jackal-man' was Draconus. "Who—who are you?"

"Don' mattah now. He get us all. You can't get away, no, nona us can. Dis all I got lef'." The woman tossed something at Fate and she snatched it from the air by reflex alone.

Looking down at the object in her hand, she felt even more confused. It was a small leather pouch with a symbol on it, crudely drawn in red. "What is it?"

The woman began tossing nervous looks over her shoulders, before whispering to Fate. "Dere's no time. The eldah Rousseau will know what t'do wid' it."

Then she began shaking her head vigorously and convulsing, as if she were having a seizure. Eyes rolled back in her head and when they came back to stare at Fate, they were different. The eyes were completely clear, like glass, with wraith-like shadows flickering in them. Just like Matthieu's had been. Just like Draconus'.

"Holy mother of crap," Fate squeaked, and pressed harder against the splintered wood, hoping to disappear. She was shaking like a leaf in the wind, torn between wanting to help the stranger and wanting to stay quiet so that whatever was attacking her didn't change its course.

Out of nowhere, black water surged up around the old pirogue. The woman screeched and began to paddle furiously, but got nowhere. The waves took form of muddy hands reaching out for their unwilling captive.

Fate pressed the back of her hand against her mouth to suppress a scream. Even though she'd always looked down on people who seemed to fall back on neglected religion during traumatic times, she found herself reaching out to her forgotten childhood Catholicism. She twisted shaking hands together as she whispered to herself. *"Hail Mary, full of grace. The Lord is with thee. Blessed art thou amongst women, and blessed is the fruit of thy womb, Jesus. Holy Mary, Mother of God, pray for us sinners, now and at the hour of…"*

That time she did scream.

Those hands latched on to the woman's shoulder and head, putting obvious pressure on her. She wailed and thrashed, but seemed to have no effect on the insidious malevolence that was attacking her. The water around the pirogue splashed and frothed as the craft listed heavily to port.

Fate watched in horror as woman and boat were dragged under the surface until nothing was left but a quiet ripple of the surface and a few bubbles. Fumbling in her pocket, she pulled out her phone only to drop it because of her trembling.

She dropped to her knees, picked up the phone with one hand, and clutched the little leather bag in the other. Hitting Matthieu's speed dial number, she didn't release the breath she'd been holding until she heard his raspy voice on the line.

"Fate?"

"You need to get here," she said, hating the shake in her voice. "Now."

₰)р

Fate told the story over a dinner of local boiled crawfish, bought from a stand up the road. Only she didn't eat. She sat on the couch, wrapped in a blanket, with Étienne's arm wrapped around her shoulders.

Matthieu was wearing a hole in the rug. Pacing and growling. Growling and pacing. Fate had just finished describing in vivid detail what she saw happen to the dark-skinned woman—even though she didn't want to think about it, much less talk about it.

She rubbed her hands over her face and sighed. "So, Doc, just how many actual buckets of crazy am I?"

Jeremiah shook his head, looking grim. "If you're crazy, then we all are. It definitely sounds like a *Lochrim* trick to me." He stepped into Matthieu's path, splayed a hand over his chest to stop his progress. "That description sound familiar to you?"

"Amara."

"I thought so too." Jeremiah looked at Drew. "What do we think here? Possession? Astral projection? Demon induced hallucination?"

"No way to tell for sure. But I think you need to find this Amara. If she's safe and sound, it will give you more of a clue."

"Did she say anything else to you?" Jeremiah asked Fate.

Fate was about to answer when she remembered the little pouch that Amara had given her. She dug it out of her pocket and looked at it more closely. It was made of worn brown leather and had a crude drawing of a hand drawn in a reddish-brown substance—God, she hoped that was mud. The hand had an image of an eye in the middle of the palm.

She held up the little bag so the others could see. "She didn't say anything other than what I've already told you, but she did give me this. There wasn't time for her to explain, but she said you would know what it was for," she answered, tossing the bag to Jeremiah.

He snagged it in midair and cursed colorfully.

"What is it?" Isla asked. All eyes were riveted to Jeremiah.

"It's a gris-gris. A voodoo object of power. This particular one is called a mojo bag, and the symbol on it is a mojo hand, which makes it kind of double-power. I'm guessing she gave it to you for protection, although I'm not sure how well voodoo works on the *auchrim*."

"What's in it?" Raven asked, reaching for it.

Jeremiah jerked his hand away so she couldn't grab the bag. "Oh, no, sister. It's major bad juju to open it if you're not the one who made it. Best leave it alone." He handed the bag back to Fate. "I'd keep that on you at all times…just in case."

"O-kay…if you say so."

Isla, Raven, and Étienne closed ranks around her, making her feel surprisingly safe after what she'd experienced. None of them had batted an eye at the craziness she had just laid on them. She wasn't sure whether to be relieved, or worried for all of their sanity.

Isla looked back and forth between the men. "You lot need to go down t' the store and check on Amara. We'll take care of Fate."

Matthieu rounded on her, baring his teeth. "Like hell I'm leaving her right now!"

Ever calm, Isla just stared him down. "Easy, tiger. Release. Retract. You know, deep down, the safest place for Fate is with us. You need to go help look for Amara. Have your brother's back."

Even Fate heard the unspoken *for once* in that sentence.

"Yeah, so run along," Raven said in a mocking tone. "We got this, bitches."

Matthieu lunged at her but Drew caught him by the shoulder. "Don't make me kill you," he deadpanned. He was calm, but no one would deny that he would follow through to protect his wife.

Jeremiah laid a hand on Matthieu's other shoulder. "C'mon, brother, let's do this right quick and then we can get back to our women."

He didn't say anything else, but the tension in Matthieu's body eased slightly. He looked Fate directly in the eye. "You okay with this?"

Her heart flipped a little at the concern. She didn't really want him to leave her, but she knew they had to find out if Amara was alive. "I'll be fine."

She watched as Matthieu strapped on his shoulder holster, secured his SOLO to his ankle, and hid the knives in his boots like he always did. While the sight of all those weapons would have disturbed her a few weeks ago, now the ritual of it was comforting. Matthieu was a constant—a solid wall between her and those who would harm her.

He followed Jeremiah, Drew, and Marduk out the door, but turned and waved at her one more time before he disappeared.

Suddenly drained, Fate slumped against Isla and wrapped her hands around the hot mug of coffee Étienne brought her. "Two days until Beltane?"

Isla nodded. "Aye."

"It's going to be a long forty-eight hours."

CHAPTER THIRTY·NINE

AMARA'S SHOP HAD BEEN LOCKED UP TIGHT AND WAS dark inside. They checked all the windows and doors for signs of a break in and found nothing. As callous as it was, Matthieu had difficulty paying attention to the search, because his thoughts were on Fate back at the cabin.

She'd looked so pale and shaken, and there was really nothing he could do to take that burden from her. This was the hand she'd been dealt—that they all had—and it just had to play out as it was meant to. But he was damn sure going to make certain they were as prepared as possible. He began going over in his head all of the things they were going to need to hand load bullets once they'd procured some of Fate's blood. He mentally catalogued everything in his arsenal and decided how to divvy up the weapons.

"Earth to Matty." Jeremiah's voice cut into his thoughts. From the look on his face, it must not have been the first time he'd tried to get Matthieu's attention.

"Don't fucking call me Matty," he grumbled.

"Whatever. You find anything? Or have you been spaced out the entire time?"

"No, dumbshit. The place is clean."

"Damn. Now we have nothing to go on. No way to know if Amara is trapped, dead, or in a warm kitchen somewhere, stirrin' up a nice filé gumbo. And no way to tell, once we take out Draconus, if she'll walk out or float away."

Jeremiah had explained to Matthieu that the *auchrim* could possess people—they could trick them into seeing things that weren't there. They'd lure them inside the *locus* so that the head honcho could feed on their life force. When a *Lochrim* was killed, the souls of the people they'd drained escape to cross over, and the people who were trapped and not yet fed on are released. Who knew into which category Amara would fall?

Matthieu sighed, suddenly tired. "Look, how do we know she didn't just close up shop to take a vacation or something? Maybe Draconus conjured up the whole vision just to screw with us."

"That's entirely possible...but I just don't see the point in showing Fate a vision of Amara if she wasn't a part of this."

Drew clapped a hand on both of their shoulders. "Seems this is a dead end, boys. Let's go back and check on the ladies."

ॐ)Cઅ

The girls had their heads together when Matthieu came through the back door, but they broke apart when they heard him.

"Interrupting something?" he asked, raising a brow.

"Just girl talk," Raven answered, her sickly sweet smile not reassuring him at all.

"Whatever." Constantly losing the battle with himself over keeping his distance from Fate, Matthieu walked over and gave her a quick but fierce kiss. When they broke away, he dropped a heavy bag onto the coffee table. "Save it for later. Right now, you're all going to get a crash course in prepping demon bullets."

"Perfect," Fate said. When she met his eyes, her expression was weary but determined. "We got the blood while you were out. Raven was amazing; no one was the wiser."

Matthieu clamped his jaw shut to keep from saying something stupid and condescending, like they shouldn't have gone without him. They were perfectly capable, and would be plenty happy to tell him all about it.

To keep himself occupied, he began unloading boxes and boxes of ammunition: .45 caliber, 9mm, 12 gauge shotgun shells. He'd decided that they wouldn't even need to hand-load to make their special *Lochrim*-hunting bullets. They could simply coat the outside of the cartridges with blood. He explained that to the others while sorting the ammunition.

"I think the quickest and easiest way to incorporate the blood will be to put a drop on the tip of each casing. We'll use as much as we can afford to. Once it's dry, we should be able to use it like normal."

He'd picked up various tools for applying the blood, and Jeremiah passed one to each of them. Matthieu slit open one of the heparinized blood bags and poured the contents into a porcelain bowl. He quickly demonstrated what he thought would be the best way to add the blood, and the eight of them got to work.

Raven made a face as she dipped a thin paintbrush into the blood. "This is so creepy," she said with a shudder.

"Creepy, maybe," Isla said, "but necessary."

Fate paused and looked over at Isla. "What did you find out today while you were out on the boat?

Isla and Raven shared a look. "It's not good news," Isla said.

"As if any of this has been. Just lay it on me."

"We believe the *locus* might actually be in open water...in the middle of the main channel."

"When you think about it, it has a twisted sort of irony," Raven said. "You being afraid of water, your friend drowning—I doubt any of that was a coincidence. It's all been leading up to this. I'd imagine Draconus thinks that having the *locus* in open water will perhaps keep you from confronting him."

"God," Fate whispered. "He wouldn't be wrong."

"Nonsense," Isla said. "He's underestimating you. That's to our advantage."

Matthieu looked up from where he'd been concentrating on priming blooded casings. "So you've got an idea where the *locus* is. Is there an actual plan for going after this bastard?"

"Well, both times we've been through this, it's been different," Jeremiah said. "The only consistencies have been the day and the hour."

"How so?"

"Each time, the final showdown happened on Samhain at three a.m.—the devil's hour."

Matthieu rolled his eyes and kept painting on blood. "So likely Beltane will pass without a whisper."

"I thought so at first, but with Fate's vision...who knows?" Jeremiah began loading the blooded bullets into magazines. "Alastore was killed by being stabbed with a knife coated in Isla's blood. Azibel actually had to ingest some of Raven's—she bit her. There's no telling which of those, if either, will work on Draconus."

"Well…" Matthieu began, slapping a magazine into his SOLO. "How 'bout I just shoot him in his fucking throat. Should get the job done either way. I'd like to see him survive that."

Raven made a noise in the back of her throat and glared at him. "Could you at least try to act like a human being for five minutes? This isn't a joke."

He only allowed himself a moment to imagine wrapping his hands around her skinny neck and squeezing, before he pinned her with a hard stare. "Do I *look* like I'm a joking? And human is the *last* thing we should be acting like, because what we're dealing with isn't."

He expected some kind of snide comment, but Raven just lowered her eyes to the shells she was coating. "You have a point. Guess I'm just a little on edge—not exactly excited about doing this all over again."

"I get that," Matthieu said, thinking of all the times he got deployed when the last place he wanted to be was back in the sand pit. Well, look at him being all well-adjusted and shit. Who knew?

Fate stood and tried to walk past him. Matthieu caught her arm and pulled her down into his lap. He could feel all eyes on him, but he just couldn't bring himself to care. Tomorrow, they could all be gone.

He nuzzled in behind her ear and breathed deep, allowing himself that simple comfort. He looked at Fate rather than Jeremiah, even though he addressed his brother. "What I don't get, is what he wants."

"I don't follow."

"We ice Draconus, we all get to keep breathing. If he wins, what's the grand prize?"

"Free reign." Jeremiah stared off into the middle distance, unfocused. "The ability to run roughshod through our world and suck it dry, one soul at a time."

"Soul?"

"Soul, energy, essence. Life force—what have you. What makes us human, what keeps us ticking."

Drew had just finished his last box from his pile of ammo. "I think Draconus escaping would have an even more deadly consequence."

"How so?" Jeremiah asked.

"Well, so far, these *'celebrity death-matches'* have gone in our favor. The *Lochrim* are oh-for-two. We let one of them get away, I'd bet the farm he's going to find a way to spread the word about what's happening. They could start picking off *praedos* before they even know what they are."

"Shit," Jeremiah hissed.

"All right, all right," Matthieu said. "We have one day until Beltane. We've blooded all the cartridges, shells, and blades we've got…so that's all we can do for right now, true?"

Jeremiah rubbed his hands hard over his face and into his shaggy hair. "I suppose so."

"Then let's climb back through the looking glass for the night and have a goddamn beer, shall we?"

"Sounds like a plan, brother," Drew said with a grin.

ℰ☽☾ℛ

Matthieu leaned back into the plush sofa and stretched out his legs. He placed one booted foot on the coffee table, crossed the other leg over it, and took a deep draw of his beer. Tonight had been...interesting. It had been a long time since he'd sat around with friends, shooting the shit and sharing beers.

The only time he could actually remember having done it was in Afghanistan, hanging with his unit during their PTO. It was different with family, though. Jeremiah had a lightness about him that hadn't been there when they were boys. It was as if, now that he had help holding up the weight of the world, he could finally be happy. Isla was perfect for him—the perfect combination of easing calm and razor sharp wit.

Drew looked like he'd walked through hell since the last time Matthieu had seen him, but he too seemed to have found a comforting balance. His smile was more genuine, his posture relaxed, and there was no trace of the affected, 'nothing-can-touch-me' playboy attitude. And Raven. Drew's Raven was snarky and completely insufferable. Matthieu kind of loved her. It wasn't every day he found someone brave enough to trade insults with him.

The group had slowly trickled out the door as the beer continued to flow. Drew and Raven had gone back to their hotel, and Étienne had flown off to parts unknown. Fate was in the bedroom calling Ridley, and Jeremiah was out on the back deck sharing a Cuban with Marduk.

That left Matthieu alone with Isla. She smiled at him as she sipped her tea, the saucer balanced on her rounded belly. "We're really glad to see you, Matthieu."

It was a comment that required no answer, just the comfortable silence of family. He was about to muster his rusty and limited "people skills," such as they were, when she let out a sharp gasp. Instantly on alert, he shot upright and slid closer to her on the couch.

"Shit, are you okay? Are you hurt?" He had one hand on his ankle holster and was twisting around to call for Jeremiah, when she stopped him with a hand on his knee.

"Relax. Don't mind me. It's just the wee one. She spends so much time kickin' me, I don't know when she bloody sleeps." She got a mischievous gleam in her eye and gave him a slow smile. "Here, give me your hand."

"Oh, no, that's really all r—"

She grabbed his hand and placed it on the side of her abdomen, just below her ribs. He didn't know what he'd expected—flutters, like fish in a bowl or something—but what he felt was a distinct thump that rolled heavily under his hand.

Isla's smile was brilliant and her laughter tinkled like fairy bells. "That's your wee niece in there."

All the things he'd done and seen, all of the places he'd been, lives he'd saved and taken...nothing compared to this. Having the power to literally grow life. An unexpected warmth flooded through him along with a fierce protective instinct that he'd only felt one other time—when he was holding Ridley.

She must have seen something in his face, because Isla's expression softened even further, and she touched his scarred cheek with delicate fingers. "You can have all of those things you pretend not to want, you know."

He started to ask her what the shit she was talking about, but she just steamrolled right over him. "Things like, oh, I don't know, happiness. Family. Love." Those gentle hands changed from a friendly caress to a quick stinging slap. "And don't give me that sodding malarkey about how you don't deserve it. You deserve it more than anyone I know."

Matthieu knew she meant well—family always did—but he had to put the kibosh on this right the hell now. "Look, Isla, you don't get it. I'm not going to make it through this showdown."

Her eyes widened and her smile disappeared. "What do you mean?"

"I am going to do anything and everything I have to do to make sure that Fate, Jeremiah, you, and that baby come through this in one piece. Anything. Am I making myself clear?"

She gave him a dazed nod but before she could say anything else, Fate came back from the bedroom at the same time Jeremiah stepped back inside. She gave him a look that told him the conversation was postponed but not over.

Deliberately looking away from her, he turned to Fate. "Did you talk to Ridley? How is she?"

The smile that lit her face was like the sun breaking through the clouds after a storm. "I sure did. She's doing wonderfully. Esme took her shopping for a new dress and she couldn't stop talking about it," she said with a quick swipe at her eyes. "I can't wait to thank Esme in person. Ridley's never really had a grandparent in her life, and Esme is just like one to her. Ridley adores her."

"Mom's great with kids." *I think.* He didn't really know anymore, did he?

"Oh, and Ridley asked about you, too."

"Yeah?"

"Yeah. She said to give you a hug for her."

He couldn't contain the smile that stretched across his face, so he gave up trying. He tried to hide it, but Jeremiah saw. That man saw everything, especially things Matthieu didn't want him to. That was one of the things that had made it easier to leave than stay all those years ago.

Matthieu could tell by the look on his brother's face that Jeremiah wasn't going to let it go, either.

"Matty, come have a chat with me outside."

"Actually, I was just about to have another beer—"

"Wasn't askin'. Bring me one, too." Not waiting for a reply, Jere turned on his heel and headed back outside.

Matthieu reluctantly got up and followed him. "You can get your own goddamn beer," he grumbled.

Once out on the deck, Matthieu stared at his brother's back. "You gonna hit me again?"

"You need to be careful," Jeremiah said without preamble.

"Eh, it's only my fourth beer. I don't think I'm at the falling-in-the-water-and-getting-eaten-by-gators stage just yet."

"Not what I meant. Falling for Fate could be dangerous for both of you."

"That is so not gonna happen, my brother."

Jere snorted and rolled his eyes, smoldering cigar clamped between his teeth. "As if you have a choice. As if it hasn't already happened."

"Seriously? How is this even your business?"

"You need to listen to me. A relationship between you and Fate could complicate the fight with Draconus."

Matthieu sucked in a sharp breath and made a circle with his fingers. "No, you listen to *me*. See this? This is the number of fucks I give about Draconus and his endgame. I don't care about the demons or the witches or the gateways or the souls. All I care about is keeping the eight of us alive." He advanced on Jeremiah, who spread his hands apart in a gesture of surrender. "So how about you shut fuck up and let me do that."

"Yeah, yeah, all right, little brother. Whatever you say."

Matthieu gave him one last glare before going back inside to spend what little time he may have left with Fate. And yes, with family.

CHAPTER FORTY

MATTHIEU KNEW IT WAS A DREAM EVEN AS HE SAT up in bed and glanced around the empty bedroom. His first clue was that he was alone. He'd gotten used to Fate beside him, both in and out of dreams. *So sue me*, he thought.

An eerie quiet had settled over the house, so much so that he could feel the absence of any other living things within its walls. In some ways, this was more disconcerting than nightmares of torture and death; this waiting for the other shoe to drop.

Reluctantly, he climbed out of the warmth of his bed. He had to figure the sooner he got things moving along to the point of the dream, the sooner he could get it over with. The great room and kitchen were equally silent as he padded through them, looking for something he couldn't identify.

There was no sign of Fate, his brother and sister-in-law, or the zoo crew. Crossing the room, he pulled apart a couple of the slats of blinds on the back window and looked out into the gloom. Nothing moved.

He turned around and stiffened when he noticed the dark silhouette of a man leaning against the kitchen bar. Matthieu took in the dark hair, slicked back and curling at the nape of his neck, and the perfectly tailored suit that screamed money-to-burn.

Before the guy even turned around, Matthieu knew it was Drake Maxwell, a.k.a. Draconus. His hand automatically reached for the pistol in his shoulder holster which, of course, he wasn't wearing. The fact that he hadn't grabbed his SOLO off the nightstand further convinced him that he was indeed dreaming.

When Draconus saw Matthieu's hand move, his mouth tipped up into a half smile and he chuckled. "Good to see you again…been a while. Relax, kid. Your guns won't work on me anyway."

"Maybe not," Matthieu growled, "but it will make me feel a lot better to blow a hole in your head—just like I did to your buddy."

"Ah, yes. Eligos. He always was a bit impetuous. I believe he's gone to ground to…recuperate. But he's not your problem right now. I am."

"Really? Because I couldn't give two shits about you or your fight."

Draconus eased away from the bar and began a slow stroll around the room, making graceful gestures with his hands as he spoke. "I believe you. However, I do think you give *two shits* about what happens to my daughter, yes?"

Matthieu's vision clouded with a red haze when the man referred to Fate as his daughter. He flexed his fingers, fighting off the urge to punch the bastard.

Making his way back to the kitchen, Draconus selected one of the Cubans from the humidor and lit it with a puff. The sweet, potent aroma of the smoke curling around his head defied logic, considering that they were in a dream…Matthieu thought. He didn't think he'd ever look at those cigars the same again.

Draconus took a deep drag and eyed him through half-closed lids. "I was surprised when I figured out you were the one who would bring my daughter to me. You were just a little child. But here we are—everything according to plan."

"I'm not going to let you have her."

The *Lochrim* cocked his head and gave Matthieu a dimpled smile—which made Matthieu want to crush his face.

"That's adorable," Draconus said with a snort. "By the time you wake up, she'll be long gone. And I'll have her. In the meantime, let's have a little fun."

The man snapped his fingers, and Matthieu experienced a lancing pain in his skull. He blinked a few times and when he opened his eyes, they weren't in the cabin anymore. They were in the bunker in Afghanistan. And Matthieu was once again trussed up and laid out on a table like a Thanksgiving fucking turkey.

Only this time, it wasn't Patang who circled him like the shark that scented blood. No, it was Draconus. It was Draconus who dragged his fingers lightly along the tray that held instruments of torture…Draconus who stuffed the dirty rag in his mouth, more to humiliate than to stifle any screams.

The demon picked up a dirty scalpel and toyed with it. Stepping closer, he wrapped a big hand around the side of Matthieu's skull to hold him still. With surgical precision, he used the scalpel to open up the scar on Matthieu's cheek, the one that he'd carved so long ago.

It may have been a dream, but he felt every bit of that blade fileting his face, hitting bone and scraping. He wasn't proud of the howl he let out, but it had been a long time since he'd last been tortured. Not long enough, but a long time still.

Draconus stepped around the end of the table so that Matthieu could see him. Chuckling, he raised the scalpel to his tongue and sampled the blood that coated it. Matthieu fought back the bile that threatened to rise, but he couldn't keep his teeth from chattering—an effect of the trauma and adrenaline.

"There are certain benefits to sharing blood," Draconus said. "I can make you feel everything as if it were real. I can keep you here as long as I want…make it feel like decades, and still have only a second pass. I can't miss my opening, after all, but I can take a moment to bond with my little pet."

To punctuate the label, he smacked Matthieu's sliced cheek so hard that spots swam in his vision. Draconus' eyes turned even clearer than usual, and the shadows inside began to thrash. He cocked his head as if he were listening to something, and then looked back at Matthieu. "Rise and shine, little brother."

Confusion cut through the pain clouding Matthieu's brain, but before he could make sense of it, he was crushed under the weight of a massive boulder.

It wasn't a boulder. It was his idiot brother. Jeremiah had apparently come bounding into the room and taken a flying leap, only to pile drive into Matthieu's blanketed body. "Rise and shine, little brother."

Matthieu, who'd been lying on his stomach, came up swinging. Twisting his body, he flipped Jeremiah over and drove a knee between his shoulder blades. With hands on the back of Jere's skull, Matthieu drove his face into the pillows.

"Mmmpff crmfm imma mmngh."

Matthieu gave Jeremiah a hard smack on the back of his head for good measure before letting him up. "The hell did you just say?"

"I *said*, you're all cuddly in the morning, Princess."

"How do you go through daily life being such a colossal ass-clown?"

"It's my cross to bear." Jeremiah sat up and made a big production of straightening out his wrinkled clothes. "So it looks like we all survived the night. Where'd Fate get off to? I want to congratulate her. You know, for being alive and shit."

Matthieu froze. A cold chill prickled the back of his neck as unease churned in the pit of his stomach. "She's not here?"

"Nuh-uh. We checked around before I came in. You know, to gently wake you."

His brother's sarcasm was lost on him, because Matthieu was busy thinking back to his conversation with dream-Draconus.

By the time you wake up, she'll be long gone.

"Oh, *shit.*

CHAPTER FORTY·ONE

FATE WAS RIPPED FROM SLEEP BY THE ONLY THING THAT could burn through her unconscious mind so effectively. A crying child. *Her* crying child. She shot up in bed, heart pounding, and her eyes darted around the room as they adjusted to the darkness.

It came again, a low whimper that cut through the dark. Then a sob and a quiet *"Mommy."* Impossible. Ridley was safely ensconced in Esme's house in New Orleans.

She was unable to stop herself—her body moved with a will of its own. She climbed out of bed, pulled on a pair of jeans over her sleep shorts, and crept out the door into the great room. She should have found it odd that she'd woken up alone, in the spare bedroom. That would have been a sign, if she hadn't been so focused on her daughter's cries.

Instinctively knowing that the sound wasn't coming from inside the house, she let herself out the back door, into the thick, wet air of the swamp night. Moisture immediately collected on her skin and her hair stuck to the back of her neck in wet curls.

With an absent flick of her wrists, she tied her thick blonde back. Hearing the cry again, she followed the direction of the noise, walking down the deck stairs until her feet hit the mossy soil at the bottom.

Her limbs felt heavy, her mind felt cloudy and her breaths were shallow. It was almost as if she was under water, and rapidly running out of air.

Dark and primitive on the brightest day, the swamp was eerie and surreal, pitch black at night. Fate could no longer feel her footfalls as she drifted through the thick forest of Cypress. Her body moved of its own accord through the dreamscape, seeking out her distressed child on a purely instinctual level.

When she entered a tiny moonlit clearing, she abruptly felt the saturated ground on her bare feet, felt the humidity on her skin once again. She immediately noticed her little daughter's small body, shaking and huddled against a tree. Her back was to Fate, but she could see the stained nightgown and the glint of blue-black hair in the moonlight.

Fate reached out to touch Ridley's shoulder, but the image disappeared just as she made contact...just dissolved like mist. Blinking, she spun around, looking for something she knew wouldn't be there.

A deep, rumbling chuckle sounded behind her. She whipped around and was faced with a man she'd never met, but knew well and feared. *Draconus*.

"Hello, daughter. How nice of you to join me."

He wore simple blue jeans and a white t-shirt with the sleeves rolled up to reveal muscular arms. The slick, jet black hair and translucent eyes managed to detract from the whole James Dean vibe he was sporting. His cheekbones and brow were sharp, his teeth were fangs, and the jackal symbol on his forehead stood out in plain contrast with his now-pale skin.

"Draconus." She refused to let her voice shake. She refused to acknowledge the *daughter* statement.

"Yes. However, I've grown rather accustomed to my human persona, so feel free to call me Drake." He bared his teeth in a smile that might have been attractive if not for the fangs. "I'm happy you came."

"You tricked me."

"Yes. You proved to be quite suggestible."

Fate's hands curled into fists and she barely resisted the urge to rake her nails across his sneering face. "Kind of a dirty trick, don't you think? Using my daughter against me."

Again, he chuckled, and spread out his arms. "Hello…Lochrim here. Dirty tricks are kind of what I do."

Standing her ground, Fate crossed her arms over her chest, though she was trembling. "What do you want from me?"

"The simple answer? Complete and utter surrender. I don't really care if you join me—in fact, I think that may have been what caused dear sister Azibel's downfall. No, I could take you or leave you, as long as you're out of my way."

"So why seek me out at all?" she asked, confused. After all, if it hadn't been for the hired hit, she would have gone about her life none the wiser. *If only,* she thought.

Drake snarled, and his hideous grill made Fate flinch away. "That goddamn Eligos jumped the gun with his ridiculous hit."

"Eligos…" she said. "Eli."

"Yes. I only needed to know where you were so I could make sure you were well away from my *locus* when I made my move. I just needed you out of the way, but Eligos had to go and get you involved. He brought his hands together and cracked all of his knuckles. "Enough chit-chat. Let's talk business, shall we?"

"I'm listening," she answered, because really, what choice did she have?

"It's simple. You will stand down. It's Beltane. The veil is lifted. I will make my way into the world and you will occupy yourself elsewhere. Right here, preferably. You won't try to stop me."

"And if I don't?"

His sneer caused her skin to prickle with unease. "Did I give you the impression that this was a negotiation? I'm being pretty lenient by not killing you outright. Don't make me regret it. Stand down or die."

Fate turned away from him with the intention of leaving. If he was going to stab her in the back, then so be it. She stopped cold when black water began bubbling up through the mud and pooling around her feet.

Turning around, she realized the same thing was happening all around her. The water rose until she was standing on a small circle of muddy ground, about three feet in diameter, and she was surrounded on all sides by swamp water.

It was as if Drake had reached into her subconscious, pulled out her deepest fear and fenced her in with it. There was no way she was going anywhere now. And yet, as usual, she had to go and make things worse. "You can keep me here, but my friends will come after you. They know what to do."

He actually rolled her eyes at her. "My brethren may have proved to be idiots, but I assure you that I am not. I know that only you can destroy me. I probably know more than you do. And even if you did figure it out, I have a little insurance policy. So your friends can't do anything but slow me down—and make me angry."

"They have my blood." *Well, damn it, Fate, you might just be too stupid to live.* She mentally scolded herself, but in for a penny, in for a pound she supposed. "Lots of it. They'll figure out a way to take you out."

Drake looked pensive for a moment, as if he was actually considering her threat, but then he pegged her with a hard stare. "Then I'll just have to get rid of them before they do."

Oh, balls. She looked up at him, ready to find some way to distract him from her friends, but he was gone. All that was left was a cloud of smoke and brimstone that smelled like rotten eggs and gunpowder.

Sweet Jesus, what had she done?

ﻍ

Gone. *Gone.* Fate had disappeared. Matthieu had lost her—*failed* her. As hard as he'd tried not to let her down, he did anyway. He always did. Ridley would be left without a mother—he would be left without…*no*.

Matthieu stared at himself in the mirror of the ensuite bathroom. His scar was red and inflamed as if it had indeed been recently ripped back open. His hands gripped the edges of the sink so hard that his knuckles turned white, and he thought he might shatter the thick porcelain. He stared at his face until the image blurred, becoming a jumble of lines and shapes, all the while breathing heavily, close to hyperventilating.

A mass of unruly black hair, begging for a razor. Frown lines furrowed in a forehead underlined with dark brows. Eyes so cold and hollow, he may as well be dead already. Red angry scar standing out in hideous contrast to the shadowy stubble covering his hard jaw.

He looked like a stranger. No, that other man was a stranger—the one that smiled and laughed and made love. That man was a temporary dream. This man in the mirror was the real Matthieu—a motherfucking piece of shit waste of oxygen. The one time in his life when he'd actually stepped up to protect life instead of taking it and he'd failed. Failed again. Fate. Dad. Dad. Fate. *Fuck*.

His vision narrowed until all he saw was the two obsidian pools of nothingness he called eyes. He *would* find her, dead or alive. And then he *would* rain agony and death down on anyone who thought to hurt her. Dead or alive. Pain, torture...killing— this was his wheelhouse.

Opening the medicine cabinet, Matthieu yanked the electric clipper from the shelf and plugged it in. He still saw nothing but his own eyes as he began to scrape the metal blade across his scalp.

Jeremiah eyed Raven as she took a swig of her second beer.

"Jesus Christ, Raven, it's ten o'clock in the bloody morning," Isla said without any real heat.

Raven gave an idle shrug. "We've just dodged another demonic bullet, so to speak, so I think I'm entitled to a little fucking celebration."

He didn't say as much, because he wasn't fool enough to side with anyone over his wife, but he tended to agree with Raven. The devil's hour of Beltane had come and gone, and the morning sun was shining bright over the bayou. They were alive. Heads hadn't rolled. That alone was worth a toast.

Sure, Fate and Étienne were mysteriously absent at the moment, but he was sure they'd turn up. When they did, they'd all relax a bit before hashing out a game plan for Samhain—they had time, after all.

A palpable chill invaded the room—so tangible that he shivered—preceding his brother's entrance. Matthieu ignored all of them, just went straight to their makeshift weapons table and began loading up. He was already wearing his shoulder holster with his pair of SIGs, and his PPK was anchored at the small of his back as usual. Jeremiah had no doubt that the SOLO was hidden somewhere on his person, too.

He strapped blood coated tactical knives to his forearms and ankles, before covering them with his black BDUs and black long-sleeved shirt. Clipping an ammunition belt low on his hips, he stuffed preloaded magazines into slots. Lastly, he holstered a sawed-off twelve gauge at his hip, and draped yet another belt across his chest that was loaded with extra shells.

Straightening, he turned toward the group of them and pointed at Marduk. "You. Wolf. Gas up the boat and be ready to head out in ten."

His voice was as raw as Jeremiah had ever heard it. Marduk gave Jere a confused look but he could only shrug helplessly. He had no idea what was happening, either. In a huff, Marduk left out the back to do Matthieu's bidding.

Raven narrowed her eyes at Matthieu as he checked his weapons. "Dude," she said in a stage whisper to whoever was listening. "Captain Crankypants is totally harshing my buzz."

This earned her a vicious side-eye from Matthieu as a muscle in his jaw twitched. Without taking his eyes off a newly shaved and weaponed up Matthieu, Drew felt around until he was able to slap a hand over Raven's mouth. "Raven," he said quietly, "Pumpkin. Shut up. Don't rattle his cage. He might snap."

"Think he already has, *Pumpkin*," she muttered under her breath.

Jeremiah heard her, and was afraid she might be right. Matthieu was gone. At least the Matthieu he'd come to know over the past couple of weeks. Old Matthieu was back—the cold, empty stranger he'd mourned through the years. The stony shell of a person that had replaced his brother after their dad had died was back with a vengeance.

Matthieu looked up from checking one of his holsters and glared at them, as if he couldn't believe they were still standing there, staring. "*Well*...weapon up and get out to the boat! I'm going to make sure the house is secure, and I'll be on out."

Drew and Raven headed out the back door to the dock, but Jeremiah hung back. He eyed his brother the same way he would a caged bear. "Look, Matty. Maybe Fate just went for a walk." He sighed and scratched the back of his head. "I mean, Étienne's gone too, right? So they're probably together, and fine."

As Matthieu jammed his last weapon into its slot, he turned around and gave Jeremiah a cold, dispassionate stare. "I know I've let you down, Jeremiah. That I haven't been the brother you wanted or needed. And I know that you probably think I have one foot in the nutbox and one in the grave...but if there's anything at *all* about me that you can trust, it's my combat instincts. You *know* this. And I can tell you right now that Fate's absence is pinging the shit out of them."

If Matthieu was nothing else, he was a soldier—and a damn good one. Jeremiah did know that was the god's honest truth. He heaved another heavy breath and nodded. "Okay."

"Okay?" Matthieu asked, looking doubtful.

"Okay. Let's go find her."

With a look of relief, Matthieu gave him a returning nod. "Go on out to the boat. I'll be out in a sec."

Reluctantly, Jeremiah did as he said, leaving his brother behind and going out to the boat. He was greeted by the familiar sounds of Raven and Marduk sniping at each other. Strange that something so annoying could also be comforting.

"I'm driving," he heard Marduk say.

"The fuck you are!" Raven retorted.

"This tub is going to be considerately more complicated to operate than your little crotch-rocket," Marduk said, referring to Raven's Ducati sport bike.

Raven bit her lip as she looked at the helm, surveying the variety of switches and controls. The throttle, the engine control, the depth finder…it did look a bit intimidating. "I can do it," she said with a shrug, and pushed one of the buttons to the left of the wheel.

"That's the radio," Marduk said with a smirk.

Raven narrowed her eyes at him. "I hate your face." She stalked off to the stern to join Isla.

Drew rolled his eyes at the antics of his wife and the shifter, and turned to Jeremiah. "How's Matty?"

"Surprisingly lucid. But…cold. He said his instincts are telling him something's fishy about Fate and Étienne being gone. I don't have any choice but to believe him." He turned to Marduk who'd manned the helm after Raven left. "We ready to shove off?"

He nodded and started to speak, but movement at the house stopped him cold. Matthieu had stomped out onto the back deck, dressed all in black and loaded with weapons. He squinted up at the sky before donning dark, wraparound shades. As he walked toward them, his utility belt laden with all manner of implements of death hung heavy on his hips, and his tags glinted in the sunlight. Jeremiah had never seen him wear them over his clothing.

He strode down the pier in a rolling, loose-hipped gate that belied the coiled tension that Jeremiah knew was underneath. He was a walking, talking war machine. Jeremiah knew he wasn't the only one who noticed as Drew let out a long whistle, and whispered, "Like a boss."

Without a word, Matthieu loosened the moorings and tossed the ropes into the boat. He stowed the bumpers, climbed in, and pushed off from the dock. He stared at Jeremiah for a long moment, his face a mixture of regret and sadness, before it went cold again. "Are we ready to do this?"

Jeremiah gave his brother a sad smile. He put a hand on Matthieu's shoulder, and one on Drew's. "Well, you know what they say, boys. *Laissez bon temps roulez.*"

Drew winked at him and smiled. "Let's kick the tires and light the fires!"

Marduk rolled his eyes. "We're on a boat, not a plane, idiot."

"I was just quoting the pillar of cinematic genius that is *Independence Day*," Drew countered.

"Guys!" Matthieu shouted. "Could we table this, please?" Ignoring the chorus of grumbles, he turned to Marduk and nodded. "Let's go."

CHAPTER FORTY·TWO

FATE BREATHED DEEPLY, IN THROUGH HER NOSE AND out through her mouth, for exactly eight counts. It was the only way to control her raging, out-of-control heartbeat. She hadn't had a panic attack in months. They were frequent during the first couple of years after her attack.

She'd never been one to take medications, so she controlled them with breathing techniques and focus exercises. Cognitive behavior modification, her therapist had called it. Little did Dr. Carson know that her techniques would be used to keep calm and get off a demon-made Swamp Island.

Fate had never even discussed her fear of water with her doctor, and yet Draconus had zeroed in on that one little flaw. He'd effectively trapped her by fear.

Looking down at the edges of the black water lapping so close to her toes, Fate's heart gave another stutter and she could feel a cold sweat beginning to form on the back of her neck. She teetered just a bit as a wave of dizziness washed over her. What the heck was she going to do?

"Okay, girl," she said aloud to herself. "It's time to nut up and figure this out. I've survived the unthinkable. I *will* survive this. I just have to figure out how to get out of here."

If Isla was to be believed, she was a *witch,* for crying out loud. Surely she had something in her arsenal to counteract the demon's magick. She held out her hands, squinted her eyes, and concentrated as hard as she could on staring at the water.

Nothing happened. Of *course* nothing happened. She wasn't *Moses*, for Pete's sake. So, upon failing to part the swampy sea, she was out of ideas. Fate jammed her hands into her pockets to keep from wringing them. She felt something rough, so she pulled it out, realizing she was looking at the *gris-gris* from Amara.

As she gripped it, she got a sense not of its history—she assumed Amara had made it just for her—but of its unmistakable power. She looked down at the crudely painted hand on the leather sack. Maybe this was what Amara had intended her to use it for. Fate summoned all of her will and concentrated as hard as she could on the mojo bag.

Feeling self-conscious and a little silly, she glanced around the swamp even though she knew no one was around. She shook her head and turned her attention back to the little bag. She focused on it so hard that her head ached.

Finally, she felt a little trembling in the air, like the faintest aftershocks from an earthquake. Her blood thrummed in her ears, sparkling with electricity. The water began to ripple at the bank of her extemporaneous island.

The water directly in front of her slowly became infused with a reddish hue. It stretched out before her like a bloody trail, waiting for her to follow. She extended her leg, intending to put her foot in the water, trusting that it would be shallow enough to wade through, but she suddenly yanked it back.

Fate's entire body trembled. She just couldn't take the step. The black water alongside the path of red mocked her. Closing her eyes, she swallowed around a lump in her throat and took a shaky breath. What if her friends' lives depended on her facing her fear? What if her daughter's did? And Matthieu's…

She squared her shoulders and squeezed her eyes shut tighter. Taking one step and then another in rapid succession, she braced for the inevitable bone-chilling feeling of sinking. It never came.

Biting down on her lip to keep her teeth from chattering, Fate reluctantly opened her eyes and looked at her feet. They were there. The water was there. And she was standing on top of it.

"I'm walking…on water," she whispered to herself. "My mother's priest would have kittens."

Shaky step after shaky step, she continued along the blood-red trail through the swamp, listening to the wind whistle through the Cyprus trees. It was still daytime but the sky had darkened with angry clouds rolling in from the horizon, and Fate could hear the nearing rumble of thunder.

Her heart leapt into her throat when she noticed a shadow in the shape of a man lurking in the gloom. The figure leaned against a tree, facing it, and appeared to be restrained. As she neared, Fate recognized Étienne, even though she could only see the back of him.

His arms were twisted behind him as if tied together, but she could see no ropes. It also appeared as if he couldn't move away from the tree. She reached out and placed a hand on his shoulder, making him startle and wince.

"Fate?" he asked, his voice high-pitched and edged with panic. "You should be back at the house. What are you doing here? Where's Matthieu?"

She was assaulted by his rapid fire questioning, and she had to cover his mouth to calm him down. "Drake lured me out here, made me think he had Ridley. And then he...trapped me," she said, looking down at her feet and realizing that she was finally on more solid ground. She told him of her dream and how she ended up on an island in the middle of the forest. "How did you get out here?"

"He did the same to me. Made me think it was my...it was Mischa," he answered, unwilling or unable to meet her eyes.

Of course, Fate wanted to ask him who Mischa was, though she had an idea, but they didn't have time for that. "Obviously he wanted the both of us separated from the others. But why?"

"I don't know. I thought he would be after you, but he just let you go."

"To hear him tell it, he just wanted to have me out of the way so that he could do whatever evil he had planned. I wasn't privy to it. Did he hurt you? She looked him over, checking for injuries. Other than being seemingly unable to move, he appeared unharmed.

"No. Not really, but he caught me while in human form. I'm weaker this way, you see. He's tied me up with mystical bonds, and I don't have the strength to counteract the spell."

"What can I do?" she asked, worried that she would have to leave him there alone.

He looked over his shoulder at her, his golden eyes wide, pupils blown. "I know you haven't had much time to sit with this, the idea of being a witch. But I need you to lend me your power."

It didn't matter if it scared her, it didn't matter if she didn't know what she was doing. All that mattered was helping her friend. She swiped a hand across the sweat on her brow and then rubbed it on her shorts. "Tell me how."

"You have to find your power. It's that tingle under your skin...that prickle of electricity you feel whenever you touch an object, or walk in a dream. Do you know what I'm talking about?"

Oh, she knew. It was as familiar to her as her own face in a mirror. "Yes."

"I need you to grab onto it. Reach inside and take hold."

She closed her eyes and concentrated. Grabbing his hands to spark her ability, she tried to keep from having visions of his life. Instead, she centered her mind on that feeling, that *need*, to delve into the history of the hands she held. "Got it," she whispered.

"Good. The rest is surprisingly simple. Just imagine pushing it into me, as hard as you can."

And she did. She forced that shimmering current out through her own hands and into him. He grunted with the impact of it, and suddenly was able to move. With a relieved sigh, he turned around and embraced her.

"I have to shift now," he said, looking worn out and dead on his feet. "I've got no strength left. Follow this path to the water's edge and you'll find my pirogue tied to a tree. Take it around the cove into the next canal and you'll find the house. Meet you there."

He didn't wait for an answer—she wasn't sure he could—before he shifted with a flash of light and smoke, and flew off into the darkness.

"Alone again," Fate said to herself. She carefully picked her way along the muddy path, stumbling on roots and running into trees as the sky had become almost completely black. And then the rain came. It blew in on furious wind, and battered her from all sides.

She was soaking wet, but kept trudging on until she made it to the canal. As promised, the pirogue waited, thrashing against its mooring as the storm violently churned the water. She gulped down a sob when she eyed the choppy water through the driving rain.

A couple of days ago, she'd refused to get on a cushy houseboat. Now she was forced to row a tiny craft around a cove in the middle of a vicious storm. *The grass is always greener, isn't it, dumbass?*

But there was no other way to get home. She slipped in the mud as she grabbed onto the side of the little boat, and tried to steady it so she could climb in. Somehow, she managed to haul her shuddering body over the edge and into the boat.

She unleashed the tie-up and pushed off from the bank. The pirogue lurched in the wind, and Fate had to fight the urge to throw up. "Get it together. You can do this," she muttered.

Grabbing the single oar, she began paddling furiously as the water sloshed over the sides. She hadn't much upper body strength, so it seemed to take hours to reach the next cove. But finally, she rounded the outcropping of swampland and made the turn into *Bayou Trépas*. Home, she thought again.

That was when the lightning came. Striking all around her, boiling the water still tossed by the wind, it lit up the canal. She could just see the house during the brief flashes, so she doubled her efforts, paddling furiously. Out of breath and exhausted, Fate was relieved when she finally drifted near the dock.

There was a blinding flash when a huge bolt of lightning struck the house. The back end was almost instantly engulfed in flames, kindled by the rotting wood of the façade. Fate was transfixed, watching in horror as the fire blazed out of control, and eventually the pier, deck, and back of the house began to crumble into the water.

Realizing she might be in danger, but unable to tear her eyes away, she blindly paddled backwards. She managed to get a safe distance away, where she let the pirogue float while she watched the carnage.

The hawk dipped out of the sky like a feathered bullet, and landed inside the pirogue. Étienne shifted back to his human form and watched with wide eyes as part of the house began to sink.

It finally occurred to Fate that people may have still been inside. "Oh my God! Matthieu...Jeremiah and Isla...the baby. I've got to go back!"

Though she knew it was futile, she picked up her oar and started back towards the wreckage. Étienne shot out a hand to still her actions, shaking his head.

"*Think!* The *Crooked Ace* wasn't there when you came up to the house, was it?"

She shook her head, his voice penetrating through the haze of her fear. "No. No, it wasn't there. I'm sure of it."

He nodded, because he'd already known the answer. "Right, so they probably all went out on the boat to look for us. Troubling, yes, because they're out on the water in this weather...but it means they weren't in that house."

She was still numb from the initial fear of thinking all of her friends were dying in a pile of rubble and ash, so she didn't answer.

Étienne turned and stared out towards the main channel, looking uneasy, so Fate followed his gaze. "I think I have a pretty good idea where they've gone."

CHAPTER FORTY·THREE

MATTHIEU TOOK OVER PILOTING THE BOAT ONCE they made it out of the canal and into the main channel, and set a heading for the coordinates they had decided upon earlier. It was their best guess at the location of Draconus' *locus*.

The wind had kicked up the minute he'd cast off, and now the sky was nearly black from the clouds that rolled in with the gale. As he drove farther into open water, the old boat was buffeted by choppy waves.

Lightning slashed through the sky, and the thunder was so loud it was as if it vibrated within his body. This was not a natural storm. This was an assault. It took all of his strength to hold the wheel and keep true.

With his eyes trained on the water ahead, he called out to the others behind him. "Raven, take Isla below deck," he shouted over the shrieking wind. "This is going to get a lot worse."

Raven stepped up beside him, arms crossed over her chest. "Let her husband take her. You can't just shuffle all the women downstairs while the men take care of business!"

Matthieu flicked a sideways look at her and growled. "Christ, we all know you're some bad ass biker bitch—you don't have to play the part all the time."

"*Excuse me—*"

He turned on her fully, holding the wheel steady with one arm and a prayer. "Think, woman. Don't *fight* me on this. Get your friend down where it's safer and *protect* her. Protect that baby."

She met his eyes and must have seen something in them, because she nodded.

Drew, who had surged forward at the use of the 'b-word' towards his wife, was glaring at Matthieu with his fists clenched. Matthieu held his gaze steadily and silently pleaded for him to get on board.

"Stand down, brother," he said in a quiet voice. "You have to pick your battles, and we've got a much worse one coming."

Drew's eyes narrowed before he nodded in kind. "All right. You're in charge...for now."

For a moment, Drew's face became Stryker's. For a moment, Matthieu was back in Afghanistan. *Not now. You can not bug out right now.* He shook his head to clear it, before acknowledging that Drew had spoken.

Drew pulled his wife in for a quick but heated kiss. When she pulled away, she grabbed Isla's hand and led her down to the cabin below deck. Jeremiah and Marduk joined Matthieu and Drew on the bridge, both of them obviously looking to Matthieu for some kind of direction.

"What now?" Jeremiah asked, flicking a cautious look between his brother and his best friend.

"Now we find this *locus*...find Draconus and hope to God we find Fate too," Matthieu answered.

Drew squinted and looked out over the bow. "What is that?"

Close to a mile up the channel, the water seemed...lighter. No, not lighter exactly—more like a different color. Red. As the boat moved closer, Matthieu could see that it was a large circular area of water that appeared to be tinted red. It was roughly fifty yards in diameter.

"Think we found it," he muttered. Pushing forward on the throttle, he gunned the engine. If there was one thing he was good at, it was throwing himself into the fray.

The boat crashed into the *locus* at full speed. Then Matthieu cut the engine so they would drift toward the center of the circle.

"Should we anchor?" Matthieu asked, looking at Jeremiah.

His brother didn't meet his eyes. Rather, he was looking off into the distance. "Don't think that's going to be necessary, little brother. We're not goin' anywhere."

As Matthieu turned his head to follow Jeremiah's line of sight, another vicious clap of thunder shook the boat. The rain blew in sideways as the wind raged.

Matthieu sucked in a sharp breath when he saw what was coming. A huge, black wall cloud was advancing toward them at a rapid clip. The thunderhead surrounded them, pushing the wrath of the storm into the locus.

"I guess we pissed the son of a bitch off."

Eventually they were surrounded by a solid mass of water, cloud, and lightning. But inexplicably, the storm calmed in the center of the *locus*, where they floated. Matthieu steered the boat in a wide circle, trying to gauge the threat.

The engine gave a powerful shudder and then there was silence. "Awesome," he said.

Matthieu caught a flash of movement out of the corner of his eye. He turned his head and looked out across the water. A silhouette of a man was moving toward them, just strolling across the water, though his feet never touched it.

He stopped about fifteen feet from the houseboat. Stopped, and just fiddled with the cuff of his leather jacket. Then he popped the collar and buttoned it up. "Crazy weather we're having, eh?"

"Draconus," Matthieu said with all the venom he could infuse into a single word.

"We meet again, young Rousseau." Draconus smiled a smile full of dripping fangs. The canines were exceptionally long, like the jackal from his *seal*. The shadows in those bizarre swirling eyes were particularly agitated. The souls, Jeremiah had told him.

Matthieu had seen plenty enough. He drew his PPK from the small of his back, racked it and aimed for Drake's head. "This is for my father."

Draconus chuckled and looked up, meeting Matthieu's eyes in a steady stare. "You and I both know that won't kill me."

Matthieu shrugged, though the pistol held perfectly still. "Maybe it will...maybe it won't. But it'll hurt like a bitch—and make me feel all warm and fuzzy inside."

Draconus lifted a muscular shoulder in a noncommittal gesture. "Do what you will, but you're wasting your time."

"I've been a trigger man for less. We'll chalk this one up to sport."

No more talk, Matthieu thought. Without so much as blinking, he sighted Drake's left eye and squeezed the trigger.

Fate and Étienne made fairly decent headway paddling together, but the storm was a constant battle. The wind and the rain had let up just a bit, but Fate could see it concentrated in one area in the center of the channel.

She pointed out at the open water. "How much you want to bet that's where we're supposed to go?"

"That would be the most likely explanation for the freak storm," Étienne said. "Are we going in?"

"We don't have any choice. I can just feel that's where they are." She looked back at him for confirmation and he nodded.

"I feel it too, *domina*."

They redoubled their efforts at rowing and the pirogue surged forward. After what seemed like hours, they made it to the edge of a thick wall cloud. It looked like a tiny hurricane, tied down and raging but unable to expand.

"Oh God, are we actually doing this?"

"Looks that way…"

"We can't just row through it, can we? We'll be obliterated."

"You're going to have to use your power. I'm still too weak," Étienne said, looking regretful.

They rowed as close as they could to the violent wall of storm cloud and then stopped. Fate dropped her oar into the bottom of the boat while Étienne kept his jammed in the water to control the direction of their drift.

She closed her eyes and gathered all of the excess energy within her, just as she had done earlier. Before she could do anything, the clouds in front of them parted just wide enough for the pirogue to enter. Someone obviously wanted them inside the *locus*.

Fate pushed outward with her power, just in case it was a trap, while Étienne rowed them through the gap. The clouds on either side of them swirled ferociously with wind and rain, but none of it touched them.

Finally, they made it through, then relaxed and let the pirogue coast. Inside the circle, it was still dark, but the weather was calmer. Fate gasped when she caught sight of the houseboat.

Matthieu was standing on the foredeck of the Crooked Ace, with a gun aimed at Draconus. The *Lochrim* appeared to be…standing a couple of inches off the water, looking like he hadn't a care in the world.

And then Matthieu pulled the trigger. There was a moment of stunned silence in which everyone held their breath, waiting to see what would happen. Then the bullet struck, and Draconus exploded into mist with a hiss and a pop.

It took a moment for Fate to collect herself. Once she realized what had happened, she started vigorously paddling until they were able to meet up with the Crooked Ace.

She saw the exact moment Matthieu noticed them. His face was etched with a mixture of relief, regret, and…something else she couldn't identify. He gave her a tentative smile while Jeremiah helped them secure the pirogue to the side of the houseboat.

"You're alive," Matthieu said quietly.

"I am," she said, smiling. "You know that Draconus is, as well, don't you? I think I'd feel it if he were dead."

"I do know. Looks like the blood laced bullets were a bust. But at least it bought us some time. There's still a chance that the knives could work—maybe it has to do with the quantity of the blood."

Matthieu reached out a hand to pull her onto the boat while Jeremiah did the same for Étienne. Fate sucked in a breath when Matthieu pulled her into a bone crushing hug. He buried his face in her hair and took a shaky breath.

"Thought I'd lost you."

"Me too. He said he didn't want to kill me. Just wanted me out of the way so that he could break out of the *locus*. He would've killed you all, though."

Matthieu nodded and squinted out over the flat water. "He's not through yet."

CHAPTER FORTY·FOUR

MATTHIEU WENT INSIDE THE COCKPIT AND TRIED TO restart the engine. He didn't hold out much hope, so he wasn't surprised when it didn't turn over. They were quite stuck.

"Everyone needs to arm up. When he comes back, he's going to be pissed." He caught Marduk's eye before continuing. "Go below and make sure Raven and Isla have weapons."

With a nod, Marduk trotted off. Shifting, Étienne took to the sky to keep an eye on things. He might be able to give them a little warning before Draconus was upon them.

Matthieu made sure they were all armed, and not a moment too soon. Across the water, he could see an oily black mass of smoke heading towards them. He deliberately placed himself between Fate and the threat, but looked back at her when she placed a hand on his shoulder.

"We both know it most likely has to be me," she said in response to his raised brow.

"He'll have to fucking go through me first, no matter what the rules are."

"*Matthieu.*"

"No." He silenced her with a hard glare. He always knew he would go down fighting one day. At least he would be sure which side he was fighting for this time. He could wear Draconus out a good bit before he got to Fate, or Matthieu's family.

That's what they were. Family. They refused to let him go, no matter how much of a screwed up pain in the ass he was, most—okay all of the time. Matthieu would *gladly* lay down his life in their defense. As the menacing cloud slipped ever closer, the occupants of the little houseboat drew their weapons and tensed for battle.

The black smoke disappeared, leaving only Draconus striding towards them in a casual gait. Matthieu was pleased to see that there was a bloody, gaping hole in place of his left eye. He wasn't healing fast, so that was something.

When the *Lochrim* finally reached the boat, he just stood there. Dabbing his wound with his sleeve, he managed to glare at Matthieu with his other eye. "Ouch."

"I warned you, didn't I?" Matthieu cringed inside. Why did he always run his mouth?

"Going to cost you," Draconus answered.

"What do you want from us, really?"

"What I *wanted* was to be left alone to go about my business, but that seems to be too much for you mouth-breathers to comprehend. Now you'll have to die."

Before Matthieu could speak another word, the demon summoned a bluish ball of energy between his open hands, and hurled it at them. For a moment, Matthieu was mesmerized. He had the absurd thought that it reminded him of a *Shinkuu*

Hadoken from *Streetfighter*. One thing was for sure—he had no idea how to block or parry the blow.

When it looked as if the ball would strike them, it was suddenly deflected, exploding back into Draconus' field of vision. Surprised, Matthieu turned to Fate who shrugged and looked behind her. Raven stood beside Drew, her arms held out in front of her, staring Draconus down.

"Bitch," he said. The blue glow from the energy ball surrounded him then, and the water below him began to churn. He gnashed his fangs at them before bending over and slamming his hand into the water. Brutal waves spiraled out from his arm and buffeted the fiberglass hull of the *Crooked Ace*.

Most of them lost their footing, until only Matthieu and Fate remained standing. Matthieu gave silent thanks that Isla was in the cabin below.

The waves increased in size and strength until with each strike, the boat was thrown almost horizontal, but righted itself at the last second. They were taking on too much water, and Matthieu knew they were only minutes from capsizing, or sinking.

"You couldn't just leave well enough alone, could you?" Draconus screeched, completely shedding his almost-human façade.

The hull gave an ominous creak, and Matthieu knew that if it split, they were done for. Draconus gathered his power, preparing for another strike. When he would have flung the blow, Fate stepped up to the prow.

"Wait!" she shouted over the maelstrom.

Everyone froze. Fate swallowed hard before continuing in a shaky voice. "I'm the only one who can kill you…so that means this is between you and me."

ഇ⊙ൽ

Fate swallowed audibly as she stepped up to the bow railing. Clutching her *gris gris*—more for encouragement now than any power it might hold—she started to climb over. Matthieu grabbed her by the elbow and tried to pull her back, but she dug her heels in.

"What are you *doing*?" he hissed.

She could see the fear and anguish in his eyes and it cut straight to her heart, but she couldn't help that just now. "Matthieu, you have to trust me. I have to meet him on equal ground...so to speak," she said as she glanced down at the churning water.

"Not a good idea, Little Sister," Raven said, her tone betraying her nerves. "These guys can't be trusted. And you've only just discovered your powers."

"What she said," Matthieu mumbled.

"You're not wrong, Raven. But you were the one who told me that it would have to be me who killed him. I want this over, without any casualties." She glanced back at Matthieu, and held his steady gaze for long moments. Finally, he dropped his hand, though his fingers automatically clenched into a fist, as if to prevent him from reaching out again.

She turned back to Draconus, and tried to drum up enough courage to make her voice steady. "You and me. Leave my friends out of it. Do we have a deal?"

Draconus raised his hands horizontally, palms down, and the water stilled. The boat stopped its incessant pitching and all was calm. "Fine. You want me, fledgling? You have to come out here and get me."

Fate had known it would come to that, but she couldn't help the shivers that crawled inside her skin at the thought of going back in—on—the water. Mojo bag in hand, she climbed over the rail and scooted as far out as she could, until her toes were hanging out over the ledge.

She screwed her eyes shut tight and took a step out into nothingness, sincerely expecting to drop into a watery grave. Instead, just like before, the water under her feet felt solid. The red that had stained her path through the swamp was there in front of her again, forming a wide circle around her, Draconus, and the boats.

Loud gasps sounded behind her because, obviously, her friends hadn't expected her to be able to walk on water as well. Wobbling with every step, she closed the distance between her and Draconus, until they were facing each other only a few feet apart.

His lips curled in a hideous sneer and he winked at her. "Do your worst, little fledgling."

Terrified though she was, the nickname irked her. "Why are you calling me that?"

"Because that's what you are." His words were so matter-of-fact, they rankled even more. "You are the uninitiated. A child compared to me. You are a fledgling witch, and I am a king. The fact that you think you can defeat me is, well...cute."

That set her teeth on edge. Fate knew he was deliberately trying to piss her off, and she was letting him. But maybe she needed to get angry to get past her fear. She hid her hands behind her back and began trying to concentrate the flow of energy in her body into her palms. It was how she imagined Draconus had created the energy ball.

While Draconus continued to jabber on about his kingliness and her peasantry, she could feel the power building between her hands. It burned but, because it was as much a part of her as her hands, it didn't cause her any pain. She tuned back into what the demon was saying, waiting for the perfect moment.

"So you see, you and your puny little human friends have no ch—"

His words cut off abruptly as she hurled the energy ball at him, striking him square in the chest. He flew backwards and skidded across the water like the perfect skipping stone.

Fate knew he would strike back hard, so she readied herself for his return blow. Keeping the energy simmering in her left hand, she drew a large hunting knife from her belt with her right. Like all of the weapons, it was coated with her blood.

Draconus stood up slowly and stared at her with a murderous expression. Fate's entire body tensed as she prepared for some kind of onslaught. Instead, he disappeared in a billow of smoke that stank of spent matches.

Fate's eyes darted around, trying to figure out where he would materialize. Turning completely around, she looked questioningly at Matthieu on the boat. He raised his hands and shrugged. They couldn't see Draconus either.

Matthieu's eyes widened suddenly, and Fate tensed to turn, but it was too late. Draconus grabbed her from behind, hooking an arm around her neck and dragging her back flush against him.

His hot breath that brushed across her ear as he spoke was nauseating. "Now I'm going to make your pit bull watch while I gut you." She could feel him raking his claw-like nails almost lovingly along her ribs, and it sickened her.

His arm tightened around her throat until her airway was completely cut off. She clawed at him, digging into his skin, but nothing could break his hold on her. Lack of oxygen was causing spots to burst across her vision, and her limbs began to unwillingly relax.

She rolled her eyes heavenward as she fought to remain conscious, and she saw a brown dot in the sky. As it neared, she realized it was a hawk nose-diving toward them. It had to be Étienne.

Instinctively, Fate lowered her head as Étienne swooped in, talons spread. With an ear piercing screech, he dug his talons into the demon's face. Draconus screamed and immediately loosened his hold on Fate. Gasping for breath, she sank to her knees and rubbed her raw throat.

She could hear the flapping of wings, screeches from Étienne, and howls from Draconus, behind her. Unable to stop the brawl, she was horrified to watch as Draconus protracted his own claws and slashed at the hawk. He finally succeeded in flinging the bird away from his face.

With a final pained screech, Étienne plummeted down into the water. Fate quickly glanced back at Draconus and saw that he had deep gouges down his face and around his eyes. Blood flowed freely as he howled and tried to clear his eyes.

Worried for Étienne, Fate tried to see where he landed. She was relieved to see that Drew was already in the pirogue, paddling toward the downed hawk. Draconus thought to use her temporary distraction against her, and grabbed her from behind again.

This time she was ready for him. She took the hunting knife she'd unsheathed and, while he concentrated on trying to squeeze the life out of her neck, she slid it between his ribs. He grunted and immediately released her. She turned around to see him stumbling backwards with his hand clutching his side. Dark crimson blood oozed between his fingers.

He was clearly feeling it, his face screwed up with a special kind of agony. But he was, in fact, still alive. She'd been led to believe that when these *Lochrim* died, they did so in spectacular fashion.

Draconus threw his head back and growled, but the sound trailed off into manic laughter—if one could call it that. His eyes were still bright and alive with swirling shadows when he stared her down.

"Good effort, fledgling. I'll give you that. But I'm afraid it's time to end this little charade. I only have until midnight to blow this Popsicle stand. There's one long black train I plan to be on."

He hurled an energy ball at her so fast, she never saw it coming. It struck her shoulder and sent her flying. She lost control of the ability to solidify the water, and plunged down beneath the surface when she landed.

Her worst nightmare closed over her head, as the dark water swallowed her up. God, she wished she'd been able to take one last gasp of breath before going down. Because of her fear of water, she never learned to swim, so all she could do was flail her arms and slap at the water around her. This was difficult, since Draconus had winged her with his demon-bomb, so she didn't have full use of her left arm.

However ineffectual her haphazard kicking and grappling, she did rise enough to pop her head above the surface to take a watery gulp of air before plunging down again. She was *so* not going out like this. She kept fighting, but she could feel fatigue setting in.

Fate was just beginning to worry that she may not make it to the surface again, when two arms surged into the water. They hooked her underneath her armpits, and hauled her aboard a boat. It was the *Double Down*. It was Matthieu.

She rolled into the boat, gasping and coughing, but didn't allow herself any time to rest. She heaved herself into a sitting position and hacked out the water that was still in her lungs. She spared Matthieu a brief glance, and wished she hadn't. His so often stoic face was a riot of emotion. He was angry with her for taking risks and he obviously felt helpless because there was nothing he could do to stop her.

"I'm sorry," she said quietly. "It has to be me." She'd said it before, and she knew he understood—but she felt like this was breaking him.

"I know." His voice could cut glass, and it cut her too…straight to her heart. "I would give my life for it to be me instead."

His words robbed her of the breath to answer, but she didn't know what she would've said. The choice was taken from her when Draconus approached the boat. "Get rid of the pit bull or the deal's off," he said. His voice was tight, as if he was running out of patience with the game. That couldn't be good. To emphasize his threat, he rippled the water with waves that tossed the pirogue a little harder than necessary.

Fate took a deep breath, grabbed Matthieu by the back of his neck and gave him a hard kiss. She ducked her head to force him to meet her eyes. "I'll be okay."

He gave her a tight nod, though his jaw remained clenched. "Be careful."

With extreme caution, she gathered her power under her and stepped back out on the water. She had to think fast to figure out what her next move should be. Blood-laced bullets were a no go. The knife was a bust. The only thing left in their arsenal that had worked for *Praedos* in the past would be forcing him to ingest her blood. *Piece of friggin' cake.*

She needed a diversion to even get close enough to Draconus for that kind of strike. Raven had said she had the power to control water, and it had worked before. Fate closed her eyes and concentrated on harnessing that ability. She could feel the energy simmering through her blood, under her skin, down her legs, into the water and back again. It was as if there was some kind of conduction between herself and the water.

This could be her diversion; she just had no idea how to pull it off. Once again, she fell back on her knowledge of CBT and called upon her experience with guided meditation. Relaxation, visualization, control.

She contracted and released every muscle in her body that she could feel. She visualized the energy pouring out of her feet, traveling through the water that was now a part of her— underneath and beyond where the demon loomed. Fate imagined that energy gathering behind Draconus, building and condensing until it spontaneously combusted.

Abruptly, a colossal geyser erupted out of the water behind Draconus, close enough to shake his footing. He whipped around to see what happened, and Fate knew that was her window. She palmed the knife with her good hand, and gritted her teeth while slicing her own palm. She figured that if this had a prayer of working, it had to be fresh blood.

As quick as she could, she came up behind Draconus, put the knife to his neck and smacked her hand over his mouth. He jolted when he felt the impact. He grappled with her, trying to get her off his back, but she clung like a swamp leech. Finally, he bit down on her hand with his razor sharp fangs and she released him with a yelp.

He staggered forward, spitting out the blood as best he could, but it was clear it was affecting him. He fell to his knees, still able to maintain his perch on top of the water. He glared up at her, eyes wild, blood dripping from his mouth.

"It would do you well to realize that I am much stronger than those who came before me." With a suspicious lack of pomp and circumstance, he sank below the surface until Fate could no longer see his body.

CHAPTER FORTY·FIVE

FATE WAS DRIPPING WET AND SHIVERING BY THE TIME Matthieu rowed them back to the *Crooked Ace*. They climbed aboard in silence, and Fate sat down on a cushioned bench to catch her breath. She smacked at Matthieu's hands when he began prodding her injured shoulder.

"I'm fine," she said.

"You're not fine, you're hurt." He shrugged out of his long sleeved shirt, leaving him in only a sleeveless undershirt, and fashioned a crude field sling for her.

She grudgingly admitted that it felt better once stabilized. She looked over to where Jeremiah, Raven, and Drew hovered at a safe distance. "Well…you guys have been through this all before. Is he dead?"

Raven scratched her head and stared out at the water. "While there's no way to be sure, my guess is a big, fat no."

"Oh." Fate was crestfallen. She thought she'd finally beat Draconus and made it safe for them all to go home. Made it safe for her daughter. "Then we're out of ideas. We still don't know how to kill him. When he had me trapped in the swamp, he said he had an insurance policy."

"Wonder what he meant by that," Drew said.

Fate was watching Matthieu, and his eyes sort of faded out for a moment, as if he was thinking really hard about something and had checked out of the conversation. His eyes widened and he suddenly snapped back to attention. She wanted to question him, but the discussion had gone on without her.

Jeremiah nudged Raven with his elbow. "We could be wrong, though. The person who would know best is Isla. The coast is clear for the moment at least. I'll go get her."

Raven plowed on with her doom and gloom. "I know Jeremiah tries to be optimistic, but I think we might really be screwed this time if Big Evil regenerates—"

Her voice cut off when the air was split with a loud clatter from below deck, as if someone had overturned some of the furniture.

"God*damn*it, Raven!" Jeremiah bellowed from the captain's quarters.

Raven flinched and Drew immediately moved to stand in front of her. Jeremiah emerged from the cabin looking like a wild man, eyes panicked, hair sticking up on end. "You were supposed to be *with* her. You just had to come up here, didn't you?"

"I—I don't understand what you're trying to say, Jeremiah."

"What I'm saying...What I'm *asking*, is where the *fuck* is my wife?"

"She's not in the cabin?" Raven asked in a small voice.

Jeremiah surged forward like he wanted to grab her and shake her, but he was body-blocked by Drew. "No. My wife and my unborn child are *not* in the goddamned *cabin*."

"How is that even possible?" Drew asked, trying to remain the voice of calm. "There's no other way out. We would've seen her."

"Not necessarily," Matthieu mumbled. There's a water access hatch that opens up between the pontoons. Comes in handy for bad weather fishing. If I remember correctly, it's in the main cabin."

"There's a *what*?" Jeremiah asked, his voice cracking on the last syllable. He opened his mouth to ask another question but was cut off by Raven's gasp.

She pointed out across the water. "Look."

Étienne's pirogue floated about thirty feet away from them. Draconus stood on the stern, perfectly balanced despite the waves that had kicked up again. Isla was seated in the bow, perched with her back straight and her chin raised, bound up like Tiger Lilly.

Fate's stomach flopped like a dying fish. This was her fault. He wanted *her*. "I'm going." Without looking back at anyone, she swung over the bow railing and hopped back onto the water.

"Wait!" Matthieu shouted.

She whirled on him, eyes on fire, so much so that he took a step back. "You can't stop me. I'm not going to let him take Isla in my place."

"I know you have to go, but I'm going with you." He didn't wait for an answer, just untied the *Double Down*, jumped in and cast off. "Want a ride?"

Grudgingly, she stepped into the boat as he rowed them out to Draconus and his captive. She could hear Drew and Raven fiddling with the stalled engine on the houseboat and hoped they could get it started. They were definitely going to need a miracle to save Isla.

Matthieu rowed with strong, steady sweeps of the paddle, his eyes nearly black as he stared at the other pirogue. "When we get out there, you think you can get me up on the water too? I'd just like to back you up."

Fate chewed on her lip. Being responsible for her own life was one thing, but Matthieu's? That was a daunting prospect. "I think so…um, you can swim, though, right?"

He flashed her a quick grin. "Like a fish. Don't worry. If you drop my ass, I'll be all right."

She let out the breath she'd been holding. "Okay. Let's do it."

Matthieu made a last push with the oar and they coasted the rest of the way to the other pirogue. Fate stood in the prow of the *Double Down* and stared Draconus down. "You said you wouldn't hurt them if I faced you alone," she accused.

Draconus rolled his eyes and glided closer to Isla. "I'm a king among demons. Demons lie."

Fate once again stepped out on the water, creating small ripples where her feet barely skimmed the surface. She untied the sling, dropping it back inside the boat, and tested her sore arm. She winced as pain lanced through her, but it would have to do. Turning back to Matthieu, she nodded. She threw all her concentration into making the water solid for him. Breathing a sigh of relief, she saw that it would hold.

"Let her go," she said to the demon.

Draconus snorted. "No."

"Damn it, come and face me like a man!" Fate shouted, her hands balled into fists at her sides.

"That would be hard," the *Lochrim* said, "as I am, in fact, not a man. However, I'll indulge you. I'm quickly tiring of this game."

"You aren't th' only one," Isla grumbled.

Draconus met Fate on the water to face off. "Walk away now, and I'll let her go."

"Don't do it," Isla said. "He'll still kill us all. It's the nature of the beast."

He turned on her and pointed. "You. Shh!"

Isla tried to speak again. Nothing but a squeak came out. Eyes wide, she clamped a hand over her mouth.

Fate used the moment his back was turned, to fire another shot of energy at him. This one seemed to momentarily paralyze him, so she was able to sidle up close and drag her knife across his throat. Blood poured, coated her hands and sprayed her. Draconus stumbled back, gasping and choking, holding his neck to try and stem the flow.

His mouth gaped like a fish as he tried to speak while he drowned in his own blood. He bared his fangs in a sick, silent parody of laughter. "You'll never kill me," he wheezed. "I'm rooted too deep. You'll have to dig me out of your own soul."

"*What the hell does that mean? You demons and your goddamn riddles?*" she shrieked.

"Silence, harpy!" he answered through a fit of coughs and gurgles. "I've told you everything you need, gods only know why. You humans have the collective intelligence of fungi—." His voice became a sickening gurgle as the arterial blood began to spurt faster.

Fate knew it wouldn't kill him, though. Nothing would. Once he regenerated, he would stamp them out like dying embers. She flinched when she felt Matthieu's hand on her arm. She turned to face him, and he closed both hands over her right one—her knife hand.

She looked into his eyes, those dark, miserable eyes, and she saw everything. Through his touch, she saw everything he'd been through, everything he'd felt. Though she had no power of precognition, in his eyes, she saw everything that would happen. It was the sheen of tears in them that scared her—that resigned yet resolute expression.

She opened her lips to form the word *no*, but not a sound came.

One of his hands came up to caress her face, to push her wet hair behind her ears, before he gripped her hand tightly again with both of his.

"It's me," he said in a voice she could barely hear over the wind. "His insurance policy. He's inside me."

"Matthieu…"

"I thought combat would take me…but now I think I was always meant to go down with this ship. Don't you see? His blood, my body."

"*Matthieu.*" She could hear the pleading tone in her own voice as her panic rose. His eyes scared her. They shone with new light…a light that looked a whole lot like relief. Release.

"I'll be okay," he whispered. "This is right. If I can save you all…maybe I'll finally be free of the demons." His voice broke.

He raised her hand which was clasped in his own big, calloused ones, and placed a gentle kiss on her knuckles. That was her undoing. The tears began rolling down her cheeks and she tried to find the words to stop this—whatever *this* was. She was too busy searching his face to notice him lowering her hand again.

"Fate, look at me." He held her gaze steadily as a single tear slid down his own cheek. He smiled, bright but fleeting. "It's how it was always meant to go down. I know that now. Tell Ridley I'll miss her."

"What—?"

Before the word left her lips, he thrust her hand forward. The hand that held the knife. The knife that was coated in her blood and her wretched father's. She watched in horrified silence, as though she was outside of herself, while the knife slid swiftly, silently, into Matthieu's chest.

Everything else unfolded in slow motion. Matthieu's hands went slack, dropping away from hers. He brought one up to brush across her cheek again. Unable to help herself, she pulled out the knife and tossed it away like it was a striking viper.

She was helpless but to watch the blood well up from the wound in her lover's heart and flow down, down into the water at his feet. She sucked in a pained breath when Matthieu's eyes closed, and she lost her hold on the water.

Fate fell backwards into the pirogue that drifted behind her. Her eyes flicked manically back and forth between Matthieu—rapidly becoming invisible as the water swallowed him—and Draconus, slowly bleeding, burning, and screaming until there was nothing left but ash dissipating into the water.

Someone was screaming. Hands, a woman's hands—Isla's, maybe—and then a man's, grabbed her as she lunged for the water. Fate strained against them, trying to follow her love as he and their enemy disappeared.

Christ, that infernal screaming. She felt her throat burn, and she realized that it was her. Thrashing against her captors, she reached for Matthieu, though all she could see now was the dark, desolate water.

ಐಶ

Matthieu knew he was dying. He'd been here before—countless times, with the breath and blood leaving his body. But this time was different. This time, it felt like the chains were falling away—the ones that had tethered him to this miserable, painful subsistence.

While he slowly floated down into the abyss, he could see that the sun had finally come out, casting a diffuse glow into the murky depths. As the *Lochrim's* blood was purged from inside him, flowing from his heart, he felt cleansed for the first time since the day his father died.

He'd done his duty; he'd protected his loved ones. The bonds were broken, the demons eked out as his blood left him. It felt like dying. It felt like redemption. He hadn't planned it this way, but now he was finally free. His only regret, as he slowly lost his grip on consciousness, was that he had to leave his family behind.

With peace in his heart, he surrendered to his fate, his watery grave. Though, as he felt the strong arms of death band around his chest, he was lifted up. And it felt a little like hope.

CHAPTER FORTY·SIX

Eight weeks later…

FATE'S STOMACH FLIPPED WITH NAUSEA AS SHE PEEKED around the side curtain to get a look at the audience. She had meant what she said to Matthieu that day, weeks ago. She didn't want to be a performer—her nerves couldn't take it, and she didn't want that life for Ridley.

But the only way to get any attention for the songs she wrote was to get out there and perform them. She knew a guy who knew a guy, and had somehow gotten an unprecedented opening spot at Tipitina's. This could really sell some songs, *if* she didn't pass the hell out first.

She scanned the audience until her eyes rested on Ridley's tiny face. She was sitting in Esme Rousseau's lap, and they were next to a handsome, dark haired older man that Fate knew was Raven's father, Ray.

Fate found it hard to be around Esme and Ray, with their looks of pity and well-meaning pats on the back, but Ridley had become attached to the both of them while she'd stayed with Esme. Fate really couldn't understand how Esme was handling Matthieu's...loss so much better than she herself was. She'd refused to ask the woman about it—she just couldn't handle it.

She had never been able to call it death—and not just because, as far as she knew, his body hadn't been found. But because she just didn't *feel* the loss of him. After he was gone from her life, she had to come to terms with the fact that she'd fallen in love with him; maybe since that first day, when he'd watched her sing and saved her life. She just wished she'd gotten a chance to tell him.

It was because of that love that she couldn't accept his supposed death. She just thought she'd feel it somewhere in her bones if Matthieu were no longer in this world. But she knew she had to face the facts. Matthieu would have come back to her had he survived the stabbing on Beltane.

But he hadn't. Fate blinked back tears and tried to get herself together for her set. She was wearing the same black gown she'd been wearing all those weeks ago, in the dive bar where they first met. But now, she was at Tip's, one of the premier uptown jazz and blues clubs.

She should feel amazing, unstoppable. But instead, she just felt empty. Once again, she kept it together for her daughter, but inside it was as if her heart had stopped beating the day she lost Matthieu.

After the set, Fate finally felt like she could breathe again. She had done a few classic blues numbers—Billy Holliday and Etta James staples—while weaving a few of her originals into her set list.

It felt like a hit. She'd been given a standing ovation and cheered on for an encore. However, she wouldn't be able to tell how much of a success it had really been until she started getting emails and calls from producers.

Glad to have the set over with, Fate waded through the crowd of blues enthusiasts waiting for the main act, accepting a few accolades on the way. Finally, she made it to the table where Ridley sat with Esme and Ray.

"Mommy!" Ridley shouted, boisterous as ever, and launched herself into Fate's arms. "You were awesome!" she squealed. It was her new word, and she was wearing it out. Everything was 'awesome' these days.

Fate hugged Ridley to her and twirled her around. Her daughter was everything to her. She had to be. Fate couldn't allow herself to fall apart, so she had to let the beautiful little girl fill up the hole in her heart.

Ray nodded politely as Fate dropped into a chair with Ridley still on her lap. She leaned over to kiss Esme on the cheek. Esme gave her the trademark Rousseau smile that made Fate's heart hurt.

"You were wonderful, dear. I'm sure all of those music types will be beating your door down come Monday," she said with a wink.

"From your lips…" Fate said. She narrowed her eyes when she noticed Esme's were sparkling with mischief. Something was up. "Something you want to tell me, Esme?"

The mischievous expression turned a bit nervous, and Esme bit down on her lip. "I just thought you could use the support of a few friends." She tipped her chin at something across the room and Fate turned to look.

Her heart skipped a beat when she saw a man emerge from the shadows. For a moment, she thought…but it was just

Jeremiah. He was escorting an extremely pregnant Isla, with Drew, Raven, Marduk, and Étienne behind them.

So, Hawkeye had survived his clash with the *Lochrim*. She'd wondered when she didn't hear from him again, but she was too afraid to ask. Admittedly, she'd closed herself off from her new found friends after Matthieu... She just couldn't be around the memories.

It was because of this that she had to put on a brave face when they approached her table. She gently lifted Ridley off of her lap and rose to meet them. She was engulfed in a swarm of hugs, kisses, punches in the arm—from Raven, of course—and she realized that it actually *was* comforting.

They all pulled up chairs and settled around the table. Isla was the first to speak. "You were brilliant up there. I had no idea you were so talented!"

Fate could feel the heat rise in her cheeks at the praise. "Yeah, I don't sing much around people I know. Too embarrassing," she said with a self-deprecating smile. "I only ever sang for..."

She couldn't finish, just cleared her throat and look at Jeremiah. "What have you all been up to?" She raised a brow as she tried to interpret a look shared between him and Isla.

"Well, actually, we've been spending a lot of time in Phoenix lately—"

"Hey, Mommy," Ridley said, tugging on her skirt.

"Honey, don't interrupt. Jeremiah is talking." She looked back at Jeremiah. "As in Arizona? What's in Phoenix?"

Isla cleared her throat and looked at her husband briefly before giving Fate a small smile. "The Mayo Clinic."

"Mommy!"

"Ridley! Hush. The Mayo Clinic? Is everything all right with the baby?" She must have looked panicked, because Isla immediately grabbed Fate's hand and shook her head.

"Yes, sweeting. The baby's just fine."

"*Mommy*," Ridley said in a mock whisper.

This time Fate just ignored her. She hated to admit it but sometimes it was easier that way. "Okay, if the baby is fine, why did you need to go all the way to Arizona to the Mayo clinic?"

There was something strange in Jeremiah's expression when he spoke, but Fate couldn't put her finger on it. "Because the Mayo Clinic in Phoenix is the top cardiovascular hospital in the country."

"I don't understand. Are you having heart problems—"

"Mommy, look!" Ridley shouted, laughing, and took off at a dead run across the dark dance floor.

Fate lost sight of her as she darted around tables and plowed through the growing crowd. "Ridley, what the heck?" she hissed. Standing up, Fate scanned the room. "Sorry guys, hang on."

She stood up and left the table. Standing at the edge of the dance floor, she searched for Ridley. She was scanning the room for her daughter when it hit her like a ton of bricks.

Phoenix. Cardiovascular hospital. Jeremiah was obviously healthy as a horse, and there's no way he'd bring his pregnant wife to a club if she had heart problems. Ray and Esme had been in New Orleans since she picked Ridley up eight weeks ago.

That only left...no. It wasn't possible. Could it be possible that no one told her? Then again, she hadn't asked, had she? She'd just surrendered to her depression, thrown herself into work and motherhood, and ignored anything that might cause her more pain.

Movement in her peripheral vision snapped her out of her stupor. She looked up, her eyes adjusting since the lights had just dimmed…and there he was.

Matthieu wove his way through the crowd with Ridley on one hip. His dark eyes found Fate's and locked on. The intensity in them knocked the wind out of her. He seemed whole and well, solid as ever, although there were worry lines on his face that had not been there before his brush with death.

He was dressed differently than she had ever seen. Instead of his trademark tacticals, he was wearing steal gray chinos and a dark blue dress shirt. The only remnants of the old Matthieu was the scar on his cheek, and the fact that he'd left his shirt unbuttoned at the neck to show his cobra tattoo.

He stopped a few feet in front of her and let Ridley slide down, though she kept her hand in his. "Mommy, *look!*" she said, unaware of the tension between the two adults.

"I see, sweetie." Fate gave her daughter a weak smile. "Ridley, Matthieu and I need to talk, okay? Go find Esme, and we'll be there shortly."

"'Kay, Mommy." Ridley rubbed Matthieu's hand against her cheek before letting go to look up at him. "Don't leave."

"I'm not going anywhere, kiddo," he said in a voice that was barely a whisper.

Fate stared at Matthieu as Ridley trotted off, leaving them alone in a sea of people. She stared for what could have been hours. He opened his mouth twice as if he would say something, but then clamped it shut. She thought he might be waiting for her to get something out.

And she was damn well going to. "How could you do this to me," she whispered. She swiped a hand across her cheek as tears fell, and then she pulled it away and stared at it.

Rearing back, she smacked Matthieu across his scarred cheek with the hand coated in her tears. Then, before his face even registered the shock, she buried that hand in his dark hair that had grown back out and dragged his lips to hers.

She poured all her pain and anger into that kiss, but also the hope and love that had sparked to a full flame when she'd seen him again. She nipped at his bottom lip to get him to open for her, and he obeyed.

He tunneled his own hands into her hair, gripping her head as if he thought she'd disappear. As if *she* was the one who already had. Still, she made love to his mouth as if she would never get the chance again, because she'd thought she wouldn't.

When they finally separated, they were both panting and looking a bit shell-shocked. Fate narrowed her eyes at him, trying to look stern, though her heart soared just from knowing he was alive. "I thought you died. Explain."

Matthieu ran a shaky hand through his hair and looked down at his feet. When he raised his eyes back to her face, there were unshed tears shining in them. "I did." He had to clear his throat to be able to get more words out. "I died."

"What? How?"

He grabbed her hand as it waved in front of him, and gently led her to an empty table. Suddenly exhausted, she dropped down into a chair. He pulled one up beside her and sat down as well.

"My heart stopped. I'm pretty sure it had to have, in order for Draconus to die as well. From what they've told me, Jeremiah pulled me out and resuscitated me. The others got you back to shore and to the hospital to treat your wounds while Jeremiah called a med-evac for me."

"Oh my God. Well, I know why they didn't tell me—I sort of cut myself off from everyone because I didn't want to th nk about...well, you. But why didn't *you* contact me?"

He hooked a finger in the collar of his shirt and dragged it down and to the side, so she could see the gruesome scar over his heart. "It was touch and go there for a while. I nearly bled out on the way to the hospital. I had to have multiple surgeries to repair my heart and, again, I nearly died—from infection that time. I didn't want to put you and Ridley through that—waiting at my bedside when I could still die, even after that.

"I was just released a couple of weeks ago, but I wanted to make sure I came to you clean, with no demons hanging over me...so to speak. I've spent this time tracking down Ward and the rest of my unit. I had to make sure all the information about me was destroyed, and I had to make doubly sure that no cne was after me."

"So you're free?" Fate asked, meaning both from his old life as a mercenary and from the demons he'd lived with for so long.

His face broke out in a huge smile, and it transformed his face. She'd never seen him look so young, so happy.

"Free and clear, baby. There's still the PTSD to deal with, but I'm working on it. I'm going to get counseling at the VA, and I plan to wear my crazy like a badge of honor."

Fate gave him a quick, indulgent smile before sobering. She still wasn't sure where they stood. Their courtship—if it could be called such—had been one crisis after the next, and they'd never really talked about the future. "What's next for you now?"

He looked deep into her eyes and cocked his head sideways in that way of his, the one she'd missed with every beat of her heart since he disappeared. "I'm going legit," he said with a crooked smile that told her he was teasing...sort of. "Raven set up a New Orleans office of her security company, Stiles & Nash, before all this shit went down. She's been wanting to expand into the P.I. business, and she wants me to head it up. I'll also be doing the engineering—general gadgetry—for the NOLA office, since their only other engineer works out of Las Vegas."

Matthieu took Fate's hand in his, and dropped his gaze to where their fingers were joined, as if he was afraid to see her reaction to his words. "I've been trying to get my life together. Trying to be worthy of you...and of Ridley. Even though I know I don't deserve either one of you."

"What? I don't...You want to be with me—us?"

His eyes snapped back to her face, and Fate saw a brief spark of anger before his expression calmed. He captured a lock of her hair and twined it between his fingers.

"How could you not know how I feel about you? You stood up to my demons, held me together when I was falling apart, and matched me push for shove when I tried to scare you away. You're the strongest person I know, and the *only* one who would put up with me." He gave a nervous chuckle, and Fate could tell he really was worried about what she might say.

"Fate, I love you more than my next breath. I want nothing more to make a life with you and Ridley, if you'll have me."

Fate couldn't help the tears that free flowed down her cheeks. It was everything she wanted to hear, and had thought she never would.

"Apparently," he continued, "according to Jeremiah, the *Bruixi* gods decided, about eleventy-billion years ago, who would mate with their *Vigilati* warrioresses. It seems as though we Rousseau's, even the honorary ones," he said with a fond look at Drew, "have been chosen for the job."

He pulled on the other side of his collar, baring his neck on the opposite side as his cobra tattoo. There was an exact replica of Fate's *signa*.

"Oh my…did you put that there?"

"Nope. It just appeared one day, shortly after I finally admitted to myself that I was in love with you, and began preparing to come find you. Jeremiah says it's called the *laqueum*, and it means we're bonded somehow. Um…how do you feel about that?"

Fate let him twist in the wind for a few moments as she pretended to think it over. After all, he *had* made her wait weeks to see him again. Finally, she took his face in both of her hands, stroking his scar with her thumb. He closed his eyes and leaned into her touch. Only the slight trembling she felt betrayed his nerves.

She kissed both his eyelids before placing her lips against his. She felt his big body shudder and then relax. He chuffed a sigh across her lips like a gentle breeze before pulling away so that he could look at her.

"Ridley decided she was keeping you the first night we met. She has sort of a sixth sense about people. Scares me to death, but she hasn't been wrong so far.

"Looking back, I think I fell in love with you that first night when I woke you from your nightmare. You seemed so defeated…lost and tired, but also grateful to have someone with you who wasn't afraid."

"So…" he prompted. "Are you keeping me too, or will Ridley and I have to run away together."

Fate gave up the charade and launched herself into his arms, capturing his mouth in a powerful kiss. "Not a chance, soldier," she whispered after they pulled apart, both breathless. "We're keeping you."

THE END